No Turning Back

"Now it's your turn," Raifer told Honor evenly as they entered his room, "to face the lion in his lair."

She smiled up at him. "Are you comparing yourself to the king of beasts?"

"King?" he mused aloud. "Alas, no, Honor. But there has been an occasional suggestion that I might fit into the category of beast." He looked down at her, entirely serious now. "Does that change your mind? I can still take you home."

She brought her hand slowly to his cheek and touched him lightly. He took her hand in his, then guided it to his lips, pressing a soft kiss to her palm.

"No," she whispered. "I haven't changed my mind."

Honor closed her eyes as he kissed her, and felt herself floating in his embrace. For a second she pondered the mystery of how he did what he did to her, how his touch could so transform her. But then she dismissed thought, and simply pressed closer to him.

This, she realized, was the secret she'd been waiting all her life to learn. Whatever lay ahead, she knew she could only embrace it with all her strength. . . .

Taylor—made Romance From Zebra Books

Whispered Kisses (2912, $4.95/5.95)
Beautiful Texas heiress Laura Leigh Webster never imagined that her biggest worry on her African safari would be the handsome Jace Elliot, her tour guide. Laura's guardian, Lord Chadwick Hamilton, warns her of Jace's dangerous past; she simply cannot resist the lure of his strong arms and the passion of his *Whispered Kisses*.

Kiss of the Night Wind (2699, $4.50/$5.50)
Carrie Sue Strover thought she was leaving trouble behind her when she deserted her brother's outlaw gang to live her life as schoolmarm Carolyn Starns. On her journey, her stagecoach was attacked and she was rescued by handsome T.J. Rogue. T.J. plots to have Carrie lead him to her brother's cohorts who murdered his family. T.J., however, soon succumbs to the beautiful runaway's charms and loving caresses.

Fortune's Flames (2944, $4.50/$5.50)
Impatient to begin her journey back home to New Orleans, beautiful Maren James was furious when Captain Hawk delayed the voyage by searching for stowaways. Impatience gave way to uncontrollable desire once the handsome captain searched *her* cabin. He was looking for illegal passengers; what he found was wild passion with a woman he knew was unlike all those he had known before!

Passions Wild and Free (3017, $4.50/$5.50)
After seeing her family and home destroyed by the cruel and hateful Epson gang, Randee Hollis swore revenge. She knew she found the perfect man to help her—gunslinger Marsh Logan. Not only strong and brave, Marsh had the ebony hair and light blue eyes to make Randee forget her hate and seek the love and passion that only he could give her.

Available wherever paperbacks are sold, or order direct from the Publisher. Send cover price plus 50¢ per copy for mailing and handling to Zebra Books, Dept. 2975, 475 Park Avenue South, New York, N.Y. 10016. Residents of New York, New Jersey and Pennsylvania must include sales tax. DO NOT SEND CASH.

Emerald Angel

Susan Sackett

ZEBRA BOOKS
KENSINGTON PUBLISHING CORP.

ZEBRA BOOKS

are published by

Kensington Publishing Corp.
475 Park Avenue South
New York, NY 10016

Copyright © 1990 by Susan Sackett Stern

All rights reserved. No part of this book may be reproduced in any form or by any means without the prior written consent of the Publisher, excepting brief quotes used in reviews.

First printing: April, 1990

Printed in the United States of America

Other titles by Susan Sackett

Island Captive
Lawless Ecstasy
Passion's Golden Fire

Chapter One

"Oh, damn!"

Raifer Farrell set down the heavy crate he was carrying and turned to find the speaker of that all-too-familiar utterance. It certainly wasn't the words that captured his attention, but rather the sound of a feminine voice in the dockside warehouse.

When he saw her, kneeling to retrieve the scattering of boxes that littered the floor at her feet, he was glad she'd spoken loudly enough for him to hear. If she'd been just a bit more discreet in voicing her anger with herself for dropping her purchases, he'd never have turned and noticed her. His eyes taking in a welter of strawberry-blonde curly hair and what appeared to be a pleasant if diminutive body, he crossed quickly to her, knelt, and hastily retrieved the boxes, assembling them into an orderly pile.

She looked up at him and smiled, and he realized he was perfectly right in making the effort. She had a firm, slightly sharp little chin, provocatively red lips, wide, prominent cheekbones, a perfect peaches-and-cream complexion turned rosy by an unseasonably brisk October wind, and the most beautiful green eyes he'd ever seen.

"Thank you," she said as she stood. "When I was little, my mother promised me I'd get to be more graceful as I aged, but I'm afraid she was vastly mistaken. If I'm not dropping things, I always seem to be bumping into them."

She smiled again, this time a bit self-deprecatingly, but with ample humor to mellow any bitterness that may have been in her words.

"You're new here, aren't you?" she asked after a moment's consideration of him.

Raifer nodded. "Raif Sean Farrell, miss," he said with his best brogue, aware that it often charmed an impressionable lady, and seasoning it with what he hoped was a disarming smile. "Raifer to my friends."

This job just might have some pleasant side benefits, he thought as he stood and lifted the pile of boxes. "And more than delighted to be at your service," he added with another smile.

"Honor Wainwright," she said, offering him her hand.

He stared at it a second, then juggled the boxes to take it and only succeeded in doing what she had done, littering the floor with them.

Honor laughed, more at the chagrin in his expression than at the fate of her purchases.

"I never thought it was catching," she told him with a grin.

"And here I was, trying to impress the boss's daughter with my charm and savoir-faire," he said, this time with no trace of the brogue. He knelt once more and swept up the boxes into a neat pile, then looked up at her. "You are Mr. Wainwright's daughter aren't you?" he asked, his expression suddenly pensive. "Not an inordinately young and pretty wife?"

Honor nodded in recognition of the compliment. "Mr. Wainwright is most decidedly my father," she answered. "A condition he'll undoubtedly regret when he finds the extent of the indebtedness into which I've placed him this afternoon." She stared ruefully at the heap of her purchases, once again firmly secure in his arms. He'd settled them in the confines of a long-armed embrace, obviously determined to take no further chance with the possibility of dropping them.

"I doubt there's any provocation that would make a man regret any association with you, Miss Wainwright," he told her soberly.

Honor stared up into blue-gray eyes that were suddenly surprisingly intense. He's very handsome, she thought almost reluctantly, realizing that for some reason she felt a bit flustered by his stare. She had to force herself to pull her eyes from his.

"Another Irishman," she scolded him softly, "like Kevin and Terrence. And Papa, too, I suppose. He's only half Irish, but I suppose that's more than enough. A woman can't believe a word from any of you."

She said the words softly, knowing that however much she might pretend she did not believe him, she felt a decided inclination to do just that, to really hope his words were something more than simply flattery.

"Farrell!"

Terrence McGowan stalked out of the warehouse office, moving directly to where they stood near the open front door. Honor looked up at him, thinking, as she had more and more of late when she'd seen her father's partner's son, that his collar must be just a bit too tight. His expression was disgruntled, as though he'd determined not to be satisfied with life in general, or perhaps, at that moment, with Raif Farrell in particular. But he brightened as soon as he recognized her standing there, trying to disguise his lapse into ill humor from her and hoping she hadn't noticed.

"Honor," he said, beaming delightedly, "what a pleasure to see you. Is your father expecting you?" He put his hand to her arm.

She shook her head. "No," she replied. "I thought I'd catch him in a spare moment, inform him of the insupportable sum of his money I've spent on frivolities to wear to your sister's engagement party, and then run off before he has the chance to get angry. That way he'll have resigned himself to the fact by the time he gets home this evening, and it will save us both some unpleasant moments."

"Shall I take these into his office, then, Miss Wainwright?" Raifer asked.

Terrence turned to him, and once again the unpleasant expression snaked its way to his face, as though he'd smelled something he thought decidedly nasty.

Honor decided she hated that, the superior attitude he took with anyone he felt not quite up to his social standing. Funny, she thought, half the city of New York seemed to spend their lives looking down on someone else. The old money, those with fortunes made more than three generations back, looked down on those with newly acquired fortunes; they in turn looked down on those struggling along the climb; and they in turn, looked down on everyone still less fortunate. The Wainwrights and the McGowans, of the second group—with secure fortunes but without the lineage to back it up—had always seemed to her to be free of such social-climbing nonsense until Terrence had finished his schooling and returned home from Harvard. Since then, Honor had found her childhood affection for him become tried to the point where it threatened to disappear altogether.

Honor saw the look he threw at Raifer Farrell and knew she was not going to like anything he was about to do or say.

"I'll take those," Terrence told Raifer sharply, reaching for the pile of her purchases. "I'm sure you must have some work you ought to be doing? After all, we don't pay you to be standing about, bothering people."

"Terrence," Honor began, hoping to distract him before he could make himself truly offensive.

Raifer, however, obviously had no intention of cowering simply because it was Terrence's father who paid him. He held firm to the pile of boxes. "Everything's done, sir," he replied smartly, the term of respect made to sound more mocking than anything else.

Honor shifted her look to him at the sound of the defiance in his voice. It was obvious he had no need for any protection from Terrence McGowan that he could not provide for himself. She was beginning to like this young man, she realized. And she was getting to dislike Terrence avidly. She turned back to him and peered at him with a sudden intentness. He'll look just like Kevin in another twenty years, she thought—all jowls and double chins—but without any humor in his eyes to make all that excess pleasant and playful. It was not an appealing thought.

"As Mr. Farrell has a firm grasp of the situation, Terrence," she said and pulled her arm from his, starting to turn toward the warehouse office, "I'll just be along and interrupt Papa as he ponders the mysteries of commerce."

But Terrence seemed unwilling to let her escape quite so easily. He put his hand to her waist and smiled at her once more.

He's going to try to talk his way out of it, she thought. He can see he's angered me, and he's going to try to make it up.

"I'm looking forward to seeing if any of the things in those boxes can make you any more beautiful than you already are, Honor," he said, ignoring Raifer's presence now completely. "And to the first dance at the party."

Honor bristled. He was beginning to make assumptions about her, assumptions that seemed to be shared by both his father and her own, and she realized she found them more and more distasteful as the months passed.

"The first dance, Terrence?" she asked sweetly, then gently backed away from his hold on her. "I'm afraid that belongs to a lady's escort."

"But I'd assumed, Honor . . ."

She cut him off. "You shouldn't have," she replied, a shade too tartly.

His eyes narrowed, and Honor felt herself beginning to squirm a bit at his stare.

"Who have you asked?" he demanded abruptly, his tone implying that he would make sure the gentlemen in question would soon find himself inconveniently

11

indisposed.

She looked up at Raifer, her eyes hopeful and a bit pleading. She found his expression sympathetic, even amused.

"Miss Wainwright has given me that honor," he said, then flashed her a slightly wicked smile. "I'm looking forward to being there." He looked back at Terrence, smiled again, and added, "sir." This time there was no question but that the address was intended to imply anything but respect.

"Now, if you'll excuse me, Terrence," Honor murmured as she pulled away. "I really do want to see Papa."

She started toward the office, conscious of his eyes watching her as she retreated, grateful for Raifer ambling along beside her, feeling that if she'd been alone, Terrence would never have let her escape so easily.

"I'm sorry," she began, turning to look up at Raifer, feeling rather awkward now, far more so than when he'd seen only her clumsiness with the boxes. "And very grateful. Thank you for not giving me away."

He was staring down at her, she found, and his expression was decidedly amused.

"Well, aren't you going to offer the invitation?" he asked. "After all, we wouldn't want to disappoint Terrence, now, would we?"

She felt a bit bewildered. "You would really do that for me?" she asked. "You needn't, you know. I could tell him something."

"Not go?" He seemed entirely bewildered at the prospect. "After telling him how much I'm looking forward to the occasion?"

They stopped in front of the door of the owners' offices, and Honor put her hand to the knob.

"He could make trouble for you," she said softly. "I wouldn't want you to lose your job because of me."

He seemed unconcerned. "A small sacrifice for the pleasure of an evening in your company, Miss Wainwright," he said softly.

His voice was low and husky, and Honor felt a small quiver inside herself.

"Honor, please."

He grinned. "Honor," he agreed. "After all, if you're about to invite me to accompany you to Terrence's party, it's only fair that you allow me to call you by your first name."

She found herself returning the grin. "In that case," she said, "Saturday evening? Seven-thirty?" She turned the knob and the door began to swing open.

"I'll look forward to it," he replied as he followed her into the unexpected solid mahogany and leather comforts of the inner office. He carefully placed the pile of her purchases on an empty chair as Daniel Wainwright looked up in surprise.

"Honor? What are you doing here?" He stared at the boxes Raifer had deposited before turning toward the door. "Although I suppose that should tell me," he finished, staring at the heap. "Thank you for your gallantry with my daughter, Farrell," he added. "I've no doubt she enlisted your help when she either tripped or dropped that lot."

"Papa!"

Raifer grinned, then nodded first toward Daniel, then at Honor as he opened the door. "It was my pleasure, sir," he said before he slipped out of the room, closing the door after him.

Honor followed him with her eyes, then stood silent for a moment when he was gone. "He's quite nice, I think, Papa," she said softly.

Daniel's dark eyes narrowed, and he stared at his daughter speculatively. She was becoming a bit of a mystery to him of late, keeping her thoughts her own a great deal more of the time than she had when she'd been younger. It was only to be expected, he thought. After all, she can't be a child forever. Still, the thought was not entirely pleasant for him.

"Is that what you've come all the way downtown to tell me, Honor?" he asked, keeping his voice stern, making a great effort to keep the humor he felt from showing in his expression.

"Oh, Papa." Honor turned back to him and smiled disarmingly. "I think it's quite obvious that I've come with the intention of luring you out to a sumptuous luncheon and then, when you're too full of foie gras and twenty-year-old burgundy to have the energy to get angry, to tell you how badly I've ruined you this morning." She flashed him another smile and waited until he returned it.

"No sane man eats foie gras or drinks twenty-year-old burgundy in the middle of the afternoon, Honor," he told her quite seriously. "And I consider myself an eminently sane individual."

Honor threw herself into the chair facing him, heedless of the way her skirts billowed out around her and revealed a goodly length of stockinged leg. "Well, none of this was really my fault, you know," she told him defensively. "You were the one who suggested this little shopping spree with Megan."

"And I was right?" Daniel asked smugly.

She nodded, albeit reluctantly. "As always, Papa. She did admire a lovely marble and gilt mantle clock in Fraiser's that will make a perfect wedding gift. But that small act of detection has cost you dearly. She practically forced me into buying a few things so that she wouldn't feel greedy about her own purchases." She stared at the pile of boxes for a moment. "Let's see," she said, rising and crossing to them. She lifted the top three boxes. "New kid gloves and a lovely beaded evening purse for the party, and the dancing slippers, which I really did need." Her expression sobered. "And a few others that were not really quite so necessary." She replaced the boxes on the pile and turned back to face him. "Papa, you're not even listening," she accused softly.

Daniel leaned back in his chair and smiled. "Oh, I've been listening, Honor," he assured her. "Kid gloves, a beaded purse, and dancing slippers." But he had to admit to himself at least, if not to her, that his thoughts had not been on her but on her mother, dead two years now, but somehow still with him a great deal, especially when he looked at Honor. She was maturing into a beautiful young woman, one who bore an uncanny resemblance to her mother when Daniel had first met her some twenty-three years before. That resemblance pleased him in many ways, but at times it also saddened him, making him think of his loss as well as of his own inevitable mortality. He shook himself, forcing his thoughts back to her.

Honor moved toward the desk and put her hand out to his arm, "Papa, are you all right?" she asked.

These moments of his, the lapses when he seemed to be falling away from her, going somewhere she could not follow, bewildered and frightened her. But Daniel put his hand to hers and smiled.

"No, I'm not," he told her, his tone jocular. "You've offered me the opportunity of lunching with a lovely young woman, and I find myself in the unpleasant position of having to reject that offer, not for something even remotely as palatable, but instead to face none other than the bewhiskered jowls of my banker across a table. Hardly a prospect that any man would find appealing."

"Must you, Papa?" Honor asked him softly. "You've been working too hard lately."

Daniel patted her hand, then pulled his own away and stood. "I'm afraid so, Honor. Once this loan is negotiated, and the *Shanghai Queen* becomes the newest asset of Wainwright and McGowan, Merchant Fleet, we will be well on our way to becoming the largest shipping company in the city." He smiled at her. "Perhaps a new house, Honor," he suggested. "Like Kevin's new mansion."

Honor grimaced slightly, then grinned at him. "I like our house, Papa. I find it suits me quite well."

"Well, then a trip to France next spring? Would that please you more?"

Honor's face brightened. "Really, Papa? Paris?"

"And Rome, too, if you like," Daniel agreed. "We can make a grand tour of it. But for now, I have to meet old man Jeffers and convince him that Wainwright and McGowan are pillars of the financial community, worthy of his confidences." He donned his hat and took his coat from the hook. "Not to mention his money. Without it, no *Shanghai Queen*. And then Kevin will never repay the loan he took to build that new pile of his." He pushed his hands through the sleeves of his coat thoughtfully. "I do this, my dear, not for myself, but for friendship." He grinned at her. "And for Honor."

"Oh, Papa," she laughed.

Daniel looked upward, to the ceiling, calling on some authority with divine powers to bear him witness. "I go, hat humbly in hand," he intoned theatrically.

"Not to mention hand humbly in kid glove," Honor muttered softly.

He threw her a perturbed glance, then redirected his eyes upward once more. "I go, hat humbly in hand, to beg succor from the ogre's table. Come daughter." He threw his arm out wide. "Kiss your father farewell for what may very well be the last time."

Honor took his gold-tipped cane from the stand in the corner and held it out to him, her head bowed as she made the offering. "Pray, brave Papa, do not go unarmed."

Daniel took the stick. "I'm relieved, daughter," he said evenly as he hung it on his arm, "that you comprehend the import of this venture." He turned to the pile of her purchases. He lifted the three top boxes and held them out to her. "You could help an old man, Honor," he suggested.

"Oh, Papa," she replied, "you'll never be old." She took the three boxes from him and watched as he organized the rest of the pile on his arm.

"You can take a cab to the bank with me," he suggested as he opened the door for her, "and then continue on uptown."

"Yes, Papa," she replied demurely as she walked through into the warehouse.

"And I expect you to dwell on the miseries I suffer for your extravagance even as you sit in the comfort of the parlor and pamper yourself with sweets. A quiet afternoon spent repenting your profligate tendencies should be in order, I think," Daniel added as he closed the door behind them and followed her.

Honor looked up at his smile. "Yes, Papa," she replied once more as he took her arm and hurried her past the huge mountains of crates that lined the walls of the warehouse and toward the door to the street.

As they neared the door, Raifer appeared and opened it for them with a sweepingly extravagant bow.

"Mr. Wainwright. Miss Wainwright," he said as they passed, but Honor saw that his eyes were firmly on her.

She responded with a smile. "Thank you, Mr. Farrell," she murmured as Daniel hurried her along.

A cold wind blowing off New York Harbor greeted them. Honor shivered slightly from the sudden blast.

"Good man, that young Farrell," she heard her father comment as they walked along the rows of warehouses that line Pike's Slip to Water Street, where they could expect to find a hansom cab. "Hard worker."

"Yes," Honor replied thoughtfully as she recalled Raifer's mischievous blue-gray eyes and dark curls. "He seems like a very good man, indeed."

Daniel turned to her and offered her a sharp look, then shrugged slightly and continued on. Honor held her silence for the moment. There would be more than enough time to tell him about the fact that his new laborer was to be her escort to Megan's engagement party. She knew her shopping spree of the morning had not upset him in the slightest, despite her comments to the contrary. But her arrangement with Raifer Farrell, she knew, would not prove so simple a matter for him to accept.

* * *

Raifer stood by the door and watched through the slightly dusty window Honor's back as she walked toward Water Street. She was the last thing he'd thought he'd find when he'd first applied for the job two weeks before. But this unexpected aspect of employment with Wainwright & McGowan quite pleased him. Just watching her as she grew slowly smaller with the distance he found a pleasantly diverting occupation.

"Farrell!"

Terrence McGowan's tone, seemingly never pleased, was at that moment decidedly perturbed, and Raifer had little doubt as to the cause. He turned and faced Terrence, not bothering to take the effort to hide the smile that had crept to his lips as he'd watched Honor's retreating form. Terrence, he found, was not smiling, not in the least.

"You made a mistake today, Farrell."

Raifer raised an eyebrow. "Mistake?" he asked, as quietly innocent as he would have been if he'd had no idea what it was Terrence would say.

"Daniel Wainwright won't be pleased when he finds out you're toying with his daughter."

Raifer remained impassive. "Toying? Now that has a decidedly unpleasant ring to it, don't you think?" He smiled amiably. "It pains me to think of anything unpleasant at the same time as Miss Wainwright." He allowed his face to sober. "And if Mr. Wainwright has any problem with me, I expect he'll let me know himself."

Terrence took a few steps forward, until he was standing only a foot or so from Raifer. He stared at him, his blue eyes blazing with anger.

"I think I didn't make myself clear, Farrell. Her father won't like you bothering Honor. *I* don't like you bothering her. If you want to keep healthy and working here, I suggest you find some excuse to give her for not being able to attend the party on Saturday. And then you stay away from her. Do you understand me?"

Raifer's lips formed a hard, humorless grin. "Oh, I

understand you well enough," he replied.

Terrence stood where he was for a moment longer, his intent quite obviously threatening. But when Raifer made no move to back away, he apparently decided discretion was the appropriate course. After all, he told himself, there was no reason for him to dirty his own hands. If this uppity worker proved to be uncooperative, he had several willing dockhands who would see that he was convinced. In the meantime, he'd said his piece.

He took a few steps back and looked around the crowded warehouse. Then he turned to Raifer and pointed to a huge pile of crates by the loading doors.

"The *Mary Louise* is due in port tomorrow," he said sharply. "She'll be carrying a large shipment of linen and crystal. You can clear that space there for it."

"There's plenty of room there." Raifer pointed to some open space just beyond.

Terrence smiled at him with humorless malice.

"You forget," he said through tight lips, "that I give the orders here. Get to work."

Raifer gritted his teeth. "Yes, sir," he spat out, repressing his anger.

Terrence stood and watched him as he began the work, and for the first time that day a look of real humor managed to make its way to his face. Then he turned away and walked to the comforts of his father's office, allowing the door to slam shut after him, the sound reverberating through the huge warehouse.

Patrick Coughlin, one of Raifer's fellow workers in the warehouse, appeared from behind a pile of crates where he'd retired for a short nap before lunch. Patrick amazed Raifer. He worked like a demon when there was something to be done, and then he could drop off to sleep with the ability of a cat when there was a free moment or two. His quiet had quite obviously been disturbed by the slamming door, and he seemed a bit displeased at the disturbance.

"What the hell was that?" he asked Raifer. "Don't tell

me His Highness has fallen off his horse again?"

Raifer laughed. "I'm afraid so," he said. "Or maybe I pushed him a bit. Either way, he wasn't real happy about where he landed."

The sound of Patrick's laughter was deep and infectious. "Is he ever?" he asked.

"I don't suppose you'd like to help me with this?" Raifer asked as he heaved a crate onto his shoulder.

Patrick watched him as he crossed the warehouse to place the crate on the floor. It was busy work, and he knew it. "No way, boyo," he replied. "You're the one who bit his arse. You can pay for the pleasure."

"Some pleasure," Raifer replied with a crooked grin. "Not my kind of meat, Paddy."

"I'm glad to hear it, boyo," Paddy told him with another guffaw. "I'd hate to have to watch my own back." He sobered then, suddenly. "But you better listen to me, Raifer, me lad. You watch yourself with young McGowan. That one's mean as a snake. And not as honest."

Raifer nodded. "I wouldn't be surprised." He lifted another of the crates onto his shoulder. "But I'm not one to allow myself to be bitten."

Honor sat in a large leather-covered chair in her father's library and idly fingered the pages of the novel she held in her hands. She wasn't really reading. Despite the fact that Megan McGowan had promised her she would love the book before pressing it on her, Honor found its plot predictable and the characters dull. Megan read nickel novels incessantly, and seemed to consider it a duty of friendship to force her passion on Honor. But as a rule, Honor found the heroines of the stories silly, rather dim-witted creatures. No matter what the circumstances in which they managed to find themselves, invariably they ended waiting for the hero to rescue them, standing uselessly by, wringing their hands and swooning, then finally falling helplessly into the waiting hero's arms.

Honor hated stories where heroines swooned. After all, she'd never once fainted in her life, and short of an elderly aunt and a cousin of her mother's who had been six months pregnant at the time, she'd never seen anyone else faint, either. She was certain that if she were ever to become involved in an adventure, she wouldn't allow herself either to swoon or to sit around like a witless, useless little ninny. And if she were ever to fall into a man's arms, she certainly hoped it would be because she wanted to, and not for any other reason.

There were, however, things about those novels that did intrigue her. They were always set in places with the most delicious sounding names, in the Vale of Kashmir, for instance, or by the Sea of Mamara, or in cities like Katmandu. It seemed impossible to her that her father's ships traveled to ports throughout Europe and the Far East, and yet she'd never been further from New York City than Boston to visit her aunts and cousins. An adventure, a real adventure, someplace far away from her own rather boring everyday world, now *that* was something to dream about, however improbable it was that it would ever happen to her.

She reminded herself that Daniel had promised her a trip to the continent if his business with the bank and the new ship turned out well. Assuming it was a promise to which she could hold him, now that was something, she thought delightedly, if not a real adventure, as close as she was ever likely to come to one. She'd see things she had read about, and maybe even meet a prince, or a baronet at the very least. If she couldn't have a real adventure, those things sounded almost as good.

She leaned back in the chair, letting the book fall unheeded to the floor, and stared around the room. Perhaps her father's joking suggestion, she mused, was not as ridiculous as it had seemed. Perhaps they ought to move to a new house. Not that she even remotely yearned for anything grander than the sturdiness of this old house on Gramercy Park. But the house held too many memories for her father, she realized, and perhaps it would be easier for him to get on with his life someplace else. After all, he wasn't that old, only fifty-three . . . still young enough to fall in love again. For an instant her thoughts brought her a small pang of guilt, as though she were being unfaithful to her mother's memory, but it disappeared quickly. She knew Daniel deserved to get on with his life, she knew her mother would have wanted that. It seemed to her that Daniel's willingness to allow her to drift into marriage with Terrence was simply his way of absolving his responsibilities to his dead wife, making sure there were no messy loose ends left about before he made any attempt to start a new life of his own. She almost felt guilty then, knowing that it wouldn't be that easy, that Daniel would not be able to find himself unfettered quite that simply. But as much as she loved her father, she knew that she could not allow herself to be simply packed off and tucked away into marriage. Not in a marriage to Terrence, at any rate.

Her thoughts were interrupted by the sound of the front door being opened and then closed again quickly against the cold blast of a leaf-rustling, bitter wind. She could predict almost to the second how long it would take Daniel to put his stick in the stand by the door, to remove his gloves, hat, and coat, and then make his way to the library.

She was standing by the liquor chest in the corner of the room, pouring the best single malt into a crystal glass, when he entered the library. She looked up at him quickly and smiled in greeting, but made no effort to speak. Daniel, welcoming what had become their evening ritual, sat in the chair she had vacated and watched her turn back to her task, measuring out the whiskey, replacing the decanter on the tray, then carefully filling the remaining space in the large crystal tumbler from a siphon before bringing it to him. He took the glass from her and sipped the drink, tasting it with a judgmental air before smiling his acceptance at her.

"Excellent, Honor," he said finally, ending the silence. "I think there is a possibility that you will make some man a reasonably acceptable wife after all."

"I think not, Papa," she replied gamely. "I doubt there's a man in the city who would stand for my spendthrift ways."

Daniel's smile vanished. "I'd thought you were to spend the afternoon repenting of the sins of this morning, Honor," he reminded her.

She smiled at him prettily. "Oh, I did, Papa," she assured him. "I even answered Aunt Elizabeth's and Aunt Louisa's letters as an act of contrition."

Daniel smiled at that, and took another swallow of his drink.

"But somehow I think I shall return to sin once more," Honor went on, "despite my better wishes." She stared at Daniel. "I fear the weakness was inherited, from my father."

Daniel grinned. "No matter. I think it only a question of time until you are not only the most beautiful young woman in the city, but one of the richest as well. I foresee no trouble in finding some young man willing to take you off my hands in return for some reasonable consideration." He smiled at her happily before taking another swallow.

"Like Megan?" she asked abruptly, seating herself in the chair opposite his.

His head snapped up. "Of course not, Honor," he said sharply. He stared at her a moment, then drained the remaining alcohol in his glass.

"I'm sorry, Papa. I didn't mean that." Honor swept the thought aside. "Am I to construe from these predictions of future fortune that your meeting with Mr. Jeffers went well this afternoon?"

Honor watched him as he stood and made his way to the liquor chest. She thought he looked decidedly tired, not quite pale, but spent. He lifted the decanter and turned to her before he poured.

"It did indeed," he replied as he half filled the glass. "I think Kevin will have a great deal to celebrate Saturday evening, the engagement of his daughter and the prospect of doubling the line." He raised his glass to her before he tasted the whiskey, straight this time, without any water, and she realized that whatever feelings her comment about Megan's betrothal had brought out, they were gone now. He was smiling, his expression become decidedly jovial.

Honor considered him for a second. He'd had a first drink, and his mood could not be better, she thought. There would be no better time to broach the subject of her escort to Megan's engagement party. And it was just as well to get it over and done with.

"About Saturday night, Papa," she began slowly. "I've asked someone to be my escort."

Daniel's brow wrinkled. "But I'd assumed Terrence . . ."

Honor cut him short. "That's just the trouble, Papa. You assume and Terrence assumes and Kevin assumes. I'm the only one who doesn't."

Daniel frowned. "Honor, you and Terrence have been close since you were children. If Kevin and I had some notion that someday the two of you would marry . . ."

Once more Honor interrupted. "Papa, he's changed. Surely you've seen it. Since he came home from school, he's so different. And I don't like the person he's become."

"Be reasonable, Honor. He's spent the last few years with the sons of some of the richest and most powerful men in this country. If he's taken on a few of their airs, it's only to be expected. That will all wear off soon enough."

Honor considered his words, then slowly shook her head. "No, Papa, I don't think it will. He likes himself now, he likes the idea that he can bully other people about. Don't say no," she added, before he had the chance to object, "because he does, I've seen it. And he changes, one moment sweet and pleasant, the next rude and demanding. I don't feel I can trust him any more. The more I see of him lately, the more I realize that he's entirely wrong for me. And there's no reason why I should let him think otherwise."

Daniel pursed his lips and stared at the amber liquid in his glass. This was not quite the sort of conversation he'd expected to be having upon his arrival home. A drink to welcome him home, another to celebrate the success of the day, maybe another just for the hell of it. Then a good dinner. That's what he'd anticipated.

He turned his glance back to his daughter and saw her face set and determined. He knew better than to bother arguing with her when she took on that look. It was far better to simply let the matter come to its own end, or she would become only more fixed and determined. If she'd decided Terrence had become a bit of a bully, he mused, he had to admit that she was probably right. And a bit of competition could only give the younger McGowan an impetus to realize what a prize Honor would be as a wife. There was no need to make too much of the matter.

"Well," he said finally, the word coming from his lips very slowly, as though it had two syllables, not one, "I suppose it won't hurt him to realize he ought to make a greater effort with you if he intends to win you, Honor. Although I do think you could have chosen a more propitious time to give him that hint."

"Papa," Honor began in exasperation, but Daniel held up his hand, and she fell silent. Let him think she was trying to make Terrence jealous, if that would keep the protests about Raifer Farrell down to a minor storm, she told herself. It would be easier to weather than a real hurricane.

"And just who is the young man you've chosen to arouse Terrence's gentlemanly fires?" he demanded.

Honor swallowed. "Someone you mentioned only

this afternoon, Papa," she told him, a shade too brightly. "In fact, you spoke quite well of him."

Daniel wrinkled his brow in concentration, but he remained at a loss. "I'm afraid, Honor, I really have no idea." He was, he realized, beginning to get an unpleasant feeling, something her expression, when he looked down at her, only intensified.

"It's Mr. Farrell," she announced, then watched as his expression changed, very slowly, from bewilderment to disapproval.

"You can't mean the new laborer at the warehouse?" he asked her finally.

"Why, of course, Papa. Do you know of any other Mr. Farrell?"

Daniel's cheeks began to color. "You aren't serious, Honor? A common laborer!"

Honor stood and returned his stare. "You yourself said this afternoon that he was a good man. And as for being a laborer, I'd never thought you based your judgments of people on the amount of money they had. I don't suppose I need remind you of all the times I've heard you tell me that you had only the clothes on your back when you met Mama."

Daniel started to speak, but he thought better of it. He stared at Honor a moment, wondering just how determined she was about young Farrell, then decided it wasn't the young laborer that was on her mind when she'd made her choice of escort, but Terrence McGowan. The sight of Raifer with Honor on his arm was sure to rouse Terrence as no young man of their own set possibly would.

"I'm not sure I quite like the game you've decided to play with Terrence, Honor," he said slowly, "but I will make no further protest than to tell you that I don't approve."

"I'm not playing any games, Papa," she told him firmly.

Daniel seemed not to notice. He took a healthy swallow of his whiskey, then put the glass down on the liquor tray, deciding he'd lost his taste for it. He turned to Honor, and he was suddenly struck with the picture of Terrence's reaction. If there was anything that could possibly prick his balloon of self-esteem, it would be this. He found himself smiling unexpectedly, then chuckling.

"Yes, Papa?" Honor asked, bewildered by his reaction.

"I was just thinking that I'm glad I'm not a young man any longer, Honor," he replied.

He offered her his hand and she moved to him, taking it, putting her hand comfortably through the crook of his arm.

"And do remind me," he said as they started towards the dining room for dinner, "to see that Farrell is provided with appropriate evening clothes. He might as well be dressed for the part you've got him playing."

"Really, Papa," Honor muttered. "You make me sound such a scheming, sly thing."

Daniel turned to her and patted the hand he held in his arm. "Well, aren't you just that, my dear?" he asked.

Honor turned away. Perhaps I am, she thought as she pictured Raifer Farrell in her mind, most especially those sparkling blue-gray eyes. If she was scheming, however, it was not quite exactly to the ends her father imagined.

Chapter Two

Raifer set the last of the crates down and moved slowly toward the office. His steps when he moved were surprisingly noiseless against the hard plank floor. Once he'd edged his way to the office door, he stood, his ear pressed against the wood, listening. He could just make out the words.

"Your trip was pleasant, I hope?"

That was Kevin McGowan, he realized, the deep timbre of his voice unmistakable.

"The *Mary Louise* is no pleasure yacht."

The response came to Raifer as a soft, slightly muffled slur, the words nearly indecipherable, obscured by the thick mahogany door as well as by a deep brogue.

"And despite her name, I'm thinking she's no lady." There was a murmur of laughter. "But we're here, and ready for business."

"And business will be ready for you, and soon, I think," Kevin replied.

Raifer realized he had been right, that the four men he'd seen disembarking from the *Mary Louise* had not been members of her regular crew. The sailors had a tired, pleased look about them, eager as they were to go home to wives and families, while these four had seemed far too uneasy, too unsure to be sailors home and on leave. Added to that was the fact that they had waited until it was after dusk to leave the *Mary Louise*, when there were few about the wharves to notice them. It seemed obvious to him that the firm of Wainwright & McGowan was importing more from Ireland than linen and crystal in the cargo hold of the *Mary Louise*, and the unlisted portion of that shipment had known enough about its destination to go directly to the offices in the warehouse and find one of the partners. Something inside told him that this extra bit of cargo from the hold was trouble.

"I wish I could make up for the discomfort by offering you some real hospitality, gentlemen, but I'm afraid that will have to wait. This evening is my daughter's engagement party, and my wife will have my hide if I'm late."

There was a gentle murmur of laughter at Kevin's words, and then Raifer heard the scraping of chairs as the occupants of the office pushed them back and stood.

"I've never known a man, regardless how fearless, who didn't stand in the most abject terror of some woman's wrath."

This, too, was spoken with a thick brogue.

"The strongest of us are all weaklings, I'm afraid," Kevin replied. "But do not think this evening a total loss. I hope to be able to convey to you word of support by this time tomorrow. Good, bankable support. Because a man's left his home doesn't mean he's lost all his feelings for it. Nor his loyalty."

"We recognize that, Kevin. And we appreciate it."

Raifer drew back quickly as he realized the footsteps from within the room were moving toward the door. He'd been stupid, he realized. There was no chance he could get out of the building now without being seen. He stole back to the pile of crates and heaved the last back to his shoulders just as the door opened and Kevin stepped out.

"Farrell!"

Raifer turned around to face Kevin, hoping his expression appeared entirely innocent. There was no one else in sight, he realized. The newcomers had stayed in the office until it was certain that the coast was clear, taking precautions even in what they assumed was completely friendly territory.

"Yes, sir?" Raider replied quickly.

"What are you still doing here?" Kevin demanded sharply.

"Just finishing up with the load from the *Mary Louise*," Raifer replied without hesitation. "Mr. Wainwright said that the crystal is to be sorted to be sent to Blackman's and to the Chicago train to Field's. I thought if I sorted it out now, it would be easier to get the Field's shipment ready Monday morning."

"Ah, yes, very good." Kevin seemed a little bewildered at Raifer's show of enthusiasm for the job. "Coughlin still here?" he asked.

Raifer shook his head. "He left a few minutes ago," he said. "If there's nothing else, sir, I'll be leaving, too."

Raifer wondered if there would be any possibility that he could get back into the warehouse once Kevin had seen him out. A look around when no one else was there might give him some idea of what the four passengers from the *Mary Louise* were up to. That, after all, was the reason he was there.

"No, nothing else," Kevin told him and he moved with him to the door, eliminating any possibility of Raifer doing any further snooping, at least for the time being.

"It's time I was leaving, myself," Kevin told him. "I should have been off half an hour ago."

"I could lock up for you, sir," Raifer offered helpfully.

But Kevin only shook his head. "Habit, lad. Certain things I've always done for myself no matter what."

Raifer nodded, taking care not to show any disappointment. After all, he hadn't really expected it to be that easy.

Kevin laid a large hand on his shoulder. "Have a pleasant weekend, lad. I'll be seein' you Monday, bright and early."

"Actually, I expect I'll see you tonight, sir," Raifer told him easily.

"Oh, oh yes," Kevin muttered. He'd almost forgotten what Daniel had told him about some quarrel between Honor and Terrence. Not that the news had come as a great surprise to him. His son had grown a good bit too big for his own breeches of late, he thought. Honor's anger could only do him a bit of good. There was nothing like a woman's ire to cut a man down to size. "Well, then, until later," he told Raifer and nearly pushed him out the door.

Raifer stood where he was for a moment, watching the door being closed behind him and listening to the heavy bolts being slid into place. He swallowed the impulse to swear. Once Kevin McGowan had finished locking up the warehouse, there was little chance he could find some easy way in. Through the years the firm of Wainwright & McGowan had managed to make the place quite secure, a necessary means of discouraging any thief from making the effort of trying to make off with the oftentimes quite valuable goods that were temporarily stored there. He'd taken an especially careful survey of all the doors and windows over the previous two weeks and found them all well accommodated with bolts and shutters.

Well, he told himself as he started toward Water Street, he still had a few weeks to find out what was going on with Kevin's four guests. There was no immediacy, at least not just yet. In the meantime, he had to get uptown and get the evening clothes Daniel Wainwright had arranged for him for the evening. He was mildly chagrined at that unexpected turn of events. Wearing ill-fitting work clothes to a laborer's job in the warehouse was one thing, but rented evening dress was quite another. He would have greatly preferred to wear his own evening clothes to the party. But he supposed if he was playing a part, he had little choice but to play it all the way. After all, a day laborer would hardly be expected to own his own black tie.

Nor would he be expected to have the funds to treat a young woman to the kind of evening he would have liked to show Honor. Shame, he thought, that he had not met her under different circumstances. And if matters progressed as he thought they would, he realized, he doubted that she would ever give him the opportunity to show her who or what he really was.

Still, he mused, things sometimes had a way of turning out in surprising ways. Perhaps there would be the opportunity of spending more than just this one evening with her. He pushed that thought away before it became too attractive to him. After all, seeing Honor was just another way for him to do his job. For all he knew, however distasteful to him the idea might be, she might very well be a part of it. And if that were the case, he would doubtless end with seeing her in jail for a good portion of the remainder of her life. At best, it would be her father sent to prison, and he the instrument that sent him. Hardly a basis, Raifer mused, on which to proceed with the expectations of performing a seduction.

Raifer had not quite reached the corner when he heard a noise behind him. He turned, curious, because he'd seen no one on the slip when he'd left the warehouse.

The single street lamp on the corner sent a dimly flickering light along the slip to where he stood. Behind him was nearly total darkness. Sunset had followed dusk quickly, and the moon had not yet risen.

His eyes adjusted quickly to the dimness. It took him only a few seconds to see them, two men cloaked by darkness hovering near a pile of empty wooden barrels. He did not know why, but he decided it would be wisest not to turn his back on those two particular shadows. He stood where he was, waiting patiently, as he did so carefully measuring the distance between himself and the barrels.

When he made no move to turn away, one of the forms slowly straightened itself and moved forward into the dim light. The man was big, Raifer saw, with hugely muscled arms that ended with hands the size of Christmas hams. Dockhand, he decided quickly. He'd seen enough of them in the previous weeks to recognize the muscles and the manner.

"You Raif Farrell?" the man asked as he moved slowly forward.

Behind him the second man extricated himself from the shadows.

"Who's asking?" Raifer demanded, his tone as gruff and raw as the other man's had been.

The dockhand smiled, revealing a row of crooked teeth that seemed to gleam with unlikely brilliance from the dark stubble of beard on his face.

"A friend, Farrell," the man told him. "I'm yer guardian angel, come to warn ya of the error of yer ways and see ya find the right path away from 'em." He smiled again, and his companion allowed a thin laugh to escape his lips.

Raifer tensed himself, but he did not step back. All he could think was that he'd been found out somehow, that McGowan had managed to learn who he really was.

"I hadn't realized I'd fallen on the wrong road," he replied softly.

"Now, there," the dockhand told him. "You need me to point out yer sins to ya. Like you shouldn't be botherin' a certain lady."

Raifer inwardly sighed with relief. This was about Honor, he realized, not about the four men he'd seen enter McGowan's offices. He allowed himself to return the man's smile, only his was somehow a good deal more menacing as he pulled his lips back tight over his teeth.

"And I don't suppose you've set out on this delicate business on your own, now, have you?" he asked.

The second man spoke for the first time. "Naw. We're just deliverin' a message, Farrell. And makin' sure you receive it."

With that, both men moved toward him. But Raifer didn't wait for them to reach him. He moved quickly, bending forward, shoulder down and braced, and raced at the first man, his shoulder meeting a beefy stomach with enough force to empty the breath from the man's lungs. The man gasped, surprised: he'd not been braced for the blow. Unbalanced, he fell backward, his weight carrying not only him to the ground, but his partner as well.

Raifer reached forward, grasped the second man's shoulder before he could scramble to his feet, and landed a quick, hard blow to his chin. There was a hard crack of bone, and then the gleam of blood on his lips as he fell back to the ground.

Raifer glanced at him quickly, assuring himself that the man was in no condition to pose a further threat, and then returned his attention to his partner.

The first man by now had managed to get to his feet, and began to swing his fists with considerable force. But he was still disoriented, and his movements were wild, tempered by his surprise at the unexpected attack. He'd been led to believe he'd have no trouble delivering his message or punctuating it with a few well-placed blows. He hadn't considered the possibility that he might be receiving, not delivering them.

His first blow landed high, on Raifer's shoulder. He never had time to deliver a second. Raifer's fist landed squarely in the center of his already painful stomach, then again against his jaw. He fell with a dull thud to the ground.

Raifer stood over him for a few seconds, gazing down at him as he thoughtfully brought his fist to his mouth and licked away the blood on the scrapes on his knuckles. The dockhand moved his own hand to his jaw, but he made no attempt to try to rise.

"Was there anything more you wanted to tell me?" Raifer asked him, his tone level now.

The man shook his head slowly from side to side, then winced at the movement.

"No," he muttered through a mouth that sounded as though it were filled with cotton.

Raifer smiled at that, deciding the man would have a bit of trouble chewing for the next few days.

"Then you can deliver one for me," he said. "You tell Terrence McGowan that if he has something to say to me, he can say it to my face, not through an interpreter. You have that?"

The man began to nod, then apparently thought better of it.

"Yea," he replied. "I'll tell 'im." He put his hand to his mouth and wiped a thin trickle of blood from his lips.

Raifer stood back. He looked down at the pair and smiled.

"Well, then, gentlemen, if we've nothing else to discuss, I'll wish you both a pleasant evening."

Then he turned and walked briskly along toward Water Street. He didn't even bother to look back to see if either of the toughs made any attempt to come after him.

The house, what little Raifer was able to see of it, held a good deal of elegance behind its rather stark stone facade. From where he stood in the entrance hall, he could peer into both dining room and parlor, and what he saw was decidedly pleasing. If the furnishings were not in the latest fashion—no rosewood or dark, heavy velvets—they were finely made and chosen with care. He found himself wondering what lay upstairs, what the bedrooms held, especially *her* bedroom.

Daniel saw Raifer's eyes lift in curiosity to the stairs that led upward, and felt the bite of indignation. He has his nerve, he thought, coming into my house, looking out expectantly for my daughter, as if he had the right.

But Daniel forced some measure of tolerance upon himself. After all, it had been at his instruction that Raifer had been made to wait, standing in the entrance hall, his hat in his hand, like some tradesman. Had it been Terrence escorting Honor that evening, Daniel would have extended him an invitation to his study and a glass of his whiskey. The lack of that offer had been intended to show Daniel's opinion of his place, a not too oblique suggestion to Raifer that he did not belong.

But now, as he stood and watched Raifer patiently wait for Honor to come down, Daniel found himself feeling a bit sorry for him. After all, it was not Farrell's fault that his daughter had chosen him to demonstrate her anger with Terrence. And he did look more than a bit uncomfortable in evening clothes. He's probably hardly even seen black tie before, David mused, let alone worn it. Although he had somehow managed to get the tie right, something Daniel found more than a bit troublesome himself.

"I'm sure she won't be long," he lied, knowing that although Honor had many fine qualities, promptness was not among them. Then, beginning to feel mean and taking a bit of pity, he added, "I don't suppose you'd like a small drink while you're waiting?"

Raifer turned and grinned at him. "I certainly would, sir."

The prospect of something alcoholic was quite obviously welcome. Daniel found himself stifling a grin. He's probably terrified about being in society tonight, he mused.

"This way," he said, opening the door to his library and motioning to Raifer to follow.

Raifer looked around, more than a little bit curious. The library was not a large room, but it had the right sort of feel to it, the right smell of leather and tobacco and books. His father's house had had a library very much like this one, and it had been, for him, the most comfortable room he'd ever known.

Raifer dropped himself easily into the leather-covered wing chair, finding the worn leather as comforting as an embrace, and watched as Daniel busied himself at the liquor chest.

Daniel was thoughtfully quiet as he measured out the whiskey into two tumblers and then added the soda. By the time he'd done, he'd decided he owed Raifer an explanation. He was far too likable a young man for Daniel to sit by and let Honor use him, and then, possibly, hurt him. Better to let him know what's going on at the start, Daniel determined, before he gets any hopes or expectations.

"Women," he began as he handed Raifer a glass, "are a bewildering lot, my boy."

Raifer swallowed the first sip of whiskey thoughtfully, appreciating the smoky, thick taste. Then he looked up at Daniel as he settled himself in a chair across from him.

"Sir?" he asked, wondering where this oddly begun conversation might lead.

Daniel looked down into the amber liquid in his glass. "They sometimes do things for reasons a man might find a bit baffling. Even the best of them are not always what they may seem."

"I'm not sure, sir . . ." Raifer began, but he was interrupted.

"Why, Papa, you couldn't have been talking about me, could you?"

Both men turned to the door and saw Honor standing there. Raifer had to admit to himself that she quite took his breath away. She was wearing a pale turquoise silk gown which hugged her waist, making it appear impossibly narrow, cut low to bare a provocative hint of cleavage and lavishly embellished with tiny seed pearls over the whole of the bodice. The strawberry-blond curls had been swept up to frame her face, a few tiny wisps falling free at the nape and temples. A collar of tiny seed pearls hung with a turquoise pendant circled her neck, and the new gloves and beaded bag she'd purchased that day he'd met her at the warehouse were in her hands.

He put his glass down on the table beside his chair and stood, unable to take his eyes from her.

She smiled at him. "Mr. Farrell, may I say you look quite handsome?"

Her eyes filled with laughter as she stared at him, but Raifer thought that there was little mockery in her voice.

"Only if you'll allow me to return the compliment, Miss Wainwright," he replied, his expression and tone quite serious. He crossed the room to her, took her hand in his, and brought it to his lips, all the while holding her eyes with his own.

Honor felt an odd flush coming to her cheeks. She could not remember when a man's touch had made her react that way before, and she found herself grow suddenly awkward. She looked down.

"Such gallantry, Mr. Farrell," she murmured, then, regaining a bit of her wits and returning her eyes to meet his once more, "and such flattery. I fear you will completely turn my head."

He raised a skeptical brow, grinning at her a moment before he released her hand from his.

"I doubt there are any words of admiration you've not heard countless times before, Miss Wainwright," he told her.

"Quite right, Farrell," Daniel said brusquely as he stood. He stared pointedly at Honor until she turned away from Raifer and toward him.

She couldn't miss the disapproval in his eyes. "Why, Papa, if I didn't know better, I'd think you were jealous," she said with a breeziness that surprised her, although she wasn't quite sure from where her sudden lack of assurance stemmed. She crossed the room to him and kissed him quickly on the cheek, reaching up to him on tiptoe. Then she dropped her bag to the table where Raifer had deposited his glass and began to pull on the long kid gloves.

"Ah," she said, looking up to the door and finding the butler entering with a sturdy tray in his hands. "Thank you, Fraser."

"What's this?" Daniel demanded. It was obvious that his feeling of pity for Raifer was fast fading, and the guarded antipathy he'd felt when he'd entered the front hall to find the younger man staring up in the direction of the bedrooms was quickly returning.

"Why, a bit of champagne, of course, Papa," Honor told him with her most ingratiating smile. "I thought we might offer a toast to Megan's future." She swept up her purse and glove as Fraser set the tray on the table and then watched as the impassive butler began to open the bottle.

"Megan's hardly going to enjoy the benefit of our good wishes if we keep them to ourselves, Honor," Daniel told her, his tone grown peevish.

She's up to something, he thought. If she's taken the effort to see that Fraser appeared with a bottle of champagne at precisely the right moment, she's undoubtedly up to something. And she looked beautiful in that new dress, perhaps too beautiful for her own good, he mused. For the first time he seriously wondered if there might be some other motive for her invitation to his warehouse help than pulling Terrence McGowan down from his high horse. The possibility did not please him in the least.

"Good wishes are never wasted, Papa," Honor chided him as she brought him a glass, then, smilingly, offered one to Raifer. "To Megan's future," she said as she raised her own glass. She let her eyes drift to meet Raifer's. "And to ours," she said softly.

Raifer smiled in reply as he sipped the wine. It was

good, just as the whiskey had been. Daniel Wainwright apparently kept a fine cellar, he mused, only the best. The best liquor, a handsome home, and a beautiful daughter, he thought. Wainwright hardly seemed to be the sort of man who had anything to gain in being involved with the types he had seen that afternoon with Kevin McGowan. Still, it was impossible to understand any other man's motives. And as long as the job let him enjoy both the liquor and Honor's company, there was no reason why he couldn't take some pleasure in them.

"Might I offer a toast as well?" he asked, raising his glass. Then, without waiting for Daniel's leave, "To new beginnings," he said, looking at Honor with the same bemused grin he'd given her at her toast. Then he turned his eyes to David, staring at him even as he finished, "And honest endeavors."

Daniel started, surprised by the words. For a moment, he felt a small flush of fear creep into his cheek, and he wondered why Raifer had chosen those words, wondered what he might know. But then he regained his control of himself and dismissed his reaction as foolish. He looked up and smiled at Raifer as he brought his glass to his lips and quickly drained the wine from it.

He's good, Raifer thought. But not quite good enough. Whatever is going on with McGowan and those unannounced guests of his, he knows about it. He kept his eyes on Daniel as he slowly drank the remaining champagne in his glass.

Honor stood between them, slightly perplexed. She'd expected her father to show some diffidence to Raifer, at least for the start of the evening, but something has passed between them that she did not understand in the slightest. They were engaged in some sort of mental fencing that completely eluded her.

She had little time to contemplate that possibility, for Daniel took the glass from her hand and, with his own, put them down on the table, depositing them with a shade too much vehemence. The small amount of wine that remained in Honor's glass sloshed about, and a few drops dribbled from its side to the shiny surface of the mahogany tabletop. An ordinarily fastidious man, Daniel seemed not to even notice.

"I think it's time we were on our way," he said abruptly. He started for the door, leaving Honor and Raifer to follow behind.

The atmosphere in the carriage was tense. Honor could feel her father's unvoiced disapproval and knew he was unhappy with what he referred to as her quarrel with Terrence.

Twice in the preceding week he'd referred to it as that, despite the fact that she'd tried to explain to him that there had been no quarrel, that her feelings, her decisions about his partner's son, were deeper and more pressing than the mere heat of a flash of anger. Her differences with Terrence were not dismissible simply because she couldn't name an instance and say he said this or he did that. But with each day that had passed of late, she had come to realize that Terrence had always had about him the hint of the incipient bully, something she'd dismissed as a child, assuming he'd outgrow it as an unfortunate aspect of his boyhood. She'd come to realize that that was not true, that the bully was growing inside Terrence, and there was no possibility that she could ever resign herself to living with it. Both her father's expectations and Terrence's own must be quashed, and the sooner the better.

Daniel's anger with Raifer, however, she'd really not anticipated. For the previous few days he'd mentioned Raifer with a sort of benignly aloof pity. But since her entry into the library and the unexpected champagne toast, she'd felt Daniel's anger grow, known it more clearly from the look of his eyes and his manner than if he'd said the words aloud.

He had expected Raifer to behave like some mannerless lout, she realized, embarrassing himself and, hopefully, her as his companion. It irked him that Raifer looked quite the elegant gentleman in evening clothes, and even more that he acted it. For a second she wondered at his apparent polish, wondering why a common laborer was not a bit more rough about the edges than Raifer seemed to be. But then she dismissed that thought, telling herself that he certainly looked handsome as he stared across the small carriage at her, his immaculate white linen stiff and pristine in the dim light that flickered through the windows from the street lamps, his blue-gray eyes shining at her with some secret amusement.

She felt Daniel shift on the seat beside her and knew without even turning to him that he disapproved of the glances she exchanged with Raifer.

"It's a lovely evening," she ventured, tearing her eyes from Raifer's and forcing a smile at her father. "The sky's full of stars."

Daniel only nodded. "Where are you from, Farrell?" he demanded abruptly. "I don't think you ever mentioned it."

Honor was horrified by her father's sudden lack of manners, but Raifer, it seemed, wasn't put off in the least.

"Upstate," he said, his tone easy, innocent. "I worked the Iron Weed mines near the Copake Flats, and read law at night with a local lawyer for the last two years with the hopes of getting into a law school and making a lawyer of myself someday. But when the iron petered out and the mines closed, I found myself without any funds and with no way of keeping myself. So I decided to come south, to the city." He grinned. "That is where a young man can expect to find his fortune, after all."

Honor felt herself smiling, almost smugly, and thinking to herself, *You see, Papa, he's a man with ambition and intelligence, and that's better than money.*

But Daniel was ignoring her still, staring at Raifer. "You intend to try to go back to reading law?"

Raifer shrugged and shook his head. "I think not. Law school costs money, and time. I'm starting to feel short of both. From what I can see, the smart thing to do is to go into trade." He grinned at Daniel. "It seems to have done pretty well for you and Mr. McGowan."

Honor could almost feel her father bristling inwardly at Raifer's words. As much as they pleased her, she knew they angered him, that he did not at all like the comparison Raifer made between the two of them.

"It's not as easy as it may seem," Daniel replied, a bit tersely, Honor thought, but not completely without civility.

"Nothing ever is, now, is it?" Raifer asked, his tone still pleasant, as though he had not noticed the ice in Daniel's manner. "But I've never been averse to hard work."

"And I think it quite admirable," Honor broke in. "Not everyone is willing to work for what he wants," she added, thinking of Terrence, who, it seemed to her, completely expected all the benefits his father's diligence had bought for him.

She turned and looked out the window to see that the carriage had drawn to a stop. "Well, it would appear that we've arrived," she announced, glad that the conversation would end now. She turned to Daniel and forced a smile. "And Papa," she admonished softly, "this is a party, after all. Smile." Then she began to laugh as he, quite obviously with some reluctance, did just that.

Raifer opened the door as soon as the carriage had halted, without waiting for the driver to climb down. He got out and stood waiting for her, offering his arm. Honor grasped it, pleased with the solidity of it beneath her fingers. *There's nothing weak about him,* she thought as he helped her down from the carriage and then tucked her hand into the crook of his arm.

They stood and waited for Daniel to follow them. Honor looked up at the façade of Kevin McGowan's new house. The impressive embellishments of carved brownstone, she had to admit, were a bit garish, but somehow they complimented Kevin's expansive style, and the reflection was in no way disparaging. As Kevin had said when he'd first shown them his newly completed home six months earlier, "I've made my bit by the work of my own brow, and I'm proud of it. Hell, why shouldn't I let the whole city know I'm now a man to be reckoned with?"

Honor remembered Terrence's glance at his father's words, the way his eyes expressed what he would not dare let his lips say, that his father's attitudes, his language, were beneath him, that he knew better than to accept such coarseness as part of himself. It had been that afternoon that Honor had come to the unpleasant realization that Terrence was not at all the man she'd thought him to be. She'd been ashamed of the fact that she had allowed her hand to be grasped by his, that she'd let him casually put his hand to her waist. She'd pulled herself away from him that afternoon, looking at him with newly aware eyes that saw him as he was, not simply as a childhood companion, but as the man he'd become. She had found she did not like what she saw.

The house had been empty that afternoon, the parquet floors echoing with their footsteps as they walked through the rooms, she and Daniel dutifully admiring the carved mantels, the stained-glass windows, the marble-appointed baths. Kevin's face had been so filled with glee, she remembered, that the excess of carved detail hardly made an impression on her, she'd been so contaminated by his pride and his sense of pleasure. The house was, however, no longer empty. Lights shone in every window that faced the street, shadowed by the swathing of newly installed draperies. Even the heavy silk could not entirely mute the sounds of music and voices from within, however, and the street held the faint echo of the party already begun inside.

Honor turned to Raifer, but her thoughts, she found, were still a bit on Terrence.

"Ready to face the lion in his own den?" she asked him softly.

Raifer peered down at her, her words reminding him of what he'd seen that afternoon, Kevin McGowan and his mysterious visitors, and he wondered just how much she might know about them. Now was not the time to ask her, he knew, now was the time to do just as she had suggested, face the lion in his own den.

"Only a coward would run now," he told her lightly.

They climbed the steps to the front door, then Raifer reached out, put his finger to the bell, and waited for the door to be opened.

Chapter Three

The maid who admitted them was clad in black and sported a neatly starched white apron stretched over an ample bosom. Immediately behind her stood a sour-faced butler who helped them remove their coats to hand them to yet another black-clad maid, this one mousy-looking and painfully thin.

It seemed only the butler was given to speech. "Mr. Wainwright. Miss Wainwright." He stared fixedly at Raifer for a moment, then turned away, apparently unsettled by the sight of a guest he did not know by name.

Honor interrupted his moment of distress. "Has Miss Megan come down yet, Potter?" she asked.

He shook his head as he handed the last of their coats to the girl and watched her disappear along a dimly lit corridor toward the rear of the house.

"Not yet, miss," he replied. "She asked that you be sent up to her rooms when you arrived, miss." His message delivered, he seemed about to return to his contemplation of Raifer's presence when his attention was diverted by the chime of the bell.

"Can I leave the two of you alone?" Honor asked Raifer and her father, her tone light, but her eyes, when they found Raifer's, quite serious.

He grinned back at her. "I'll make every effort to behave myself, Miss Wainwright," he promised. He lowered his voice so that only she could hear him. "I'll try not to disgrace you." With that he winked at her, then turned to follow Daniel, who'd offered them both nothing more than a disapproving glance, into the swell of the party, presumably toward the bar.

Honor watched them disappear, then told herself nothing much could possibly happen in a crowded ballroom. She turned to the tall flight of stairs, firmly grasped the ornate newel post, and started to climb.

Once she'd reached the second floor, she turned right, going directly to Megan's room, passing on her way a half dozen closed doors until she reached the one at the end of the thickly carpeted hall. She knocked softly, then opened the door.

"Megan? Can I come in?"

Megan McGowan sat at her dressing table, fumbling with a handful of emerald green satin ribbons. A maid stood behind her, obviously afraid to venture too close, her hands shaking as she reached out with the ivory-handled brush she held, but not quite managing to bring them to Megan's curls before the offending strands, indeed, the whole head, moved away in exasperation.

"This is impossible," Megan moaned desperately as she reached up to correct the misplaced curl and only succeeded in dislodging several others. "I can't go down there. Half the city is here, and . . ."

"And what?" Honor asked, firmly forcing herself to keep from laughing as she crossed the room. "If you don't go down, you shall miss your own engagement party."

Megan turned and saw her approach, and the panic began to slowly drain from her expression. "Honor. Thank goodness. Mama's so useless, I sent her away, and Mary can't seem to do anything right tonight." She lifted her hand to the slightly off-balance hairdo.

Honor gently pried the brush from the maid's frozen hand. "Why don't you go down to the below stairs dining room, Mary?" she suggested brightly. "I'm sure there will be some punch and cakes there in honor of the occasion."

The girl managed a weak smile of relief, then bobbed a quick curtsy. "Yes, miss. Thank you, miss," she murmured before she fled.

Megan frowned after her. "That girl's completely incompetent," she sniped. "Just look at my hair." She turned back to face her dressing mirror and scowled.

Honor put a firm hand to her shoulder. "If you don't hold still, it will stay that way," she warned. "And I don't suppose you could possibly think of any reason that Mary's a bit nervous this evening?" she asked coyly. "She gave every indication of being in fear for her life."

Megan quieted and stared up at Honor's reflection in the glass. "You can't understand how I feel, Honor," she said softly. "You're so pretty. And it always seems so easy for you. You can't understand what tonight means to me."

"Hush," Honor told her firmly as she began to carefully resettle the wild red curls. "Tonight, Megan, I can assure you, you are absolutely beautiful."

Honor found that the words were far more than simply well-intentioned flattery or mere comfort to settle her friend's obviously frayed nerves. Ordinarily Megan's sharply angular features, so very much like Terrence's, appeared completely undistinguished, if not absolutely drab. What appeared boyishly handsome in Terrence only seemed overly masculine on Megan, the sharp, just-too-long nose, the solidly square jaw and slightly pointed chin. But that evening none of those things seemed to be particularly noticeable about Megan when Honor looked at her. Her thin body seemed to have suddenly blossomed, perhaps owing to the softly disguising drape of the gown with which both she and the dressmaker had taken such pains, and either nerves or a maidenly contemplation of her forthcoming marriage had brought a blush to what were usually wan cheeks. The only disturbing feature was the unruly mass of red curls which Honor set about taming with determination.

When the last of the curls had been brought into some semblance of respectful behavior, Honor pushed away the green ribbons that matched the trim of Megan's pink silk gown and chose instead a half dozen tiny satin roses, which she pinned among the curls.

"There," she said as she stood back to admire her handiwork. "If one look at you doesn't make George Cavanaugh wish that he were being wed this evening, not simply announcing his intention to do so, I don't know what will."

Megan stared at her reflection in the glass for a long moment, seemingly surprised at what she saw there, then turned to face Honor once more. This time there was pleasure in her expression, not panic.

Honor smiled at her. "And I, for one, think he should consider himself decidedly lucky to catch you."

"I'm the lucky one, Honor," Megan told her softly. "I never thought any man would ever want me, never mind one so smart and handsome as George."

"I wish you only happiness, Megan," Honor told her gently. She tried not to think of the things her father had told her, about the settlement George Cavanaugh had demanded from Kevin to accompany the pledge of marriage. Daniel had seemed upset at the arrangement, feeling that the young law clerk's insistence upon making the marriage a cut-and-dried business arrangement was cold-hearted and mean. But Kevin had seemed willing to buy his daughter a husband with the same unstinting extravagance he'd shown with his new house. And Megan, as aware of the arrangements as was Honor, seemed entirely willing to ignore the less romantic aspects of her forthcoming marriage. She was, apparently, entirely taken with her fiancé and willing to accept him upon any terms whatsoever.

Megan, it seemed, could read Honor's thoughts, and she determined to dismiss them. She stood abruptly.

"Despite appearances to the contrary, Honor, I really

didn't ask Potter to send you up so that you could help me dress this evening."

"What better way to flatter a friend than to make her feel needed?" Honor asked. She seated herself on the small velvet-covered stool Megan had vacated as her friend crossed the room to a tall pier mirror and inspected her reflection one last time.

Megan bit her lip thoughtfully, a habit that screwed up her cheeks and lips and made her appear decidedly wizened. "It was that I needed to talk to you, Honor," she said.

"Well, that's flattering, too," Honor told her offhandedly as she brushed away a red hair that had fallen from Megan's brush and clung to her skirt during her stint as hairdresser. She folded her hands neatly in her lap and looked up at Megan.

Her friend had begun to pace the far side of the room. She was no longer biting her lip, but her face was still settled into the odd expression that meant she was deep in thought. Honor watched her in silence for a while, waiting, but it soon became apparent that Megan needed a bit of a push to begin.

"Megan, sweet, if it's about George . . ." she began tentatively.

Megan turned quickly and stared at her. "No, it's not about George," she sputtered, and her cheeks took on a heightened splotch of red. But whatever had spurred her anger disappeared quickly. She crossed back to Honor, sat on the edge of her bed facing her, and held her hands out to her.

Honor stood and crossed the few steps between the dressing table and the bed, taking Megan's hands and sitting beside her.

"I know what you think, Honor," Megan said softly, "that Papa bought George for me . . ."

"I never. . . ." Honor protested, but Megan merely shook her head and put a thin-fingered hand to her lips.

"I know you don't quite approve of him. And I know

your disapproval stems from your love of me. So don't feel that you can't admit it, Honor. And there's no reason why you shouldn't. After all, it's true—Papa did buy him."

Honor felt numb with embarrassment. These were hardly the words she had expected to exchange with Megan, certainly the last words she'd expected to hear from her on this particular evening.

"I don't know what to say, Megan," she admitted softly.

"There's not much to say about the matter," Megan replied brightly. "It was just that I've gotten past the point in my life where I can expect some miracle to happen to me, where I could expect some hero to appear out of nowhere and fall madly in love with me. I'm not the sort who inspires great passions. And heroes, I think, almost never simply appear out of nowhere. I entirely approved of Papa's paying George to marry me. I'm very fond of him," she said, and the blush reappeared. "More than fond. Although I realize he'll never feel that way about me, I've decided it really doesn't matter. He'll doubtless have other women. But I can deal with that. At least, I think I can. Mama has for twenty-seven years, and I'm sure I'm no less strong than she. But that's not what's important, you see. I'll be his wife and bear his children, and I'll be the mistress of his house. No miracles, Honor. I wanted this to happen, and I simply asked Papa to make it happen."

Honor's embarassment had fled during Megan's short speech, but it was quickly replaced by a dull feeling of depression. It had always been Megan who was the romantic, the one who lost herself in the nickel novels, the one who'd so often scolded Honor for her cynical pragmatism. And now she calmly spoke of her father's arrangements for her marriage as though the matter of going to sleep in a man's bed was no different from the business of importing Irish lace, while Honor listened with disbelief and the growing awareness that

Megan had somehow managed to change into a person she hardly recognized, and done it right before her eyes.

"But it's not me I wanted to talk to you about, Honor," Megan continued. "It's you. You and Terry."

Honor let a sign of exasperation escape. "Not you, too, Megan," she pleaded.

Once more Megan held up her hand. "I know," she said quickly, so as to interrupt any flow of protest. "He's been acting like a complete pig lately. For quite a long while, actually. I wonder that you've put up with him as long as you have. No, it's not that you won't have him that puzzles me . . . it's the matter of the other man, this Raif Farrell."

"You know about him?" Honor asked, completely bewildered.

Megan shrugged. "Certainly. Terry's done nothing but rant about him for the last three days."

Honor looked down to the hands in her lap. "And what has he said?" she asked.

"That doesn't matter, Honor. What *does* matter is that Terry isn't the sort who'll let it pass. I know him better than you ever will. And if this Mr. Farrell means anything to you . . ." She paused, the question in her intonation unmistakable.

Honor looked back to her, letting their eyes meet. She slowly shook her head. "I hardly know him. I don't know that he means anything to me," she said, even as she realized that the words were not entirely true. Raifer Farrell had begun to fascinate her, and she was acutely aware that her hand still tingled from where he'd held it earlier. "Besides," she added quickly, "I don't know that I mean anything to him, either."

Megan's dark brown eyes grew sharp and perceptive, but she made no attempt to refute Honor's words, despite what she saw in her expression. "If he really means nothing to you, Honor, if this is just some way of telling Terry things he ought already to know, then perhaps you shouldn't see Mr. Farrell again after this evening. Because I think there is a possibility that my brother might decide to arrange something unpleasant for him as a way to dissuade him from seeing you."

Honor drew back. "You can't be serious, Megan," she countered. "He may be bad-mannered at times, and act a bully, but he wouldn't . . ."

"Oh, yes, he would," Megan told her firmly. "He's incensed that you would prefer the company of a hireling to his, and even angrier that you chose to display that fact publicly by bringing him here tonight. I've never seen him quite so irate about anything before. And the last thing I want is to see you being hurt by him."

Honor stared at her for a long moment, wide-eyed and silent. "What's happened to us?" she asked finally. "Have we all changed so much? It seems we're all strangers to one another."

Megan smiled wryly and shook her head. "Not you, Honor. But we have, Terry and I. Perhaps the need to grow up isn't quite so strong with you, the need to let go of some things and cling too tight to others. I suppose it's just the way we are. Maybe we inherited it from Papa. We want our own way. And we each try to find some way to get it." She stood and held out her hand to Honor. "Perhaps I'm just seeing shadows, Honor. I really didn't mean to frighten you." She smiled then. "And I'm the one who's sworn to give up believing in anything I can't put my hands to touch. I think I've not done being fanciful, after all."

Honor laughed at that. "Surely not you, Megan," she said with a tone of unrestrained irony. She, too, stood and let Megan link her long, thin arm around hers.

"Let's go down," Megan said firmly. "I think it time we show New York's bachelors the opportunity they've all lost."

Honor turned to her sharply. If Megan felt any bitterness, however, she hid it well. Together, they left the room and started toward the party in the ballroom below.

Raifer sipped a glass of champagne. He stood quietly in the shelter of a large potted palm at the side of the room, hoping he was properly inconspicuous. He'd really not counted on the luck the evening would bring him. But from where he stood he could scan the room easily. And much of what he saw, he realized, would bring a gleam of delight to his captain's eyes when it was reported to him.

The small groups of men who huddled in conversation at the edges of the ballroom quite fascinated him. The guests included most of the city's rich Irish, he realized, men like Dennis McCarthy, who'd made a fortune as a liquor dealer and by peddling political influence; Thomas Brady, whose law practice somehow managed to finance one of the largest mansions on Fifth Avenue; as well as Kevin Murphy and David Donoghue, who'd wrested fortunes from their more Anglican competition on Wall Street. We Irish have done well by ourselves, Raifer thought glumly, one way or another.

He watched Kevin McGowan work the room, circulating from group to group, playing the part of the effusive host to the hilt. But he noticed Kevin somehow managed to take a few moments of rather intense conversation alone with some of the men, conversation that seemed far too heated to consist solely of mere pleasantries. And each conversation ended with a slap on the back and an enthusiastic handshake. He wondered what sort of a deal Kevin was closing at his daughter's engagement party. Something told him that it had to do with his visitors from the *Mary Louise*. If that was true, he felt sure it could only mean trouble.

"Penny for your thoughts, Mr. Farrell?"

He turned, surprised to find that Honor was beside him, staring up at him and smiling. He'd not even seen her approach.

"Or are they dire thoughts?" she asked him, the

smile gone now, her expression quite serious. "They certainly seemed portentous from where I stand."

He grinned lopsidedly at her. "Dime thoughts, decidedly, Miss Wainwright," he told her. "But now that you're here, they've escalated in value. Looking at you, I have only silver-dollar thoughts." His expression grew suddenly mournful. "But if you don't call me Raifer, I fear they'll be valueless."

"Yes," she agreed with a nod, "I had thought we'd gotten past the Miss Wainwright Mr. Farrell nonsense that first afternoon. Definitely Raifer."

"Good," he replied flatly as he put down his glass on a small table behind him. "Because it would pain me were I to take a woman in my arms and not even have the liberty of her given name."

"Take me in your arms, Mr. Farrell?" Honor asked, her expression showing some pretense of shock. "Whatever can you be suggesting?"

"Raifer," he corrected her quickly.

She pursed her lips primly, then nodded. "Raifer," she agreed with a grin.

"Better," he allowed, his tone now as serious as hers had been. "And I meant, of course, the first dance which you promised me. I'm quite shocked to think you'd think me so crass as to even consider anything dishonorable."

He held out his arm to her. When she put hers in its crook, he clapped his own atop it, holding it firmly.

"At least here," he added, "with half the city looking on."

"And were half the city not here as well?" she prodded.

He raised a slightly cocky brow and stared at her intently as he led her to the dance floor. "That, my dear Honor, raises some decidedly intriguing possibilities. But as there is little chance that we might be allowed to explore them here and now, I think it best we leave the discussion of them until a more propitious moment."

With that he put his hand to her waist, took her right

hand in his own, and swirled her onto the floor amidst a score of other couples.

Honor found he quite surprised her. After his recitation in the carriage of his past spent working in a small-town iron mine, she hadn't expected him to display any prowess in the art of the waltz. But his hand, where it rode at her waist, was firm, his grasp secure, the gentle cues his fingers offered completely without hesitation. She liked that, she decided, the warmth of his hand to her waist, the way he held her close, perhaps a bit too close for the critical eye her father was no doubt casting in her direction at the moment, but she decided she didn't care, that the sensation was decidedly to her liking, and she had no intention of pushing herself away.

He was silent. When Honor looked up at him, she realized that his attention seemed caught by the huge room, with its gaslit sconces and the huge crystal chandeliers, the long rows of gilt chairs along the wall and the thick opulence of heavy brocade draperies at the windows. All this crystal and gilt, she mused. How excessive it must seem to someone who's not had much in his life. Or how magnificent. She was really not sure if he was impressed or merely amused by it all. She waited until his eyes had completed his scan of the room and returned to find her own. She smiled up at him.

"Grand, all this, isn't it?" she asked. "Imagine, having a ballroom in your own home."

He stared at her a moment, then the corners of his lips turned up into a slightly sardonic grin. He nodded. "Grand," he agreed. The one word, no more, and then he looked up once more to his survey of the room.

Honor bit her lip. He hates it all, she thought. And he hates me for bringing him here.

Honor's evaluation of Raifer's silence, however, could not have been further from the truth. He was far from indifferent to the warm and lithe body he could feel moving just beneath the layer of silk that separated it from his hand. A long and interested research into the matter had taught him a great deal about a woman from the way she felt when he held her to dance. For instance, at that moment he could say quite definitely that Honor wore no corset, something of which he felt she had absolutely no need in any case, and that the gentle curves her dress advertised were indeed her own and not the result of painfully laced whalebone and canvas. Before his thoughts could travel too far in that direction, he put an abrupt stop to them. However attractive he might find Honor, and there was no use trying to tell himself that he did not because his body was giving him indications to the contrary and had been since he'd first taken her in his arms, he had a job to do—one that might very well find her involved in a matter he not only knew was illegal, but one he also found personally repugnant. It was one thing to feel the physical urgings of lust, quite another to let thoughts wander too far away from his real purpose simply because he found himself charmed by a pretty face.

Even as he scanned the ballroom and located Kevin McGowan's now familiar, bulky form hunched toward one of his guests in heated discussion, however, Raifer knew that what he was beginning to feel for Honor was not to be so easily dismissed. He found himself wishing, above all things, that she was ignorant of whatever it was McGowan and her father were up to with their unheralded guests in the warehouse. The thought that she might be involved had become more than unappealing to him, it had become something painful to contemplate.

He looked down at her finally as the music ended and saw she was staring up at him with a bemused expression.

"You don't approve of any of this, do you?" she asked him abruptly.

He was a bit taken aback by that. Whatever she'd seen in his expression, she'd interpreted it as disapproval.

"Envy," he told her quickly, hoping she'd accept his words and not try to pry too closely into his thoughts about her. "Simple envy shaded by the unpleasant suspicion that I shall never have my share of it."

She shook her head slowly at his words. "I don't believe you," she said flatly. "I don't believe you the sort of man who would envy another man's possessions. And I don't believe that you think there's anything you won't someday earn for yourself." She stared at him then, wondering why she'd burst out that way, not knowing quite what it was she wanted to see in his eyes and even more bewildered at the realization that it seemed to mean a great deal to her. He made no reply, and Honor turned away, puzzled at the small twinge of despair she felt at his silence.

"Perhaps you'd like to meet the happy couple?" she asked, forcing herself to keep her tone light, to seem as indifferent as he'd seemed to her.

He put his hand to her arm, stopping her as she turned to the long receiving line that had formed at the far side of the room just after Megan had made her entrance.

"If she's at all like her brother, I'd just as soon forgo the honor of Miss McGowan's company," he said, his tone a bit sharp.

Honor turned to him, surprised once more by his show of antipathy. But then he smiled at her, his eyes softening, the blue-gray glinting with promises and secrets that seemed both intriguing and mysterious.

"Besides," he told her, his tone once more lightly playful, "there's not a woman in the room who doesn't disappear when she stands beside you."

She colored slightly at the compliment. "More blarney, Mr. Farrell?" she asked, but still she knew she was pleased with it.

He shook his head slowly. "Upon my honor." Then he grinned. "What little there is of it."

Honor stifled a smile. "You're all alike," she said,

then added, "Megan is a lovely woman, not at all like Terrence in her ways, if that's what's bothering you."

"In that case, I'd be delighted to offer her my best wishes and congratulate the lucky fellow who's to wed her," he replied.

They began to cross the ballroom as the music started once more. Before they reached the long line of guests waiting to convey their wishes to the engaged couple, Raifer took her arm.

"Honor, we'll be standing in that line forever. Let's dance instead."

There was something about the way he looked at her, Honor found, a look of yearning that took her by surprise. So he's not put off or indifferent after all, she thought as she put her hand to his and nodded. That knowledge sent a long, pleasant finger of satisfaction through her, a reaction that bewildered her a bit as she'd seen the look quite a few times before in the eyes of a goodly number of men and never once before done anything but dismissed it. At that moment, when he once more put his hand to her waist, she felt as though she were floating on air. She had the answer to the question Megan had posed to her earlier that evening, an answer that entirely pleased her in a way she'd never been pleased before.

This time he seemed to have only one matter on which to concentrate as he danced with her, for his eyes never left hers. Honor felt the pressure of them, as palpable as the warmth of his hand on her waist. As they danced, she felt the music flowing through her. It seemed to her as though all the other people in the room had simply disappeared. This, she thought, was the sort of man she wanted, one who was strong and able and willing to work for what he wanted, a man who knew no shame for the poverty of his past or the extent of his ambition. If he was not the sort of man her father would have chosen for her, it did not concern her. He had far more compelling attractions, not the least of them more than apparent to her as he held her in his arms.

Raifer directed the two of them across the width of the room, toward the long line of French doors that led out to the garden. From the moment when they'd started for the receiving line and he'd seen Kevin McGowan lead Daniel Murphy through the door at the far side of the ballroom and into what appeared to be a small study, he knew he had somehow to find a way to listen to their conversation. A quiet moment with Honor just outside the library window, he'd decided, was the easiest way to accomplish that end. After all, there was no one who could possibly question his motives for wanting to spend a moment alone in the dimness of the garden with a young woman as handsome as Honor. But as they danced and he stared down at her, Raifer found himself in the uncomfortable position of feeling the necessity of telling himself quite firmly that his purpose in making his way out to the garden was not simply to be alone with her. It was an act of will to convince himself that his motives were strictly concerned with McGowan and Murphy. And in the end he knew it was a lie.

He forced his thoughts to what he knew of Daniel Francis Murphy. It was a good deal, actually, for, like any man who'd managed to provide himself with a fortune and some amount of power, Murphy had also accumulated a few enemies through the years, some of whom had made their own way into power. That, no doubt, explained the police dossier he'd read on Murphy. Raifer forced himself to concentrate on remembering what he'd read, rather than on the sweet, subtly enticing scent that emanated from Honor.

Murphy had emigrated to New York some forty years before, and in the course of those forty years had managed to make himself something of a legend. He'd earned his first fortune through the Tammany political machine, trading votes for favors and jobs for the newcomers who'd come to New York to flee famine in Ireland. But he'd managed to catch the scent of impending scandal and doom that had intruded on Tammany Hall, and transferred his talents and his small fortune to the equally risky gambling table called Wall Street in time to evade public censure. He'd come out a winner, indeed, one of the most impressive winners in an age of big gamblers. But his wealth had not completely separated him from his past. He remained staunchly loyal to his Irish heritage and just as staunchly outspoken in his criticism of the treatment of the Irish by the English. He'd backed up his position by personally funding the immigration of literally hundreds of Irish peasants. And, a fact that was a good bit more sinister, there was ample suspicion, if no concrete proof, that he was funding and arming Irish insurgents.

Kevin McGowan's warehouse guests and now a meeting with Daniel Murphy, Raifer thought. It all became curiouser and curiouser.

He made no mention of any of that to Honor, of course. Instead, when they neared the French doors, he edged them through the small group of idlers at the side of the room.

"A bit of fresh air, Honor?" he asked.

Hardly waiting for her answering nod, he put his hand to her waist and guided her out to the balustraded veranda. Large, ornate cast-iron planters were neatly arranged along its edge, all sporting the last of the autumnal chrysanthemums that patiently waited the killing bite of the first winter frost. The sky was dark and brilliantly clear, sprinkled with pinpoints of stars, and the air chill enough to make him regret the necessity of taking Honor from the warmth of the ballroom. He put his hand to her waist, and they began to walk along the deserted veranda towards the study he'd glimpsed Kevin and Murphy enter.

"Are you cold?" he asked as he pulled her a bit closer.

She looked up at him, and when he saw the moonlight turn her hair to gold and her skin to pale, iridescent silk, he felt a sudden lurch within himself.

"No," she told him firmly, her eyes wide, her expression a bit expectant. "Not when you hold me this close."

They were, he saw, close to the edge of the library window, away from the sharply reflected light from the ballroom, standing in one of the muted shadows cast by the more subdued library lamps. He turned to her and put his arms around her.

"Perhaps this might be a bit better?" he asked softly, moving her back a few steps, further into the shadows and closer to the ajar library window. Then, allowing her no time to answer, he lowered his lips to hers.

At first his attention was riveted to the conversation he could just discern from within the library. Murphy's questions, "Then they think ten thousand will suffice? There's a chance?" were quickly followed by Kevin's response, "They seem to be sure this will work."

Raifer pondered those words for an instant before his thoughts became tangled, then hopelessly lost to him. The touch of Honor's lips to his own, he realized, was not something to be quite so easily ignored as he had anticipated. There was a growing heat that began to fill him; he doubted he could have dismissed it even if he'd wanted to. But then, there was no thought in him to dismiss it. Instead, he pulled Honor closer and buried his lips against the warmth of her neck.

Honor found his touch simply intoxicating. There was, she decided, no other word for it. She felt a rush, like the rush she'd felt when she'd had the champagne earlier in the evening, only a thousand times stronger. She let her head fall back and brought her hands to Raifer's neck. For an instant she stared up into the black velvet of the night sky. Then she closed her eyes and gave herself over to the lush liquid flow that filled her, the heated warmth that she knew came from the contact of his lips to the bare flesh of her neck. Somehow the chill of the evening air seemed to have disappeared. She was filled with a pleasant, tingling heat. She didn't question it, didn't fight it. This was a new, undiscovered mystery that she instinctively knew was her first real lesson in womanhood. As she felt Raifer's dark curls beneath her fingers and the heady warmth of his lips against her flesh, she knew she was ready and eager to learn.

She wanted, at that moment, nothing more than to stand there with her eyes closed, her senses filled with the feel of Raifer's lips warm against her neck. But something seemed to be willing her to open her eyes, to let the outside world in. It was a silent command she had no desire to obey, but apparently no will to deny.

When she opened her eyes, she wished she had ignored the urge. Terrence McGowan returned her stare. He was standing behind Raifer, and there was such anger in his eyes Honor could not help but recall Megan's words of warning.

She pulled back from Raifer and whispered, "Terry!" Then she froze with fear.

Chapter Four

Raifer released Honor and turned. Terrence McGowan's hands were clenched into white-knuckled fists, and his lips were drawn tight.

"Get away from her, you bastard," he snarled. "Keep your filthy hands off her."

"Terry," Honor began as she stepped forward, trying to place herself between the two men.

But Raifer put his hand to her arm and drew her back, behind him. "What is it you want, McGowan?" he asked, his voice even and cold and assessing. "To give me a warning? Like the one your two friends tried to give me this afternoon?"

Honor saw Terrence's cheeks color, a dark red stain of anger and embarrassment.

"What two men?" she asked, trying to push herself forward.

Neither men answered, but Terrence's face went a shade darker and Honor needed no other answer. Horrified, she could do nothing but stand as she was and stare mutely.

"I gave them the only answer they deserved this afternoon," Raifer went on evenly, his eyes on Terrence's. "I'll be glad to offer you the same." His fingers quickly unbuttoned his jacket and he pulled it off, throwing it carelessly to the balustrade. "Shall we end this once and for all, now, like gentlemen?" he asked when he stood in vest and shirtsleeves.

"Gentlemen?" Terrence sneered. The unnatural blush had faded and left his face pale, his freckles sharply contrasted against the fair skin. "I wouldn't lower myself to dirty my hands on the likes of you."

Raifer's lips grew thin and tight, then turned up into a humorless grin. "No," he said slowly, "I don't suppose you would. You'd rather pay someone else to fight your battles. You don't have the stomach for doing it yourself."

"Are you calling me a coward?"

Raifer merely shrugged in response as he watched Terrence pull off his jacket.

"Stop it, the two of you," Honor shouted at them. She felt her voice shaking and knew it only mirrored the sensation of fear she felt. She put her hand to Raifer's arm. "Please don't do this," she begged him softly.

Terrence saw the gesture, her hand to Raifer's arm, and whatever wavering he might have felt disappeared. "Keep out of this, Honor," he told her flatly. "This doesn't concern you."

She turned her back to Terrence, wanting only to convince Raifer, to somehow get him away before some real damage was done. "Please, Raifer," she begged him softly.

But he put his hand to hers and gently drew it away from his arm, motioning her aside.

She felt a surge of anger of her own then. "I won't be fought over like a bone by two dogs," she told him sharply.

Raifer stared at her silently for a moment, then shook his head. "He's right, Honor," he told her softly. "This isn't just about you. It's a matter between the two of us." He put his hand to her arm and drew her back, to keep her out of danger.

Just as Raifer turned away from her and back to face him, Terrence lunged forward, landing the first blow to Raifer's cheek. Raifer staggered backward, the blow coming unexpectedly, before he was ready. But when

Terrence attempted to follow through with another, he found that Raifer had more than recovered, blocking his fist with his arm and landing a powerful jab of his own to the stomach, then following it with another to the jaw. Terrence staggered backward, momentarily stunned. Then both men stood facing each other, each with a pale trickle of blood trailing from his face to the pristine white of his shirt, Raifer's from the first, unexpected blow to the cheek which had left a bright slit just above his cheekbone, and Terrence from the corner of his mouth.

"Where the hell do you two think you are? In some back alley?"

The shout startled the two of them, and both men turned to find Kevin had vacated the peace of his library and stormed out onto the veranda. Honor had never seen him so angry. In fact, she realized she'd never seen him really angry before at all. But there was no dismissing the wrath that seemed to leap out from his eyes at the two men. She fell backward, a bit more into the shadows, unconsciously hoping to avoid his anger.

Kevin seemed to be completely occupied with his consideration of Raifer and his son, however, with seemingly no thoughts to waste on her at that moment.

"I don't care what this is about," Kevin continued, glaring at both Raifer and Terrence, "and I don't care which one of you is the injured party. I will not have brawling in my house. As of this moment, the matter is settled." He sent a warning glance toward Terrence. "And you will abide by that ruling. I will not have you ruin this evening for your sister. Is that clear?"

Terrence nodded numbly, unable to argue with his father but clearly unhappy with the outcome of the situation. Raifer, though, recovered immediately. He took his handkerchief from his pocket and held it to the dripping red trickle on his cheek. Then he turned to Kevin.

"I wish to apologize to you, sir," he said, his tone

genuinely earnest. "My conduct was unbecoming. I'll leave immediately."

His words seemed to mollify Kevin, for he shook his head and put a hand quickly to Raifer's arm. "No, no, my boy. That's not necessary. I'm sure there was provocation." He cast a quick glance at Honor, and then a long, meaningful one at his son. "The two of you shake hands, and there will be no more said about it."

Raifer grinned sardonically as he put his hand out with mock amiability. "Well, McGowan, shall we be done with it?" He stood then smiling, his hand extended, completely aware that he was only feeding Terrence's anger.

Terrence knelt and grabbed his jacket from where he'd dropped it on the ground. "To hell with you," he muttered angrily as he turned and stalked away.

Raifer slowly lowered his hand. Honor felt as though she were surrounded by a thick, uncomfortable silence. Finally Raifer broke it.

He turned to Kevin. "Perhaps I had better leave after all," he said.

Kevin considered him a moment, then nodded. "Perhaps you had better," he agreed. Then he too turned and left.

"Raifer." Honor moved to him slowly, reaching up to the cut on his cheek.

He pulled back. "It's all right, Honor," he told her. "I'm sorry it turned out this way."

He was too, he realized. It was more than just the awareness that Kevin knew he had been outside the library window, that eventually he would realize that he might have been overheard. He genuinely regretted not being able to spend more of the evening in her company. If he'd had any doubt about his growing feelings for her, it was swept aside by their kiss. He could still feel the tingling warmth, the pleasant softness of that contact. Staring at her once more brought on the throb of heat he'd felt as he held her in his arms. He found himself cursing the circumstances that had dictated the impossibility of a relationship between the two of them. He'd mourned missed opportunities before in his life, but he'd never felt the loss quite so deeply as he did at that moment.

"I don't understand why you had to fight with him," Honor told him as she took the handkerchief from his hand and used it to daub at the now thickening blood on his cheek. "He's foolish and childish, but that's no reason why you had to act the same way."

Raifer brought his hand to hers and drew it away from his face. "Men never act reasonable when it comes to a beautiful woman," he told her evenly.

He knew that that was only part of the answer, that if he'd refused to fight Terrence the younger McGowan would consider him weak, and find a way to see that his employment at the warehouse would be terminated. He would have failed miserably at his assignment. Now, at least, Terrence knew he would not give in easily, and Kevin would not allow him to be fired because of a misunderstanding over Honor, whatever his son's insistence. But that was very little comfort for the more immediate regret that filled him.

He looked down to where his hand still held hers, staring at it a moment before releasing it. "I must admit that I feel the fool now," he told her, "having to leave you here, prey to the upstanding Terrence's attentions while I return to my lonely room to spend the night with only thoughts of you to comfort me."

Honor stared up at him, wondering if he was laughing at her. She quickly decided that she didn't care if he was. "I'm aghast, Mr. Farrell," she told him primly. "And I took you to be a gentleman."

"I'm sorry that little exchange with McGowan has altered that opinion," he told her soberly.

She shook her head. "It wasn't that," she replied. "It's your willingness to simply leave and abandon me here. I thought a gentleman would never leave a lady to find her own way home unescorted."

Raifer grinned. "Your father?" he suggested.

She shook her head. "You are my escort tonight," she reminded him. "I should think you'd consider it your duty, however painful."

"Are you sure you won't mind missing your supper?" he demanded, no longer attempting to hide the smile that had been slowly tugging at his lips. "I've no doubt I could offer anything that might compete. I'll bet it'll be a handsome spread. Caviar, champagne, all manner of dainties, no doubt."

Honor laughed. "No doubt. Kevin wouldn't dream of stinting, especially not tonight. But I really think I've already drunk enough champagne this evening. And the truth is, I don't like caviar." She looked thoughtful. "I really think I'm in the mood for something sturdier."

He looked at her quizically. "Corned beef and cabbage?" he asked.

She laughed. "Well, perhaps not that sturdy."

"In any case," he replied, holding his arm out for her and waiting for her to put her hand in the crook, "I suppose we can manage to find something to please you."

She placed her hand on his arm, and the warmth of the hand he laid over hers quite pleased her. "If we go this way," she suggested, pointing to the library door Kevin had left ajar when he'd come out to the veranda, "we can avoid all the fuss in the ballroom."

He nodded. He found he had little inclination to face Terrence again at that moment, and there was little chance he could learn anything more that evening. A discreet departure was decidedly the most intelligent course.

The stars were sharply bright, with the brilliance of a chill fall evening. Honor snuggled into the fur drape of her evening cloak. She wondered where the cold had come from, remembering that she'd not felt it in the least just a few moments before when she'd stood in

Raifer's arms on the veranda. She smiled to herself. The warmth she'd felt then had come from within, something he'd lit inside her. If he took her in his arms once more and kissed her again, she was sure the night would seem pleasantly balmy despite the brisk wind she now felt on her cheeks.

She wished he'd do just that, take her in his arms and press his lips to hers, just so she could feel that odd surging liquid heat within her. But the avenue, it seemed, was sacrosanct. Raifer held himself, if not apart from her, no closer than society would consider proper.

"Well, Honor," he said, pressing her hand gently where it rode on his arm, "what takes your fancy? Shall it be Delmonico's?"

Honor shook her head. "Oh, no," she replied quickly. "It's so big and bright." And expensive, she thought. He certainly can't afford anything like that. "I'd thought we might find someplace quieter." She smiled up at him coquettishly. "Perhaps a bit more dimly lit?"

Raifer looked down at her and thought how pleasant it would be to take her to someplace like Delmonico's, to treat her to the sort of evening she no doubt enjoyed with others, with champagne and extravagant food and music. But if he was acting the part of a hired man, he could hardly be expected to have the sort of funds such an evening would cost. Not for the first time that evening he wished he didn't need to act a part with her.

"I know a few dark, dimly lit little places, Honor," he told her. "But not a single one is fit for the presence of a lady."

She was unperturbed. "Well, I happen to know of one myself," she told him brightly. "And I've been there before, so either it's fit for a lady, or else I can't use that appellation. In either case, it really doesn't matter." she smiled. "And the food is quite good."

"All right," he agreed, and raised his hand to hail a passing cab.

She put her hand to his. "It's not very far, and I

rather like walking with you. Besides, if I don't force you to spend all your money this evening, perhaps you'll see fit to ask me another evening." She stopped suddenly, and stared up at him. "Was that terribly forward?" she asked.

He nodded, his expression very sober. "Yes," he replied, but then he smiled. "Which way?"

She pointed away from the avenue, toward the west side. "Five or six blocks," she told him.

And another world, he thought. Five or six blocks separated Fifth Avenue with its mansions from struggling, poor neighborhoods where people fought to find enough money to feed their families. A strange city we live in, he mused.

The lights of the great houses along the avenue faded behind them until only the gas street lamps lit their way, aided by silvery moonlight and a few flickering lights from an occasional window.

"You were right," he told her when they'd gone about two blocks. "It is pleasant to walk."

He dropped his hold of her arm, and instead put his own around her waist. It was pleasant, he found, to feel the slope of her waist beneath his palm, the gently evocative awareness of what lay beneath the folds of her cape and the silk of her dress.

"We turn here," Honor told him, directing him toward one of the side streets. It was lined with small storefronts, mostly shuttered, all dark, barred and quiet in the late-night absence of customers. Butcher shops, he realized, and small groceries. They had a European feel to them, the same sort of shops he remembered lining the sides of a market street of a small town in France or Italy. The air still held the waning scent of yeast from the bread ovens in the basements of the bakeries, and the hint of bitter, sweet pungency that he knew could only be fresh blood from the butcher shops. Funny, he thought, how the scent of a place can bring back more memories than one would expect. It had been years since he'd spent that summer tramping through France and Italy after his final college year. But the sight and the smell of this street brought it all back to him with surprising vividness.

"Where are we?" he demanded, turning to look for a street sign.

Honor laughed. "In Brittany. At least that's what Claudine says," she told him. "Maybe someday I'll be able to agree with some measure of certainty," she added, a bit wistfully.

Raifer furrowed his brow. "Claudine?" he asked.

She nodded. "Claudine Charpentier. She runs the restaurant. Well, she and her husband and her sons and their wives. It's a family affair. It's really Claudine, though, who keeps it all together."

They'd reached nearly the end of the block, and Raifer noticed a small storefront that was not shuttered like its neighbors. A tentative finger of candlelight managed to make its way over fussy lace curtains that swathed the lower half of the windows. Raifer looked over them into a small room cluttered with a welter of tables squeezed too closely together, just about all of them occupied. People seemed to be as concerned with the food on their neighbor's plates as they were with their own.

Raifer hastily decided that tolerant resignation was the proper demeanor to take in his guise as untraveled laborer. From the glimpse he caught of the faces at table, however, he had quickly decided the food would be more than adequate.

He groaned just loudly enough for Honor to hear. "I'm prepared," he said, making his features stoic. "Do your worst."

Honor laughed and tugged at his arm, pulling him to the door. "You'll love it," she promised.

He opened the door and followed her inside. The place was noisy with a babble of rapidly spoken French. Claudine, it seemed, fed mostly her own nostalgic countrymen. The scents of wine-stewed meat and vegetables greeted him, and he could feel his stomach react with expectant pleasure.

An ample, gray-haired woman turned at the clatter of the tin bell as he pushed the door closed behind them. Her face lit quickly into a delighted smile as she recognized Honor.

"Mamselle *On-orr*," she drawled, her voice loud enough to momentarily interrupt the flow of two dozen conversations as she pushed her way through the maze of tables toward them, oblivious to the fact that she jostled a dozen of her patrons in her wake. They cast displeased glances at her, to which she was also totally oblivious, then went back to their food.

"Je suis ravi . . ." she began with a breathily exuberant enthusiasm as she approached. She halted in midword, however, and began again, this time in a heavily accented, studied English. "What pleasure to see you."

Honor smiled at her and took the hand she offered. "And it's a great pleasure to see you, too, Maman Claudine." She turned and motioned to Raifer. "I've brought a friend. I think he's rather hungry, Maman. Could you spare a crust for us?"

Raifer realized he was being openly and critically inspected. Claudine's large eyes swept up and down, and he found himself uncomfortably wondering what he would do if he did not pass muster with her. But once her examination was complete, she seemed satisfied and became amiable once more.

"But of course, ma cherie," she said, smiling now at Honor. "When has Maman Claudine ever turned away a hungry man from her door?" She grinned. "And a handsome, hungry man at that?" She turned toward the back of the room, where two young men in aprons and shirt sleeves scurried about with steaming plates in their hands. "Charles, Jean, une table. Vite! Vite!"

The two did her bidding immediately, clearing a table near the window, spreading a fresh blue-and-white checked cloth and setting out cutlery and two stiffly starched white napkins. As the younger, Jean, lit a fresh candle and brought glasses, Claudine bustled

Honor and Raifer to their chairs. Charles appeared, filling the glasses with dark red wine he poured from a small earthenware jug and then set it on the table while his mother surveyed the preparations before deciding that all was as it should be.

Raifer soon discovered that there was no menu, that Maman cooked what she liked each night and was even determined to make the choice of what she would serve them.

"Tonight is cassoulet and boeuf carbonnade," she said. "Both are good, but the cassoulet is better."

Honor nodded up at her obediently. "As you think, Maman," she agreed.

"And to start," Claudine went on as if there were no need for even Honor's small interruption, "salade des moules, and tarte tatin for dessert." She looked around the room, mentally counting the number of patrons and comparing it to the quantity of tart she had prepared that afternoon. She leaned forward conspiratorially. "I will see that the tart is saved for you," she said and smiled at Raifer. "You will like it."

Her decisions made, Claudine hurried off to the kitchen to personally supervise the preparations. Raifer studied her ample retreating form.

"That was easy," he said as Claudine disappeared and he turned back to Honor. "At least I think it was." He grinned at her. "What am I about to eat?"

Honor lifted her glass and sipped the wine. "Piggies' noses and chicken's toesies," she replied, then laughed when she saw his reaction. She set down her glass and reached out a comforting hand to his. "That's what Megan called it when I brought her here. It's not caviar or champagne, but it's good, I promise you. Just simple country food." She smiled and lowered her voice. "Megan's a bit spoiled, I'm afraid. Not that it's really her fault."

Raifer tasted his wine. It was young, a bit raw and slightly tannic, but pleasantly fruity, far from unpleasant. "And you, on the contrary, are not?"

Honor shrugged. "Oh, I suppose I am," she replied, not the least put off. "But I wouldn't dream of letting it keep me from a good dinner."

He laughed at that. "And Maman Claudine? Was she your nanny or some such thing?"

Honor shook her head. "The maman is strictly an honorific. She's 'Maman' to everyone, I think. Actually, she was one of my students."

That seemed to surprise him. "Your students?"

She nodded as she sipped some more wine. "I teach English classes at the settlement house downtown to immigrant women newly arrived here. Wednesday and Sunday afternoons. Actually, Wednesday there are few students. Most of the women work, you see. But Sunday I often have as many as fifty students in class. They all work so hard, they want so much to be able to do something more than spend their lives sewing piece goods ten hours a day. But for anything else, they need English."

"I didn't know that rich, spoiled young women concerned themselves with immigrant women's lives," he said thoughtfully.

She peered at him, her eyes narrowing. "Perhaps there's some small part of me that isn't quite so bad as you seem to expect me to be, Mr. Farrell," she replied slowly.

He reached his hand across the table to hers. "I doubt there's any part of you I'd call bad, Honor. It's just that you constantly seem to surprise me."

She blushed slightly, and looked down to where his hand covered hers.

"Pardonnez moi, monsieur."

The words were spoken a bit sharply, as though Claudine intended to remind them that however important romance might be, food was just a bit more important. Honor blushed once more, and, looking up to watch the older woman set down two plates of mussels and a basket of bread on the table, she wondered just how long she'd been standing there before venturing to disturb them.

"Maman Claudine was one my best students," she said to Raifer as Claudine refilled their glasses. "I think she taught me a good deal more than I ever taught her, though."

Claudine smiled with pleasure at the words. "Bon appetite, monsier, Mamselle *On-orr,*" she trilled as she left them to their food.

Honor lifted her fork and sampled one of the mussels, aware that Raifer was still watching her. She smiled at him reassuringly, put down her fork and reached for the warm loaf from the basket. "Be brave," she laughed as she pulled off a piece for herself and one for him.

He took the bread from her hand and looked down at his plate. "I thought fishermen throw these things away," he said diffidently as he forked one of the mussels.

"They probably do," she agreed. "Right into Maman's shopping basket."

They were good, Raifer decided, briny and pungent with the taste of olive oil, lemon, parsley, and thyme. And the bread, too, was just as he remembered it, thick crusted and chewy, with a slightly sour bite. Honor was staring at him expectantly, he found, and he smiled at her, dropping all pretense of hesitation.

"It's good," he told her. "I bow to your greater wisdom on the subject of comestibles." He forked another mussel. "How did you come to teaching the classes?"

This information had quite surprised him. After all, it was not the usual way rich young women amused themselves.

She swallowed a bit of bread. "My mother did it for many years. When she died, I just took her place. I had a good bit of French, and a smattering of Italian and German," she grinned. "The result of being totally inept at embroidery. Miss Porter's School for Young Ladies had to give me some graces in its place, so they settled on languages."

"And you like doing it?" he asked, totally intrigued.

She nodded. "We have so much. It's little enough to do for others, to try to help them make their own start. And then there are always students like Maman who teach me." She held up a mussel on her fork. "I really have learned a great deal from them," she added with a mischievous smile.

They both fell silent, concentrating on the mussels, and then the savory cassoulet that followed. Raifer found that she was more and more of an enigma to to him. A young woman with a social conscience, he mused. He wondered if she might be more than peripherally involved in her father's and Kevin McGowan's deal to send illegal weapons to the Irish insurgents. For that, he decided, was what the conversation he'd overheard between McGowan and Daniel Murphy had been about.

The possibility of her being part of the illegal traffic made the emotions he felt stirring within him when he looked at her all the more dangerous, and he knew it. He stared at her as she lifted her wineglass to her lips, letting his eyes catch hers. This is insanity, he told himself, even as he realized he was trying vainly to swim against a current over which he seemed to have absolutely no control.

"Good night, Honor," Raifer whispered.

Standing in front of her door, he realized that those were the last words he wanted to say. Come with me, sleep in my bed, let me make love to you . . . those were the words he really wanted to say.

"I had a lovely evening," she replied as she stared up at him.

It was late, she realized, very late, and her father would not be pleased. But it had been a lovely evening. They had lingered over the promised tarte tatin, neither anxious to leave and end the evening. Maman

Claudine and her family had accommodated them, magically conjuring up glasses of Armagnac to be sipped after the tart was eaten, and then leaving them to themselves, quietly clearing up the restaurant around them long after all the other patrons had gone. Eventually they'd become aware that they were the only two left in the establishment, that Jean and Charles were both sitting at the far side of the room, yawning and hopeful that Raifer might look their way, but afraid to make any outright suggestion that they leave for fear of invoking Claudine's wrath. Blushing with embarrassment, Honor had thanked them and Claudine for the fine meal as Raifer paid, then scurried out into the street on his arm, a bit shamefaced that she had not even noticed that the hour had grown so late.

Now, as they stood by her door, she realized she would gladly have the evening go on and on, that it was far too soon for it to end. She felt a bit lightheaded, she realized, aware that she'd drunk a good bit more than was her habit, but somehow sure that it was something else that made her feel slightly giddy, something wonderful and a bit terrifying. She'd never felt as comfortable or as happy in a man's company before, or as pleasantly on edge, in a way unsure of herself and yet still breathlessly expectant.

This is what it's like to fall in love, she told herself as she stared up at him. She wanted to shout the words aloud, to tell the world that she was in love. Instead, she put out her hand to Raifer and waited silently while he took it in his own.

He pressed it gently between his hands. "Good night, Honor," he said again as he reached for the door knocker and sounded it once, without much enthusiasm. Then he looked down at her hand and smiled crookedly. "This is no way to say good night," he murmured as he put his arms around her and drew her close to him, pressing his lips eagerly to hers.

Honor was aware of the same flood of heat that had

filled her while they'd stood on the veranda of Kevin's house when he'd kissed her, the same warm, liquid feeling that flowed through her, leaving her anxious and weak and wondering and breathlessly expectant all at the same time. She had never felt this way when Terrence had put his arms around her. She'd never felt this way before. She snaked her arms up and around his neck, pulling herself to him, hungry for the pleasant throb.

When she felt the gentle probe of his tongue to her lips, she parted them. She was aware she was trembling, but that it was not from fear. The tremor was rather the result of the tidal flow that surged within her. She was not quite sure she understood it, but she had no thought to question it. The gentle thrust of his tongue was only a spur to that throb. It was heady, the taste of it sweet from the tart and Armagnac they'd shared, but the sweetness, she found, was more than in the taste of it. She seemed to feel it, as if it could pass through her, fill her. She wished the feeling would never leave her.

But it did. There was the sound of the latch being drawn on the door, and Raifer hastily dropped his hands and drew back from her. Honor felt dazed, somehow cheated. When she looked into Raifer's eyes, she realized the sensation was not hers alone. There was a fire in his blue-gray eyes, and she instinctively knew she had set it burning.

"Miss Honor."

Fraser was dressed in his robe, a dark green velvet affair of which he seemed most proud as he he changed into it immediately when his regular hours were done and wore it even to open the front door, as he now did, for late-night, unexpected guests. Honor expected this was as much to show it off as to discreetly remind unannounced guests that late visits only cast doubt on their manners.

Honor nodded to him and turned to face Raifer once more, offering him her hand. "Good night, Mr. Farrell," she said softly, aware that the words sounded foolishly inappropriate in her own ears, that she could feel the flush and excitement his kiss had roused in her.

He caught her eyes with his own, and raised her hand to his lips, touching them softly to the gloved fingertips. "Miss Wainwright," he murmured, smiled at her, then released his hold of her hand and backed away.

He stood and watched her disappear into the house and the door close behind her. He didn't move for a long moment, even after she was gone, but stood there in the chill, clear October night, pensively watching the door as if he would will it to open once more and her to step through. Finally he turned abruptly on his heel and walked quickly away, disappearing into the dark shadows between the light of the street lamps.

Honor, of course, saw none of that. She was too occupied from the moment she entered the house even to think of peering out the window beside the door to watch him walk away. For as soon as Fraser had taken her cloak and disappeared with it, she found Daniel had somehow silently materialized and stood staring at her.

She smiled at him pleasantly. "Papa. What are you still doing awake?" she asked easily as she slowly pulled off her long kid gloves.

Daniel's eyes followed the motion of her fingers as they nimbly unfastened the row of tiny pearl buttons. "Where have you been, Honor?" he asked, ignoring her question, his tone filled with concern and a hint of disapproval. "When you weren't at dinner, Kevin told me that he'd found young Farrell and Terry brawling, that the two of you left. I came home assuming to find you here. I've been worried to death about you."

Honor walked quickly up to him and stood on her tiptoes to kiss his cheek. "Dear Papa. I should have told you before we left, but it seemed politic at the time to avoid Terry. He was behaving like such a fool. Mr. Farrell took me to supper, that's all." She smiled at him.

"And a very good one at that."

Daniel scowled. "I don't pay him enough to allow him to take you to supper," he told her archly.

Honor laughed. "I introduced him to Maman Claudine," she replied. "I dare say he was a bit bewildered by the food, but not completely put off."

Daniel's brow furrowed a bit deeper. "Honor, I applaud the sentiment that leads you to teach those classes at the settlement house, but I can not understand why you feel you must mix with those people. Just as I don't understand your apparent fascination with this Raif Farrell."

Honor's face drained, and whatever trace of her smile lingered was quickly made to disappear. "Those people, as you call them, Papa, are the same as we, no better and no worse. The only difference is that your father had the good luck to come here when he was young and theirs did not."

"Honor!"

But even the tone of warning in Daniel's voice did not still her. "I won't listen to you denigrate them, not the ladies in my class, and most certainly not Raifer Farrell, Papa." She turned away from him and strode quickly to the stairs. As she put her hand to the newel post, she turned back to face him. "And I won't stay here any longer and let you ruin what was the most wonderful evening of my life." With that she quickly turned and ran up the stairs.

"Honor!" Daniel called to her, but she ignored him. He stood at the foot of the stair and stared up after her, calling out her name once more, only to be answered by the sound of her bedroom door slamming behind her.

Daniel was, he found, more than a little surprised with her defense of Raif Farrell. He'd been so convinced that she had been using him to get to Terrence McGowan that until that moment he'd not really considered the possibility that she might actually have any real feelings for him. At that moment the possibility came home to him with a painful certainty that things he would not like were about to happen.

He wandered into his study and made his way straight to his liquor cabinet. He poured a large tumbler of whiskey and then sat with it in his hands, staring into the dark, amber-colored liquid. If Honor was forming some attachment to this Farrell, he told himself, he must see that it was stopped before anything serious came of it. He would not see his daughter wed to a nobody like that. The whole situation entirely bewildered him. If he'd known his daughter to be independent and occasionally stubborn, he'd never thought her willful before, never considered the possibility that she would purposely do something she knew to be contrary to his wishes. But that was what she seemed to be doing now, and flaunting her disregard for his opinion to boot. Yes, he told himself as he sipped his whiskey, this friendship with Farrell must be ended, and the sooner it was concluded, the better.

How to do it, he realized, that was most important. Young people were more apt to jump in precisely the wrong direction if pushed too hard. It would not be a simple matter to have her think the break came from her own reasoning, not his. Or, even better, if Farrell could be induced to cooperate, he mused thoughtfully. That might be the best way of all.

Chapter Five

Police Captain Michael Ryan sat with his feet propped comfortably on his desk. From where he sat, Raifer could see little more than the bulge of his belly stretched against the white of his shirt and the heels and soles, both well worn, of his boots.

The small, cramped office was silent, save for the noise of an indrawn breath and the occasional sound of paper rustling as the captain slowly made his way through the pages of Raifer's report. Raifer knew that he was sucking on his lips, an action that connoted deep thought, for he could hear the older man's sharp, liquid intake of breath. It was not a habit Raifer found at all appealing when accompanied by the view of Ryan's indrawn, red-splotched cheeks. At that moment, with Ryan's face hidden from him and only the view of his belly and feet to accompany the sound, Raifer found it even more annoying than usual.

For a while he tried to distract himself, trying to remember what it was he had written on those pages Ryan now inspected with such studious attention, but that part of the night, when he'd returned to the unpleasant rooms he'd rented to enforce his disguise of Raif Farrell, laborer, seemed blurry and indistinct to him. All he could remember with any clarity was the way Honor had looked as she bade him good night, her lips and cheeks colored with a warm rose blush from his kiss, her eyes wide and betraying her regret at his leaving. He'd been haunted by that image of her all the previous night, his conscience nagging at him and making it impossible for him to sleep. His conscience, and something else.

Ryan finally removed his feet from the desk and swung them heavily to the floor. Then he sat forward and let the pages of the report drop to its surface.

Raifer took a long swallow of the coffee from the cup in his hand. It was still too hot, and it scorched his tongue. "It's Sunday morning," he said abruptly before Ryan could speak. "Hasn't it occurred to you that a good Irishman belongs in church on a Sunday morning?"

Ryan smiled, and there was a distinctive spark of humor in his eyes. "But I've never claimed to be a good Irishman, Raifer. Unlike our friends," he tapped the sheets of paper, "McGowan and Wainwright. They are, I assume, safely tucked up, occupying themselves with public displays of humility and prayer in the company of their loved ones, Wainwright at Trinity's Episcopal, and McGowan uptown at Saint Pat's." He looked thoughtful. "How come these two, a Catholic and a Protestant, can manage to get along so well, while across the pond they're hot for each other's blood?"

Raifer shrugged. "Perhaps instead of exporting rifles they might send over a few lessons in brotherly love?"

Ryan chuckled. "Well, that is an idea. I don't suppose you'd care to make the suggestion to them?"

Raifer made no answer, and Ryan went on.

"No matter. Well, we'll know what they've been up to soon enough. I've got a few watchers looking after them, and a couple across the street from the warehouse as well, in case those friends of McGowan's decide to make a little pleasure tour of the city." His eyes narrowed and he looked at Raifer sharply. "That news doesn't seem to please you. Could it be that the thought of someone else trailing around after the beautious Miss Wainwright upsets you, my boy?"

Raifer looked up at him sharply. "I don't like any of

it," he burst out. "I don't like lying to her. I don't like pretending to be something I'm not. And most of all, I don't like knowing that I'm helping you to put her father in jail." He leaned forward toward Ryan. "I think I want out of this one."

Ryan shook his head. "Too late for that, Raifer. We can't get someone else in there at this late date. Whatever happens will happen soon, and you know it. You knew what you were getting into when you began this. You'll just have to swallow whatever objections you have to the assignment . . . and get your mind back on what you're supposed to be doing and away from Honor Wainwright's ample charms." He smiled genially. "Or is it those two grubby little rooms you're in for this one? All you really want to do is go home to the niceties a working-class type like me can't afford. It must be tough on you, to have to rough it out like the rest of the peons do."

Raifer kept control of his anger. He knew Ryan resented the fact that he had a private income, that there was more than a bit of envy for the money he'd inherited. But he also knew that despite the envy, Ryan knew he was very good at his job, and that he respected him for that. He endured the gibe silently until the anger passed, aware that even the silveriest lining oftentimes was surrounded by a dim gray cloud.

He smiled when he could honestly say the rancor had disappeared. "If you're trying to ask me for a loan, Captain, you're going about it in all the wrong ways," he said, but his tone was light, and he knew Ryan wouldn't take it amiss.

Ryan, too, smiled. "Yesterday was payday," he replied. "I'll think about sweet-talk come Wednesday. In the meantime, I suggest you get back into guise." He leaned back in his chair and stared at Raifer as he stood. "Somehow I like thinkin' of you in work clothes," he drawled, "raisin' a good, healthy sweat."

Raifer grimaced and turned to the door.

"Farrell," Ryan called. Raifer turned to face him.

"Remember those two men I have watching the warehouse. They're within easy call. Like I said, something's bound to happen soon. You may need them." His eyes narrowed as he watched Raifer nod in acknowledgment of his words. He did not know why, but he felt an unpleasant suspicion of something wrong about to happen, a kind of itching at the back of his neck that would not be appeased. The feeling did not sit well with him. "I don't suppose," he continued, "that I need bother tell you to be very careful about this one?" His expression grew thoughtful. "I did mention that our own beloved Chief Fitzpatrick plays cards occasionally with our wrongdoer, didn't I? If anything goes wrong, I have an unpleasant feeling Wainwright and McGowan have enough influence to have both our asses in rather uncomfortable slings."

Raifer grinned, but there was no humor in his expression. He was more than well enough aware of the political infighting that marked the taut relationship Ryan shared with Chief of Police William Fitzpatrick. He wondered for a moment how much Ryan's dislike of his superior had influenced his decision to pursue the information he'd received about Wainwright and McGowan. It would please him, Raifer thought, if he could prove that two of Fitzpatrick's friends could be implicated in something unsavory. No matter, he thought. Wainwright and McGowan were harboring the Irish terrorists. He had no doubt about that.

"I believe you might have mentioned that fact," he replied as he reached for the doorknob.

"And Raifer," Ryan said, stopping him once more, "for your own good, stay away from the young lady. Unless I miss my guess, she's nothing but poison for you."

His eyes caught Raifer's, and he was suddenly aware that those particular words were not ones that Raifer wanted to hear.

Honor sat beside her father and stared up unblinkingly at the sanctimonious face of the Right Reverend Jonas Mather. It was a pose she had taken for each Sunday for the past several months, and she did it, she realized, simply because she knew it made Mather uncomfortable. Each time his eyes scanned the sea of upturned faces in his congregation, they inevitably hesitated when they found Honor's. Often he'd stumble over his words then, and occasionally a splotch of red would appear in his otherwise wan cheeks. Honor realized that the only reason she did not beg Daniel to allow her to stay home on Sunday mornings was that her presence disturbed Mather. That, and the realization that she would have a hard time explaining to him exactly why she'd rather remain at home than accompany him to church.

Actually, it had all begun innocently enough. Mather was new to the church, having recently taken the place of old Father Hayes, who'd died of influenza the previous winter. When she'd first met him, Honor had thought Mather a friendly enough person, if innocuous, with a tall, bony solidity about him and the kind of dark, shining eyes that bespoke suspicion and the ability to see hell and damnation wherever he looked. But he'd been more than pleasant enough with her, often grasping her hands between his own as he greeted her and Daniel each Sunday after services, usually lingering to talk with them far longer than the requirements of his position dictated. She'd come to the conclusion that he was genuinely bound to his vocation, albeit a bit overzealously if his sermons were any evidence of his vehemence. She'd decided he was genuine enough, pleasant if he desired to be, and more than a bit old-maidish in his outlook. All of which only showed her how wrong she could be as a judge of character.

It had been a Wednesday afternoon, right after the class at the settlement house, that the idea had come to her, to ask him if he might consider asking the parishioners to find places for her more advanced students. Domestic work had to be better than laboring in dank factories for ten hours a day, she reasoned, and it would help them improve their language skills if they were forced to speak English. She'd decided to broach the subject with the new minister immediately, wondering why the idea had not occurred to her before.

She'd gone directly to Trinity and made her way to Mather's office. He'd greeted her pleasantly enough, and she'd reminded him of her work at the settlement house.

"Of course, my dear," he'd replied as he put his hand to her arm and drew her into his office.

But Honor had known something was wrong as soon as she'd seen him push the door closed firmly behind them. She turned sharply to find he'd thrown the bolt. It was only then she'd recognized the alcohol on his breath.

"I knew you'd come to me sooner or later, Honor," he'd sputtered. "I knew you could feel the same mystical bond that I feel, the same force pulling us together."

There'd been a horrible moment when she felt his hands snaking around her and his lips touching hers. Then she'd recovered from her amazement and put her hands to his chest, pushing against him, pummeling his rail-thin torso until he'd let her go.

"The only mystical bond you've felt emanated from a bottle of whiskey," she'd sneered at him as she'd backed toward the door.

When he'd moved after her, she'd shouted at him. "Come one step closer and I will scream rape, sir. And I will continue to scream it, and into the ear of every one of the elders of this church."

That had stopped him, at least long enough for her to unbolt the door and run out of the room and down the long hallway that led to the door to the street. When she'd reached it, she'd heard him following her, running after her and crying out for her to stop, to listen to him, to let him explain. One quick glance back at him, however, had been enough to convince her that explanations were not quite what he had in mind. She'd run out to the street and hailed the first passing hansom she'd seen, climbed into it, and not looked back again until it had started down the street.

She sat back then, thankful for the escape, and thought. She'd realized almost immediately that there was really nothing she could do about what had happened. In the end it would be his word against hers. He would be sure to mention that she had come to him unchaperoned, alone, late in the afternoon, when it was most likely he would be alone in the church. So she'd said nothing, not even to Daniel, and had contented herself with sitting in church Sunday mornings, staring up at him and smiling, watching his embarrassed reaction whenever his eyes met hers, and reminding herself that he was one of the weaker and more odious vessels of religion, the exception, not the rule.

At the moment, however, even the sign of Mather's embarrassment could not distract her from her thoughts, and she simply wished he would hurry. Daniel had been tense and quiet with her during breakfast and the trip to church, and she knew he was working his way toward a definite discussion of her activities of the previous evening. She had, however, little intention of allowing him the opportunity. She simply did not have the time for it.

That morning she'd realized she'd lost an earring the night before. It was not just any earring, but one of a pair that had been her mother's, and her mother's mother's before her, a small shower of diamonds and tiny baroque pearls set in gold. It hadn't taken her many moments' concentration to decide where she must have dropped it. The more she thought of it, the more clearly she recalled having felt a small tug at her ear as Raifer had drawn away from her when Terrence had disturbed their kiss. If she'd not been so surprised — and, yes, frightened, at that moment — she would have realized it at the time. As it was, she'd had other things on her mind.

But now she realized how much she would hate to lose the piece of jewelry, how neglectful of her own heritage its loss would seem to her. By rights and tradition, the earrings should someday belong to her daughter and then her granddaughter. Losing the earring was unthinkable.

She had just enough time, she decided, to take a cab uptown to McGowan's, claim the earring if it had already been found, otherwise search the veranda for it, then take a cab back downtown to the settlement house. She should be just in time for her class if she didn't waste too much time finding the missing piece of jewelry. She would not have to spend any time with chatter, as Kevin and his family would be still at church, and the servants would have their hands full with the debris from the party. All of which quite pleased her. At that moment, she realized, she had little desire to see either of the McGowan men, neither Kevin nor Terrence.

When the final hymn was sung, therefore, she stood immediately.

"Papa, I must be off," she told Daniel crisply. "I've an errand, and then I must get to my class."

He reached up and put a firm hand to her arm. "You can't just run off, Honor," he began. "I want to talk to you. And it's impolite to just bolt out of church."

"I'm sorry, Papa—really, I am. But if I don't hurry, I'll be late for my class. And you can offer my very best wishes to Father Mather," she added with a slightly malicious smile.

But Daniel didn't release her arm. "And does this errand have anything to do with a rendezvous with that Farrell person?" he demanded suspiciously, his tone hushed but the words drawn through tightly clamped teeth.

Honor forced down the immediate reaction of anger at the way he referred to Raifer. "No, Papa, I have no intention of meeting Raifer Farrell," she replied, her lips drawn as tight as his had been.

Daniel stared at her an instant longer and then released her. He didn't like any of this, he decided. He thought it wiser, however, not to make a scene there in the church, to draw any attention to the two of them. "I'll see you at home, Honor," he said finally as she edged her way from the pew.

She nodded, then slipped down the carpeted aisle, making her way through the crowd that was beginning to drift toward it and to the door.

Mather, she found with a good deal of relief, had not yet taken his place by the door. She darted through it and out into the startling brightness of a sunny October morning.

"Miss Honor?"

Honor almost enjoyed the unusual, almost unprecedented display of Potter's surprise. It seemed she had managed to unsettle him twice within two days, first by appearing the night before on the arm of an absolute stranger, and now by simply appearing.

"Good morning, Potter," she told him crisply as she entered the foyer. "I'm sorry to disturb you. I've no doubt you're all quite busy, so I won't get in your way. I think I lost an earring last night."

"No one has mentioned finding an earring, miss," Potter told her.

"Oh." Honor felt a bit disconcerted by that, and her certainty wavered. She'd been so sure she'd lost it in that tense moment just before Terrence and Raifer began their unfortunate argument. Now she was beginning to feel a good deal less positive. "On the veranda?" she suggested. "I was so sure I'd lost it there."

Potter shrugged as if to distance himself from any false impression he might have given. "Oh, I don't think anyone's been out there yet this morning, Miss Honor. There's been so much to do."

Honor felt a wave of relief. "Then I'll just take a quick look around myself, Potter," she said, turning toward the ballroom.

The huge room seemed somehow a bit sad now, in the morning light. Half-emptied glasses littered the tables along with tiny crumpled linen cocktail napkins. The gilt chairs were partially stacked, and a half dozen servants were busily clearing things away on large trays and attacking the scuffed floor with enormous buckets of soapy water.

"Do watch your step, miss," Potter warned, scurrying after Honor as she skirted the already damp portions of the floor. "I can have Patrick help you look, if you like." He motioned toward a young man who was energetically stacking the gilt chairs along the side of the room.

Honor shook her head, rejecting his offer. "Don't disturb anyone, Potter. I'll just have a quick look myself. If I can't find it, perhaps I'll take advantage of your offer, but I hate to bother you. It looks as if you've your hands full as it is."

The butler seemed more than relieved at that, and halted his pursuit of her, letting her go on alone. He turned to a critical inspection of the work being done as Honor crossed the remainder of the room and slipped out one of the French doors to the veranda.

It seemed incredible to her that the afternoon felt so pleasantly warm. In the enclosed space of the garden, protected from any wind, the sun had heated the bricks underfoot and the iron balustrade that edged the veranda. It felt as warm and sultry as a summer afternoon might, and it brought back the pleasant memory of the warmth she'd felt the night before, another kind of warmth, that strange heat she'd found growing within her when Raifer had taken her in his arms.

She closed her eyes and imagined herself once more in his embrace, remembered the feel of his lips pressed against hers, the even more enticing sensation of his tongue touching hers. Just the memory brought back the odd liquid feeling, and added to it was the strange, pressing regret she'd felt when he'd left her at her door.

She forced her eyes open and began to walk toward the library doors, searching amongst the bricks for the missing earring as she stepped carefully forward, and telling herself that she was acting like the sort of lovestruck little fools who peopled the novels Megan pressed on her. Unexpectedly, she realized she was smiling as she made the comparison.

Then she pictured one of those heroines engaged in the sort of kiss she'd shared the evening before with Raifer. There had never once been the description of that sort of kiss in any of those books, not one. Heroines, it seemed, were permitted only one chaste kiss, mouth closed and lips dry, she was sure, at the very end of the novel, when the adventure was completed, just after the hero had proposed. It was, she decided, a highly unsatisfactory way to entertain the prospect of marriage. She earnestly hoped that a real love affair was not as dry and as passionless as those described in Megan's novels. And then she laughed out loud at the thought, the probability of a haplessly helpless heroine, with only the experience of a single, chastely modest kiss, engaged in the sort of embrace she and Raifer had shared. As she laughed, she spotted a glinting reflection of sunlight gleaming sharply from the near edge of the veranda just beside the door that led to Kevin's library. She stepped to it and knelt. There, close to the side of a large cachepot, was the lost earring.

"What's that? Who's there?"

The sound of Kevin's voice was completely unexpected, and it quite startled her. It had not even occurred to her that any member of the family might be home, rather than uptown at Saint Patrick's.

"It's me, Uncle Kevin," she said as she slowly got back to her feet. "Honor."

She peered in through the glass door to the library, squinting in the brilliance of the sunlight and trying to see into the far dimmer room inside. With her eyes narrowed and adjusted to the differences in the light, she realized that Kevin was not alone in the library, that the huge mahogany desk was surrounded by four other men as well, men who sat in their shirtsleeves and leaned over the papers that littered the shiny, dark surface.

Kevin sat for a moment, staring at her. His cheeks colored slightly, as though he'd been caught doing something he oughtn't. Then he stood abruptly and made his way to the doors, opening them to her with only the slightest show of reluctance.

"Honor," he said as she smiled weakly at him. "What a surprise to see you here."

Honor held up her hand to him and opened it. The earring lay on her palm. "I lost this during the . . ." she paused for a moment, realizing that the situation was as difficult for him as it was for her, "the misunderstanding last evening. It was Mama's, and I hated to lose it, so I thought I'd come see if I could find it."

As she spoke, her eyes drifted to the four men who sat by the desk. They were, she noticed, staring grimly at her.

"I'm sorry to have interrupted you," she said quickly, beginning to back away, to return to the veranda.

Kevin seemed relieved at the prospect of her immediate departure, but one of the three rose and made his way across the room to them.

"Ah, now, Kevin," he said, putting his hand out to greet Honor as he moved, "you aren't about to allow this bonny creature to leave, and me without an introduction?" He grinned at her pleasantly.

Honor found herself staring into a pair of handsome dark eyes. He was not tall, only an inch or two taller than she, but his walk was a powerful stride, and there was no mistaking the strength of his arms and shoulders. There was something vaguely predatory about him that quite puzzled her. She found her hand quickly grasped in his firm, callused grasp.

"Brian Flannagan, miss," he introduced himself, his

thick brogue seeming to linger in the air even when he'd finished speaking.

Kevin quickly collected himself. "Excuse my manners," he muttered, but Honor noticed he stared at Flannagan with an oddly sharp expression, one that said he took no pleasure in making the introduction. "Honor, this is Mr. Brian Flannagan, the son of an old friend of mine. He's here on a short visit. Brian, this is Honor Wainwright, the daughter of my partner and best friend." He waved vaguely at the three other men who were still seated. "And his friends, Mr. Donoghue, Mr. Moynahan, and Mr. Burke."

Three heads nodded toward Honor, but no one spoke, nor did they make any motion to rise. Honor had the distinct feeling that she had interrupted something she ought not to have, that all five men were decidedly displeased with her presence.

"You're visiting from Ireland, then?" she asked with a wan smile, trying ineffectually to make some sense of what was happening around her and not succeeding in the slightest.

"From County Cork," Flannagan replied with another intense grin that somehow made Honor feel only more ill at ease.

"I hope you're enjoying your visit, Mr. Flannagan," she ventured. "Will you be staying long?"

He shook his head dolefully. "Alas, no, Miss Wainwright. Had we known there were such powerful attractions here, we might have arranged for a longer stay." He smiled at her once more. "But as it is, I'm afraid we must be returning in just a day or two more."

The pleasantries obviously completed, Honor decided she'd best take her leave. "I'm sorry to have interrupted," she said again to Kevin. "I found my earring, and now, I'm afraid, I must be off or I'll be late for my class." She carefully placed the object of her search in her purse, then drew its silk ropes tight to close it.

"Oh, yes," Kevin muttered absently. "That class you

teach to all those Germans and Poles." There was a note of derision in his voice, but Honor purposely ignored it. He put his hand to her shoulder and guided her towards the door. "I don't want to keep you, my dear."

"It was a great pleasure to make your acquaintance, Miss Wainwright," Flannagan said.

Honor paused and turned back to him. "Yes, a pleasure," she replied.

"Perhaps there'll be an opportunity some day to make up for the unfortunate brevity of this visit." Flannagan was once more smiling at her, and his voice sounded hopeful as he made the suggestion.

"I'll look forward to it," she answered quickly, then felt the pressure of Kevin's hand on her shoulder.

"Your class, Honor," he reminded her.

"Yes, certainly," she murmured, turning back towards the door. As she turned, her glance fell to the papers on Kevin's desk. They were spread out on its surface, nearly covering the whole of the desktop, and to Honor's surprise, they looked decidedly like building plans. Odd, she thought as she nodded to the three still silent men sitting beside the desk, why would Kevin be showing them the plans to his house (something he'd done with great pride and excitement countless times to both her and Daniel while the mansion was still under construction) when he had the finished article and need only show them around? She was so perplexed she hardly even noticed the intent stares all four strangers leveled at her as she left.

When she'd gone and the door was safely closed behind her, Flannagan turned to Kevin. "Your partner's daughter," he mused aloud. "What kind of tales will she be bringin' home to Papa?"

Kevin's hand slammed loudly on the desk top. "No tales!" he shouted. "And even if she did, it would mean nothing to her. You're the son of an old friend from Ireland. She knows nothing."

"We may have to deal with her. She might have seen

something, noticed something," Flannagan persisted. He motioned to the pile of papers on the desk.

"She saw nothing," Kevin insisted. "That young woman is dear to me, do you hear? As dear as my own. And my son intends to marry her. If you've any thoughts about her, you can forget them, and now." His voice had grown to a low bellow.

Flannagan stared at him a moment longer, then reseated himself beside the desk. "As you like," he said finally, and once more he smiled. "It would be a terrible waste to have to deal with her, in any case." His expression became completely benign as he looked up at Kevin. "Terrence's intended, is she? Then we've nothing to fear from her. So we'll just forget about her little visit and get back to work, shall we?"

Kevin stared at him uncertainly, wondering if he could take his words at face value, but there was nothing else to be said on the matter. He took his seat once more, bending over the large diagrams that covered the top of his desk, as did the other men.

"Here," he said, taking up a pencil and pointing to a particular point on the plans, "this is where you can wait undetected until the right moment."

The four others silently nodded.

Chapter Six

Honor had an oddly expectant feeling all during the class, and for the first time in her memory she was really eager for it to end. She did not know why, but she had the distinct feeling that something was about to happen, something important, something wonderful. She felt like a child on Christmas morning, lying awake in bed in the dark, waiting for the hour to grow late enough for her to creep down the stairs to the parlor to see the tree without waking the still sleeping adults and arousing their anger. She remembered that childish anticipation, the dry, harsh taste in her mouth, the anxious lump in her stomach that precluded any thought of hunger, and realized she felt precisely those symptoms although she was decidedly no longer a little girl and this was certainly not Christmas morning.

She wondered what was wrong with her, why she felt so jumpy and on edge. She started to raise her watch to look at it for the third time in a quarter hour, then dropped her hand, telling herself she was behaving foolishly and must stop it.

"No, Miss Proski. We say I am, not I is."

Honor didn't realize how sharp and impatient her tone had been until she saw her student wince with embarrassment and shame. The girl looked down at her feet and seemed unable to utter another word. Honor was conscious stricken. Marla Proski was unnaturally shy at the best of times, and Honor knew it took all the girl's courage just to appear in the class at all. She was horrified at the callous way she'd corrected her.

In an effort to make amends, Honor moved quickly down the aisle of chairs to the girl's side and took her hand, squeezing it in an effort to be encouraging.

"Let's try it just once more," she suggested gently.

The girl hesitated for a moment, but then looked up at Honor. There seemed to be a hint of reproach in her eyes, but she managed to start once again.

"I am at school," she said slowly, enunciating each word carefully, placing a special emphasis on the verb as she corrected her mistake. "After, I go Aunt Helena's. We eat supper." Her speech completed, she dropped into her chair as though overcome with exhaustion.

Honor smiled at her. "Excellent," she pronounced. The girl seemed to glow with the praise. "And you even helped me start the next part of today's lesson," Honor continued. "You will go to your aunt's house after class. You will eat supper. That is the future tense. You will go, you will eat." She smiled, then looked up at the class in general. "Tomorrow is Monday. Who can tell me what they will do tomorrow?"

Half a dozen hands rose into the air, two with energetic assurance, the others with a good deal more trepidation. Honor made her way to the front of the classroom, determined to keep her mind on her work, no matter how painful the effort. She nodded at a pleasantly anxious girl, thin and round eyed, like Marla Proski, but with none of the other girl's reticence. She'd have pink roses in her cheeks, Honor thought, if she ever had the opportunity to leave the garment factory where she worked and spend some time out of doors.

"Yes, Miss Tannenbaum?"

The girl stood. "Tomorrow I will go to work with

my sister Rena . . ." she began, carefully pronouncing each word.

When she walked down the steps of the old brick building and saw him there, she turned to him and smiled as though she'd expected all along to find him waiting for her.

"You could act a bit surprised," Raifer said, straightening and pulling himself away from the pillar against which he'd been leaning.

"If you like," Honor laughed. She forced herself to sober up quickly. "Mr. Farrell. What a surprise it is to see you here," she said with an attempt at seriousness that did not sound in the least genuine.

He strode the three steps that divided them and took her arm, putting her hand in the crook of his arm and continuing down the remaining steps to the street.

"How did you know I'd come?" he asked her.

Honor shrugged her shoulders and shook her head. "I don't know," she admitted. "I just knew."

And she had, she realized. When the class had finally ended, she'd practically bolted for the door, somehow sure she'd meet him.

"Odd," he said as they moved slowly along the sidewalk. "I didn't know where I was going until I got here and realized this must be the place where you taught."

She smiled up at him gaily. "Perhaps I'm clairvoyant," she suggested. Her voice softened, and her eyes found his. "Or perhaps you came here because I wanted you to."

They stopped for a second, and he stood staring down at her. He oughtn't to have come, he heard a voice in his head telling him firmly, a voice that sounded suspiciously like Captain Ryan's. He silenced it quickly, telling himself that Ryan didn't know everything, least of all the way he felt when he was with her.

"Are you in a hurry?" he asked her. "Shall I take you straight home?"

"I've no obligations," she told him, even though she knew her father was doubtless waiting, ready for that little talk of which he'd spoken before she'd left the church. "I'm free for the remainder of the afternoon."

Raifer grinned. "Well, then, Miss Wainwright, perhaps you'll do me the honor of having tea with me?" he asked. "That is right, isn't it? Ladies do drink tea about this time of the afternoon?"

She smiled and nodded. "But you needn't feel you have to ply me with goodies, Raifer," she told him. "Just a walk by the river would be fine."

His eyes narrowed. "Afraid to be seen in public with me, Honor?"

"On the contrary," she told him, hugging his arm with her own. "It's just that Papa told me last night that he doesn't pay you enough for you to buy me dinner. I've felt quite guilty all day."

He grimaced. "I'm not quite as poor as you think me, Honor."

She looked up at him thoughtfully. "No, I dare say you're not. You're far richer than Terrence, for instance, in many things that matter, confidence and ambition and determination. In many ways, you're already quite a rich man. And I've no doubt but that you'll be materially wealthy some day as well." She stopped walking, and he did, too, when he felt the tug of her hold at his arm. "We could share a simple tea," she said. "We could go to your rooms, and I could prepare it if you like."

Honor was surprised. Even as she heard herself say the words, she was not quite certain how they'd gotten said. Certainly a lady would never make such a suggestion. But the thought of being alone with him was there in her mind, and she somehow realized that regardless of what a lady would or would not do, that was what she wanted.

He brought his hand to cover hers. "Is that what you would like to do, Honor?" he asked her slowly. "What you would really like to do?"

She nodded gravely. "Yes, Raifer. That is what I would really like to do."

It wasn't far. They walked uptown a few blocks, just beyond the tenement houses where the women she taught in her classes lived, whole families of six or eight all in a single room. The streets grew a bit cleaner, a bit less crowded, but still poor, the townhouses still decorated with long lines hung with laundry at the windows, the noise of children echoing sharply in the streets.

When he finally stopped before a dark, stone-faced building, Raifer stared up at it in distaste. "I think you won't like this, Honor," he told her. "I'm not sure that I could blame you."

But she started forward, towards the door, tugging at his arm. "I will like it," she promised. "I want to see where you live. I want to learn all about you, Raifer Sean Farrell."

His lips slowly formed into a crooked grin. "I don't know that there's much to be learned that might be interesting," he said evenly. "And I doubt that you could learn anything from those rooms even if there were."

Honor was surprised at his reluctance. Surely she had not been mistaken in what she had felt when he'd held her in his arms and kissed her the evening before, in what she saw when she stared into his eyes. But then she certainly was a good deal less experienced in such matters than no doubt he was. Perhaps she had imagined the warmth of his kiss, the heat of his touch, because that was what she'd felt, what she wanted him to feel as well. She felt suddenly foolish, and horribly forward. Perhaps he was repulsed by the very fact that she seemed so willing to be alone with him. After all, it certainly was not a thought a lady would permit herself, certainly not on such short acquaintance. But somehow she knew the sudden feeling that had sprung up in her for him was what she'd been waiting all her life to feel. It was almost as if she were afraid to let it slip away without learning more about it, afraid that if she did not cling to it, embrace it, it would simply disappear.

She turned and stared at him, letting her eyes find his, searching in them for some assurance that he, too, felt this mysterious impetus.

"If you'd rather not, Raifer . . ." she began, then grew silent as a flood of awkwardness seemed to engulf her.

He put his hand to her chin, slowly caressing her cheek with his thumb. Then he suddenly dropped his hand and stepped back from her.

"Wait here," he said brusquely. "I won't be long."

With that he turned away from her, walking quickly. As Honor stood numbly and watched, he disappeared around the corner.

She'd never felt more foolish or more awkward in her life. For a moment, she thought only that she should leave, that he would not come back as he had promised, but had left her there as a lesson. She turned on her heel, finding the sight of the corner where she'd last seen him somehow painfully telling, a message she didn't want to hear. She stared up at the dark façade of the rooming house where he lived, seeing it as he must see it, a mean necessity, a fact of life that promised little that a man was unwilling or unable to fight for. How garish and excessive her life must seem to him, she thought. And how cruel for him knowing he must come home to the dim rooms he occupied in this bleak building on this noisy and crowded street.

The bump came before the "Pardon, miss," the force of it far out of the proportion to the size of the boy who had fallen against her as he'd chased after his ball. His friends on the far side of the street were sneering at him, and Honor could see his real regret was for having missed the catch, not for having precipitated the mishap. He was staring down to the hem of her skirts where the ball nestled, obviously wondering if he dared simply stoop and grab it, or if she might take that amiss, especially after the unsettling impact of his small body against her legs.

"May I?" she asked as she knelt and retrieved the ball from where it had finally settled near her shoe. "This was a foolish place for me to stand," she admitted with a smile as she handed it to him.

He only scowled in agreement as he took the ball from her, turned, and threw it across the street to his friends. His whole body bent forward, following the ball in its flight. He started after it, darting into the traffic of the street, ignoring the angry shout of a man driving a milk wagon.

When he'd reached the far side of the street, however, his friends laughed, then one, taller and obviously older than the rest, took the ball and heaved it once more in the direction of where Honor stood. This time she was watching, and she reached up and caught it just as the small boy, running to catch it, collided with her a second time. He landed against her with a heavy thump, his arms waving in the air, but too late to catch the ball.

"I think your friend did that on purpose," Honor told him as she held the ball out to him.

He nodded sagely. "He does it cause he's bigger," he confided. "He laughs if I fall."

"Not a very nice friend, is he?" Honor mused aloud. "Shall we laugh a bit instead?" she asked the boy. She walked with him to the edge of the curb.

He looked up at her suspiciously. "How?" he demanded.

Honor looked pointedly down at the ball in her hand, "You could throw it back to him" she said. "Or I could."

He stared at her thoughtfully and then, for the first time, smiled. "You, miss," he said.

Honor considered his expectant expression, and hoped she hadn't led him to believe too much in her. Then she pulled her arm back and heaved the ball with all her might at the startled group of eight- and nine-year-olds on the far side of the street.

The tall one, the one who had laughed, jumped up, managing to deflect the ball's path but not quite catch it. He started off down the block, eventually stumbling over a large garbage pail before he finally retrieved it.

Honor's new friend smiled up at her delightedly. "Thank you, miss," he said as he took off across the street, joining the group of little boys who were now laughing and motioning excitedly at the unseemly position of their self-styled leader, pointing to where he sat, surrounded by garbage, on the sidewalk.

"I had no idea you had such hidden talents, Honor. Perhaps Abner Doubleday might be interested."

Honor laughed, more from relief that he had really returned as he'd said he would than from the words. She turned to face Raifer.

"Nor had I," she confessed. "Do you think there's some future for me?"

He looked into her eyes. "I wouldn't doubt but that there are some great possibilities for you, Honor," he told her, his voice low and husky.

Honor felt her heart begin to pound at the sound of his voice. I wasn't mistaken, she thought. He feels just as I do.

Raifer almost felt the heat inside her, almost knew what it was she was thinking, and he knew it all was true. Somehow a bond had sprung up between them, and it was far stronger than anything he'd ever felt before. Damn you, Ryan, he thought, for getting me into this mess. And damn her father and McGowan for making it necessary. He tore his eyes from hers and nodded across the street, to where the small group of boys were waving before they ran off.

"Seems like you've made a conquest, Honor," he said. "Another conquest," he added softly.

Honor felt the warmth of a blush creep into her cheeks. "I think that big one is a bully," she said. Then, thinking of Terrence, she added, "I hate bullies, people who try to push others around, simply because they're bigger or richer or more powerful."

Raifer considered her silently. Was she thinking of the British in Ireland, he wondered, was that why she was involved in whatever it was McGowan and her father had planned? Or was his notion precipitous? What if she really knew nothing about the strangers in the warehouse, or the undeclared shipments of arms his people suspected were being made from it? More than anything else he wanted to believe that she knew nothing, that she had no part in any of it.

"What's that?"

Her question brought him back to attention. She was staring now at the parcel he held under his arm.

He grinned at her. "One can't have tea without tea," he told her sagely. "Or a teapot."

"Oh." Honor felt a stab of guilt. She really hadn't wanted him to be put to any expense, for her father's warning about his wages really had made her unconsciously aware of the scarcity of his finances. But he seemed unconcerned as he took her arm and they started to climb the front stairs of the stoop.

"Now it's your turn, Honor," he told her evenly, "to face the lion in his lair."

He was repeating the words she'd used the evening before, but this time there was a hint of amusement in his expression.

She smiled up at him. "Are you comparing yourself to the king of beasts, Raifer?" she asked him. She tried to repress the smile that tugged at her lips.

He opened the large double doors of the building entrance before he answered, considering her thoughtfully before he answered.

"King?" he mused aloud. "Alas, no, Honor. But there has been an occasional suggestion that I might fit into the category of beast." He looked down at her, entirely serious now. "Does that change your mind?" he asked. "I can still take you home."

She brought her hand slowly to his cheek and touched it lightly. He brought his hand to hers, then guided it to his lips, pressing a soft kiss to her palm.

"No," she replied softly. "I haven't changed my mind."

The interior hall was dark, lit only by the meager light that managed to filter its way through the dirt-smudged windows of the door through which they'd passed. There was the stale odor of old meals lingering in the air, the scents of onions and cabbage and fish. Somewhere behind a door a baby was crying.

Raifer took one quick look at her face, then hurried her toward the stairs. "This way, Honor," he said as he took her arm. "For some reason it's worse down here."

He was right, Honor realized. By the time they reached the second floor landing, the odor seemed to have receeded, most likely because she'd become accustomed to it. Raifer withdrew a latchkey from his pocket as they made their way to the end of the hall. Then, while she stood and waited, looking around at the chipped, dirt-streaked paint on the walls, he unlocked the door. His hand to the knob, he turned to face her.

She could see him searching her face, looking for the hint of condemnation or repugnance he obviously expected to find there. Instead, she smiled at him.

"Are you sure, Honor?" he asked her softly one last time.

She nodded in response. He pushed the door open, then stood aside to let her pass. She entered and looked quickly around, finding herself in a small, dark room, its window facing a tiny, wild garden below and immediately after the brick and dark wooden back of yet another building just like the one they were in. A small, bare oak table stood in front of the window, flanked by two hard, straight chairs. On the far wall was a well-worn, small couch, its cushions lumpy, the ancient maroon velvet of its upholstery showing spots worn completely bare. Beside it a table held the one lamp in the room. Just beyond, an open door revealed a wrought-iron bedstead and slightly rumpled bedclothes. On the opposite wall there was a curtain obscuring what she supposed were the kitchen and bath. It was all scrubbed and clean and starkly bare, so bare it hardly seemed possible that anyone actually lived there.

"You were right," she said as she turned to find him behind her, closing the door to the hall.

He faced her. "Right?"

"You said I wouldn't learn anything about you from this place. All I can possibly gather is that you're either very neat or you don't spend much time here."

He grinned. "Right on both counts."

She smiled back at him as she pulled off her gloves. "I suppose that means I shall have to ask you countless questions in lieu of making some compromising discoveries all on my own," she told him.

He raised a brow. "Compromising discoveries?" he asked as he took the container of tea and a small white porcelain teapot from the bag he carried and set them out on the table by the window. "Is that what you've come for?"

She watched him as he turned back to face her, and asked herself the same question, wondering why she had come, why she'd insisted he bring her there. She knew, she realized, down deep inside she knew it was simply that she was afraid to lose the part of herself she'd discovered in his arms, that somehow if she didn't act quickly, Terrence or her father or Kevin or someone would see to it that he disappeared from her life. He had been the one part of her existence that hadn't been according to plan and expectation, the single deviation to an agenda that seemed to have been laid out at her birth. When she was with him she felt as though she were embarking on some breathtakingly wonderful adventure, and she was not about to let the chance slip through her fingers.

She looked up, letting her eyes find his. "No," she admitted softly. "That's not all I've come for." She took one brave, determined step toward him and then stopped, suddenly awkward and afraid.

Raifer, it seemed, had no fear, no need for hesitation. From the moment he had closed the door behind them, he had known. He moved to her and took her in his arms, enfolding her in his powerful embrace as his lips found hers.

Honor closed her eyes and felt herself floating, buoyed on a wave of liquid desire. The fear and uncertainty had disappeared at his touch. She'd never felt anything close to the way she felt when she was in his arms. All thought that it might be wrong, that what she did, what she had done with such seeming determination to bring herself there to be alone with him, all of it faded into oblivion. All she knew was that when she was in his arms nothing else mattered, nothing else could intrude, not thoughts of her father, of Terrence, of the differences between them that Daniel had gone to such trouble to point out to her. All that mattered was that she was with him, close to him. And somehow she simply knew it was right.

Heedless, she dropped to the floor the gloves she still held and brought her palms to his shoulders. They were wide and hard and strong, and made her feel terribly vulnerable, yet very safe. The contact of his lips to hers sent slowly undulating waves of liquid warmth through her.

She felt the darting probe of his tongue and opened her lips to it, tasting it with pleasure, aware that the contact seemed to roil the waters on which she floated, leaving her breathless and dazed. When he pulled himself from her, she only knew she wanted more.

Raifer slowly unfastened the buttons of her coat, aware of the flush that had crept into her cheeks, of the heat of her eyes on his as he released her from the warmth of the heavy folds of fabric. Finally he drew it off, dropping it to the couch without taking his eyes from hers. She stood before him, staring at him as though she were dazed, pliant to his touch but seemingly without volition of her own.

He returned to her, putting his arms once more around her and drawing her close to him. He brought his lips to her earlobe, then to her neck, aware of the shivers that passed through her at the contact.

"I want you, Honor," he whispered softly, his lips close to her ear. "More than I've ever wanted any woman in my life, I want you."

His tongue darted to touch the lobe, then traced the inward spiral of her ear. Honor trembled at the touch of his tongue and his lips, then wrapped her arms around his neck, pulling herself closer to him. She wanted him, too, she realized. That was what the liquid heat that was coursing through her meant, the hot flow of desire. She dropped her head back and stared up at him.

"Yes," she said softly. That was all, just yes.

He lifted her in his arms and carried her toward the bedroom, letting his lips find hers as he walked, aware only of the feel of her in his arms, of the realization that what he'd told her was true, that he'd never before felt about a woman as he felt about her. But when he stood beside the small, wrought-iron bedstead, he hesitated.

This is not how it ought to be, he thought. Not here, not in a place like this. For a second the image of Michael Ryan passed through his mind, the police captain's sharply knowing eyes staring at him, warning him. What's happened to me, he wondered, puzzled by the wealth of feeling that now filled him, sweeping aside what had always before been a distant objectivity.

"Raifer?"

She was staring up at him, her expression puzzled, wondering, her eyes filled with trust. This is wrong, he thought. I'm using her, stealing from her something I've no right to take. But then she put her hands to the back of his neck, drawing his face to hers, pressing her lips to his. Whatever doubts he had had, whatever nagging probes of conscience, vanished.

He lay her down on the worn cotton spread, then followed her, once more finding her lips with his, letting his hands cup the soft, beckoning mound of her breast.

Honor lay back, her head against the pillow, her hands moving cautiously as her fingers touched his face, snaked their way through his dark hair. She hardly noticed his fingers releasing the buttons of her blouse, but when he drew back the linen and brought his lips to the vee of exposed flesh, she felt the liquid fires within her burn hotter and brighter. For a second she pondered the mystery of how he did what he did to her, how his touch could so transform her. But then she dismissed thought, and simply pressed herself to him.

This, she realized, was the secret she'd been waiting all her life to learn. Whatever lay ahead, she knew she could only embrace it with all her strength.

Raifer drew back the soft white linen of her blouse, gently touching the pale skin of her cleavage, first with his fingers, then with his lips and tongue. He felt her tremble beneath him, and the awareness of her excitement spurred his own.

With impatient but practiced hands, he drew away her clothing, first the blouse and skirt, and then, far more slowly, letting his hands linger against her skin, her petticoat, stockings and chemise. He pulled reluctantly away from her, shrugging quickly out of his own clothing before returning to her.

She smiled up at him as he lowered himself to her, reaching out to him and taking his face in her hands, pressing an anxious, curious kiss to his lips. He smiled at that, and she saw it.

"Am I so clumsy as that?" she asked him, letting her hands trail down his chest, reveling in the touch, the feel of hard muscle beneath the skin and the mat of wiry curls.

"Your naiveté, my beautiful Honor," he replied, "at this moment is the greatest spur I've ever known."

He moved closer to her, and Honor felt the hard press of him against her thigh, ample evidence that what he'd said was true.

"I shall be a very attentive pupil," she replied with a breathless smile. "I'm eager to learn."

He smiled as he lowered his lips to hers, as eager to teach as she was to learn.

He pressed a hard, knowing kiss to her lips, letting his tongue flirt with hers. And then he moved them to her neck and slowly downward to the soft valley between her breasts, and then to each rosy mound, letting his tongue tease her breasts and trace her nipples until they grew hard with want. His hands gently stroked her, taking delight in the satiny smoothness of her skin, letting them caress her breasts and her thighs, pleased when he felt the responding heat that sprang up wherever he touched her.

Finally he brought his hand to the soft thatched vee between her legs. Her immediate reaction was surprise, and he felt her muscles tighten. But before he had the thought to withdraw, she looked up at him and smiled, then coiled her arms around his neck.

"I love you, Raifer," she whispered against his ear, pulling herself close to him, telling him as much with her body as with her words that whatever he wanted of her, she would give to him gladly.

Once again he brought his lips to hers, positioning himself over her, spreading her legs with his own and holding himself against her. Then he wound his fingers in her hair and kissed her once more, his tongue playing with hers, darting, probing, seeking the honeyed warmth, as he slid inside her.

Whatever Honor had imagined it would be like when she'd considered the act—and she'd considered it quite seriously on a goodly number of occasions, as any normal young woman would—its actuality in no way compared to her imaginings. She had expected hurt, but there was none, only the sweet, hard press of the liquid fire inside her, a fire that snaked its way through her body, melting it until it seemed to her that she was no longer separate, a thing apart, but part of Raifer and he part of her. She felt him close to her, inside her, and his hands gently caressing, guiding her, but the distinctions seemed blurred, all part of a single sea of feeling that had swept through her. The waters seemed to surge, higher and higher, each wave stronger, more powerfully pressing. She gave herself up to them, willing to drown in them if that was to be her fate. She'd never felt like this before, never thought she could feel so much, so close to another human being. Raifer had released a flood within her, something she knew had always been within her but never recognized before, never even imagined. She moved with him, aware only of the sweet, hot flow within her, aware of nothing save his body and hers and the impossibly narcotic magic of the lovers' dance.

Slowly the tidal flow within her grew, each wave higher than the last, until she felt as though her whole body were shattering. She heard a moan, a distant, disconnected sound, unaware that it came from her own lips. She felt her body arch to Raifer's and buried her lips against his neck, clinging to him, lost save for the solidity of his body close to hers.

She lay close beside him, clinging to him, her breath still a ragged panting and the sound of her heart throbbing within her still filling her ears. There was the feeling of Raifer's arms around her, his hands gently stroking her thigh and his eyes turned to her, waiting for hers to find them. She looked up at him and smiled.

He pushed a damp curl away from her cheek. "I've been waiting my whole life for you, Honor," he whispered.

"And I for you," she replied. "Waited my whole life for you to come so I could fall in love."

His eyes seemed to fill with sadness then, something she could not understand. She wondered what she had said, what she had done, to elicit the mournful sadness she saw in his eyes. She reached up to his face, putting her palm to his cheek.

"Have I said something, done something wrong, Raifer?" she asked him, terrified that she had.

He shook his head slowly. "No," he replied softly. "If there is any wrong, it is mine."

He rolled to the side, then lay beside her, staring up at the ceiling. "I should never have brought you here, Honor. Never have let any of this happen."

Bewildered, she could only protest. "But I wanted it, Raifer," she told him, aware of the lump of panic that seemed to have sprung up within her.

He turned his eyes until they found hers, then pulled her to him, until she was close to him, facing him.

"And I wanted it. More than I've ever wanted anything else in my life," he told her gently. He raked the tangle of her curls with his fingers, feeling the silken mass against his palm, wondering at its thick, weighted softness. "And now I only want you more, Honor," he said slowly.

"Then it's not wrong," she told him, feeling the panicky feeling ebb, sure of herself once again.

He stared up at her, and thought only that in the end what had happened between them would make her hate him all the more. The thought filled him with a sinking, sickening dread.

"If only it were that simple, Honor," he said.

She lowered her face to his, letting her hair fall forward, a silken curtain that enclosed the two of them. "It is," she assured him before she brought her lips to his.

Raifer told himself he shouldn't let it continue, that he ought to take her home, anything to get away from the cramped, dreary room. But at the touch of her lips to his, he knew he was lost before he made the attempt. His body reacted to hers with an immediacy that bewildered him. He wanted her, he realized, and the taste he'd had was nothing more than a spur to the hunger.

He put his arms around her, letting his hands slide languorously along the naked skin of her back to her haunches, then back up to her shoulders. Then he wound his fingers in her hair and pulled her head back and stared at her, at the deep blush in her cheeks, at the passion he saw in her eyes. If there had been a moment for indecision for him, he knew it was past.

He pulled her down to him, telling himself as he pressed his lips to hers that consequences didn't matter, that he would face them when he must. But for now, there was nothing else for him but the feel of her body in his arms.

He kissed her, feeling the heat in his body grow and the answering fire it lit in her. His senses seemed to become more acute, more responsive, as though his fingers, his eyes, his lips were all drinking in memories that would someday be too precious to be forgotten, as though these moments that he shared with her would have to satisfy him for the rest of his life.

He pulled her down, then turned until he was

positioned atop her, and stared at her as though he were seeing her for the first time. He stared at her, memorizing her features and fixing them in his mind, the feel of her skin to his fingers as he slowly stroked her breasts and shoulders. Then he lowered his lips to them, storing away in his mind the taste of her skin beneath his lips, the sweetness like a hint of honey on his tongue.

Slowly his lips traveled downward, trailing through the small valley between her breasts, along the softly jagged line that her ribs made, to the small, round core of her belly. This, too, he tasted, all the while marveling at the wonders of her body as if he'd never seen a woman before, as if it were all new to him and undiscovered. Then he buried his lips in the pale golden mound of curls between her legs and, finally, found her moist warmth.

He heard her moan softly and felt her fingers in his hair. At that moment, he wanted nothing more than the knowledge that he had pleased her, that he had made her feel something of the way he'd felt when he'd made love to her. It was foolish, he realized, to think that in some way the passion might mitigate what he knew would come all too soon between them; but love follows its own logic, its own reason. He knew only that he had to please her.

He felt her body tremble, then arch toward him. He raised himself, brought his face close to hers.

She stared up at him, her eyes glassy and unsure. "What have you done to me?" she asked him softly, reaching her hand up to his cheek. "What magic have you that you can so totally transform me?"

He shook his head. "I have no magic, Honor," he whispered, thinking how much he wished he had, how much he would give if he could change circumstances so that there might be some possibility for them.

"But you have," she told him, her words throaty and warm, as she pulled his face down to meet hers.

"You've made me fall in love."

Then he was kissing her lips once more, his tongue touching hers, the sweet taste, the hint of honey, filling his senses as he slid inside her.

He made love to her slowly, drawing out each movement with deliberate precision, wanting to feel the heat growing inside her, wanting to know that he was giving as well as taking. He buried his lips against her neck, feeling the beat of the pulse there, strong and growing steadily sharper and faster. And then, just as he realized he could control the powerful tides no longer, he felt her tremble beneath him, her whole body pressing to his, and he joined her in the sweet delirium of release.

"We never had our tea."

Honor felt Raifer's smile as much as saw it in the growing dimness of late twilight. They walked slowly along the stone-paved walk, content with the contact of their bodies brushing close as they moved, the steady hold of her hand on his arm. She found she quite regretted the sight of her own house as they neared it, wished that it might recede a bit into the distance so that the two of them could continue walking alone together, as the late afternoon shadows gathered around them.

"I wasn't really thirsty," she admitted with an answering smile. "Perhaps we might postpone it for another time. After all, you did buy that pot."

He covered the hand on his arm with his free one. "Not to mention the tea." He looked down at her and his face sobered. "I'll keep it safe, in the hopes that you may some day agree to share it with me," he told her.

His expression puzzled her, for it seemed so hopeless, so apart from her. It was not the first time she'd noticed that pained, distant expression that afternoon, and she could only think that she had in some way caused it, however unknowingly. He stopped and she saw they were standing in front of her house.

"Will you come in and have dinner with us, Raifer?" she asked.

He looked away from her, up at the stern, Federal façade. "I think I'd better not, Honor," he replied without turning back to face her. "I think your father might not approve."

And he'd be right, Raifer told himself. Daniel may disapprove of me for all the wrong reasons, but in the end, he is right.

"He'll come round," Honor told him firmly. "He's not unreasonable, just stubborn. And when he knows you, really knows you as I do . . ."

He looked down at her finally. "Just what do you know about me, Honor?" he demanded sharply. "How can you place your faith in a man who is nothing more than a stranger to you?"

She drew back, hurt by his words, and frightened by them. "Is that what we are, Raifer?" she asked, her voice trembling. "Are we no more than strangers?"

He hadn't realized until that moment what he'd done, how easily he could hurt her. He hated the callousness he'd shown her. He brought her hand to his lips, brushing it softly.

"For now," he said gently. "I only hope you'll grant me the opportunity to become something more." He smiled then. "But for now, I think I'd better see you to your door and leave. I'd hate to have my memory of this day ruined by a disagreement with your father."

He walked her to the door, then stopped with her there, putting his hand to her cheek and kissing her fleetingly on the lips before drawing away. Then he turned to raise the knocker.

"Good-bye, then," Honor said, suddenly feeling very awkward, wanting more than anything for him to stay but aware that he was probably right, that his presence would not please Daniel.

He turned back to her and grinned a crookedly lopsided grin. "I've never enjoyed having tea quite so much as I did today, Honor," he told her.

She returned the smile. "And I'd never thought something so mundane could be so surprisingly exciting," she replied.

She leaned a bit toward him, wanting more than anything for him to take her in his arms one final time, to kiss her once more before he left her there, but just then the door opened and Fraser stood in the doorway, a stern-faced sentinel guarding her public honor. Rather than a kiss, she was forced to content herself with a quick press of his hand to hers, then she watched as he turned and walked away from her, feeling as though she were losing a small part of herself at the separation.

This is what it feels to be in love, she thought, this pain at parting, this feeling of loss. She turned and walked into the house, her expression bemused.

Fraser considered her as he took her coat, wondering what it was about her that seemed different to him and unable to quite define it.

"Your father is waiting for you in the library, Miss Honor," he informed her when she'd shed gloves, coat, and hat.

She nodded, pursed her lips in concentration, and turned to the library door. He's been there all afternoon, she thought, fuming, waiting for that talk he'd mentioned in church. There was nothing for her to do but face it.

She pulled the door open and walked through, forcing her lips into a purposeful smile. "Good afternoon, Papa," she said, then stood waiting for Daniel to look up at her.

Daniel considered her as she crossed to him, dropping his book into his lap, aware he'd hardly concentrated on a word he'd read in the preceding hours, not enough to remember more than a phrase or two, at any rate.

"Good evening, Honor," he answered pointedly, his tone terse, then paused, waiting for her to make an explanation of her belated return home.

Instead, Honor seated herself on the couch across from him, silent, a bit remote. When she made no move to speak, Daniel went on in a slightly accusing tone. "You're rather late home from your class this afternoon, aren't you, Honor?"

She glanced up at him, and then away, well aware that his tone meant he was not the least pleased with her at the moment. "I hope you weren't worried about me, Papa," she replied absently. "I didn't think to send word. After all, I've had tea with Terrence or Megan quite a few times in the past after class. You never worried then."

"But I was worried," he informed her. "And you weren't having tea with either Terrence or Megan."

She looked up at him once more and found his look sharp, accusing. "I know, Honor. I made inquiry."

"No," she replied slowly. "I didn't have tea with Terrence or Megan." She stood. "Shall I make you something to drink, Papa?" she asked as she started toward the liquor cabinet.

"Sit down, Honor," Daniel told her sharply. "I do not want a drink. I want you to tell me where you were, and who you were with. Or do I already know? Were you with that Farrell person?"

"Don't, Papa," Honor begged him softly, not wanting to hear him say the things she somehow knew he would say. "Please don't."

"For God's sake, Honor, can't you see this man only wants one thing, and that's money? He as much as told you so last evening. He's ambitious, a fortune hunter, and you're a quick way to get him what he wants, nothing more."

Honor felt the rage inside her, hot and bitter and a vicious thrust of hurt. "Stop it, Papa," she shouted. "I won't listen to this, do you hear? I love him, and I won't listen to any more."

She was shocked that the words had come out in a spurt of anger, when she wanted more than anything for him to understand, for him to be happy for her. But hearing the words, hearing the echo of them there, in her father's house, somehow made what she felt inside seem all the more real to her. It was one thing to murmur them when she was in Raifer's arms, when she was in his bed, and quite another, she realized, to hear herself say them to her father in the midst of his study.

She saw Daniel's reaction, the way he seemed to draw back from the words, as though they'd been a blow she'd leveled at him. Then the pain disappeared from his eyes, and it was replaced with anger. She answered, feeling her own ire welling up inside her. She stood, then, glaring at him, daring him to say any more.

Daniel felt her anger like a missile, realizing for the first time just how far she'd grown from him in so short a time, aware as he had not been until that moment that she was no longer simply his child, but a woman, a woman he realized he hardly knew.

"It's true, Honor," he told her, this time gently, wishing the look of pain that he saw slowly creeping into her expression and seemingly shattering her features would somehow disappear.

"No," she shouted. "I won't listen. I love him and you can't say anything that can change that."

Daniel shook his head slowly. "But does he love you, Honor? Can you say with any certainty that he loves you?"

She stared at him, frozen, letting the hours she'd spent with him play themselves quickly in her mind. She'd said the words, she realized, but as much as she wanted to remember him saying them to her, she could not.

"You're young, Honor," Daniel said softly. "It's easy for a man like that to fool you, to use you."

"No," she gasped, refusing to hear any more. She turned and ran to the door, fleeing the room as though it were the den of an ogre and he the dreaded beast.

Daniel sat in his chair, feeling shaken and miserable. It had gone so much further than he'd thought, he realized. She'd said she was in love with this upstart Farrell. And if it was true, he had no doubt but that that love would take her from him entirely if he let it go on.

He felt a stab of loss. She was all he cared for, he realized, all he loved. Resolve settled into him as solid as stone. He'd put a stop to this nonsense before there was the opportunity for this infatuation of hers to get out of hand. She'd thank him for it one day, he told himself, squashing down the feeling of remorse that nagged at him, that told him he would be hurting her.

He rose and went to his liquor cabinet and poured himself a large drink.

Chapter Seven

"You sent for me, Mr. Wainwright?"

Daniel turned and looked up at Raifer. He could understand why Honor had become so infatuated with the man, he thought. He did have a rugged kind of handsomeness, he supposed. And an air of arrogant independence. But surely none of those things was the basis for love.

"Surely you're not surprised by that, Farrell?" he asked.

Raifer considered Daniel's expression. He wondered what had happened between Honor and her father the evening before.

"No, sir," he admitted slowly. "I suppose I'm not."

"You're aware, then, that my daughter has come to the decision that she has fallen in love with you?" Daniel asked, but he wasn't really asking, he was stating something of which he knew they were both equally aware. "You won't be surprised to learn that I am not particularly pleased by this turn of events," he went on purposefully. "It seems to me that there are several avenues open to me." Daniel turned away from Raifer and faced the tall bookshelf that backed his office. "I could fire you, tell you to get out and never see Honor again. That's the most obvious thing for me to do, but I don't think it would be the wisest." He turned back to Raifer then, his brow raised in question. "You would simply defy me, as would she, and go on seeing one another. She would believe I was persecuting you and only become more infatuated with you. A woman always idolizes a man she thinks has martyred himself for her." His eyes narrowed contemplatively. "And so, Farrell, I choose to take another tack."

"Mr. Wainwright . . ." Raifer began.

Daniel held up his hand. "Let me finish, Farrell. I'm willing to pay you, to pay you handsomely, if you agree to leave."

Raifer felt himself color with anger. "I don't want your money," he spat out between tight lips. "This has nothing to do with money."

His words seemed to amuse Daniel. "Oh?" he asked. "I somehow find that hard to believe." His tone was dry and distant, and he stared at Raifer with unforgiving eyes. "But if it is true, then you will not be upset to learn that should she marry you, Honor will be penniless, and she will stay that way, even at my death." He smiled grimly. "Does that in any way alter your attitude, Farrell?"

Raifer returned his stare. "What I feel for Honor has nothing to do with your money," he said hotly.

Daniel stared at him silently for a moment, then his expression softened. For some reason he did not quite understand, and against his better judgment, he found he believed Raifer.

"If that's true," he said, "if you really care for her, then you must realize that you can never give her the kind of life she deserves. If you really feel anything for her, break it off with her and let her get on with her life."

Raifer felt as though he'd been struck. It was not so much Daniel's suggestion, for he'd told himself much the same thing a hundred times the night before, but the sudden feeling of loss, the absoluteness of it.

"You're right," he said softly. "It's the only way."

Daniel seemed shaken by that, his easy acceptance. "Then you'll break it off, end it?" he asked, quite bewildered by the ease of it all.

"Yes," Raifer agreed and he turned to the door. "I'll leave, too."

Daniel found his conscience had begun to pain him. Perhaps Farrell was not the fortune hunter he'd believed him to be, perhaps he was better than he'd given him credit for being.

"No," he said suddenly, almost surprised as he heard himself utter the word. "No, that isn't necessary. You've proved yourself a good worker here. I don't want to take your livelihood from you. You can stay, if you give me your word concerning my daughter."

Raifer turned back to him and it was obvious from his expression that Daniel's words were unexpected to him, too. He was there to do a job, he told himself. If he couldn't have Honor, and he knew the impossibility of that, had spent much of the night telling himself that even the thought was absurd, he should at least finish what he'd begun. He let his eyes meet Daniel's.

"Very well," he said slowly. "You have my word."

Daniel heaved a sigh of relief. It was done, he thought, and far more easily than he'd have expected it to be. He moved out from behind his desk and crossed the room to where Raifer stood beside the door, his hand extended. "You understand, Farrell, this is nothing personal against you."

"I understand," Raifer replied.

"I've always accepted a man's handshake as his bond," Daniel said.

Raifer nodded. "So have I."

Daniel grasped his hand firmly and the two of them stood a moment, hands clasped, silently considering one another. The bargain was sealed.

A simple enough way, Raifer thought, to end a love affair.

* * *

"He should be fired. And the sooner, the better."

Daniel leveled a contemplative glance at Terrance McGowan. This is what has driven Honor away from him, he thought, and into the arms of the likes of Raifer Farrell. He tried to distance himself from Terrence, to forget that he had known him since the day he'd been born, tried to forget that Terrence was his best friend's son. He began to realize, however painfully, that he did not like what he saw, but he forced away the thought as quickly as it had come to him and told himself Terrence was young still, and just needed a bit of time to mellow.

"I accepted his word, and until he proves false to it, I see no reason to terminate his employment."

"How can you be so naive, Daniel?" Terrence persisted. "The man is nothing more than a fortune hunter. He should be sent packing, and the sooner the better."

Daniel managed to squelch the trace of a smile that itched at the edge of his lips. Terrence was behaving like an affronted old maid; even his tone of voice had the sort of unsatisfiable whining note to it.

"If you ever want to win Honor back," he told the younger man firmly, "sending Farrell into the streets is not the way to do it. I'm afraid, my boy, you'll simply have to make a greater effort with her."

Terrence did not like what Daniel was saying to him, but he had the presence of mind to realize that any further argument was valueless. He put his hands to his thighs and pushed against them as he stood.

"Perhaps you're right," he admitted slowly as he turned toward the door of Daniel's office. "Perhaps, in a way, all this has been my own fault. I do love her."

Daniel felt a wave of relief. He hadn't been wrong about Terrence after all. If the boy had been a bit thoughtless of late, it was only because he'd had his attention too firmly mired in the business, only because he hadn't realized how fragile a woman's feelings could be. This little misunderstanding could only have a good effect upon him, make him more aware of Honor's sensitivities. He'd be more gentle with her in the future, more understanding, and make more of an effort to make her happy. That was all he really wanted, Daniel decided, to see his daughter happy. Nothing was more important than that.

Daniel moved around the desk to him, putting a firm hand to his shoulder. "I know that, my boy," he said. "All you have to do is make her understand it as well." He smiled encouragingly, wanting to let Terrence know that he was on his side. "And don't worry about this Farrell. I honestly think he realizes that he can only hurt her. He'll stay away from her now. He's given me his word."

Terrence grimaced slightly, as though to say that Farrell's word might satisfy Daniel, but that he couldn't be quite so accepting. He said nothing, however, and Daniel went on.

"You can talk to her this afternoon. She's to join me for lunch today, but I suppose I could make myself busy, too busy to join her, and force you to the duty of providing escort for her. How does that sound?"

Terrence nodded and smiled. "Nothing would please me more, sir," he replied.

Daniel grinned. "I've promised her a tour of the continent this spring," he went on thoughtfully. "But I fear my own wanderlust has long ago faded. If you could persuade her to marry you by then, my boy, I'd be delighted to offer the trip to the two of you, as a small wedding gift."

Terrence's smile broadened. The spring, he thought . . . by spring everything would be settled, and the prospect of an extended wedding trip in Europe with Honor offered a pleasant outlook.

"That sounds most enticing, Daniel," he said before he put his hand to the doorknob.

Most enticing, indeed, he mused as he opened the door and passed out into the more mundane precincts of the warehouse.

"Hello, Raifer."

Honor felt, for the first time in her life, completely self-conscious. She had expected him to come by, or at least send her a note, and had waited each day for some word from him. When a week had passed and there'd been no word from him, she had slowly come to the realization that she really meant nothing to him, that what had happened between them meant nothing. It was not an easy matter for her to accept, that she'd been used and then cast aside.

She'd tried to make excuses for him in her own mind, excuses that slowly faded, to be replaced by a dull acceptance and a nagging misery. It pained her to realize that she'd allowed herself to become a foolish, malleable fool like the ones she'd so easily detested in Megan's novels. But that was exactly what had happened to her, she realized. She'd let herself act like a silly, brainless child, letting a man charm her and take her to his bed only to dismiss her once he'd had her.

Nothing, it seemed, would ever salve the shame she felt.

She'd thought that if she ever saw him again, she'd only feel scorn, sheer hatred. But as she entered the warehouse out of the damp chill of a drizzly November morning to find him standing there facing her, she felt her anger and pain suddenly seem to recede to be replaced by the heated warmth she'd felt when she'd lain in his arms. The eyes he turned to her smoldered, and she told herself that those inner fires were for her, only for her.

"Miss Wainwright," he replied to her greeting, and

nodded his head slowly as he stared at her.

"Miss Wainwright?" she whispered, stepping a bit closer to him. "Have we become strangers, then?" she asked. "Miss Wainwright, Mr. Farrell?"

Raifer was shocked by the power of remorse that filled him at her words, remorse for the pain he saw in her eyes. He told himself, just as he had a hundred times in the previous days, that it was better that she hated him, that it would have come anyway sooner or later. And if what Michael Ryan believed actually was true, it would be sooner. But still, there was the remorse, the urge to reach out to her, to touch her, to hold her in his arms. He had to force his hands to remain by his sides. He looked up and saw Terrence McGowan at the far side of the warehouse, knew there would be only a moment with her before Terrence saw them and approached.

"I never lied, Honor. I never told you we were anything but strangers," he told her in a hoarse whisper.

He watched as she backed away from him as if the possibility of contact with him had suddenly become an odious prospect. He realized then just how much he had dreaded seeing her the past few days. There was almost a sense of relief, now that it was done. Now, he told himself, he could get on with his job, with his life. He'd been a fool ever to allow any of it to get as far as it had.

She stared at him with a mixture of disgust and disbelief as he stood motionless, watching her. Then he nodded once and turned away, completely ignoring Terrence as he passed him.

Terrence approached her slowly and put his hand to her arm. "Honor, my dear, are you unwell? You look a bit pale."

Honor bit her lower lip, but managed to respond calmly, "I'm quite all right, Terry," she said as she watched Raifer's back move away from her. "It's just this vile weather, I think. I must be taking on a bit of a chill."

She wondered how her voice could sound so entirely normal in her own ears, how she could appear so calm, so unmoved. She felt as if she were crumbling inside.

She turned away, absently pulling her arm from Terrence's grasp. "If you'll excuse me, Papa's waiting for me," she muttered as she began to move stiffly away from him.

"I'm afraid not, Honor," Terrence told her.

Honor looked up and only then realized he'd followed her, that he was once more at her side.

"He asked me to convey his regrets, and tell you he was called away on a meeting with that banker, Jeffers, at the last moment." Once more he put his hand to her arm. "He asked me if I might take his place and buy you some lunch, a duty I was only too delighted to accept."

Honor looked up at him, her eyes focusing on his face for the first time since he'd joined her. For the previous moments, she realized, she'd thought of him absently as a mild nuisance, as one would a buzzing fly, something to be waved away and then avoided. The prospect of spending the next hour or two alone with him, she found, appalled her.

She shook her head, as though that might clear it. "I think you were right, Terry," she said slowly. "I think I may not be feeling quite well after all. If Papa's not here, I might just as well go home." She looked down at her arm where his hand held it, dismissing him once more in her mind, thinking only of the determined hand that held her.

"I'll see you there, Honor," he told her. He paused for a moment, as though he were trying to order his words in his mind. "I know I've made mistakes, Honor," he went on slowly. "I know what's happened between us has all been my fault. But I want to mend it now, before it's too late. You know how much I love you."

Honor felt as though she were dizzy. Terrence's words were the last ones she wanted to be forced to think about.

"Please, Terry," she murmured as she raised her hand to the side of her forehead. "Not now. I have to go home. I have to be alone."

"You aren't well," he told her as he turned her back to the door. "I knew it when I saw you. There'll be time enough for all this later. For now, let me take you home."

She nodded in agreement, thankful for whatever respite he was willing to give her, knowing only that she needed to be alone, to think, to try and understand why Raifer had done what he'd done, to try and deal with the rending feeling inside herself. She let him lead her back out into the cold drizzle, unaware that Raifer had turned and watched the two of them leave, oblivious to the look of pain that crossed his features as he saw Terrence put his arm around her.

She withdrew into herself, numb to everything save her thoughts, unaware even of the way Terrence sat close to her in the carriage, the way he put his hand to her waist as he walked her to her door.

"I'll come by tomorrow, Honor," he told her before he left her.

Honor only nodded, not ready yet to waste the effort of her thoughts on him, still trying to understand what had happened, wondering how Raifer could have been so cold to her, so indifferent. When Terrence had gone, she wandered into the parlor, still dressed in her hat and coat, oblivious to the stares Fraser offered her when she made no move to remove them. She sat, huddling herself into the warmth of her coat, and closed her eyes, recalling the image of Raifer's face, the dark, smoldering look in his eyes when he'd spoken to her. There was regret in his eyes, she told herself, regret and hurt.

The more she thought of it, the more she determined that he'd not wanted to say those cutting words to her, that he'd felt as much hurt as she when they'd been uttered. Perhaps Terrence or her father had somehow forced him to act that way, she told herself, perhaps they'd convinced him that his poverty meant he was, as they saw him, unworthy of her.

She found herself wavering, wondering. Surely he would realize that money meant nothing to her, that she didn't care about it. Surely he would see through such arguments. Perhaps he didn't really care enough. But then, what if he'd been convinced, if Daniel or Terrence had made him really believe that wealth was a requisite for a husband? Or perhaps he'd simply decided he didn't want her.

She felt herself seesawing back and forth, ascribing one motive to his words and then another. Whatever the reason, she told herself, she had to have it out in the open, she had to know if he'd simply decided he didn't care about her or if her father or Terrence had forced him to agree to something he didn't really want to agree to. If she were to cope with the thought of losing him, she realized, she had to be sure it was really what he wanted.

She stood abruptly and walked out to the hall, calling out to the butler.

"Fraser, have a carriage brought round," she told him when he appeared. "Immediately. I've something very important to do."

Raifer turned the lock pick carefully, then withdrew it when he heard the familiar click sound that told him the door was open. He replaced the pick in his pocket, then put his hand to the heavy, iron-bound door and tried the lock. The knob turned easily in his hand, he found, and the door creaked open at his touch.

"I wouldn't be goin' down there, boyo, if I were

you."

Raifer turned to find Patrick Coughlin behind him. He cursed under his breath. He'd watched the others leave for their lunch, entirely forgetting that Paddy had retired to the rear of the warehouse for his pre-lunch nap half an hour before.

"Where does this go to, Paddy?" he asked. "I've never seen this door opened before."

"I've never see it left open either, boyo. And for all I know, it goes down to hell." Paddy's eyes narrowed. "If you're smart, you'll forget you ever saw it open."

Raifer tried to look bewildered. "What's the big mystery, Paddy?" he demanded. "There can't be anything down there so important it has to be locked up like that."

"There's things and there's things, boyo. And sometimes it's healthiest not to even ask questions."

Raifer wrinkled his brow, and he made a show of pulling the door closed. "I've got enough on my plate with his lordship after my ass," he muttered. "I guess it wouldn't be too bright to bring anything more down on my head."

Paddy's expression eased and then he offered Raifer a toothy grin. "I keep tellin' you, Raifer my lad, to simply stay out of his highness's way. If you keep your head down and your arse covered, he won't have anything worth aimin' at."

Raifer laughed. "I'm afraid my ass is a better target than yours, Paddy. Or at least little Terry's more determined to find the mark."

Paddy echoed his laughter. "The burdens of beauty, Raifer my boy, the burdens of beauty. I fear I can extend nothing more than my condolences." He clapped his cap onto his head. "And will you be joinin' me for a pint or two while the cats are all away?" he asked. "We could just take a short amble down to the corner saloon and be back before anyone's the wiser."

Raifer shook his head. "You go on, Paddy," he

replied. "If any of them comes back while you're gone, I'll tell them you've gone to help a sick old woman who collapsed on the sidewalk, true charitable Christian that you are."

"Ah, laddy, you know me like a brother. I'll raise a short one to your kind and generous nature."

With that, he buttoned up his jacket against the cold and turned away, strutting to the door, whistling as he crossed the wide warehouse. Raifer wandered away from the heavy, iron-bound door, hoping he portrayed the proper aspect of indifference to Paddy when the older man turned to him and nodded farewell before he left.

"Sure you won't join me for a mugful, lad?" Paddy called out one last time before he opened the door.

"You go on," Raifer replied. "If we leave the place empty and someone finds out about it, there'll be all manner of hell to pay."

"Right you are, lad," Paddy agreed, then he left, pulling the door closed against the wind that blew a splash of rain into the warehouse in his wake.

When Raifer was sure he'd gone, he turned back to the heavy door, crossing to it quickly, and pulling it slowly open. The door creaked slightly as it opened, revealing a dark, downward set of narrow, rickety stairs. There was a small, rusted lantern hung on a peg by the entry, and this Raifer took down and quickly lit before starting down the flight.

It's down here, he thought as he took the steps slowly, careful to make no sound. Whatever McGowan and Wainwright have been up to, the proof is down here. He could feel it.

He was filled with an expectant excitement, the way he always felt when he was about to solve a case. This time, however, there was little elation for him in the awareness of the feeling as there usually was. This time, he knew, when it was over, he'd be left with less than he'd had when he started.

He thought fleetingly of Honor, and wished it had

all been otherwise.

Honor was surprised at the silence that filled the warehouse as she entered.

"Raifer?" she called out expectantly, but her voice seemed lost and muffled in the cavernous room. She took a tentative step forward, realizing that she hoped to avoid Terrence if he'd returned. The wisest thing for her to do would be to go directly to the rear of the warehouse. She was sure she would find Raifer somewhere there.

As she started forward, however, she saw him just disappearing through a door near the rear of the building. Funny, she thought as she slowly approached it, she'd never noticed it there before, in all the years she'd been visiting the place once or twice a week. She put her hand to the latch, then drew the door back and peered into the dim shaft, staring at the downward flight of stairs that were made just discernible by a flickering ray of lamplight that managed to snake its way from whatever was below.

She looked around once, to be sure there was no one else there, no one who might tell her why Raifer had gone down there. Then, deciding there was no one about, she carefully began the descent of the unsteady stairs.

The flight led down to a cavernous basement, dark and dirt floored and very damp. The air was filled with an unpleasantly musty odor, moving wraithlike shadows, and, as far as she could see at least, seemingly little else.

Honor stood at the foot of the stairs, staring into the dim darkness, wondering what sort of creatures might have crawled out of the mire that edged the river to find a more agreeable home in this underground vault. The thought of river rats roused a feeling of panic in her. She was terrified by the mere thought of such things, and she squinted into the darkness, trying to see.

"Raifer?"

His name had come out as a mere whisper. She found she was unable to force her throat to make the sound any louder. If she had any sense at all, she thought, she'd go back up to the warehouse and wait for him. Seeing him come down to this dark hole, however, had raised a finger of suspicious fear in her, something she did not quite understand, but seemed solidly unshakable, something that would not be simply explained away. Much as she wanted to turn around and climb back up the flight of rickety wooden steps, she found she couldn't before she'd discovered what it was he was doing down there.

She took a single, tentative step forward, then tried once more to call out his name, finding she had no more success on second try than she'd had the first time. There was nothing for her to do, she realized, but move forward, toward the place from where the dim light seemed to be coming, far to the rear of the dank room. Except for a wealth of shadows from the area where the light shone, the basement seemed to be empty.

Moving quickly as she dared, and trying not to think about the creatures that might be lurking in the darkness around her, she started toward the flickering light. In the back of her mind she was dimly aware of soft, scurrying noises, but she refused to allow herself to dwell on them. Nothing can hurt me, she told herself firmly. After all, I'm not alone.

When she finally reached the light, she almost wished she was. Raifer was standing with a crowbar in his hands, leaning over the forced open top of a large crate. All around him, nearly surrounding him, were more large wooden boxes, randomly heaped in a disorganized pile. For a second Honor was struck by the strangeness of that, the fact that there seemed to be no order to the boxes. Everything in the warehouse above was neatly ordered, for locating a specific shipment quickly was often a priority, and that meant strict control of cargoes that were temporarily stored there.

"Raifer?" she ventured, taking a step closer to him. Her movement seemed to stir the air, for the light cast by the lantern flickered with an eerie shimmer, setting the shadows that lined the wall behind Raifer to move with grotesquely exaggerated motions. They were, she realized, by the far side of the basement, near the wall that would border the river. Here the whitewashed bricks had long ago turned a shiny gray-green with mold and dampness. Honor could see quite clearly the huge body of an enormously fat spider, suspended in the corner in an enormous web.

"Raifer?" she tried again, for although he'd straightened, he hadn't turned around to face her, and she wondered if he'd heard her. This time, like the previous ones, her voice sounded like a harsh, pale croak, hardly recognizable as hers, even to her own ears.

He had heard, though, for this time he put down the iron crowbar and turned slowly to face her. She was stricken when she saw the pistol in his hands. She gasped and drew back, shocked and frightened.

"Honor?"

Raifer sighed audibly, then tucked the pistol firmly into his belt. "What are you doing here, Honor?"

"I could ask you much the same question," she told him, staring pointedly at his waist, where he'd placed the weapon, "especially as you've that."

Her fear, she found, had gone as soon as he'd spoken to her. But her curiosity had only grown. She stepped forward to him.

"What is this?" she asked as she stared into the opened crate.

"About what it looks like, I should think," he said dryly as he moved aside, letting her peer into the rough wooden box.

Honor straightened up and turned to him. "But those are rifles," she said in a frightened whisper. "Why are there rifles down here?"

He considered her apparent shock, wondering if it could possibly be genuine, or simply a well-feigned act. "Perhaps you could explain that more easily than I," he replied.

"I don't understand," she protested. "How could I know? Papa doesn't deal in arms. Why should there be a crate of rifles down here?"

"Not one," he replied. "Dozens." He made a sweeping movement with his hand. "All these, it would seem, are filled with rifles or ammunition."

Honor looked dazedly around. She realized that several other boxes had their tops loosely pried open.

"That's impossible," she told him slowly. "I told you, Papa doesn't deal in arms." Her voice had sunk to a near whisper as it occurred to her what the presence of the armaments implied.

"So you said," Raifer answered dryly. "But then, perhaps upon a bit of reflection you might recall that he has a single, special customer for whom he might do a favor or two, perhaps even an illegal favor?"

Honor looked up at him sharply. "That's not true," she hissed between tight jaws. "Papa wouldn't do anything like that."

He shrugged, complacent. Then he dropped the top back on the crate.

"Perhaps then we should simply ask him to explain it to us," he said as he took her arm firmly in his hand. "To us and to a few representatives of New York's finest."

"What are you saying?" she demanded, her voice rising now, as she tried to pull her arm away from his grasp.

But before he could answer, there was the sound of a rough, grating noise from the far side of the basement. A long flicker of light appeared in the distance. Raifer dropped her arm and quickly extinguished his lantern.

"What . . . ?" Honor began.

He interrupted her with a harshly hissed "Be quiet!" as he pulled her back, away from the heap of crates and into the darkness.

Numb, Honor let him pull her against the cold, damp wall, his body pressing close against hers. She stared toward the light that had grown larger as a door opened and a man stepped through into the large basement room and looked around in the darkness.

"Kevin? Is that you out there?" he asked into the darkness.

His voice seemed vaguely familiar, and after a second pondering, Honor realized it was Brian Flannagan, the visitor from Cork she'd met at the McGowan house the morning she'd gone to retrieve her earring. He was outlined by the light from the small room behind him. She could just make out a rumpled cot and a table with the remnants of a meal in the room, the details sharp and comparatively brightly lit beside the dark wall of the basement that surrounded her and Raifer. His dark eyes seemed to glow with a sharp tenseness as he stared into the gloom.

"It's nothing but a rat, I'm tellin' ye," came a voice from behind him.

Flannagan turned and began to close the door behind him as he retreated into the relative comforts of the lighted room.

"But that's Kevin's friend," Honor said and started to move forward.

Raifer clamped a hand over her mouth, stifling any further noise, and drew her back into the shadows. She struggled for a second, not understanding why he would treat her like this, why he would want to hide from Kevin McGowan's friends. But the hold on her arm tightened until it hurt her, and she ceased fighting him, frightened now, far more so that she had been when she'd first found herself in the damp darkness of the basement.

"I tell you I heard something," Flannagan said, addressing the man who'd spoken to him, then turning back once more to face the darkness.

"Here."

The second man appeared at Flannagan's side bearing the lighted lantern. Donoghue or Burke? Honor tried to recall which face had nodded to which name as Kevin had quickly introduced her to them, but couldn't remember and gave up the effort.

"If you find yourself facin' a giant rat, just give a holler and I'll come out and give a cheer for your side." There was laughter in the man's words and manner as he held out the lantern to Flannagan.

Flannagan only scowled in response, turning back to stare into the dark recess of the cellar, obviously more intent upon the noise he'd heard than on anything his companion could say. He reached his hand into his jacket and withdrew it bearing a pistol.

Honor watched as he took the lantern, then her glance returned to the pistol and she found she could not draw her gaze away. The strangeness of what was happening seemed to be growing on her, filling her with confusion and a strangely chilling fear. Why would Kevin's friends be staying down here, in this grim cellar of whose existence she'd never even had an inkling? The basement itself most certainly had existed as long as the building above it, but the little furnished room at the end, when had that been put there? Surely it couldn't be a pleasant place to stay, so why would Kevin house them there, rather than in his home? And, even more mystifying, where had the rifles and ammunition come from, and why were they there?

She had no time to think of any of that, however, for Raifer was drawing her slowly back, away from the heap of crates, back into the shadows even as Flannagan slowly approached them, his lantern held high, a dim beacon into the darkness. Twice he paused and seemed to listen, and when he did, Honor could feel Raifer pull her close to him in warning to be silent, his hands on her waist rough, with no gentleness to them, only the immediacy of the warning. She complied with his silent orders, too terrified and bewildered to do anything else.

Luckily, Flannagan's attention seemed centered on the crates of rifles, not on any stirrings that might come from the far corners of the dark basement, for he moved directly towards them after only a cursory glance around him, inspecting the heap. Apparently, he found it much as he had left it for he shrugged, seemingly satisfied with his inspection, and then lifted the lantern once more, and peered again into the darkness.

Honor stood silent, watching him, hearing only the sound of her heart beating sharply within her. She was afraid, she realized, afraid of Raifer's intent, uncaring grasp, but also afraid of the possibility of discovery by Flannagan, a fact that completely bewildered her. After all, she told herself, she had no reason to fear the man—he was a friend of Kevin's.

Flannagan started to turn back to the room he'd come from, and Honor felt Raifer relax his hold of her arm a bit. She too was conscious of the ebbing of her own fear. But then Flannagan suddenly stopped, his eyes apparently finding something that puzzled him. He set down the lantern but kept the pistol ready as he lifted the crowbar from the top of the bar where Raifer had placed it and stared at it for a second.

"Damn," Raifer hissed, the sound barely audible to her even though his lips were close to her ear. Once more he tensed sharply beside her.

They stood in frozen silence as Flannagan inspected the bar, then, apparently satisfied nothing was amiss, he replaced it on the top of the crate, took up the lantern once again and made his way across the dark cellar to his room.

"What was it?" came the voice from within. "A giant river rat, I'm guessin'."

The man's tone still held the hint of humor that it had shown before, but Flannagan's answer showed none.

"I don't know," he said slowly as he entered the room, pulling the door shut behind him.

"Now," Raifer whispered sharply to Honor, pushing her towards the rickety flight of stairs. "I think we get out of here now."

She moved as he directed, catching up her skirts in her hand as she climbed, aware of his presence immediately behind her, still too bewildered to protest his orders. She was aware that Flannagan might decide to come out for another look and find them. The thought of the pistol he carried chilled her.

When they were once more in the relative brightness of the warehouse, Honor felt the fearful thudding in her chest begin to ease. She watched as Raifer turned and bolted the door carefully behind him. Then he turned back to face her.

"Now, perhaps you can explain this?" she asked him sharply. "What is going on down there?"

His face seemed to harden as he returned her unblinking stare. "I suggest we get a little help in finding out," he said, taking her arm with his hand and starting to the front door. "Or would you like to go back down there and ask your father's friends alone?"

This time she balked, jerking her arm away from him. "Friends?" she demanded.

The words he'd muttered below came back to her, his suggestion that her father was doing something illegal, that he should explain his actions to them and a few representatives of New York's finest. Those were the words he'd used, New York's finest, and that could only mean the police. Slowly awareness began to seep into her, like a finger of bitter poison.

He nodded complacently at her. "It would seem, from appearances, that your father is engaged in a bit of smuggling, Honor. Could it be that shipment of rifles is being sent to the rebels in Ireland?"

Honor felt a bitterness growing in her, could taste it on her tongue. "You're a policeman, aren't you?" she asked him, barely more than whispering the words. "That's why you're here. That's why you made love to me. You just wanted to spy on my father, to see if you could learn anything from me."

His face seemed to crumble at her words, at the look of hatred she levelled at him. "That's not true, Honor," he said evenly.

She wouldn't let him say any more. "It is true," she shouted at him. "The only thing that's not true is what you're saying about my father."

"Honor, listen to me," he began, reaching out to her, trying to take her arm once more with his hand.

This time, however, she would allow none of it. She balled her hands into fists, striking at him, thinking only that she hated him, that she wanted to hurt him any way she could, to hurt him as much as he was hurting her.

He let the blows fall, one after another, but when she'd struck him several times and made no indication that she'd vented her anger, he caught her wrists with his hands and held them roughly.

"I've no time for this now, Honor," he told her sharply. "You can tell me just how much you hate me later. For now, I've got work to do."

With that he started toward the front of the warehouse, shuffling her along beside him.

"Stay here," he ordered her sharply when they'd reached the front door. Then he pulled it open, stepped out, and waved his arms in the air.

Honor watched as two men, roughly dressed idlers who lazed among the heaps of barrel staves and piles of rope that littered the slip, suddenly became uncharacteristically animated, running along the length of the slip to where Raifer waited for them.

"Coriarty, see to reinforcements. We've got the weapons and, I daresay, a few of the types who hope to use them."

The first man nodded and took off at a run toward Water Street. The second man followed Raifer into the warehouse.

"There," Raifer told him, pointing to the barred door that led to the cellar. "That's the only exit. Let me know if you hear anything, McBride." The second man moved toward the door, and Raifer took Honor's arm once more. "You come with me, Honor," he told her. "There are a few things I intend to do while we're waiting."

"No," she said, trying to twist away from his grasp only to find the effort useless.

"I'm afraid, Honor, you really haven't any choice. I can't allow you to go off and warn anyone at this juncture."

"Warn anyone?" she repeated, incredulous. "Who would I warn? Those men down there? I don't even know what's happening."

"Then you wouldn't have any objections to coming with me," he insisted.

"Why don't you just have me arrested?" she taunted him.

He stared at her coldly. "I hope I won't have to do that, Honor," he replied. "I really hope you have nothing to do with any of this."

She found she couldn't believe him, not his words, not his cold indifference. "You're serious, aren't you?" she asked him, aware that she was suddenly beginning to believe that what seemed to be happening actually was happening. As impossible as it might seem to her, it was all horribly real.

"Deadly serious, Honor," he told her grimly.

Defiance slowly ebbed out of her. Honor allowed him to lead her to her father's and Kevin's offices.

"Sit there," he said, pointing to a chair that faced her father's desk.

She dropped into it, thinking of all the times in the past when she'd sat in that very chair, wondering how it suddenly seemed so completely strange to her, how the familiar room had suddenly become so foreign. Then she watched in silent fury as Raifer began to open her father's desk drawers and rifle through the papers he found in them. He was invading her father's precincts, her father's life. And she knew she had helped him find his way there.

Chapter Eight

"You can't go in there."

The shouted warning was followed by the sounds of a bit of muffled scuffling. With only a glance at Honor, Raifer strode to the door.

"Stay where you are," he told her.

"And just where do you expect me to run to?" she asked him.

He ignored her and pulled the door open.

Honor peered into the warehouse. Just outside the room where she sat, she saw her father, his arm being held by the man Raifer had called McBride. His cheeks were flushed with anger and embarrassment at his relative helplessness as he struggled against the younger man's hold.

Ignoring Raifer's instructions to stay where she was, Honor rose and ran past him to Daniel's side. She began to tug against the policeman's arm.

"Leave him alone!" she shouted at McBride. "You bully!"

Her words seemed to surprise the young man. His cheeks colored at the accusation, and he stared at her with an owlish, wide-eyed shame. But he made no move to release Daniel's arm.

"It's all right, McBride," Raifer told him and nodded to him to free Daniel.

The young man did as he was directed, and nodding curtly toward Honor before he left to return to his place by the door that led down to the basement.

"What is this all about, Farrell?" Daniel demanded, his tone strident. He made a brushing motion with his hand against the sleeve that McBride had held, as though he could somehow wipe away the contact. "What do you think you're doing here?"

"He's been searching your desk, Papa," Honor said before Raifer could answer. She took her father's arm and stood beside him, staring at Raifer as one would at a deadly enemy.

"My desk?" Daniel seemed more bewildered than affronted. "What are you talking about, Honor?" But he turned to Raifer for an explanation, not to his daughter.

"Perhaps we might go into your office and discuss this quietly, sir," Raifer suggested, his manner courteous, but far from obsequious.

Daniel's eyes narrowed speculatively. "Young McGowan has been urging me to fire you, Farrell. I am on the point of obliging him," he said.

Raifer allowed himself a wry smile, then shrugged and motioned toward Daniel's office behind him. "If you please, Mr. Wainwright."

Honor glowered at him. "He's a policeman, Papa," she said. "He thinks you're smuggling arms, and that's why he's here."

Daniel's brow furrowed. "Policeman?" he asked.

"I'm afraid so, sir," Raifer told him and once more motioned toward the office door. "Shall we?"

Honor and Daniel entered the office, then turned as Raifer followed them, closing the door firmly behind him. Once the door was shut, he turned to Daniel.

"If you make this easy, sir, I think I can see that

Honor isn't involved."

Honor could hardly believe her ears. "What?" She cried. "Make what easy? And just how am I supposed to be involved?"

"You nearly managed to warn them, Honor," he said to her evenly. "Don't try to deny you would have if I hadn't stopped you."

"Warn who?" she cried. "You're mad. You can't think I was trying to warn that man. I'm not involved in anything. And neither is my father." She turned to Daniel. "Tell him, Papa," she said. "Tell him how insane this is."

Daniel put a placating hand to her arm. "Of course it is, Honor." He turned his glance to Raifer. "I think, young man," he said, his tone icy, "that you've made a very unfortunate mistake."

"I wish I had," Raifer replied. "Believe me, I take no pleasure in any of this." His glance strayed momentarily to Honor, and then his gaze quickly returned to meet Daniel's. "But I'm afraid we are, quite literally, standing on the proof." He pointed to the cellar below. "If you make a clean breast of it now, before my superiors arrive, I think I can intercede in your behalf. Hopefully, we can arrange matters so that Honor's name remains out of it entirely."

"Damn it all, Farrell, I don't know what you think you're doing, but I can assure you there's no way you can involve me in anything even remotely illegal. As for your suggestion that I trade my daughter's good name for a spurious confession, that's an insane as your ridiculous accusations."

Daniel's cheeks had become colored with a dark red flush of anger. "And I don't suppose I need remind you that I am not entirely friendless in this city. I play cards with your chief of police. I would say, Farrell, you've gone to a great deal of trouble, and all it's going to do is get you fired."

Raifer remained impassive. "Shall we simply sit tight and wait until my superiors arrive, then?" he asked calmly. "Then, I suppose, we'll both learn if that's true or not." His eyes wandered to meet Honor's for a second, and he found the disgust he saw leveled at him from hers completely unsettled him. He turned away quickly, aware that he didn't blame her for the hatred she quite obviously felt for him. He was filled with a goodly measure of his own self-loathing . . . not that he hadn't known that this moment would come sooner or later. Still, anticipating it had in no way prepared him for the hurt he felt at the pain he was causing her. He ventured a sideways look at her. I'm sick to death of this job, he thought, as he felt the waves of her hatred seem to leap out and engulf him. Even the certainty that he was right, that what he'd done was necessary and right, gave him no solace for the loss he felt.

They hadn't long to wait. In less than fifteen minutes the slip outside the warehouse was filled with policemen and the office had become suddenly crowded with the addition of several uniformed policemen and a large, touseled-haired man wearing a rumpled brown suit.

"Let's have it, Farrell," he said brusquely after he'd leveled a quick glance at Daniel and a slightly more lingering one toward Honor.

"This way, Captain," Raifer said, making his way out of the office. "There are two of them that I know of, maybe more. And they're armed." He moved into the warehouse toward the bolted door, the other police following close behind him.

Daniel and Honor rose and began to start after

the others. Raifer had just drawn back the bolt when he noticed them.

"You stay here," he told Daniel.

But Daniel just shook his head. "I believe I have the right to know what it is I've been accused of doing, haven't I, Farrell? Or is that no longer common police practice?"

"The men down there are dangerous," Raifer replied.

"What men?" Daniel asked, unimpressed. "I know of no men. All that's below this warehouse is a damp and empty basement, so far as I know."

"Captain?" Raifer turned to Ryan, expecting him to make the ruling.

The big man only shrugged. "Mr. Wainwright seems to be filled with the pious indignation of the innocent," Ryan replied. "Let's see just how long he can maintain that image." His tone implied that he thought it would not be very long at all.

"Papa," Honor whispered as she put her hand to Daniel's sleeve. He turned to face her. "Perhaps it would be better if we waited here."

Daniel only shook his head. "I think I ought to find out what's going on on my own property, Honor," he replied. "You go back to the office and wait there."

She shook her head. "No," she said, leveling a sharp glance toward Raifer. "I'm staying with you," she said, her eyes telling Raifer that she never should have trusted him, that she should have believed Daniel in the first place.

Raifer had no time to ponder the unpleasant reaction he had to her words and her expression, for his attention was drawn to the large front door, which had been opened with a bang and followed by the loudly vocal entry of Kevin McGowan and, of all people, Chief of Police William Fitzpatrick. Raifer saw his captain cringe at the unexpected swell of ranks. He knew there was little love lost between the two men, and at Fitzpatrick's entry he found himself wondering if he'd somehow become caught in the constant power struggle that the two men pursued with singularly intent perversity.

"What's going on here?" Fitzpatrick demanded loudly as he approached Ryan. He eyed the other man's rumpled suit and unkempt hair with distaste. Perfectly groomed himself, Fitzpatrick liked to think of himself as a gentleman, and openly looked down on his less pretentious subordinate officer.

"Damn," Ryan muttered under his breath, and he threw a sharp glance at Raifer, one that said quite plainly that someone in the office was reporting to his superior behind his back. He managed to force down his dislike of the man as he turned to face him.

"We've had some information, sir, that illegal arms intended for the Irish insurgents are being hidden in this warehouse," he answered, his words grimly determined. Somehow he'd managed to make the word *sir* sound more like a disparagement than a term of respectful address. "We were just about to investigate."

Kevin's cheeks grew bright red. "This is absurd," he shouted angrily. He looked at Honor and Daniel. "Surely you've told them what drivel this is?"

Honor caught the note of unnatural bluster in his tone. *He's lying*, she thought. *He knows all about whatever is going on down there.* But she kept her silence, knowing that to condemn Kevin was to condemn her father as well.

"Of course I told them," Daniel replied. "It didn't seem to serve much purpose."

Fitzpatrick leveled a sharply probing glance at Ryan. "You had better be sure of what you're about, Captain," he said through tight lips. "I will not have officers under my command abusing their positions and making false accusations." His eyes narrowed. "I don't suppose you need to be reminded that these two gentlemen are personal friends of mine?" he asked.

"I'm well aware of that fact, sir," Ryan replied.

Honor could feel the hatred that flowed between the two men. She wondered how much that hatred had influenced the situation they all now faced, how much Ryan's dislike of his superior had prompted his investigation of her father and Kevin as friends of Fitzpatrick's.

"You don't suppose you would like to offer Mr. McGowan and Mr. Wainwright an apology and be done with this nonsense, do you?" Fitzpatrick pushed.

For a moment Honor thought the police captain might do just that, that he might turn around and forget about the whole matter. She felt the flow of a tide of relief within her. But then she realized that Fitzpatrick had made a mistake, that by urging Ryan to dismiss the accusations against his friends, he had only pushed the police captain to pursue them all the more intently.

Ryan's features grew leaden. "I think, sir, it would be more in the interests of the law to investigate the matter," Ryan replied evenly. He turned quickly to face Raifer. "If you'd care to show us all, Detective Farrell?"

Raifer only nodded, then made his way through the small crowd to the bolted door. He drew aside the thick bolt, pulled the door open, and started down the dark flight of stairs.

Honor reached out for Daniel's arm as they followed the others. "What's happening, Papa?" she asked him in a tense whisper. "What is going on here?"

"Nothing, Honor," he said firmly.

She darted a glance at the policeman, McBride, who stood near them. "But if there was something down there, Papa?" she asked cautiously.

"There's nothing there, Honor," he told her evenly, patted her hand absently, then turned away.

She found that would have to content her, for it seemed he would tell her nothing else. She wondered at his certainty that nothing would be found, wondered that he'd not seemed to notice the false tone in Kevin's voice.

Raifer found himself once more in the huge, dark cellar. The darkness, however, quickly ebbed as others followed him carrying lanterns. It did not take much light in any event, for him to realize that something was wrong. He started directly for the side of the cellar where the crates of arms had been only half an hour before. But even in the darkness he could see that the shadows that had marked them on his previous trip were missing.

"Well, Raifer?"

Raifer realized Ryan's voice was thick with tension. He wished he had something to say to ease that tension, but he was without any words his captain could find comforting.

"They were here, right here," he said as they reached the spot the crates had occupied. "More than a dozen crates." He looked around at the bare dirt floor. All that remained were scraped-up marks and a muddle of footprints in the damp dirt at his feet. "They were here," he repeated as his eyes roved over the empty, mold-bespeckled wall, fruitlessly looking for some mark that might mean a door existed in the wall nearby, something that could explain the missing crates. There was nothing.

"Well, Ryan?" Fitzpatrick's tone was edged with sarcastic chiding. "Am I to assume these arms you mentioned are invisible? Or did they suddenly develop legs and walk off somewhere?"

Raifer turned away, towards the far end of the cellar where the room with the light had been. "They must have taken them there," he said, pointing to the dark, far wall.

"Where?" Fitzpatrick demanded, his tone unchanged. "Am I to believe there is more to this fantasy?"

Raifer made no reply to him. He was moving quickly across the wide, empty expanse of the cellar, stopping on his way only long enough to requisition the lantern one of the uniformed policemen held.

The door was easy enough to find, stained white batten, with dark iron hinges. But even as he drew it open, Raifer knew that what he sought would not be there. Somehow the men who had been down there had been warned, somehow they'd managed to get the crates out and get away.

But how, that was the question. There was no exit from the basement except the way by which he'd entered, through the warehouse above. And he'd had McBride stationed by the door the whole time. They couldn't have gotten out that way. Unless, he mused, unless there was a way out through the small room, they couldn't have gotten out at all.

He'd been a fool to give them the time, he thought, the realization as accusing as the look Ryan leveled at him. He should have tried to take them as soon as he'd become aware that they were down there, not given them the time. It had only been minutes, and he'd had Honor's safety to think about, that if she'd been hurt in the cross fire, he'd have been responsible.

Finally he told himself that his thoughts and excuses were valueless. He pulled open the door and tensed the hand that held his pistol, part of him still fervently hoping that the men were still there, that they'd offer some resistance, part of him knowing that they would be gone.

The room was empty. Save for a large crate that lay upended on the floor by the wall, there was nothing, no cot, no table, no lamp, no armed men. Just the crate and a tall row of poorly constructed shelves lining the far wall, and they, too, were bare and empty.

He moved slowly around the edge of the room, holding the lantern up high, examining the walls, hoping to find something, anything that would tell him how the men had escaped and instead finding only solid, unmoving wall for his bother.

"Well, Farrell?"

Raifer looked up to find the small room had become fairly crowded. Ryan, Fitzpatrick, Daniel, Honor, and three of the uniformed policemen had managed to fit into the room's confines. They all stood and looked at him curiously, a few of their expressions indicating the thought that he might be just a touch unbalanced. He tried to ignore them, all save Honor, but she turned away as soon as she realized he was looking to her for some word that would verify what he'd said was true. He realized quickly that there would be no sympathy for him there, that the last thing she'd do was offer him her help.

"Farrell?"

This time Fitzpatrick's summons was sharp.

Raifer tore his eyes away from Honor, aware that the hurt he felt at her rejection was far deeper than that which sprang from his apparent failure.

"They were here," Raifer replied to Fitzpatrick's unvoiced question. "At least a dozen crates of arms. And two men, maybe more. And from where I stood, it looked as though they were living in this room."

Fitzpatrick smirked. "Well, it would seem they are not living here now, wouldn't it?" he asked.

Raifer made no reply.

"Come, come, Farrell," Fitzpatrick pushed. "Perhaps you or Captain Ryan might be so kind as to explain what happened to these supposed terrorists and their contraband armaments?"

Ryan, too, Raifer found, was staring at him now, his eyes asking the same questions.

"I don't know," he replied heatedly. "They were here."

Fitzpatrick shrugged. Then he turned his back to Raifer and Ryan and faced Daniel, Kevin, and Honor. "I can only offer my apologies," he said, "and hope that you can see your way to dismissing this whole matter as an unfortunate mistake."

"Of course," Kevin replied, his manner effusive. He sent Raifer a look of smug victory. "I suppose any one is allowed a mistake." Then he smiled. "You may, Farrell, of course consider your employment here terminated." He smiled pleasantly, pleased with his small joke.

His remark seemed to give Fitzpatrick an idea, for he turned back to Raifer and Ryan. "And you both may consider yourselves under suspension pending investigation of this matter," he said. He smiled smugly at Ryan before he turned, and led Daniel and Kevin out of the room and towards the stairs.

For a moment Honor stood where she was, staring at Ryan, watching the way the anger that had swept over him colored his cheeks and clenched his fists, completely unaware of the uniformed policemen who walked by her as they emptied out of the small room.

"I guess you've done it now, Raif, my boy," Ryan said miserably as he, too, turned and left.

It took her a second before she realized that she was alone with Raifer, that his eyes were on her, watching her, waiting for something, some words, some explanation. She felt a wave of shame and guilt, aware that she could have helped him, that she could have substantiated his story, and yet had stood by and let him be thought a fool and an incompetent. I don't care, she told herself, filling with a sharply vicious anger of her own, remembering what he had done, that he'd made love to her simply to get close enough to her to learn something that might help him entrap her father. He deserves whatever happens to him, she thought. She had no reason to feel responsible for his disgrace.

He seemed to read what it was that was in her mind. "It would seem you have your revenge, Honor," he said softly. "I hope it pleases you." His face was entirely without expression, without remorse or distaste or even disappointment with her at her lack of support. Instead he stared at her impassively, as though he were looking through her, at the blank wall beyond.

She found she couldn't stand there feeling the cold of the icy look in his eyes. Who was he, after all, to blame her after the things he'd done?

"I never want to see you again," she spat out at him. "Never."

Then she turned on her heel and followed after the others, leaving him alone in the grim, empty room.

Honor sat silently in the large leather-covered chair in her father's library and watched as Daniel and Kevin spoke. She hardly heard the words, she realized, and could scarcely register any of the meaning of the thin hum that was their voices, but she really wasn't interested in what it was they had to say to each other. If there was to have been any word of explanation, it would have happened long before this, while they were still in the carriage that had taken them home from the warehouse. There had been none then, and there would be, she knew, none now.

But that fact did not bring her to the conclusion that none could have been made. There was, she knew, too much of the good-humored pleasure Kevin displayed at parties or when he intended to impress people about her father's partner's manner. He knew something, she realized, possibly everything, where the crates and the men had gone, what their presence there had meant in the first place. Otherwise he wouldn't be so pleased with himself, so complacently smug. The awareness rankled at her, for she honestly cared for Kevin as she would for a favorite uncle. It pained her to think that he was involved with those two men in the basement, with the smuggling of arms.

There was nothing else for her to believe. After all, she'd seen the man Flannagan in Kevin's home. He knew what was going on. He was doubtless part of it. To believe otherwise would mark her as a naive fool, and she'd felt herself entirely too much that of late. She'd been a fool with Raifer. She wouldn't let herself behave that way ever again.

When Kevin finally left, she roused herself. She stood and crossed the room, staring out the window at the cold, deadened garden.

"Honor? Are you not feeling well? You look pale."

Daniel had returned from escorting Kevin to the door, and now he seemed to be looking at Honor for the first time since they'd returned home. She turned to face him, her expression set and determined.

"What is going on down there, Papa?" she demanded. "What were those men and those crates of rifles doing in the basement of your warehouse?"

Daniel stared at her for a long moment without answering, searching for something in her eyes, it seemed, and unable to find it.

"I don't know what you're talking about, Honor," he replied finally. "You were there. There were no men, no crates of rifles."

She nodded slowly. "Yes, I was there. I was there with you and once before, with Raifer. And the first time there were men and there *were* guns."

Daniel swallowed, his Adam's apple moving uncomfortably in his throat. His glance grew uncertain, and after a moment it skittered away from her face as though it could not bear any longer to meet hers.

"I don't know what you're talking about, Honor," Daniel said finally. "That Farrell is deluded and dangerous. I told you that in the very beginning."

"No, Papa," Honor countered. "You told me no such thing. You said he was using me. And as it happens, I now find myself agreeing with you, if that brings you any comfort. I shall not see him again. But I saw what he saw in that basement. I could have substantiated his story, but I didn't. In a way, by not speaking I lied. I lied to protect you, Papa. And I think that lie should be paid for with an explanation." She peered at him sharply. "Now, are you going to answer my question? What is going on in that warehouse? What are you and Kevin involved in?"

This time Daniel only shrugged. "I have no idea, Honor," he said as he turned to the liquor cabinet. "As far as I know, nothing is going on there but business. Just ordinary business."

Honor watched him as he poured whiskey into a tumbler, half filling it. Whatever he knows, she thought, he feels he can't tell me. She was reminded of her experience with the Reverend Father Jonas Mather. Perhaps it was something like that, she hoped almost desperately. Perhaps he's blameless, in a compromising position, and unable to change it. Perhaps it's all Kevin's doing, and he has been saddled with a situation of which he's had no part. She could understand his unwillingness to tell her, just as she'd been unable to tell him about that unpleasant afternoon at the church. There was nothing, she realized, she could do to change matters after all.

"Terry! What are you doing here?"

"Why, I came to see you, of course, Honor."

Honor had been in the act of deciding if she would simply go straight up to her room after dinner, offering the excuse of a headache, or stay with Daniel in the vain hope that she might be able to induce him to confide in her after all. She saw Daniel look up at the sound of Terrence McGowan's voice. He, at least, she realized, was more than pleased with the diversion of an unexpected visitor.

Terrence entered the room and made his way directly to her, with little more than a nod in Daniel's direction.

"I heard what happened today, Honor, I came to assure myself that you were as well as Father assured me you were." His expression grew anxious. "It must have been horrible for you."

Honor was quite taken aback with his unexpected show of concern for her welfare. For the previous several months she'd thought him completely incapable of thinking of anyone but himself. Perhaps she'd misjudged him, she thought as a wave of guilt swept over her. It did not seem to be quite as impossible as she'd have considered it a few weeks before. After all, it was more than apparent that she'd misjudged just about everything and everyone else of late.

"I am, as you can see, absolutely unscathed, Terry," she replied with a laugh and a small smile. "I fear your mission of charitable comfort was quite unnecessary."

He took her hand and ceremoniously raised it to his lips. "Any expedition that leads me to you, Honor, can not be unnecessary."

Honor's eyes wandered to Daniel's pleased expression. She wondered just how spontaneous this visit of Terrence's actually was, and just how much of a hand Daniel might have had in arranging it. Whatever the reason, she told herself, still he'd made the effort to come to see her, and she ought not to appear ungrateful.

She brought her gaze back to meet Terrence's. She didn't know why, but his glance made her uncomfortable. Was it guilt, she wondered, over what she'd shared with Raifer, over the fool she'd been about a man who was only using her? She wondered suddenly what Terrence would do if he knew, if he'd be quite as solicitous if he were to learn she was no longer the innocent he believed her to be.

"Will you stay and have dinner with us, Terry?" Daniel asked. "We're quite alone this evening and without diversion. I think Honor could use a bit of company just now," he added pointedly. "Company a bit more interesting for her than her father's."

"Papa," Honor chided. It seemed he was purposefully trying not to be alone with her and subject to her questions. She was not at all pleased with the prospect of being required to keep up polite conversation when she was far more interested in finding a way to induce Daniel to confide in her.

The two men ignored her. Terrence accepted the invitation with no hint that he was aware of any friction between her and her father. During dinner he made a manfully gallant attempt to be as entertaining as he could, ignoring Honor's occasional absent lapses and Daniel's descent into a moody thoughtfulness. Had Honor been given to consideration of the circumstances, she would have realized he was taking far greater pains than he had with her in months.

When finally dinner was finished and the last of the dishes had been cleared from the table and the bottle of port and glasses set out, Honor stood, greatly relieved to be able to get away from the two of them. She wanted, more than anything, she realized, to be alone, to have a chance to think.

"If you gentlemen will excuse me," she murmured the ritual leave taking as she dropped her napkin to the table at her place and backed away from the table, "I'll leave you to your brandy and cigars."

But Terrence jumped up as well, apparently of a mind to end his meal with something other than tobacco and alcohol.

"If you don't mind, Honor, and with Daniel's permission, I'd like to talk to you."

"I'm really terribly tired, Terry. It's been, to say the least, a trying day."

Despite her protest, he seemed unwilling to allow her the excuse. "It will take only a few minutes, Honor," he insisted as he moved around the table to her.

In vain Honor looked to her father for some support. Daniel, however, was reaching for the decanter of port Fraser had set in front of him, and seemed entirely indifferent to her silent pleas.

"Very well, Terry," she agreed finally.

Terrence took her arm and led her into Daniel's library. Honor felt as though she were trapped as she watched him shut the door behind them.

"Shall I pour you a brandy?" she asked him, pulling away from his hold rather than simply sitting where he indicated on the couch. She moved to the liquor chest as if she might somehow find a way out of the room through it.

"I've no need of spirits when I have you to look at, Honor," he replied with a small smile.

Honor turned to him, and despite herself, found herself grinning. "Such poetry, Terry," she said. "And such blarney. What prompts you to such raptures of flattery, if I might ask?"

His smiled disappeared. "I suppose I deserve your doubts, Honor," he told her, his tone quite sober now. "I've treated you badly of late, and you have every reason to question my feelings for you. But I realize now what a fool I've been, and I want only to make amends." He crossed the room to her, his hands extended as though in supplication.

Honor backed away from his grasp as he neared her. "Please, Terry," she begged him softly. "I don't think I can bear to go on with this conversation. Not now, at any rate."

He stopped and dropped his hands, then nodded. "I understand, Honor. And I have no desire to press you in any way if that will push you away from me rather than bring you to me. I came tonight only to tell you that I'm here, waiting for you whenever you find yourself ready for me. That, and to give you this." He put his hand into his vest pocket and drew out a small, embossed leather box. This he opened and held out to her on his outspread palm.

Honor stared at the ring, an ornate setting with a central sapphire surrounded by a collar of diamonds. But she made no move to reach for his gift.

"I can't, Terry. I can't take something like this from you," she told him softly.

"Think of it not as a pledge of love, Honor, but one of friendship, if that is easier for you. I know right now your feelings about me are less than what I would have them be. I realize that Farrell has left you confused and hurt."

"Terry, please!" Honor fairly shouted at him, interrupting the flow of his words, hating to hear him mention Raifer, feeling the name in her ears like a splash of dark poison that worked its way inside her with a breathless speed only to choke her and fill her with pain.

Terrence took a single step closer to her, then took the ring from the box and grasped her right hand in his.

"A pledge of friendship only, Honor," he told her as he slipped the ring on her finger. "In the fervent hope that it will soon grow to something more."

He leaned forward to her and planted a chaste kiss on her cheek, then released her hand and backed away from her. She stared at him mutely, numb, not really sure what had just happened between them and not willing at that moment to so much as offer the energy of thought to the matter.

Terrence smiled at her. "Good night, Honor," he said softly as he backed to the door.

Then he was gone and Honor remained, staring dully after him. It was only when she'd been alone for several minutes that she looked down and found the ring he'd put on her finger.

Chapter Nine

Honor came down from her room late the following morning. She found Daniel seated at the dining table, the morning newspaper in his hand and the scraps from his breakfast on the plate he'd pushed to the side.

"I thought you'd be gone by now," she said as she slid into her place and put her napkin in her lap. It was only when the words were spoken that she realized that she wished he had gone, that she was not up to seeing him if they were only to continue with the distant pleasantries they'd maintained the evening before.

Daniel made no answer. He was, it seemed, entirely absorbed by the article he was reading in the newspaper. Honor only shrugged, and reached for the coffeepot that had been left near her place, concentrating completely on filling her cup as if it were an unprecedented feat. The sharp, piquant bouquet of the coffee filled her nostrils as the dark liquid flowed in a stream from the pot's spout. And Honor's gaze drifted from the brown flow to her hand and the shining adornment that was still on her finger where Terrence had placed it.

The realization that she was still wearing the ring startled her somewhat, and the coffeepot trembled in her hand, sending a few drops of dark brown onto the white damask cloth. The sight of them was enough to steady her thoughts, and she carefully straightened the pot and returned it to its place. Only then did she allow her glance to wander back to the ring on her finger.

She'd return it, of course, she told herself firmly, at the very first opportunity that presented itself. She had no intention of allowing her misery over Raifer to send her into willy-nilly into Terrence's arms.

Raifer. The unbidden thought of him sent a painful finger of hurt and anger through her. I can't think of him now, she told herself firmly, not yet. Just as she had told herself a thousand times through the previous, sleepless night. I can't think of him now, she'd told herself as she lay in the darkened room. But it was a useless resolve, for thoughts of him had nagged at her ceaselessly, leaving her filled with remorse and anger and the miserable realization that her heart was broken.

She reached unsteadily for her coffee cup, but when she saw her hand was shaking so much that liquid sloshed over the rim when she lifted it, she set it down immediately in its saucer. She looked up at Daniel.

"Papa," she said, forcing herself to settle her thoughts, "I'm afraid we have to talk."

Even the strident quality of her tone did nothing to dislodge Daniel's attention from his newspaper. Honor stared at him, wondering what it was that had so caught and transfixed his attention. It was only then that she noticed the paleness of his cheeks, the uncertain way his long fingers clung to the sheet of newspaper.

She stood and walked around the table to where he sat, then leaned over his chair and scanned the page that so completely held his attention. The headline fairly leaped out at her: *Attempt to Assassinate Prince of Wales Meets with Failure.* Beneath the bold letters was a profile picture of the prince, his stare fixed and almost bemused, a dark bristling moustache separating a rather long nose from full, firm lips. Not so much handsome, she thought, as one certain of his destiny and the power he would one day wield.

Her eyes fell down to the long rows of print, and she read the words hungrily, with a kind of transfixed fascination.

> The Crown Prince of England, Prince Edward, Duke of Cornwall and Prince of Wales, narrowly escaped death last evening as he entered his hotel, the Saint Pierre. Just as the prince left his carriage to mount the front steps of the hotel, a shot rang out, missing the prince by only inches, and striking instead a night porter who held the door for him. The porter, Harold Mahon, was taken to Daughter of Mercy Hospital for treatment of the gunshot wound to his shoulder.
>
> Prince Edward, in the city following a goodwill tour of the provinces of Canada, intends to meet unofficially with President Cleveland before he returns to Great Britain sometime next week. When asked about the attempt on his life, a spokesman for the prince said Edward had cavalierly dismissed the matter, suggesting it may have been a case of mistaken identity.
>
> Chief of Police William Fitzpatrick, however, was far more concerned. He explained that the New York Police intend to keep a careful eye on the prince for the remainder of his visit. "The gunman may have escaped this time," he said, "but we don't intend to give him a second opportunity. I will not have murderers on my

patch." The prince will have, despite his official escort, an honor guard of New York's finest while he is here, Fitzpatrick added, suggesting that news of such a guard will discourage any further attempts on the prince's life while he is here.

There was a good deal more, most of it speculation tying the assassination attempt to recent disturbances in Ireland and rumors of threats sent to the crown promising worse if conditions in the area did not ease.

When she'd finished scanning the article, Honor's eyes narrowed, and she looked down at her father suspiciously.

"Papa," she demanded, "what do you know about this? You must tell me."

Daniel turned his eyes, finally, to meet hers. Honor was surprised by them, found they were dazed with shock and disbelief.

"I never thought," he murmured, then fell silent once more, as though he could not bring himself to say the words he held in his mind.

His appearance surprised Honor and bewildered her. It seemed as though he had suddenly grown terribly old, something she'd never thought him before that moment, old and defeated. She knelt down beside his chair.

"You never thought what, Papa?" she asked him softly, afraid of how he might answer, but aware that she had to know.

"There was never to have been any gun play," Daniel murmured, not to her, really, but to the part of him that clung to his own innocence. "They were to come and collect this shipment of rifles, that's all. No one was supposed to be hurt."

There was a dull awareness in her now, that the

men she'd seen at Kevin's house, and then again in the warehouse, had been the ones who had done this thing.

"This shipment, Papa?" Honor pushed, even more afraid now, but relentless.

Daniel nodded. "Kevin has been sending illegal arms for the last three years." He held his hand out to her, a small gesture of supplication. "There was nothing I could do about it, Honor. Kevin's so deeply involved in this thing. He had already begun with it, without my knowledge, when I found out. But there are others in the city, so many others, contributing money and influence." He fell silent once more, putting his head to his hands, retreating into himself, still telling himself he was in no way responsible for the attempt on the prince's life, even as he knew deep down that it would never have happened without his silent compliance.

Honor drew back from him slowly, feeling with the distance from him her revulsion for the assassins growing. If she had not interferred the day before, she realized, if she'd not appeared when she had and kept him from his duty, Raifer would have had those men arrested, and there would have been no attack, no attempted murder. It struck her with the thickness of a blow that Raifer had been right all along, that both her father and Kevin McGowan were involved in a business that was not only criminal, but dangerous as well.

"How could you, Papa?" she murmured as she clumsily seated herself in the chair beside him. "How could you let me believe you innocent? Do you trust me so little as that?"

Daniel looked up at her sharply. "It had nothing to do with you, Honor. Just as it had nothing to do with me. There was never to be any gun play."

She drew back from him, shocked at his persistence. "How can you say that, Papa? What use are guns ever put to? You knew about it and did nothing to stop it."

"What could I do?" he cried out.

"You could have made Kevin give it up, for both of your sakes!"

He only shook his head and returned his face to his hands. Honor stared at him in dumb silence for a moment, then she realized suddenly that she had seen the terrorists who had made the attempt, she knew their faces. There was still something she could do to make up in some measure for what Daniel had allowed to happen.

She stood abruptly and started for the door.

"Honor!"

Daniel's voice was sharp and his eyes piercing when she turned to face him.

"Where are you going?" he demanded.

"To find Raifer Farrell," she told him flatly. "I saw those men. I can describe their faces, identify them."

Daniel stood shakily at his place and leaned forward, towards her.

"You can't, Honor. You don't understand. There are other people involved in this. I told you. It's not just Kevin. There are others, important people, people who don't like things getting in their way."

"Is that what I'd be doing, Papa?" she asked him softly. "Getting in their way? Well, I don't care if I'm an inconvenience to these important people, whoever they are. I intend to do what I know is right, and you can't stop me."

With that she turned away from him and stalked from the room. Daniel stared after her, sinking back into his chair only when he heard the front door open and shut behind her. He had never, he realized, felt quite so beaten in his life.

Some of Honor's sense of indignant righteousness seemed to fade as she entered the police station. It was noisy and dirty and rife with an aura of the unpleasant knowledge that man was, intrinsically, lawless and evil. Honor felt uncertain and a bit afraid.

"Can I help you, miss?"

The question was hardly unusual, nor, considering her confused manner, even surprising, but still Honor felt herself nearly jump before she turned to find the young uniformed officer who had addressed her.

"I'm looking for Raif Farrell," she managed to reply once she'd gathered her wits together.

"Detective Farrell isn't here," he said, his tone just a bit sharp. Then his eyes narrowed a bit and he stared at her as one does at someone one has met but isn't quite sure how to place. "You're Miss Wainwright, aren't you?" he asked after a moment.

Honor, too, realized she had come into contact with him, for his features were familiar but somehow did not fit in her mind with a police uniform. Then it came to her, he'd been the young officer Raif had set to guarding the door at the warehouse, the one who had tried to restrain her father when he'd entered. She vaguely remembered calling him a bully and his resulting embarrassment. He looked far more certain of himself in his neat uniform with its bright brass buttons than he had in the dirt-stained work clothes he'd worn the day before. And she felt a good deal less certain than she had when she'd so volubly attacked him.

He was sitting in a large, leather-covered wing chair, dressed in vest and trousers and wrinkled white linen, but no jacket, holding a large glass of what appeared to be whiskey on his way to raise it to his lips.

He lowered the glass. "I'd have thought they'd have told you I'm suspended from the force just at the moment, Miss Wainwright. In part, thanks to you, I might add."

He raised the glass once more, towards her in a mocking salute, then brought it to his lips and swallowed thirstily.

"I have to talk to you, Raifer," she told him as she moved, unbidden and uninvited, into the room.

The butler turned and started towards her. "I'm sorry, miss," he began, putting his hand out to her arm.

But Raifer waved him away. "Inasmuch as Miss Wainwright is so determined, Creighton," he said, "it would seem to be ungentlemanly to send her away unappeased." He raised the glass to his lips once more and this time he drained it. "After all, she thinks me less than a gentleman now. I'd hate to reinforce that impression any further."

The butler scowled a bit, but nodded. "As you say, sir," he murmured before leaving the room, closing the door silently behind him.

When he'd gone, Raifer turned to the tray bearing a decanter and glasses on the table at the far side of the room. "I don't suppose you'd be interested in a display of my hospitality, would you, Honor?" he asked without turning to look at her.

"Isn't it rather early in the day for that?" she asked him tartly.

He poured his drink, refilling his glass carefully and returning the decanter to the tray before he turned to face her.

"A gentleman of leisure drinks whenever the whim strikes him, Honor. And as I suddenly find myself a gentleman of complete leisure, the whim seems to be striking me quite a bit." He sipped the whiskey once more, defiantly this time, keeping his eyes on hers.

She watched him, silent, numbed by his show of diffidence as well as by the unexpected luxury of his circumstances. Nothing was quite as she had expected to find it.

"Well, do you intend to simply stand there, Honor?" he asked her finally. "Didn't you come here to tell me just how much you hate me?" He stared at her, painfully expectant.

Honor shook her head slowly and took one tentative step towards him before she stopped.

"No," she said, her voice scratchy and raw. Her throat was suddenly tight, and it seemed a feat to her to force even the single syllable from it.

"I'd forgotten," he told her thoughtfully. "You said you never wanted to see me again. It must have been something important to force you to such an extreme." He stared at her, his expression growing colder by the second. "After all, you're a woman wronged. I seduced you, used you, mistreated you."

She found her voice suddenly, and the words exploded from her lips as though driven. "You did," she cried. "You know you did."

He dropped the glass onto the tray and started to move toward her. "No, Honor, I didn't. I give you my word, what passed between us was apart from the rest."

Honor felt an uncomfortable thudding in her chest. She wanted to believe him, more than anything else she wanted to believe him. She could taste the salt of tears in the back of her throat and felt the uncomfortable lump that presaged them. She fought to hold them back. She'd been a fool, she realized, to think she could see him again and feel nothing.

"You lied to me," she managed to force past the catch of tears in her throat. "It was all lies. How do you expect me to believe anything you tell me now?"

He moved to her, and put his hands to her arms, holding her. "It wasn't lies, Honor. I didn't tell you I was a detective. And that was a lie of omission, I'll grant you that. But all the rest, that was true."

She shook her head slowly, then motioned to the luxuriously furnished room. "How do you explain all this if you told me no lies?" she demanded weakly. Her resolve was beginning to totter, she realized. She wanted more than anything else for him to convince her. "You worked in the mines, you said. A miner does not live in a house like this one."

He stared down at her, aware, once his eyes found hers, that she was begging him to make her believe.

"This isn't my house, Honor," he told her evenly. "It belongs to a," he hesitated only for a second, "a friend who lets me live here when he is not in the city. And those things I told you were true. I did work in the lead mines. And I read law for a while."

Honor felt herself wavering. "But what happened between us," she pushed, knowing that her persistence was perverse, that if she wanted to believe in him she ought to simply accept his word, "that was simply so you could spy on my father."

He tightened his grip on her shoulders as though his hold on her might force her to accept his words.

"That first night, I wanted to see who would appear at McGowan's party. I did accept your invitation for the very reason you say, to see if I could learn anything about who else was in this thing with McGowan and your father. But it ended there, Honor. I swear to you, from the moment we left McGowan's house, it was between us, strictly between us."

Honor felt the press of his hands to her arms, but it was no more unsettling to her than were his words. "You still think my father is involved with arms smuggling?" she asked him faintly.

He dropped his hands away from her and took a step backwards. "You were there, Honor," he told her, his tone turned harsh once more. "You saw those crates."

She could hear his unspoken accusation, that she could have spoken up, could have attested to what she had seen before Ryan and Fitzpatrick. She looked down, no longer daring to meet his gaze with her own.

"What would you have had me do?" she demanded. "Condemn my own father?"

"It was he who condemned himself, when he got into the business of smuggling arms to terrorists."

There was anger in his tone now, and derision. She found herself looking up once more, her eyes seeking his, only now they were beseeching, not demanding.

"It wasn't his fault, Raifer. I swear to you, the fault was Kevin's, not Papa's."

"Then you admit it now?" he asked.

She nodded slowly. "Yes. He told me this morning. Kevin has been secretly sending arms for three years now. There was nothing he could do."

"And he just looked the other way?" Raifer

pressed, his tone tinged with scorn.

She looked down once more, aware that in his eyes what her father had done was as evil as what Kevin had done, that by ignoring the situation, Daniel had allowed it to flourish.

"Please, Raifer, please listen to me. I came here today to beg you for my father's freedom. I've seen the terrorists. All of them. I came to trade their descriptions, identify them if need be, if you will promise to keep my father from being prosecuted."

Raifer stared at her, his blue gray eyes growing hard and knowing. Once more he neared her, once more he put his hands to her arms and held her.

"Is that all you came to me for, Honor?" he asked her.

His hand left her shoulder and moved slowly to her cheek, his thumb moving softly against her neck, the contact fleeting, gentle strokes that sent unexpected waves of liquid heat through her.

"Yes," she murmured, trying to fight the feeling, aware, even as she made the attempt, that the effort was useless.

He lowered his face until his lips were only inches from hers.

"Was it, Honor?" he asked again, his voice low now, and husky, the warmth of his breath touching her skin like a caress.

"Yes," she managed to murmur once more.

They both knew it was a lie.

His hand moved to the back of her head, his fingers coiling themselves in the heavy silk of her hair, while his other hand slid around her waist, pulling her close to him. He kissed her slowly, intently, his lips first pressing hers, hard and warm, then his tongue parting her lips and gently probing. She felt herself melting against him, yielding herself to him, as much an admission of defeat and repentance for the wrong she had done him the day before as any words might have been. But she found she could not think of that, of what had passed between them, only of the way she felt in his arms, of the fire the warmth of his body close to hers lit in her, of the gentle, heady pleasure of his tongue seeking hers.

"Was it, Honor?" he whispered once more, his lips moving from hers to her neck, then settling, warm and insistent, close to her ear.

The contact filled her with shivering tremors, and she knew that any further attempt at denial was useless.

"No," she cried softly. "I had to see you, I had to know the truth about what happened between us. I had to hear you say it, one way or another."

He pulled away from her and stared at her as she spoke, and realized for the first time how tortured she'd been by the thought that they'd shared nothing more than a lie, as tortured as he'd been at the thought that he must lose her. It seemed impossible to him that it could be so simple, that the wrongs they'd done each other could be so simply cast aside.

She was staring up at him, her eyes still tinged with doubt, with the thought that he had, perhaps, only lied to her once more. Words, he thought, words were useless. He would prove his intent in another way.

He took her in his arms, lifting her even as his lips once more found hers. Then he made his way across the room to the heavy leather couch that faced the hearth. When he'd set her down, he followed her, his lips seeking hers once more, with no thought in his mind now but the single one that he wanted her.

Honor felt his hands and lips and the heat of his body pressed close to hers. She, too, lost all trace of thought, of time or place. It was as though she were floating, adrift on a sea of liquid fire. She reached up to him, pulling him close, filling with the timeless, eternal need.

Somehow, she was not quite sure how, she awoke to find herself undressed, her skirt in a heap on the floor beside the couch, her blouse unbuttoned and disheveled. Raifer, too, was partly undressed, his shirt unbuttoned. She realized she must have performed the task of baring his chest, but she could not quite remember.

She smiled up at him. "This is foolish, isn't it?" she whispered.

He pulled back, perplexed by her words until she began to pull off her blouse. He smiled and followed suit.

She lay back on the couch, and then he was beside her, his hard, muscled flesh pressing against her, his hands, moving knowledgeably along the slope of her waist and the rise of her hip, sending rivulets of fiery desire flowing through her.

Honor wrapped her arms around his neck, pressing her body close to his, wanting to lose herself in him, wanting him to lose himself in her. That was what she needed, she realized, to know that he had given himself to her completely, that he offered himself to her, to become part of her just as she longed to feel herself become part of him. That, and only that, she realized, would mark the bond between them, would erase all the doubts she had harbored about him.

She felt his lips as he buried them against the soft flesh of her neck, felt her own pulse reverberating, then echoing with the throb of his. She spread herself beneath him, eager for him, welcoming the first fiery thrust.

There was nothing else for her, no world outside the circle of his arms, no feeling save for the honeyed, sweet flow that filled her as he loved her. She'd been a fool to try to think she had come to him for anything else but this. From the first moment she'd spoken to him, she'd known somehow that her body needed him, would be complete only with him. Somewhere deep within her was some primal, knowing part of her where, deep seated and buried at birth, was knowledge that was not hers alone, but of her mother and mother's mother and a thousand more before, passed on to her. It was this part of her that had spoken to her and brought her to him. Whatever doubts she had had of him, whatever lies she'd heard from him, they all faded in the one, single, and absolute truth that she loved him.

She felt herself floating on the tide of her passion, free of thought, free of everything except feeling, aware only of the thunderous waves that buoyed and carried her, each washing higher until one swept her up and left her with crashing force where she lay, spent and disoriented, in his arms.

Raifer held her close. He could feel the ragged stir of her breath against his skin as she snuggled against the damp, warm curls on his chest, felt the oddly pleasant sensation when she playfully kissed, then licked his damp flesh. He waited silently for a moment, until the thudding of his heart had begun to subside, then he rolled over onto his back, leaned back into the couch, and pulled her on top of him. He reached up and took a long lock of her loosened hair between his fingers, then held it up to the stream of sunlight that snaked its way through the long window at the far side of the room. The reddish gold strands coiled themselves around his fingers, thick and shimmering lustrously in the shaft of light.

Honor looked down at him thoughtfully, with passion-glazed, adoring eyes. They lay together, silent, simply staring at one another, delighted with the pleasure that comes with spent passion. But after a moment, Honor's eyes roved the room around them.

She pushed herself hurriedly away from him.

"What is it, Honor?" he asked, surprised at her sudden panic.

"What have we done?" she demanded as she stood. "What if someone should come in here and find us this way?"

Raifer grinned. "Then, I suppose I should be Honor bound," he grinned at his small pun, "and we should be thrust without further thought of opportunity to protest, into the dreaded chains of matrimony to thereby salvage our good names."

He was grinning, his expression belying the dark cast of his words, but Honor didn't notice his expression. She heard only the words, the comparison of marriage bonds to chains. She felt herself shiver inside and told herself that it was no matter, that she did not need marriage or permanancy to sanctify her passion, but she knew she was lying to herself.

She turned away from him and began to cast about the heap of clothing that had fallen to the floor, retrieving her own and hastily beginning to don them. Raifer watched her lazily.

"I'd never thought you to act like a frightened mouse, Honor," he said with a wide grin.

She turned and looked sharply at him. "Is that how I'm acting?" she asked as she pulled on her chemise and rifled for her blouse. "Like a frightened mouse?" Or is it more like a fool, she asked herself silently.

Reluctantly, Raifer sat up and leaned over to take up his own shirt. "No one will come in here," he told her. "Since the unpleasantness yesterday, I'm afraid I haven't been acting very nice. I think they'd just as soon avoid me as not. Even the admirable Mr. Creighton."

Honor finished doing up the buttons of her blouse. "But that's past," she told him. "I can help you find the men who tried to assassinate the prince." She peered at him evenly. "That should help you buy your way back into Chief Fitzpatrick's good graces."

Raifer shook his head. "I think not, Honor. We've no proof that the men who were in the warehouse were the ones who took that shot at Edward." He reached for his trousers, stood, and pulled them on. "And I doubt they'll take another try and let us catch them in the act."

She settled her skirt at her waist and then paused before buttoning it, staring at him, at his curious expression, wondering what he thought.

"But why else would they be here?" she asked him. "Why else come all that way?"

He returned her stare. "Why else, indeed?" he asked.

"I can identify them," she persisted. "In return for a promise that my father won't be involved."

Raifer shrugged. "If it's deals you want to make, Honor, I suggest you find someone empowered to make them. Perhaps Chief Fitzpatrick."

Honor stared at him dully. "But you promised,"

she said.

Raifer shook his head. "No, I didn't promise. And if I had, I couldn't have honored such a promise." His eyes narrowed as he peered at her. "Is that what this was all about?" he asked her, his voice grown suddenly cold and distant. "Just a way to sweeten the deal?"

She stepped back from him, sick that he could think her capable of that, feeling as though he'd struck her with the words.

"No!"

He could not doubt the intensity he saw in her eyes, nor question the truth of her response. It was there, mirrored in the shock and disgust on her face. He realized that he was acting like a fool, that he'd hurt her again, and needlessly. It was an odd dance they did, one step coming together, one step apart.

"Listen to me, Honor," he said, his voice soft now, without any trace of accusation. "Ryan, my captain, and Chief Fitzpatrick are in the midst of some kind of war. At first I thought it was just personal, Ryan bitter and vengeful because he was bypassed for a job he felt he deserved, some kind of a political tiff between the two of them. But now I'm not so sure. Something's going on, something far more important than some petty infighting between a couple of public servants. And this thing with McGowan and your father was right in the middle of it."

Honor stared at him, suddenly wide eyed. "Papa said something like that," she said finally, her voice low, barely more than a whisper. "That there were important people involved, people who wouldn't like having anything get in their way."

Raifer listened to her words intently. "What else did he say?" he demanded.

She shook her head slowly. "Nothing, just that about important people being involved."

"He knows more than that, Honor," he said sharply.

"No!" She fairly shouted at him. "He had nothing to do with it. He couldn't. He hates guns. His brother was killed in a hunting accident. He couldn't be a part of any of this."

For the first time, Raifer realized, he actually believed that she was totally ignorant of what McGowan and her father had been doing, that she really did believe Daniel was completely innocent. In many ways it was a relief to him, to be absolutely convinced that she was herself without involvement or guilt. At least Daniel had done that for her, he mused.

He made no effort to refute her then, knowing it would only lead to an argument. Instead, he sat back down on the couch, but leaned toward her.

"What do you suppose those men were brought here to do, Honor?" he asked her slowly.

She cocked her head in thought. "Not to collect those crates of rifles," she said finally. "There would be no need for that. The *Mary Louise* makes regular trips to Liverpool, and usually stops at Dublin. There would be no need to have those men illegally enter the country simply to bring the arms back to Dublin."

Raifer smiled and leaned back into the couch. "My thoughts precisely. So why would those men have bothered to come here?"

Honor shrugged. "To kill the prince," she replied quickly.

But Raifer shook his head. "No, that's not logical, Honor. Think. If you were planning to have a man assassinated, how would you go about it?"

She scowled in distaste. "I wouldn't."

"This isn't just a game, Honor," Raifer told her sharply. "How many men did you see at McGowan's house?"

"Four," she answered promptly.

"And if you were sending a sniper to assassinate someone, would you send four men to do it? Think," he prodded, "or try to think the way a terrorist would think."

Honor sat mutely and did as he had bid her. "No," she said finally. "I'd send one man, a well-trained marksman, but only one."

Raifer smiled at her and nodded. "And how do you come to that decision?" he demanded.

She was bewildered by his continued questions, but Honor obliged him and answered. "It seems only obvious that each man added to such a mission increases the risk of discovery, a chance word said to the wrong person, the opportunity of one man of the group being seen by the police or the like. So it seems obvious you'd send only as many men as it would take to do what you wanted done." She scowled once more, her distaste quite evident. "And it takes, after all, only one man to pull a trigger."

Raifer grinned at her with pleased admiration. "Exactly," he told her. "Now, if we can reach such a conclusion, it would be foolish to assume the terrorists could not do the same. If their aim was to kill the prince, they'd have sent one man, and one only, and he wouldn't have missed that shot last night. I think we can safely assume that if the intent had been to kill Edward, the headlines this morning would not have told us of his lucky escape, but rather his untimely and unpleasant demise."

Honor was more bewildered now than ever. "But I

don't understand," she said. "If their intent wasn't to kill the prince, then why the attempt last night?"

Raifer shrugged. "There are two possibilities," he replied. "One, that it was a completely isolated incident, having nothing to do with the terrorists, someone with his own grudge against the Crown, or even Edward, a disgruntled husband he's cuckolded or the like." He grinned at her quickly, then went on. "And the second is that it was our friends from the warehouse, and that they intended the attempt to fail. As easy as it would be to accept the first, it seems too unlikely, and besides, it doesn't explain the presence of those four men. They went to too great a bother to get here for there not to be a reason, and a strong one, for their being here. The only thing that makes any sense is that they used the attempt as a tactic, a diversion for whatever it is they really intend."

"Which is?" Honor demanded.

Raifer only shrugged. "There I'm at a loss. I've been trying to ponder that very question ever since I read the newspapers this morning, and could force myself to think of anything but you." He smiled at her seraphically. "That is, until you arrived and provided me with an extremely pleasant diversion yourself."

Honor looked away from him and down at her still bare feet. That's all I am to him, she mused, a diversion. The realization was wrenchingly painful.

"If whatever it is they plan succeeds, and something happens, something horrible, and it comes back to Papa being involved . . ." Her words trailed off, her throat catching.

"Then it seems it is in our mutual interest to try to stop them," Raifer told her evenly. "I, for my job, and you for your father's good name."

Mutual interest, Honor thought. That's all he cares about, getting his damned job back. And when the voice inside her asked her what else she had expected, she had no answer, only the knowledge that she would have wanted something more.

Slowly, she let her eyes drift back to meet his. "Yes," she agreed, forcing herself to keep her voice steady, "it would be in our mutual interest."

Raifer stared at her for a moment in silence, not quite understanding the distance he saw in her eyes, the coolness he heard in her tone. He stood, then, and pointed to her unshod feet.

"Why don't you find your shoes and apply them to the proper appendages," he suggested. "I don't know about you, but I'm hungry. If you let me buy you lunch at Madame Claudine's, perhaps we can spend the time trying to make some sense out of his senselessness."

As she reached for her shoes, Honor became aware of a growing feeling of leadenness inside her. He was offering her the opportunity to help her father, but it seemed more than apparent to her that that was all. Whatever hopes she might have secretly harbored for salvaging the feelings she had for him crumbled away into nothingness. She'd gotten what she had told herself she had come to him to find.

Somehow it seemed an all-too-hollow victory.

Chapter Ten

Brian Flannagan moved toward the other man who stood across from him in the tiny, cramped room. Thomas Moynihan was a decidedly large young man, and every inch of him, Flannagan knew, was muscle. But the younger man's rosy complexion and wide-eyed, persistent smile always seemed to generate trust in the people who came in contact with him, overshadowing whatever hint of fear his size might otherwise evoke. And that, Flannagan knew, was precisely why Moynihan was with him at that moment, precisely why he was the right person for the job they were about to do.

Moynihan's bulk somehow seemed to fill the steward's room on the sixth floor of the Saint Pierre Hotel, towering over the shelves laden with stacks of fresh white towels, sheets, and nappery. The little man who lay cramped in the corner, trussed and gagged and quite evidently frightened nearly witless, seemed more like a gnome than ever when compared to the man who was about to take his place.

"There," Flannagan said as he adjusted Moynihan's bow tie and then, with the fussy sort of motion a grandmother would use, picked a small bit of lint off the sleeve of the younger man's black jacket. "Don't we look the part, young Thomas?" he said with a pleased grin.

Moynihan ventured a concerned look toward the old man who lay staring up at them from the corner.

"You needn't worry about him," Flannagan quickly assured him before he could ask the question he seemed so obviously on the point of asking. "As long as he's quiet and cooperative, we've no quarrel with him." Flannagan turned toward the corner and looked down. "And I'm sure he'll be quiet and cooperative." He had lowered his voice until it became sharply vicious, a clear threat. "Quiet and cooperative."

The old man nodded his near-bald head furiously in agreement, his only means of conveying his good intentions, ignoring the fact that the motion caused him twice to knock his head against the wall behind him. Flannagan smiled, apparently satisfied with the old man's efforts.

"You see," he told Moynihan, "we have no need to worry about our friend here with us in service." He grinned, then, at his words. "We're all of us in service today, to our most noble prince."

Moynihan apparently had no thought for levity, for he eyed the table that occupied what little space remained in the room that he did not require. It had been set with a long, draping white linen cloth and was covered with dishes and crystal and a good number of silver serving pieces, all neatly covered with silver domes. A large ice bucket sat to the side, waiting for its burden of champagne.

"Do you think it will actually work, Brian?" he asked nervously.

Flannagan narrowed his eyes and stared at him. Moynihan was nervous, and doubtless frightened, as frightened as the old man they'd tied up and dumped in the corner. He wanted to be reassured.

For a second Flannagan considered giving him what he wanted, then decided that a bit of fear could only spur him in his efforts. He grinned a bit maliciously.

"It will either work, Thomas my boy, or we will all end up, I've not one doubt, on the gallows. I think Her Highness will not have much pity on us when we've tried to kill her favorite boy."

Moynihan paled visibly. "There was never any intention to kill him, Brian," he managed to protest. "It was just to get the police watchin' outside, not thinkin' about what's goin' on in here."

Flannagan grinned once more, and there was a bit of real amusement in his expression this time. "I don't think Victoria will be in the mood to listen much to reason, Thomas. So unless we both want to end up with uncomfortably long necks, I suggest we stick precisely to the plan. If I didn't think it would work, I wouldn't be here with you, now, would I?"

Moynihan swallowed, then turned to look at a large button on the call board, the one marked for suite A. The largest suite in the hotel, Flannagan had said, with a grand view of the pack. Only the best for Eddy, Flannagan had said. Although he knew it would be at least an hour still, Moynihan stared at the disk marked with the large letter A. He wished it were time, wished the waiting was over. He swallowed again, suddenly conscious of the feel of his throat, the awareness of a stiff thickening at the back of his tongue. The gallows, that's what Flannagan had said. He closed his eyes and silently began to pray: "Hail Mary, full of grace . . ."

Edward, Duke of Cornwall, Prince of Wales, and

heir to the throne of England, sat up in bed, leaned contentedly back against the padded headboard, and stared past his own naked body to the one that lay beside him.

He lifted his hand and, with a well-formed habit of which he'd long since lost all notice, touched the edge of his neatly trimmed moustache with the back of his left index finger. Then he smiled.

"I can't tell you how much this means to me, Diana, seeing you again."

The woman at his side lifted her face from the pillow and stared up at him. She smiled at him for a second, and then the pleasure seeped out of her large, dark eyes.

"You mean this one last time, Eddy, before you go home to Mama and the duly sanctified connubial bliss of the Princess Alexandra's frigid arms?" she asked, her tone suddenly grown spiteful, mean.

He drew back. "I never lied to you, Diana," he said. "You knew from the start. It's not as though she means anything to me."

She lowered her head once more, putting her cheek to the white linen cover of the pillow. "I know," she whispered. "Future kings marry princesses, not actresses." There was a note of self-pity in her words now.

"It's not as though we can never see each other again," he told her. "We can arrange things. Like this afternoon." He leaned forward and kissed her bare shoulder. "You mean everything to me, Diana. Everything."

She lifted her head once more, this time with a shake to the mass of her dark curls.

"I wish I could believe that, Eddy," she told him.

He leaned back and took a small, narrow box from the bedside table. "Would this, perhaps, persuade you?" he asked as he opened it and held it out to her.

Her eyes found the string of diamonds quickly, and whatever bit of peevishness that had lingered in her eyes quickly disappeared.

"Oh, Eddy," she gasped as she sat up and threw her arms around his neck, then thanked him with an enthusiastic kiss.

He chuckled tolerantly when she released him. "Here," he said, and removed the necklace from the box. He pushed aside the hair that shrouded her neck.

Obediently, she twisted around and moved her arm so that she held the curls away from her neck. She touched the stones lovingly as he fixed the necklace at her throat.

"Now, let me see you," he said when he'd settled the string of diamonds securely. He put his hands to her bare shoulders and turned her back to face him. The long tear-shaped pendant nestled between her naked breasts. "Lovely," he whispered as he leaned to her and kissed first one rosy nipple, then the other.

She leaned her head back. "I wish it could always be like this, Eddy," she told him.

He looked up at her and smiled. "It can, my sweet. I promise you, it can."

She looked down at the shiny tear, realized that the stone was a bit cold against her skin. "I know it's foolish," she said softly, "but a woman somehow can't help but hope that she'll be able to spend her life with the man she loves." She waited until her eyes met and held his. "Not like this. Not sneaking about, hoping not to be seen."

"But I sent them all away, just as I promised. There should have been no one, no guards, no police, to see you enter."

She smiled at his pained expression. "And there was no one, just as you said, love. It's just that I worry, for both of us." Not that it really mattered, she thought. No one would have been able to recognize her even if she had been seen, not with the heavy dark cape and wide-brimmed, thickly veiled hat she'd worn. But then, this would hardly be an afternoon to wish to be recognized, at least not just yet. Her eyes strayed to the desk, where Eddy's valet had set out half a dozen photos in silver frames, among them one of a pale young woman with a longish snub nose and small dark eyes. Then she swung her gaze back to his. "But I won't think about any of that any more. We have so little time. Let's not waste it with harsh words or unpleasant thoughts." She put her hand to the necklace, fingering it gently. "Have them send up some champagne, Eddy," she suggested. "And I'll thank you for this small token." She smiled at him, her eyes and lips silently saying more than her words could.

The suggestion seemed to please him. "As you like," he said as he rose from the bed. He reached down to the foot and found a silk robe and pulled it on quickly. "I won't be a moment," he told her, leaning down to her and kissing her cheek before turning and walking to the bedroom door.

She watched him leave the room. When he'd gone she climbed out of the bed and strode to the desk. She reached for the picture that had caught her eye before and stared at the pale face that smiled out at her.

"So this is who'll warm your bed in the future, Eddy," she whispered. "Do you really think she'll please you as well as I do?"

There was noise in the next room, and she crept silently to the door in time to see a tall, heavily built young man set down a tray bearing an ice bucket and glasses, then lift the bottle from the bucket, quickly pull off the foil and wire cage, and release the cork with a loud pop.

"That will be all," she heard her lover say. "I'll pour."

The young man nodded and started for the door. Diana stood and watched Edward lift the bottle and fill two glasses. Then, as he started back to the bedroom, she ran quickly to the bed and resettled herself there just as he pulled the door open wide.

"Champagne for my lady," he told her brightly.

She smiled up at him with expectant pleasure.

Diana hadn't thought it would act so quickly. Upon a bit of consideration of the matter, she realized that she hadn't thought about it very much at all, not this part of it at least.

She carefully took the glass from Edward's now unsteady hand and put it on the bedside table. Then she placed her own untouched wine beside his.

When she turned back to him, he was slumped forward, his eyes closed, the pale white flesh at the side of his neck contrasting with the dark silk of his robe where it had pulled back. She decided quite suddenly that she really hated the whiteness of his skin. It seemed weak to her, weak and selfish. At that moment she was glad, glad that he wouldn't simply be able to return to England and marry his precious Alexandra, glad that she'd managed to help start something that should serve to unsettle his complacent, ordered life a bit, glad that the next time he saw her name on a theater marquee, perhaps he wouldn't think of her simply as his whore.

She climbed gingerly out of the bed, pulling the sheet around her, moved quickly to the next room, and pulled the rope for the steward, just as she had been told to do. It seemed only seconds before there was a knock at the door. She opened it slowly, realizing that her hand shook as she grasped the knob. Until that moment, it had not occurred to her just how dangerous the thing she'd done could be. She realized then that she was afraid.

But then Flannagan and the other one, the big, young one, were in the room with her, and there was no time for her fear. She could feel the younger one's eyes on her body, her bare shoulders and her leg where the sheet did not cover her. She flashed a quick smile in his direction, ever willing to perform for an appreciative audience.

"It all went well, luv?" Flannagan asked as he moved the rolling table from the corridor and into the center of the room.

She nodded. "He drank it and just seemed to nod off," she replied.

"And a good night's sleep to him," Flannagan said, moving across the room to the door to the bedroom. He pushed the door open and stared in at the slumped figure on the bed.

"Poor old Eddy. He's about to see what the real world is really like." Flannagan grinned. "And he isn't even able to keep his eyes open and watch it all begin for him."

With that he motioned to Moynihan and the young man followed him into the bedroom. They emerged a few moments later, carrying the unconscious body between them. Diana had cleared the table of the dishes and glassware for them, and drawned up the long cloth that covered the sides. With the masking linen pulled away, it was immediately apparent that the base of the table had been fitted with a large, empty box.

"Will he fit?" she asked, staring at the empty space as Flannagan drew back a hinged door.

He smiled up at her pleasantly. "Like a wee babe in his mother's arms," he told her as he motioned to Moynihan to lower Edward to the floor beside the table. The two men proceeded to fold the limp body, bending knees and tying hands to them, then placed a gag to Edward's slack mouth.

"Is all that necessary?" For the first time there seemed to be a touch of concern in Diana's words. She realized that although she could tell herself she hated him, she had shared far too many beds like the one in the next room with him, received too many gifts like the necklace that hung around her neck, for her to be completely indifferent to his fate. "He won't be hurt?"

"No need to take any chances," Flannagan told her brusquely. "How much time do we have?"

She glanced at the mantel clock. "His valet should be here at one to dress him for his luncheon with the president," she replied. "Forty-five minutes."

Flannagan nodded. "Just time enough," he said. He turned to Moynihan. "All right, Thomas, my boy."

The two men then proceeded, with evident effort, to lift the limp, still body and pack it into the crate below the table. Diana winced as they casually knocked Edward's head against the tabletop, then pushed it down into a cramped position before forcing him into the box. Despite her discomforture at their cavalier treatment of him, however, she made no move to object.

Flannagan closed the box, securing it with a small lock he took from his pocket, and then finally dropped down the linen cloth to cover the sides of the table. He straightened up.

"Right, then," he said, turning to Diana. "Remember, drink your wine and get into bed. And whatever questions you're asked, you simply don't know any answers. You and Eddy were having a pleasant little reunion, had a bit of wine, and then it all went black."

She nodded. "You're sure it's safe?" she asked. "The drug, I mean."

"A couple of hours sleep, and then a wee headache, luv," Flannagan assured her. "That, and the sure knowledge that you've helped a fine cause."

She pursed her lips primly. "I don't give a damn for your cause," she told him. "I just wish I could be there when the sweet princess learns about the circumstances of his disappearance."

Flannagan grinned. "With a lovely, naked actress in his bed?" he asked. "Won't that be pleasing to her, don't you think? Not to mention Mother?"

The two men pushed the table toward the door. Just before he opened it, Flannagan turned back to Diana.

"Remember, luv, the two of you drank the wine, and that's all you remember."

Diana nodded, then moved close to him and wrapped her arms around his neck. "We drank the wine and that's all I remember," she repeated before she kissed him.

Flannagan let his hand stray down the length of her hip as he casually returnd the embrace, then pushed her away. She stood aside as the two men wheeled the table out the door and into the long, carpeted corridor. Then she closed the door behind them and returned to the bedroom.

She settled herself on the bed and took her glass of wine. The sheets, she found, were still warm from where Edward had lain on them. She lifted the glass in salute towards the picture on the desk, then brought it to her lips.

"To you, my dear princess," she said pleasantly, then she drained the contents of her glass.

"Wait here."

Moynihan looked at Flannagan as if he weren't quite sure but that he'd turned a bit mad.

"Here?" he asked hoarsely. "Now?" He looked down at the linen-covered table, sure the prince would wake at any moment and somehow get free.

Flannagan grinned at him, his expression more than a bit superior. "Just keep your head about you, Thomas, my boy," he said softly. "I won't be but a moment."

Flannagan opened the door of the porter's room and slipped in quickly. His eyes found the old man, just as they had left him, tied and gagged in the corner. The look of terror returned to the old porter's eyes as he watched Flannagan approach.

" 'Tis indeed a shame," Flannagan said as he sidled along a tall row of shelves laden with bedding. "Had I any choice in the matter, believe me, I'd just as soon matters could be settled otherwise. But as it is, you're a loose end, old man, and I can't afford to leave any loose ends."

The old man seemed to realize what Flannagan's words meant, for he struggled a moment, uselessly, trying to get to his feet, to somehow get away. But he'd barely moved when Flannagan returned to him, a thick feather pillow in one hand, a pistol in the other.

"Like I said, I can't afford any loose ends left behind." He aimed the pistol and then held the pillow firmly in front of the barrel before he pulled the trigger.

There was very little noise, the shot being muffled by the wadding of the pillow, and that followed by the old man's jerky movement as the bullet hit him. That, too, ended quickly, and he lay suddenly still.

"What was that for?"

Moynihan's voice was choked with shock and revulsion. His tall, muscled body seemed to be shaking.

"You were to stay with our package," Flannagan snapped at him sharply.

But neither his tone nor his words seemed to make any real impression on the younger man. Moynihan stood, pale and still shaking, staring at the old man and the dark red rivulet of blood.

"It had to be done, Thomas," Flannagan said firmly, his tone cool now, controlled. "He could have told them, could have described us. We can't afford to leave any loose ends." His explanations completed, Flannagan's face hardened once more. "Now we've a job to finish. I suggest we get on with it."

Flannagan put his hand to the younger man's shoulder, urging him back into the carpeted silence of the empty corridor. The table was there, still and untouched, exactly as it had been left.

"Shall we get on with it, Thomas?" Flannagan asked as he saw Moynihan seem to hesitate, the look of shocked revulsion still lingering in his expression. "Or have you forgotten so easily how your father and brother died? Have you forgotten why it is we came here in the first place?"

He'd struck the proper chord, as he knew he would. Moynihan's expression settled. He put his hands to the table's edge and began to push it along the corridor. Flannagan nodded to him, rewarding him with a small smile, then hurried along to be sure the way was clear.

Raifer pulled a bit of bread from the piece in the basket on the table between him and Honor and dropped it into the garlic-and-herb-flecked butter that remained beneath the half dozen empty snail shells on his plate.

"What I can't understand," he said as he put his fork to the bit of crust and used it as a sop to the butter, "is why they'd even want to give the appearance of condoning an attack on Edward. They've been vocal enough voicing disapproval of the system, certainly, even sniping at passing troops when the opportunity arose and considered it fair sport. But the royal family has always appeared to have the aura of being sacrosanct until now. They may hate Victoria and hers, but they're still royalty and thus inviolate. Why the sudden change of attitude?" He brought his fork to his mouth, and chewed the bit of bread meditatively

Honor swallowed a sip of wine. She stared down at her own plate of country paté, virtually untouched, realizing she had no appetite. She could only wonder at his coolness. After all, her own thoughts and emotions were far too roiled for her to eat. She settled herself forcefully and brought her eyes back to meet his.

"What good could they get from his death?" she asked.

Raifer pursed his lips. "That's just it. None, at

least not that I can think of," he replied. "Now, if they were holding him and could use a threat of ending his life as a means of forcing concessions, that would be different . . ." His voice trailed off, then he suddenly glanced sharply at Honor. "What do you remember about that empty box that was left in the warehouse cellar?" he asked her abruptly.

Honor wrinkled her brow, not following his train of thought. "Nothing," she replied. "Just that it was large."

"That's just it," he told her. "It was large. Too large for guns or anything else your father's firm imports. A crate of rifles that large would be too heavy to lift." He grinned at her with sharp awareness. "But it wouldn't be too heavy if it were to contain something else," he said slowly, "Something like a body."

Honor put her glass down on the table. "You can't be serious," she said.

"I'm damned serious, Honor," he insisted. "Just think. If they were to kidnap him, if they were holding him, they might be able to force Gladstone to do something more than talk about reforms. There's already a movement in Parliament. With Victoria's coerced support, this could be the deciding factor."

She shook her head. "Then why the sniper attack?" she asked. "It's not logical."

Raifer shook his head. "But it is. An attack would have the police looking elsewhere, for something different. If they're protecting him from a sniper, they'll be looking outward, for an attack. They won't be expecting the prince to be snatched from right beneath their noses."

Honor looked unconvinced. "All right, just for the sake of argument," she said, "say they do manage to kidnap Edward. You don't mean to tell me that they intend to put him into that crate and ship him out of the country like a box of barrel staves?"

He stared at her intently. "That's exactly what I do think they intend to do, Honor. Unless we stop them."

He put down his fork and raised his hand to summon the waiter and call for the check.

Jean, Madame Claudine's youngest son, scurried over immediately.

"Oui, monsieur? Il y a quelquechose de mal?" Jean looked with concern toward Honor.

Before she could respond, however, Raifer replied. "Non, non, c'est tout excellent. Mais il faut que nous quittons. Il y a un rendez-vous que j'ai oublié." He drew some bills from his pocket and put them on the table. "Dites à Madame Claudine que nos allons retourner aussitôt que possible."

This explanation seemed to mollify the young Frenchman, for Jean backed away, not quite convinced, it seemed, but with his conscience clear that he had done nothing to offend his mother's favorite customer and teacher. Meanwhile, Honor eyed Raifer contemplatively as she dropped her napkin to the table and slowly stood.

"I'd no idea you spoke French," she murmured thoughtfully as he took her arm.

What other secrets did he have, she wondered. What other lies had he told her? Wasn't there anything she thought of him that she could trust? Anything, that was, except for the fact that he was determined to get his job back however he could.

"I suppose I'm not quite the unschooled country bumpkin I usually impress people as being," he told her offhandedly. He seemed unaware of her doubtful glance as he helped her into her coat and hurried her out into the street.

They started out quickly toward the avenue, skirting the heap of goods that seemed to tumble out onto the sidewalk from the row of shops that lined the street. Honor found she had to run to keep step with him. Once on the avenue, however, Raifer hailed a passing hansom. He handed her into the carriage and then settled himself beside her after telling the driver to take them to the Saint Pierre Hotel.

"Why are we going there?" Honor demanded once he was seated beside her.

"To warn Captain Ryan," he told her. "That is, if Chief Fitzpatrick doesn't have him clearing out his desk already. And if anyone will believe me."

His lips settled into a firm, thin line, and Honor could see the tense, determined look that had hardened his features. For a second she thought him a complete stranger to her, one to whom she'd never so much as spoken a single word. He seemed so distantly apart from her, so hard and certain. Even as she stared at him, she felt herself growing weaker, less sure that the bargain she had struck with him would in any way help her father. What if he was just using her, just as he had used her before, she mused. What if she was once more nothing more than a means for him to get information he wanted? How could she allow herself to be such a fool as to play his game and by his rules?

The doubts that nagged at her were all the more disconcerting as she realized she really had no choice in the matter, no choice at all.

"I tell you, we were here, together. We drank the champagne. And then I woke with the valet shaking me, and he was gone, and there were all those people milling around."

Diana Wells put a pale, tentative hand to the collar of the robe she'd wrapped about herself, pulling it just a bit tighter to cover the creamy white, rounded mounds that spoke of amply enticing breasts. She seemed not to notice, however, when the robe fell back, leaving her endowments as vulnerably unprotected from the eyes of the policemen who milled in the room, if not moreso, than they had been before her efforts at a display of maidenly modesty.

Chief of Police William Fitzpatrick, who was sitting on the couch at her side, made a gallant effort to calm her obviously distraught nerves. He reached for her hand, which lay trembling slightly now in her lap like a small wounded bird, grasped it, and patted it reassuringly.

"Of course, Miss Wells, there's no need for you to trouble yourself any further . . ."

"To trouble myself?" she burst out. "How can I be anything but troubled? My beloved Edward! What could have happened to him?" She disengaged her hand from the police chief's and brought it to her temple. "And what will the queen think of him when she learns of my presence here with him? She never approved of me. That was why I came here, to end the trouble my love for him to meant to him." She looked up then, her eyes pleading as they found Fitzpatrick's. "Only love is not so easy a thing to end. It does not listen to reason. It knows only its own sort of logic. That was why he came to New York. That is why I came to see him today. For at least one last good-bye. And now, to have it end like this . . ." Her words faded into a tearful choking sound, and she buried her face in her hands. "I know what you think of me, and I don't blame you. But how could I do otherwise? I love him."

Having obviously completed her speech, or perhaps overcome with emotion, feigned or otherwise, she slumped back into the cushions of the couch. Fitzpatrick sat beside her, his expression speaking as much of lechery as it did of gentlemanly concern.

"I can assure you, Miss Wells," he told her, "no one could possibly think anything but the noblest thoughts of you, a woman of your beauty and talent, one who's brought so much pleasure to us all. Your portrayal of Juliet was superb. I doubt there was a person who saw it, man or woman, who left the theater dry-eyed."

Diana immediately brightened. "You saw my Juliet?" she asked. "I thought, when I agreed to take the role, that I had grown a bit too old to play her. After all, Juliet was but a child. But the director, Mr. Crystaldi, said that emotion was more important to the part than the matter of a year or two."

She was smiling now, and staring into Fitzpatrick's eyes with the kind of singular directness that spoke of a great many things, mostly far too intimate to be uttered aloud in the presence of so many others. Once more Fitzpatrick reached for her hand. She allowed him to take it between his own, this time making no effort to withdraw it.

"Of course," he assured her, "emotion is all in a role such as Juliet."

"And should the necessity arise to cast the role once again, I'm sure Miss Wells will find herself amply qualified. But at the moment, there is the small matter of the prince's disappearance."

Michael Ryan's gruff tone seemed to settle over the pair on the couch like a shower of ice water.

Diana removed her hand from Fitzpatrick's grasp and pointedly pulled the robe firmly and tightly closed, eliminating any further possibility of any of the officers in the room availing themselves of the task of contemplating her more evident charms. Fitzpatrick stood abruptly, the glance he offered Ryan as he did so clearly expressing the wish on the part of the police chief that he'd taken the effort to fire his subordinate before matters had come to that point.

Ryan's only response was a grin, one of obvious pleasure.

"It seems we've come too late, Honor."

Raifer entered the room first, with Honor trailing a bit behind him, her mind still absorbed in the snatches of the conversation she'd heard as she'd hurried along the long carpeted corridor from the lift to the prince's suite. It had seemed odd to her that they'd been challenged only once, by a policeman who had never met Raifer, and he'd seemed content with a quick glance at Raifer's badge and hastily uttered assertion that he was a detective. Until the moment they entered the suite and faced Fitzpatrick's withering glance, their presence had gone, if not unnoticed by the number of police who thronged the hall, at least ignored.

But Fitzpatrick, it was only too apparent, was about to change that circumstance. The police chief stood glowering at Raifer.

"What the hell do you think you're doing here, Farrell?" he demanded in a tone that required absolutely no interpretation. "Need I remind you, you are under suspension pending investigation of that fiasco yesterday. And would it be too much to ask why you've brought that woman with you?"

Raifer was quite clearly unmoved. "Perhaps you've

forgotten Honor Wainwright?" he asked. "I believe you met her during that untimely advance into the basement of her father's warehouse?"

Fitzpatrick seemed a bit ruffled as he darted a glance toward Honor, then he smiled. "Of course, Miss Wainwright. Under these circumstances, you are the last person I'd expect to see here." He smiled at her once more, then turned and offered one more smile to Diana in seeming compensation for the defection to another camp. The niceties apparently completed, he turned his attention back to Raifer. "But that does not explain your presence, Farrell. Or that of Miss Wainwright, for that matter."

Raifer directed his attention past Fitzpatrick to Ryan. "Miss Wainwright was struck with the idea that possibly the malcreants who'd squatted in her father's property might be there with the intent of carrying out a plan to kidnap the prince. It seems her thought was valid, if a bit tardy."

Honor noticed that he'd referred to the men in the warehouse as squatters, not as guests, and she found herself oddly elated that he'd made that effort to distance her father from them. Perhaps, she thought, he really meant to keep his word to her after all. But before she had much chance to contemplate that, Fitzpatrick's sharp words caught her attention.

"It is a shame, then, that Miss Wainwright's prescience comes too late. As you can see, the prince has already been removed from the environs. And your presence here is not only unnecessary, it is entirely unauthorized."

Raifer caught Ryan's eye for a moment, the two men exchanging some wordless communication. Then he turned his glance back to Fitzpatrick.

"As you've made only too obvious," he murmured. Then he shrugged, turned and took Honor's arm.

"But we can't leave," she objected.

He cut her off before she could say anything more. "Our presence, as Chief Fitzpatrick has pointed out, is not needed here, Honor," he said firmly.

Cowed by his tone, Honor let him marshal her back toward the door. She managed to turn, to catch a quick last glance at Diana Wells, who had risen to stand beside Fitzpatrick. Then Raifer's hand at her back urged her forward.

"Raifer," she began, hoping he'd at least give her the opportunity to voice her objections.

He didn't. "Not here, Honor," he hissed at her under his breath. "Not now."

Honor felt herself bridle at his manner, at the way he virtually pushed her along the corridor toward the door to the lift. She could not for the life of her understand why she allowed him to bully her, to order her about. That first afternoon she'd met him, however clumsy she'd been, still she'd felt herself to be in control of herself, sure with him. As long as she'd thought him to be penniless, somehow there had been the feeling of assurance about her, the sureness that she could, in the end, control the way she felt about him, the way she could allow herself to tell herself she was in love with him, aware, in the end, that she, and no one else, dictated to herself. Suddenly that sureness was gone.

She'd lost whatever control she'd felt, and his power over her seemed to have grown with the awareness that he was far more complicated than the small-town, ambitious young man she'd thought him to be. So she hurried along at his side, allowing him to marshal her into the lift, making no effort at protest, not even daring, at that moment, to question his authority.

Once in the open, busy lobby of the hotel, however, she managed to grasp a bit of her lost self-assuredness. She pulled herself away from the hold he had of her arm and turned and faced him.

"Why didn't you tell them about that large crate, the one in the cellar?" she demanded. "Why didn't you tell them what you think they'll do with the prince?"

He gave her an exasperated glance, then took her arm once more. Before he tried to force her forward once more, however, he seemed to relent a bit.

"All right, Honor. Why don't we find a quiet corner and talk about this?"

Honor felt herself stamping her foot. "There's no time to sit and talk," she told him.

"I'm afraid there's no time for much of anything else," he told her.

His grasp on her arm tightened, and Honor felt herself giving in to his certainty, his sureness, once more. She allowed him to lead her off to a pair of thickly upholstered chairs in the corner of the lobby facing the exit from the lift. She sat obediently, and stared at him, waiting.

"Look, Honor. Didn't you find anything strange about the conversation we overheard up there?" he demanded. "And didn't you think it odd that no one seriously challenged our presence until Fitzpatrick did?"

She shook her head. "I suppose I assumed they all knew you were a policeman," she told him. "And that was why they let us pass."

Raifer shook his head. "Security was lax, suspiciously lax, that's only too obvious. And it was most likely just as insufficient this morning. If I had been in charge of Edward's security, I certainly wouldn't have allowed his little tryst with an actress to occur, at least not without making sure no one and nothing entered that suite while they were alone there together. As much as I dislike him, I can't believe Fitzpatrick so great a fool as to order matters handled any differently than I'd have them."

Honor shook her head as though she were trying to clear away a feeling of fuzziness that had managed to creep into it. "But you're saying that you think Miss Wells was a part of it," she said. "And Chief Fitzpatrick, as well."

"Whether Diana Wells was part of it or simply used doesn't really concern me. I, for one, didn't believe that sobbed little speech she gave about love. Not when I saw her eyeing the good police chief when she is supposedly distraught with grief over Edward's disappearance."

"She sounded so torn," Honor murmured.

"For God's sake, Honor. The woman is an actress. She earns her livelihood making people believe feelings that are feigned." He thought it politic at that moment to refrain from adding, "in bed or out of it." "As for Fitzpatrick, I'm in no position to make any accusations. All I'm saying is that he made a mistake, one that seems to have had rather dire consequences."

Honor lowered her gaze, feeling herself rather self-consciously chastened. "All right," she whispered. "What do we do now?"

He grinned at her gamely. "We wait. For not long, I think, but we wait."

Raifer's estimate that they would not have long to wait proved entirely accurate. Honor had only three or four minutes to sit and fume silently at his superior manner when the lift door opened and

Captain Michael Ryan stepped out into the lobby. He stood for a moment, scanning the large room. Then he located Raifer and crossed quickly to him.

Ryan eyed Honor with a look of mild irritation as he pulled up a chair close to Raifer's. "Perhaps Miss Wainwright might excuse us while we have a little chat, Raifer?" he suggested, his tone mild, but his displeasure with her presence obvious.

"Miss Wainwright has decided to cooperate," Raifer told him, "and as she has a vested interest in this matter, I think it only fair that she be included, Captain."

Ryan seemed unconvinced, but he shrugged, apparently willing to allow Raifer the privilege of making the choice. He leaned back in his chair and allowed himself a smile. "Well, now, Farrell," he said amiably, "was that look you threw me upstairs to tell me you had an empty place on your dance card, or was I to infer that you have something to tell me? Although, from your patient presence here and Miss Wainwright's presence as well, I assume it's the latter, not the former." He leaned forward and put his elbows to his knees. "And would it be too inquisitive of me to ask you where you acquired the knowledge that the prince was to disappear?"

Raifer considered him judgmentally. "Perhaps you'll be kind enough to tell me first just what is going on up there?"

Ryan shook his head. "Damned if I know." He looked up hastily at Honor, nodded to indicate his regret for using profanity in her presence, then returned his attention to Raifer. "Fitzpatrick took personal charge of the prince's safety, apparently as a display of his disfavor with my work and that of my men of late." His eyes grew steely as they found Raifer's, assuring himself that the reference had not been lost, then he continued. "Fat lot of good that did. Nothing but rookies up there, and no one to so much as tell them what they ought to be doing. From the looks of things, I'd almost say our chief of police was on the side of the kidnappers." His own words seemed to surprise him, because he stopped suddenly and turned to offer Honor an appraising glance. Then he turned back to Raifer. "I hope you know what you're about, Raifer, my boy. Or else I should think I've just been talking a bit too much for my own health and doing it in front of a member of the enemy camp."

Honor bristled. "I am not the enemy," she hissed angrily. "I came to help."

Raifer turned to her. "I don't think we have any time for this sort of thing," he said firmly. He turned back to Ryan. "Miss Wainwright has offered her help, and she has convinced me she is sincere."

"And her father?" Ryan asked pointedly.

"Has nothing to do with any of this," Honor retorted. Her cheeks colored, and she found she was grasping the arms of her chair with needless intensity. Had they been anyplace less exposed, she realized she would have shouted her response to Ryan, would have done anything she could to make him believe her.

"Something I am inclined to believe as well," Raifer added.

"I hope you've good judgment, Farrell," Ryan said, and his face settled into a grim expression. "Because if the kidnapping weren't enough, whoever did it did not stop there. One of those nincompoops up there just found the body of the floor porter, shot dead. These men who took Edward, whoever they are, are not playing any games."

Honor's face paled. "Dead?" She felt a stab of

numbing, sickening shock. Oh, Papa, she thought desperately. What sort of people have you allowed yourself to become involved with?

Raifer, too, now looked grim. "You don't really think Fitzgerald could have had anything to do with anything so crass as murder, do you?"

Ryan shrugged. "I'm sure he'd rather keep his hands clean. But the best-laid plans and all . . . it could have been a spur-of-the-moment act. After all, Fitzpatrick wouldn't have been there when it was done. All I know is, he's sitting up there in the prince's suite with his arms around the beauteous Miss Wells, offering whatever comfort he can to the poor, frightened lady, while his men are chasing around like a troupe of clowns. That circus up there, it makes too good a show. And it doesn't do a damn bit of good. It almost seems as if he was putting on an act, as good an act as Miss Wells's protestations of grief over her lost Eddy." His eyes narrowed. "Now, do you suppose you might tell me how you knew he was kidnapped? No one has been up there except police and private security guards. Who told you?"

Raifer's voice lowered, although there was little chance that they might be overheard in the general hubbub of the busy lobby. "That crate in the cellar of Wainwright and McGowan told me," he said evenly. "Do you remember it?"

Ryan nodded. "Large. About six feet long. Fairly sturdy." He grinned humorlessly. "And empty. No trace of illegal arms."

"Right," Raifer agreed. "Large. Large enough for Edward, I'd venture. And what easier way to make a man disappear than truss him up, nail him into a crate, and ship him out of the country, just another bit of freight?"

Ryan considered Raifer's words for a moment and then his ruddy cheeks turned pale. "By God, you may be right. And if you are, we haven't much time."

"Can you get a few strong-arms?" Raifer asked him.

Ryan nodded. "But it will take a bit of time. I wouldn't trust any of Fitzpatrick's lackeys. I'll have to round up a few of my own men."

"All right," Raifer replied. "Why don't you take Miss Wainwright and do just that? I'll meet you at the warehouse." He stood.

Honor got to her feet and stood facing him. "I'm going with you, Raifer," she said sharply.

"No, you're not, Honor," he told her firmly. "You'll just be in my way. Stay with the captain, and I'll see you in a while. With any luck, we should have this thing all neatly cleared up by this evening." He started out into the flow of traffic that surged through the lobby.

"Raifer!"

Honor started after him, but she found the hand that held her arm completely ungiving.

"He's right," Ryan told her. "You would just be in the way. Now stay here for a moment while I go up and act surly enough to Fitzpatrick so that he'll find it necessary to dismiss me from any further duty." The prospect seemed to please him, and he grinned. "It shouldn't take more than a minute or two. Then we've got a busy half hour or so rounding up a few good men."

He dropped her arm and stood towering over her until she acquiesced and sat down once more in the chair she had vacated. That seemed to satisfy him, for he nodded at her, then turned away and made his way to the lift.

Honor sat watching him until the door of the lift opened and he disappeared inside.

The warehouse was silent. Patrick Caughlin's jacket hung from the rack that stood near the door, a wary testament to the fact that he was in residence for the day, but his missing cap told Raifer plainly that someone had suggested he take a half hour break. In his mind's eye, Raifer could see the burly, redheaded Patrick crossing the wharf and heading toward the public house near the corner, his dark cap rakishly angled, his stride cockily jaunty in anticipation of imbibing a pint or two and that on the company time.

Raifer recalled Patrick's warning, offered to him what seemed months, not a few weeks, before, that there were some things a man was better off not knowing, not questioning. It seemed Patrick took his own advice seriously. Whatever was going on at the warehouse that day, Patrick considered himself safe in his conscious ignorance.

The fact of Patrick's absence, however, told Raifer that his suspicions had been right, that something unusual was going on, unusual enough for the warehouse to be left empty. And if the lack of human activity weren't enough, the fact that the door that led down to the basement stood warily ajar only intensified that supposition.

Raifer crept cautiously to the door and paused for a moment, listening, beside it. There were, unquestionably, sounds coming from below, human sounds, the noise of voices raised in indistinct argument. That somehow pleased Raifer, those indecipherable sounds of discontent. At least, he thought, they weren't as polished and as perfect as the smooth execution of their plan at the Saint Pierre would seem to indicate.

He made his way to the tool cabinet where crowbars used to open cargo crates were stored, and chose a hefty one, all the while cursing himself for having come without a revolver. It's not as impossible as it might seem, he told himself. After all, he didn't have to arrest the lot, just make sure they stayed where they were until Ryan arrived with reinforcements.

He returned to the door, slipping through and onto the narrow stairs, moving carefully, being sure he made no sound. When he'd descended half the flight, he paused and let his eyes grow accustomed to the dimness of the light. Then he continued downward until he stood at the stairs, surrounded by the darkness, letting his eyes find the one source of light in the long, low-ceilinged expanse.

It was not unexpected to him that the light as well as the sounds of the agitated voices he'd heard above were coming from the small room at the end of the cellar. The batten door had been left wide opened. As he crept carefully forward, Raifer could see into the room, could see a half dozen men, two of them facing one another, gesturing angrily. As he stared into the room, Raifer suddenly realized that behind the two who argued so voluably where the rickety row of shelves had been, there was now an opening into a dark, damp-walled tunnel beyond. So that's how they got the rifles out of here so neatly, Raifer thought. There's a tunnel, leading, no doubt, to the water. An easy access to whatever boat happened to be tied up at the wharf. And what's more, at night or even in late dusk, it would be virtually impossible to see any activity from the streets above.

Raifer moved a bit closer. He could hear the voices quite distinctly now, and if he'd felt surprise when he'd seen the tunnel, he felt even more as he recognized one of them to belong to Daniel Wainwright. No matter what he'd told Honor and Ryan, and despite his determination to try to clear Daniel, he'd never really believed Honor's father to be innocent of the smuggling and whatever else was taking place in his warehouse and aboard his ships. Now Raifer sidled off to the side of the door, pressing himself against the damp wall, hoping the few feet's distance and the darkness would keep his presence a secret, and listened.

"You swore to me, Kevin," Daniel was saying. "You promised that no one would be hurt, that you were only helping people who needed help. And I was enough of a fool to let you go on with it, not wanting to allow myself to think, to know. But this has gone too far. I can't stand with my eyes closed any longer."

"For God's sake, you're no fool, Danny," Kevin retorted sharply. "You knew what I was doing, even if you wouldn't admit it to yourself. And that was fine with me; just as long as you didn't make a fuss, as long as you didn't get in the way. And it'll still be fine with me, just as soon as you get yourself out of here and forget what you've seen." There was a short, sharp sound, a snort of disdain. "That's the way it's always been, hasn't it? Me doin' all the real work while you were the outside man, the talker, the polished one who didn't need to be gettin' his hands dirty. Well, your hands ain't soiled now, Danny. Just get yourself along."

Raifer's attention was distracted just then by a sound of movement, the sound of footsteps hurriedly crossing the width of the open cellar. He turned to catch a glimpse of Honor running forward, toward the opened door of the small room and the light.

He groaned inwardly. Then he started forward, hoping to reach her, to get to her before she made so much noise that the others would become aware of her presence. But he was too late. Just as he started for her he heard her shout.

"Papa!"

There was a flurry of movement as men streamed out of the room. Raifer turned and raised the crowbar threateningly, not sure he could do much good, without much hope but aware that he had, at the least, to try. He swung, letting the weight of the bar carry his arm into the chests of two of the men who tumbled forward toward him, even as his eyes focused on the glint of the pistols in their hands.

Then there was the sound of a shot and the burning sensation in his arm, followed by the rattle of the dropped crowbar against the floor. He hardly felt the blow to the back of his head, only the sensation of falling.

The last thing he heard was the sound of Honor's scream.

Chapter Eleven

Honor hardly even noticed the hand that was clamped over her mouth. All she could see, it seemed, was Raifer's body where it lay dumped on the floor in the corner of the small room. There was blood on his arm, a lot of it, and a thin trickle of red oozed from a cut on his head. It filled her mind, that and the image of her father's tense and white-faced stare, his obvious disbelief. Nothing seemed to have any meaning for her at that moment, especially as her eyes kept returning inexorably to Raifer and the dark puddle of red that seeped to the floor near where he lay.

"Take your hands off my daughter!"

It was Daniel's voice, outrage finally managing to outweigh his shock, and the words made their way slowly into Honor's mind. Then Flannagan, his face close to hers, too close, close enough so that she could smell the hint of whiskey on his breath, forced her attention, putting his hand to her chin and holding it until her eyes finally found his.

"If I have him release you, will you give me your word to be silent?" he demanded.

Honor nodded, then let her eyes drift back to Raifer. Flannagan stood back and nodded to the faceless body behind her that held her still and silent.

"Let her be, Tommy."

The hand was withdrawn from her mouth first, then the arm that held her around the waist loosened and finally released its hold. Without bothering to turn to the half dozen faces that anxiously watched her, she crossed the room and fell to her knees beside Raifer, reaching a frightened, shaking hand out to his cheek.

"Raifer," she whispered, uselessly, for he didn't stir.

Daniel turned to Kevin as he moved to Honor's side. He seemed to have regained his confidence now, buoyed, perhaps, by Flannagan's direct acquiescence to his demand that his daughter be freed. Whatever the reason, he stood now, apparently sure of his ground, and faced Kevin.

"This is the result of your little games, Kevin. How much more blood has to be shed before you accept the consequences of what it is you're doing?" He looked meaningfully at Flannagan, then at the pistol in Flannagan's hand.

Kevin followed his stare, then moved to Flannagan. "There's no need for this," he said, putting his hand to the barrel of the pistol. His eyes were on those of the younger man's, challenging, angry now at the bother the violence he'd precipitated had caused.

Flannagan felt the hot flush of his own anger, but he swallowed it, telling himself this was not the time, that he was too close to let an old man's stupidity get in his way. He released his grip on the pistol butt, letting the weapon fall into Kevin's hand.

Kevin turned back to face Daniel. "None of this was intended," he told Daniel calmly. "No one was supposed to be hurt. And if he hadn't come snooping around, it wouldn't have happened. But now

The Publishers of Zebra Books
Make This Special Offer
to Zebra Romance Readers...

AFTER YOU HAVE READ THIS
BOOK WE'D LIKE TO SEND YOU
4 MORE FOR *FREE*
AN $18.00 VALUE

NO OBLIGATION!

ONLY ZEBRA HISTORICAL ROMANCES
"BURN WITH THE FIRE OF HISTORY"
(SEE INSIDE FOR MONEY SAVING DETAILS.)

MORE PASSION AND ADVENTURE AWAIT... YOUR TRIP TO A BIG ADVENTUROUS WORLD BEGINS WHEN YOU ACCEPT YOUR FIRST 4 NOVELS ABSOLUTELY *FREE* (AN $18.00 VALUE)

Accept your Free gift and start to experience more of the passion and adventure you like in a historical romance novel. Each Zebra novel is filled with proud men, spirited women and tempestuous love that you'll remember long after you turn the last page.

Zebra Historical Romances are the finest novels of their kind. They are written by authors who really know how to weave tales of romance and adventure in the historical settings you love. You'll feel like you've actually gone back in time with the thrilling stories that each Zebra novel offers.

GET YOUR FREE GIFT WITH THE START OF YOUR HOME SUBSCRIPTION

Our readers tell us that these books sell out very fast in book stores and often they miss the newest titles. So Zebra has made arrangements for you to receive the four newest novels published each month.

You'll be guaranteed that you'll never miss a title, and home delivery is so convenient. And to show you just how easy it is to get Zebra Historical Romances, we'll send you your first 4 books absolutely FREE! Our gift to you just for trying our home subscription service.

BIG SAVINGS AND FREE HOME DELIVERY

Each month, you'll receive the four newest titles as soon as they are published. You'll probably receive them even before the bookstores do. What's more, you may preview these exciting novels free for 10 days. If you like them as much as we think you will, just pay the low preferred subscriber's price of just $3.75 each. *You'll save $3.00 each month off the publisher's price.* AND, your savings are even greater because there are never any shipping, handling or other hidden charges—FREE Home Delivery. Of course you can return any shipment within 10 days for full credit, no questions asked. There is no minimum number of books you must buy.

4 FREE BOOKS

TO GET YOUR 4 FREE BOOKS WORTH $18.00 — MAIL IN THE FREE BOOK CERTIFICATE TODAY

Fill in the Free Book Certificate below, and we'll send your FREE BOOKS to you as soon as we receive it.

If the certificate is missing below, write to: Zebra Home Subscription Service, Inc., P.O. Box 5214, 120 Brighton Road, Clifton, New Jersey 07015-5214.

FREE BOOK CERTIFICATE

4 FREE BOOKS
ZEBRA HOME SUBSCRIPTION SERVICE, INC.

YES! Please start my subscription to Zebra Historical Romances and send me my first 4 books absolutely FREE. I understand that each month I may preview four new Zebra Historical Romances free for 10 days. If I'm not satisfied with them, I may return the four books within 10 days and owe nothing. Otherwise, I will pay the low preferred subscriber's price of just $3.75 each; a total of $15.00, *a savings off the publisher's price of $3.00*. I may return any shipment and I may cancel this subscription at any time. There is no obligation to buy any shipment and there are no shipping, handling or other hidden charges. Regardless of what I decide, the four free books are mine to keep.

NAME _____

ADDRESS _____ APT _____

CITY _____ STATE _____ ZIP _____

TELEPHONE ( ) _____

SIGNATURE _____
(if under 18, parent or guardian must sign)

Terms, offer and prices subject to change without notice. Subscription subject to acceptance by Zebra Books. Zebra Books reserves the right to reject any order or cancel any subscription.   049002

GET FOUR FREE BOOKS
(AN $18.00 VALUE)

ZEBRA HOME SUBSCRIPTION
SERVICE, INC.
P.O. BOX 5214
120 BRIGHTON ROAD
CLIFTON, NEW JERSEY 07015-5214

AFFIX
STAMP
HERE

we've got to deal with it. Get Honor out of here and forget what you've seen."

Daniel put his hand to Honor's shoulder. "Just what is it you intend to do?" he demanded.

"Well, now, I don't think you should be worryin' about such things, Mr. Wainwright."

Flannagan had pushed himself forward, in front of Kevin. There was no longer any emotion in his expression, nor was there any hint of anything except command in his manner. If Daniel had had any doubt as to who was in charge, the young Irishman or Kevin, it was suddenly completely dispelled.

"Just be assured that matters will be handled so that you and yours, and Mr. McGowan as well, of course, will be completely protected. No trace, no hint of involvement, will ever come back to you."

His words seemed to strike Honor, settling into her with a startling clarity, cutting through the fuzziness that had blurred her observations in the previous moments. She looked up at Flannagan and as soon as she saw the expression on his face, she knew what it was he intended.

"You're going to kill him," she said flatly. She turned her glance to Kevin, accusing him with her eyes. "And you're going to let him."

"No," he told her. "He'll disappear with the prince for a few weeks, nothing more. When it's over, none of it will matter."

Honor shook her head slowly. "You're going to let that man kill him," she said evenly.

Her words shocked Daniel, so sure, so unarguably lucid. More than that, they seemed to galvanize him. How could he have stood by and let things go this far, he wondered. How could he have shut his eyes to what he knew was happening around him? His own daughter was not afraid to face the truth. How could he do any less?

He started toward Kevin, his eyes on the pistol Kevin had taken from Flannagan, his intention clear.

"It's over, Kevin," he said as he grasped his partner's hand, the hand holding the pistol. "You end it all now, or I'll end it for you."

Kevin pushed against him, struggling. "Don't be a fool, Danny. No one is going to die. Do you want to send us both to prison?"

But Daniel wasn't listening. His hand squeezed tighter around Kevin's, increasing the pressure against the steel of the pistol where it bit into his skin.

"I won't let you do this," he cried sharply. "I won't..."

The sound of the shot was not as loud as one that had been fired in the open space of the cellar. There was no loud reverberation, no echo of the noise coming back to them. Instead, it was a bit muffled, the concussion partly swallowed by Daniel's chest as was the bullet as it entered it.

Horror filled Honor as she watched her father stagger backward and then fall. Disbelief was the only emotion available to her. The words formed in her mind, congent and precise, this can't be happening, none of this can be real. Then she scrambled to her feet and ran to him, kneeling beside him, barely aware that Kevin knelt beside her.

"Papa," she moaned softly, touching him, his face, his neck, his chest. Then, as the sure knowledge that he was dead settled into her, she turned glazed, wild eyes to Kevin.

Suddenly she could see only one thing, Kevin's hand against her father's neck, looking vainly for a throb of a pulse. And the thought of his touch became suddenly unbearable to her.

"Don't touch him!" she screamed as she beat against Kevin's arm, pushing it away. "Don't you touch him!"

Kevin drew back, dazed by her reaction as well as by the sickening realization of what it was he'd done. "It was an accident, Honor," he pleaded softly, trying to make her understand. "I didn't want this to happen. You can't think I intended for this to happen."

She refused to listen to him. She leaned forward, over Daniel's body, moaning, calling to him, the single word, "Papa," whispered over and over, as though it might have the power to call him back to her.

Flannagan approached them, standing over them, staring down at the three of them as a remote derision filled his expression.

"Now you see where your good intentions lead you, Kevin. Now I'll have three bodies to dispose of, not one."

Kevin looked up at him, focusing sharply on Flannagan's cold expression.

"No!" he shouted. "No more blood!"

"When are you going to learn, old man, that you've no more say in the matter than a fly on the wall? You're a fool. You let sentiment get in the way and mistakes happen."

Honor heard his words and she began to shake. No only her father, but she and Raifer, too, were to die. She looked down at Daniel, at his still, slack features. His face seemed to wear an expression of mild surprise, as though he, too, could not believe what was happening.

"No!" Kevin was shouting. "I said no more blood.

This woman is my son's intended. There will be no more killing. There was never to have been any killing."

Flannagan only shook his head. "Don't you understand, old man?" he asked softly. "No more sentiment. It will only end with you at the end of a hangman's noose. If she lives, it's over for you."

"No, no," Kevin interrupted. "I can leave. Fitzpatrick can hold it off for a while, and I can sell the business, the fleet. And I'll give you half the proceeds of it all, a small fortune for your cause. Only no more killing." Then he stared at Flannagan, realizing that the words he'd offered up in his panic were the one rational argument the terrorist might accept. His cause was everything to Flannagan. He'd kill for it. To finance it, he'd even refrain from killing.

Flannagan mulled over his words for a moment in silence. "How long would all that take?" he demanded softly.

"Not long," Kevin replied quickly, anxious to assure him. "You can take them back with you on the *Mary Louise*. A few weeks, not much longer. You were planning to hold Edward that long anyway. Just no more killing." He was pleading now, his voice reduced to a near whine, but Kevin didn't care. He looked down at Honor and Daniel, his best friend and his best friend's child. He'd killed the man, but he'd die himself before he allowed anything more to happen to Honor.

Honor turned and looked up at him, her eyes filling with hatred, blame, and more than anything else, the accusation of betrayal.

"You won't get away with it," she told him, her words hot with defiance as she stared first at Kevin, then turned to Flannagan. "The police will be here within the hour. You'll hang. You'll all hang."

As soon as she had uttered the words, Honor realized how foolish she'd been. But it was too late to call them back. Flannagan leveled a hard, cold stare at her, then seemed to rouse himself abruptly.

"All right then, old man," he said to Kevin. "You've a deal. Half what you can salvage in exchange for their two lives. Now, if we can believe the young lady, I think we had better hurry."

He motioned to the tall, young Irishman who had held Honor and brought her into the small room only a few moments before.

"Thomas, my boy, you will have the pleasure of taking care of Miss Wainwright." He motioned the others into action.

Honor struggled weakly against the hands that held her. They tightened perceptibly, and Thomas Moynihan leaned forward to her and whispered in her ear, "Don't make me hurt you, miss. I don't want to hurt you."

Honor quieted, giving up to the realization that it was useless anyway. The young man had seemed dazed at first by the sight of Daniel lying dead on the floor, as though the body had brought him face to face with ghosts of his own. After a moment, however, he'd recovered more than enough to perform as Flannagan order him sharply, taking her out to the damp, dark tunnel and holding her there while the others removed her father's body and Raifer, dumping them both like so much refuse into the wet mud of the tunnel floor. Raifer had stirred, and for a moment Honor had felt a tinge of hope, but they'd quieted him with another blow to the back of the head before he'd completely regained consciousness, then tied his hands and feet and gagged him so that they need not be put to the bother again while they were otherwise occupied. He lay now on his side, his face partially in the mud. Honor's eyes kept straying to him, to him and the large, bearded and moustachioed man who sat beside him, trussed and gagged like a large comical fowl, his bare arms and legs extended from soiled white linen underwear, the only clothing he wore. It seemed impossible for her to believe that this dirt smudged creature was Edward, Duke of Cornwall, Prince of Wales, and heir to the British Crown. Were it not for the obvious terror she saw in his eyes, she would have found him only clownish as he sat in the mire.

She could not allow her eyes to wander to her father's still body. That was one thing she could not accept, not yet, not if she was to retain any semblance of her wits. And she knew she had to think, to try at least, if there was to be any escape for her and Raifer. However slim the chance, she must not let it slip away. So she turned her eyes toward where Raifer lay, trying to will him to regain consciousness with her thoughts, to somehow have him rise up, break the ropes that bound him, and overpower this group of ruthless men who surrounded her.

They all stood, silent and listening to the sounds in the small room they'd just vacated, the thin wall and the rickety shelving that divided it from the tunnel where they waited allowing the sounds of the men searching there, Ryan's men, to come through fairly distinctly, even Kevin's words of shocked outrage and dismay, then anger, all clear enough for her to understand.

It didn't last long, the noise in the next room,

only a few moments and then it was followed by the shuffling sound of departing footsteps.

"No," she screamed. "Don't go. We're here. Don't leave us." The sound, loud and clear in her head, was nothing more than a thin, weak murmur, muffled nearly to extinction by the hand against her jaw, a hand that tightened its hold at the first pale sound that managed to escape her, and the handkerchief Moynihan had forced to her mouth. Silent tears of impotent fury fell, unheeded, to her cheeks.

They stood as they were for several moments after the noises had all faded. Then Flannagan motioned to Moynihan to release her. The big young man released the hand at her mouth, and she spit out the handkerchief.

"Now, that wasn't so bad, was it, miss?" he asked as he released his hold of her waist, his tone sounding oddly concerned, as though he felt guilty for what he'd been required to do. She turned and stared at him, her look filled with derision. Then she screamed.

It was foolish, she knew, to think that Flannagan would let it go on for very long, but her cry seemed to completely amaze Moynihan. He stood, stricken, wondering apparently what it was he had done wrong. Then Flannagan, aware that the young man seemed incapable of stopping the noise, moved to her quickly and slapped her lightly on the cheek. The slap seemed more intended to gain her attention than to hurt her. She kept up the scream. Flannagan then put his hand to her mouth and forced her roughly against the moldy wall of the tunnel. He turned to Moynihan.

"Don't just stand there, boy," he snapped. "We've an hour or more to wait here until dusk. We can't have her wailin' like a banshee. Get some rope and tie her up, and gag her. When we have her aboard the *Mary Louise* and we've set sail, she can scream her bloody head off. Until then, I hold you responsible to keep her quiet."

With that, Flannagan pulled her away from the wall and thrust her into the young man's arms. Moynihan caught her, and held her as Flannagan tied a gag around her mouth, then he forced her to sit down, with her back against the wall. He tied her hands together firmly, then her ankles, his motions jerky, seemingly angry as he worked with the rope.

"I didn't want to hurt you," he whispered sharply as he pulled the last of the ropes taut. "Now be still, or it'll go worse for you." His eyes seemed sad as he sat back on his haunches and uttered his last words. Then he turned away, obviously too guilty to face her.

The minutes dragged on slowly. Where she sat, Honor could feel the cold and damp from the floor and walls seep into her body, but they made little impression on her. It was all she could do to sit there and see her father's body lying only a few feet away.

After a while Raifer regained consciousness. Their guards seemed unconcerned with his return to wakefulness. They made no effort to help him as he rolled over onto his back and then struggled to a sitting position, a far from simple feat with his hands and ankles tied together. If Honor had expected some superhuman, heroic feat from him, she was soon disappointed. The effort he'd expended and the loss of blood from the injury to his arm had obviously taken their toll. He sat on the far side of the tunnel from her beside the prince, his breath labored and audible, his glance occasionally meeting hers.

They were, the three of them, incapable of affecting in any way the outcome of Flannagan's plan. And Daniel had died because he had made the effort. Honor was sick with the burden of grief and the guilt she knew she bore for the part she'd played in bringing him there, in leading him to his death.

Finally Kevin appeared, opening the door from the small room slowly and peeking into the dark length of the tunnel.

"It's dusk, getting dark quickly. You can be off," he said. His voice was cold, businesslike, as though the shipment the *Mary Louise* was about to take on were no different from any of the others she'd carried in the previous years. But then he approached Honor and stood over her, and his expression grew gentle and sympathetic.

He hunkered down in front of her. He tentatively reached out his hand to the gag at her mouth, but then drew back, as though he decided it best if he not hear whatever words she might have for him.

"Don't worry, Honor," he whispered. "They won't hurt you. I have Flannagan's word. Just do as you're told and you'll be home in a month or so, safe and sound. You and Terrence can be married. You'll be all right."

She peered daggers at him, her eyes momentarily leaving his and moving to Daniel's body, then returning.

Kevin took the meaning she'd intended, and he winced. "I can't bring him back, Honor. Much as I would wish it, I can't. And you needn't worry. You won't ever see me again. As far as you are concerned, I'm dead from this moment. God knows I never wanted any of this."

He stood then, turning away from her with obvious relief, and faced Flannagan. "Remember," he said. "We have a bargain."

Flannagan grinned at him, his face eerily malignant in the light thrown up by the oil lamp near his feet. "Aye," he agreed. "A very profitable one. You needn't fear for her or the other one. I won't lose so much that the cause can make good use of."

Kevin seemed to bridle at his response. "That's all it is to you, dollars and cents," he said sharply.

Flannagan's expression turned hard. "Don't be lecturing to me about money, old man," he snarled. "When you see your wife and children without food or a roof over their heads, then you can deride my beliefs. I'm fighting for my people in the only way I know how."

Then he turned his back on Kevin and motioned to two of his men. They followed him, and Kevin stood for a moment, watching as they brought the large, empty crate Honor had seen with Raifer on their first trip down into the cellar. Kevin turned one last time, offered Honor a final glance, and then disappeared into the small room in the cellar, closing the door silently behind him.

When Kevin had gone, Honor was treated to the spectacle of watching the heir to the throne of England, gagged, tied, and dressed only in his underwear, being forced into a large wooden crate. He was, as she had so derisively suggested to Raifer that afternoon at lunch, to be carried aboard the *Mary Louise* like a crate of barrel staves.

This act was carried out with complete silence on the part of the conspirators. The only noise was the sound of muffled groans as they escaped Edward's lips, and the sounds of the crate lid being secured. Then the four Irishmen hefted the large container and carried it down the length of the tunnel until it disappeared from her view.

When they were gone, Honor managed to edge her way slowly to Raifer's side. His shirt, she saw, was soaked with clotted blood from the hole in his arm, and his gaze seemed disjointed to her. She wanted to touch him with her hands, to speak to him, but all that was impossible. Her eyes found his, begging for comfort, wishing she could feel his arms around her. She was terrified and in need of comfort.

Flannagan and his men returned soon, now relieved of the burden of the crate they'd used to bear away Edward. Flannagan approached them and stood over Honor, staring down at her with his oddly impersonal, cold, dark eyes. In his hand was a large, heavy sack.

"Your turn, Miss Wainwright," he said with mock politeness. Then he bodily lifted her and covered her with the sack.

Honor felt herself being handed away, then thrown over a thick, strong shoulder. The complete darkness, the obvious uselessness of her struggles, it all terrified her, as did the awareness that she had no idea what was happening to Raifer.

Eventually she was set down, and the thick canvas of the sack drawn away. She was, she realized, on board the *Mary Louise*, in a tiny, portless cabin. Moynihan had put her down on a hard, narrow, bunk and now stood staring down at her. He seemed indecisive for a moment and hesitated, but then leaned down to her and drew away the gag from her mouth.

"Please," she begged him hoarsely. "Please let us

go."

For a minute she thought that he might, for there was indecision and obvious regret in his expression. Honor pressed her point.

"I've done nothing to you. Can't you see what you're doing is wrong, that it can only lead to worse? The British won't stand for what you're doing to Edward. They'll hunt you down. Kill you."

She quickly realized that she had taken the wrong tack with him, trying to dissuade him from what he considered his cause. His expression hardened.

"We sail in a few hours," he told her. Then he retied the gag, stood, and made his way to the cabin door. He turned to face her. "You should try to sleep," he said before he turned away from her, letting himself out of the cabin.

Honor heard the sound of the bolt being thrown. She sat for a moment, listening to the sounds of the ship, the creaking of the planks as the *Mary Louise* rode at anchor, the gentle groaning of the rigging. She tried to concentrate on the noises, to keep her mind dull and empty and lull herself to the escape of sleep. But it was useless. Each time she closed her eyes, the sight of Daniel's body filled her mind. For the first time she became aware of the finality of her loss, of the fact that she had not allowed herself to accept until then, the fact that he was actually dead. Added to that was the dull, hurtful pain of the knowledge that she was partially to blame for his death. Tears welled up in her eyes and fell to her cheeks, oddly silent tears as the gag muffled her moans of misery and loss. Eventually, exhausted and bereft of comfort, she sank into an uneasy sleep.

Chapter Twelve

Honor awoke the next morning to the sound of heavy footfalls on the wooden floor outside her tiny prison and the bolt being thrown on the door. Moynihan entered and strode immediately to where she lay still on the narrow bunk. Behind him, Flannagan strolled smugly into the small cabin and leaned against the wall as the younger man knelt in front of her and removed the gag.

Honor gasped and brought her hands to her aching cheeks and chin. Her hands, still tied together at the wrists, were stiff and a bit numb, but their discomfort, she realized, was small compared to the ache in her jaws.

Flannagan watched her with his dark, impersonal stare. When she looked up and noticed his gaze, Honor felt a shiver pass through her. The man has no feelings, she thought, no pity, not even any fear. His lack of emotion, she found, frightened her more than anything else she could imagine.

She turned her eyes away, back to Moynihan, who was peering, she realized, at the dark red marks the gag had left on her cheeks.

"Give me your hands, miss," he told her, "and I'll untie them."

Obediently she held them out to him, and watched as he took a knife and carefully slit the rope.

"Aren't you afraid that I'll scream?" she asked him. Her voice was hoarse, but there was no mistaking the note of derision in her tone. "Or run away?" she added as he slit the rope that bound her ankles.

"We're ten hours out to sea," he replied with a pleasant grin. "No one to hear you scream. No place for you to run."

Honor rubbed her ankles and wrists thoughtfully. "Then you aren't going to keep me locked up in here?" she asked. She turned her gaze to Flannagan, for it was he, she knew, and not the boy, who determined her fate.

"I've decided to let you have the freedom of the ship as long as you cause no trouble," he told her absently, his eyes still peering in that oddly intense way at her.

For the first time Honor felt a surge of hope, and she fought to keep from showing it. But Flannagan went on, crushing the surge as quickly as he had let rise.

"If you think you can rouse some of the crew to help you, Miss Wainwright, let me suggest that the effort would be futile. I have already seen to it that they were told you are, shall we say, a trifle unstable, and prone to wild and fantastic stories. You are being sent, so they believe, to a hospital in England in the hopes that you might be helped. The crew is instructed to humor you as far as behaving pleasantly, but to ignore the more outlandish tales you might bring them."

Honor looked away from him, knowing the disappointment she felt showed in her expression and not wanting to give him the satisfaction of seeing it.

"And Mr. Farrell and the prince?" she asked

softly.

"Below, in irons," he replied.

"And just how did you justify that?" she snapped at him.

He grinned at her oddly, with the first real humor she'd seen in him, and brought his hand to his breast pocket, withdrawing a small leather wallet and opening it to display a badge.

"I am, as you see, a detective in the New York City Police Department," he said as he held it out to her, "extraditing two criminals to face trial for rape, murder, and robbery. I assure you, the crew are all quite happy to avoid such despicable types completely and leave their care to my men. All very neat. And ironic, don't you think?" He seemed quite pleased at that. "All the more believable, thanks to Mr. Farrell's own police badge."

He chuckled softly to himself. Honor felt a wave of impotent anger. "May I see them at least?" she managed to ask through her ire.

Flannagan's face resettled itself into its previous remote blandness and a humorless grin spread to his lips. "I'll do better than that, Miss Wainwright. I'll even let you play nurse to our good detective's wounded arm. After all, I gave my word that you'd be well cared for. I intend to keep it." He turned to Moynihan. "If you will, Thomas, my boy, see Miss Wainwright to her fellows. I'll send along some bandages and disinfectant."

He left, presumably completely pleased with himself and the situation he had engineered so masterfully.

"Damn. My own shield," Raifer muttered. "How could I have been such an incompetent as to let this happen?" Raifer scowled, then his face contorted. "Ow. That hurts, Honor."

"Just hold still a minute longer," Honor admonished him as she finished swabbing the gory wound in his arm with antiseptic. She was more than peripherally aware that she had not burst in when she had, he would most likely never have been captured by Flannagan's men. But the sight of her father and Kevin fighting had been too much for her to stand, especially when it had become apparent to her what their argument was about. If she'd had the presence of mind to stop and think, she'd have realized that she could only give Raifer's presence away to the terrorists. But she'd rushed headlong in without thought. And now they were all paying for that act—she, Raifer, and the prince as well.

She forced her attention back to the hole in Raifer's arm, knowing that regrets would in no way help change the situation.

"The bullet passed through your arm, Raifer. If the wound doesn't infect, I think it should be all right," she told him as she dropped the unappetizingly stained bit of bandage she had been using to clean the wound onto the small table where she'd set out the limited medical kit Flannagan had sent for her use.

"I'd already figured that out," Raifer told her, his tone petulant. "I'm not all sure infection might not be preferable to what you're doing to it now, though." Despite his words and the fact that he flinched with pain, however, he made no move to pull away.

"Don't be such a baby," she snapped, her tone harsher than necessary. That, too, she realized, was due more to her sense of guilt than to any ill feeling she bore him at that moment. It was all she could do to keep herself from gagging as she stared at the gory mess.

She forced herself to concentrate on what she was doing, making an effort to be more gentle as she wrapped bandages around the wounded arm. As she worked, she glanced nervously at Edward, who sat facing the two of them on the bare plank that served as his bed in the cramped, locked portion of the hold that had been given over to the makeshift jail.

"No reason to blame yourself," he was saying mildly to Raifer. "Under the circumstances, I should say you performed admirably."

"Should the opportunity arise, Your Grace," Raifer told him grimly, "I'd appreciate an endorsement of that variety to my superiors."

"Certainly, certainly," Edward agreed, amiably enough, nodding his head for emphasis. "When all this is over, I shall be glad to do whatever I can."

Honor was quite surprised by the prince's manner. Of the three of them, he seemed the most at ease. Dressed now in rough pants and shirt, he no longer appeared the terrified, owl-eyed fool he'd seemed to her as he'd sat trussed and gagged in the mud of the tunnel floor. Of course, she told herself, the addition of clothing could only reduce his feelings of inadequacy and fear. But she somehow realized that he had become confident that Flannagan had no intention of seeing any of them harmed, that they were of more value to him alive and well, and he had determined to consider the experience an unlikely adventure. She could only hope that his confidence was well founded, as she felt none herself. But his calm and Raifer's simple anger served to alleviate her own fears a bit.

"I could try to get some of the crew to help us, I suppose," she mused aloud as she finished tying the bandage. "Although with Flannagan's story of my supposed insanity firmly in their minds, I don't know how much good it will do."

"And you such a level-headed, thoughtful person," Raifer murmured with wry humor. He shrugged into his tattered, stained shirt, then offered her a lopsided grin.

Honor turned away, suddenly full of tears wanting to be shed.

"I wish I were mad," she burst out. "I wish I had imagined this whole awful thing." The first of the tears filled her eyes and there was a heavy, thick weight in her throat. "I wish my father were still alive," she managed to gasp.

Raifer rose and went to her, turning her to face him and folding his arms around her. "I know, Honor," he said softly.

Honor let herself melt against him and released whatever hold she'd managed to keep on the tears. She let them pour out, a sudden, hot spring of them, not caring at that moment where she was or how she had come to be there. All that was real to her at that moment was the loss of her father and Raifer's arms around her. At that moment she realized how much she needed his strength to find her own, how much comfort the feel of his body close to hers gave her. She knew it was all meaningless, that all he cared about was his job, and getting it back, that he'd only used her. She told herself that she meant nothing to him. But her heart told her something else, something that had no basis in reality, in what she knew to be true. She'd cling to that, she told herself, only so long as she needed to, only until she could face the tragedy of Daniel's death and come to cope with what was happening to them. When the time came, she promised herself, she'd be able to face what she must. But for the present, she allowed herself what comfort she could find in his arms.

When the tears were finally gone, she realized that they had helped, that somehow those tears, shed in his arms, healed her a bit and eased the hurt, unlike the ones she'd shed alone the night before.

"No need to fear, Miss Wainwright," Edward told her gently as she pulled herself away from Raifer's arms. "If the Royal Navy doesn't manage to rescue us while we're still at sea, I've no doubt but that we'll be quickly found once we reach British-controlled soil." His moustache bristled with confidence and he raised a finger to it to help it into a cheerful upsweep.

Honor managed to repay him for the gesture with a wan smile. Then she set about cleaning up the mess of the medical kit, returning the bottle of antiseptic and unused bandages, dropping the soiled pieces she'd used to clean away the mess of dried blood and dirt and the makeshift bandage Raifer had fashioned from a torn piece of his shirt, sweeping the mess into the bowl of warm water that was clouded now, and soiled to a dull copper color. It was easier, she realized, to force herself to some task than to stand idle and just think.

"Then you believe, Your Excellency, there's nothing we can do for ourselves?" she asked. Edward's words seemed to imply that there was nothing for them to do but sit and wait for help to come to them.

"Nothing I can think of at the moment," Edward told her with a smile.

Raifer waited until she'd turned her gaze to his for confirmation. "You can, Honor," he told her soberly, "do your damndest to keep out of Flannagan's way. The others simply do as they're told, but he'd different. He's smart and dangerous. Don't underestimate him."

Honor was still considering his words when the door to the men's jail was opened. Moynihan stood in the entry. Behind him another of Flannagan's men stood with his rifle aimed and ready, lest either the prince or Raifer decided to take advantage of the situation.

"It's time you left, miss," Moynihan told Honor. He picked up the small medical kit and put it under his arm, then put his free hand to her wrist.

She squirmed away from his grasp. "Don't touch me," she snarled at him and proceeded toward the door, head high and defiant.

Moynihan seemed so dazed by her response to him that he let her go on alone, following sheepishly behind, bearing the small bag of medical supplies.

When they were gone and the door was closed and locked behind them, Edward turned to Raifer. He was grinning mildly. "The young lady, it seems, is a bit strong willed," he said pleasantly.

Raifer laughed. "I would say, Your Excellency, that Honor could only be described by the word *hellion*. I almost feel a bit sorry for Flannagan." His expression sobered as he thought about his words. "Almost," he added judiciously. "But not quite."

It's Captain Keenan, Honor thought as she looked up to the bridge of the *Mary Louise*.

She'd badgered Moynihan into allowing her to

walk out on the deck for some fresh air and a bit of exercise, and he'd agreed with only minor reluctance. He was, she soon realized, becoming quite pleased with his role as her babysitter, and his manner with her had begun to grow easier, even a bit worshipful. She had not time to fully consider the possible use of his admiration for her, for she'd only just become certain of it, of the way he smiled at her, the way he looked when his hand touched hers. She realized now that she could crush him with the accusation of having hurt her. But despite all that, he was doggedly faithful to his orders from Flannagan not to let her out of his sight except when she was firmly locked in her cabin.

She let that thought trail off as she looked up to where Captain Keenan consulted with one of his men by the great wheel. She'd met him once, fleetingly, but she did remember him and could hope that he might remember her. It was a stroke of luck that he had drawn the *Mary Louise* on this particular trip. If she could only get away from Moynihan long enough to talk to the captain, she told herself, she was sure she could convince him that Flannagan was not at all what he pretended to be.

She turned back to stare thoughtfully out over a gray, white-capped ocean, allowing her hand to drift casually close to where Moynihan's held the rail beside hers. He turned immediately and looked at her, apparently surprised that she did not withdraw her hand immediately when she made the contact. Instead, she smiled at him, and he, in turn, returned the smile with open pleasure.

"Nice afternoon, don't you think, miss?" he asked.

Honor inhaled the salt-tinged air and looked up to pure blue sky punctuated with soft white balls of clouds. The sun shone fiercely, and except for a steady, sharp wind, it was an absolutely beautiful afternoon.

"Yes, a lovely afternoon, Thomas," she agreed with a warm smile. He blushed a bit, she noticed, both at her use of his given name and at the smile that seemed unmistakably intended for him, the first she had offered him in the two days since the *Mary Louise* had sailed. "I should hate to be sent below by the cold of the wind," she added and shivered a bit, then drew the collar of her coat up in case he missed the point.

Moynihan quickly removed his heavy jacket. He draped it around her shoulders, letting his hands linger a moment as he surrounded her with the thick woolen fabric.

Honor looked up to let her eyes find his. "Oh, I couldn't let you do that," she told him quickly. "You'll catch your death out here like that." She began to reach up, to remove the jacket and return it to him.

He put his hand to hers to stop her. "I can get something else," he said. He smiled at her, and Honor could read the look of open adoration in his eyes.

"Please," she begged him gently. "I'll wait right here for you to come back."

He seemed to hesitate for a moment, aware he was not to leave her alone, so she prodded him with another smile, this one saccharine and cloying. It seemed to be all he needed.

"I won't be but a moment," he said as he backed away from her. "You won't leave this spot?"

She smiled yet again and shook her head. "I'll

wait for you right here," she promised and huddled contentedly into the warmth of his jacket.

He turned and ran to the hatch that led to the lower cabins, and Honor watched him go with the same seraphic smile on her lips. Once he had disappeared, however, her expression changed, as did her manner. She dropped the thick jacket and started at a run toward the bridge. She climbed the stairs quickly and was already beside Captain Keenan before any of the sailors on the deck stopped to consider that she might not belong there.

"Captain Keenan," she said breathlessly as she approached him.

He turned and looked at her, his expression puzzled.

"Captain Keenan, do you remember me? I'm Honor Wainwright. We met last year, in my father's offices."

Keenan nodded. "I am well aware who you are, Miss Wainwright," he told her evenly.

"You must help me, Captain," she went on breathlessly. "That man, Flannagan, he's not a policeman. He's a kidnapper—a terrorist."

Keenan cast her a doubtful glance. "I'm sure that you believe that, Miss Wainwright," he replied with absolutely no inflection to his words.

"You must believe me, Captain. They've imprisoned the real policeman in the hold. And Crown Prince Edward."

Keenan smiled. "If you please, Miss Wainwright, I've work to do, and you are not permitted on the bridge."

Honor drew back, realizing how he must see her, how impossible her story must seem to him. "I am not insane, Captain," she said firmly. "Regardless of what he's told you, what I am saying is the truth."

Keenan only shrugged and let his eyes wander to the deck, obviously looking for Moynihan to retrieve her so that he might be rid of her.

"Listen to me, Captain," Honor continued, grasping his arm. "If what I'm saying isn't true, then why did they smuggle one of those men on board in a crate? And me, gagged and tied, in a sack? And why would the *Mary Louise* be used to extradite criminals? It doesn't make sense."

"More sense than your fantasies, Miss Wainwright. The request for the *Mary Louise* to provide transport for the extradition of criminals is not so unusual, as we are the first ship to leave New York bound for the Isles since their capture. Moreover, Mr. Flannagan has presented me not only with his own credentials, but official papers ordering the transport."

"They're forgeries!" Honor exclaimed. "And the badge isn't his, but Raif Farrell's, one of the men he has locked up in your hold."

Keenan held up his hand to stop her flow of words, then went on calmly. "Although I was not on board when you were brought on the *Mary Louise*, Miss Wainwright, I was personally assured by Mr. McGowan that he escorted you to your cabin himself. I've no reason to doubt his word. And a good many reasons to consider your tale of mistreatment as being rooted in your imagination, not reality." He stared at her calmly, through her, it seemed to Honor. "Now, if you'll excuse me." He turned away, his dismissal obvious, shaking off her hand from his arm.

"Kevin McGowan is part of Flannagan's group," she countered, but it was apparent that he was ignoring her now. Honor was not about to give up quite so easily, however. She took on her most authoritative tone. "Captain, my father employs you. You will give me the courtesy of a fair hearing."

The words were already spoken when she realized they weren't quite true, that Daniel was dead and no longer anyone's employer. She felt a sharp, painful contraction in her throat, that Daniel was dead and she'd momentarily forgotten. She somehow managed to control herself, to stare at Keenan unwaveringly as he turned back to face her.

His expression was grim. "Mr. McGowan employs me, Miss Wainwright. I've met your father only twice, and fleetingly. But I've known Mr. McGowan quite well for more than eight years. I will tell you quite frankly, if you insist upon badgering me or my crew any further with these stories, I will be forced to have you confined to your quarters. Is that entirely clear, Miss Wainwright?"

That was it, then, Honor thought. There would be no reprieve for her, not by the captain's hand, at any rate. For the first time she started to understand how things had gotten so far out of her father's hand that Kevin McGowan could arrange for the smuggling of arms while Daniel could only stand by and watch it happen. Once he had given up the day-to-day running of the business and concerned himself only with the financing and contacts that brought Wainwright and McGowan their business, he had, in fact, abdicated his control. If he'd not been so reluctant, as Kevin had accused him of being, of getting his hands dirty, none of it could have possibly happened.

Keenan looked up and pointed. "You," he called loudly.

Honor turned. Moynihan was climbing up the

ladder to the bridge. His expression was decidedly displeased as he mounted the last of the steps and moved to her and Keenan.

"I am under the impression that you are charged with overseeing Miss Wainwright's behavior while she is on deck," Keenan told him coolly. "I would appreciate your assurance that she will not find her way to my bridge again."

Moynihan's cheeks colored brightly and he nodded. "She won't be botherin' you again, sir," he said. Then he put a firm hand to Honor's arm. "This way, if you will, miss."

Whatever pleasure he might have displayed at the contact only a few minutes before was gone now. Honor realized that his anger had severed any power she might have been able to wield on him. Feeling beaten and miserable, she allowed him to lead her back to her cabin.

When he'd heard of her small adventure, Flannagan became irate. He took his initial bout of anger out on Moynihan, calling the boy stupid and incompetent. Then he'd informed Honor that she would be confined to her cabin for the remainder of the voyage, except for an hour each afternoon for exercise on deck. Her privileges to visit Raifer and the prince were revoked. She was, essentially, to be treated as a prisoner herself.

This sentence was harsher than it might have seemed to him. The fourth day out of New York the seas grew rough and continued to be so for the remainder of the trip. Honor spend most of her time alone, locked in the tiny cabin, weak and heaving with seasickness. What comfort she had been able to take in Raifer's and the prince's encouragement was now denied her. She felt alienated, alone, and abandoned, her misery completed by the constant discomfort caused by the *Mary Louise*'s lurching on uneven seas.

For his part, Moynihan came to treat her with a biting diffidence that she knew was caused by her misuse of his trust. Whatever sympathy she had come to expect to see in him during the first days was gone. He even refused to talk to her, answering only what questions he deemed necessary with monosyllabic responses. He kept his distance from her when he escorted her to deck for her solitary walks, ensuring that the members of the *Mary Louise*'s crew did the same. She came to see herself as the sailors must see her, as a pariah, deranged and unstable. Were it not that the open air gave her some relief from the sick feeling in her stomach, she would have forgone her walks on deck entirely. As it was, they allowed her to change one misery for another.

The trip came finally to as unspectacular a conclusion as its beginning. It had already grown dark when Moynihan unlocked the door to her cabin and entered.

"Get your coat," he told her roughly. "We're putting ashore."

"Have we reached Dublin?" she asked.

"Neither Dublin nor London," he told her, then stood stolidly silent, making it clear to her that he would answer no more of her questions.

Realizing that she could expect nothing more from him, she stood and donned her coat, her fingers working the buttons absently as she watched him, wondering what it was that went on in his mind, wondering if his anger with her was so complete that she had lost whatever protection he might have afforded her from Flannagan. For once they reached land, she knew, Flannagan's control of his prisoners would be complete, unhampered by the need to present some reasonable explanation for his actions to Captain Keenan. She cursed herself as a fool for having so completely squandered whatever slight advantage she might have had with so little result.

She wordlessly allowed him to marshal her out of the cabin and up to the deck, moving with a resignation that would not have seemed possible to her two weeks before. She looked around, searching in the darkness for the shoreline, bewildered to find only a half dozen flickering lights and the indistinct outline of a rock-strewn coast. Moynihan had not lied to her, that was more than apparent. They were certainly nowhere near a large city.

Moynihan marshaled her to the side of the *Mary Louise* where a skiff hung, already suspended, waiting to be lowered into the water. In the darkness that seemed only barely broken by the half dozen lanterns scattered around the deck, she could just make out the shapes of four men already seated in the skiff. As she neared them, she found Raifer and the prince were the two in the stern. Flannagan's two men sat facing them, holding rifles aimed at their chests. The two prisoners were both haggard looking and dirt smudged, and, to Honor's horror, manacled. The rigors of the trip had been hard on them, she realized. She did not realize, however, how hard a toll it had taken on her until Raifer reached out a manacled hand to her when he saw her. A look of stricken concern came over his face.

"Honor?" he said softly.

But Flannagan stepped forward quickly, stopping

any possible exchange she might have with him.

"Get her in the bow," he directed Moynihan, and the younger man urged her forward with a forceful nudge to her back.

She moved on numbly, doing as she was bidden, climbing into the skiff as quickly as possible so as to keep from rousing either man's anger any further.

When Flannagan and Moynihan had settled themselves in the skiff as well, four of the *Mary Louise*'s crew lowered the small boat into the choppy waves, then lowered themselves by means of ropes to take up the oars.

Honor looked up at the bridge of the clipper as the skiff moved away from the *Mary Louise*. Captain Keenan was standing there watching, and a sudden wave of anger engulfed her. He could have done something, she thought. He could have helped us if he'd given me half a chance. Forgetting her fear of Flannagan, she half stood and shouted, "You've been a fool, Captain. And you've made a terrible mistake."

Somehow the words managed to fill the air before Moynihan grabbed her and forced her back to the hard plank seat. Honor saw the edge of anger in Flannagan's eyes, and she quieted, wondering if she'd transgressed too far, wondering if she'd have to pay for the words. She turned her eyes to the beach, to what appeared to be a half dozen flickering torches. An odd reception committee, she thought hazily. Then she turned back to the bridge of the *Mary Louise*, to her last glimpse of Captain Keenan, who watched them draw away with stoic indifference.

When they reached the shore, they were greeted by a half dozen men carrying lit torches. The wind tore at the flames, carrying them from side to side. They gave the appearance, in the darkness, of tormented ghosts, darting from the hands of inky, blurred specters who carried them.

The sailors jumped out of the skiff and pushed it the last few feet to the shore. Then Flannagan marshaled the prince and Raifer into the shin-high icy water. They moved clumsily, hampered by the manacles at their hands and feet, something that seemed to amuse Flannagan more than anything else. Finally Moynihan climbed out into the swirling lip of water, then lifted Honor out and set her down onto the damp sand with a clumsiness that made him seem unusually awkward. His hand firmly holding her arm, they made their way up onto the beach and to the small knot of men who waited with the others.

The group then stood and watched the skiff turn back to the *Mary Louise*. In the darkness Honor edged her way a bit closer to where Raifer stood.

"I'm not pleased with you, Miss Wainwright."

Flannagan's voice came from behind her, and when she turned she found his eyes on her, hard and unpleasant.

"You made a mistake back there."

Honor tried to ignore the threat she heard in his tone. "Is it that you're afraid Captain Keenan will think about what I said?" she asked him. "Are you afraid he'll realize eventually that it was the truth?" she smiled at him in the darkness, pretending to be as sure as her words seemed. "He will, you know. And when he does, he'll send the authorities."

Flannagan stared at her thoughtfully in the darkness in silence. And then he laughed. "You're right, Miss Wainwright. But it won't matter. By the time any of that happens, it will be too late."

He pushed her, and she stumbled, nearly falling into Raifer, who managed to catch her, despite the manacles on his hands. He put a protective arm around her shoulder. Honor found the warmth of his body close to her oddly calming.

"Leave her be, Flannagan."

Despite the manacles, despite the obvious hardship the journey had been to him, there was still some threat in Raifer's tone.

"My, how brave we are, Mr. Farrell," Flannagan hissed as he moved forward and stood facing Raifer. "Need I remind you, my bargain with McGowan was for your life. It made no mention of the condition you were to be in."

"Brave words, Flannagan," Raifer snarled back at him. "Are you brave only when your opponent has chains on his hands and feet or when you're dealing with a woman?" He pushed Honor gently behind him and he stood facing Flannagan, full of defiance.

"You presume too much, Farrell," Flannagan snarled. Then he drew back his fist and swung.

Raifer danced aside, avoiding the blow, deflecting it with his elbow. Then he lowered his head and ran forward, forcing his shoulder into Flannagan's stomach. The Irishman grunted and fell back into the sand, landing with a dull, unbelieving look on his face.

Raifer's advantage was short lived, however. Moynihan and one of the strangers who had met them on the beach raced after him, catching him by the shoulders and holding him firm.

Flannagan got slowly to his feet. It was obvious from his expression that he was unhurt, save for his ego. And that, Raifer quickly realized, was

255

probably the most dangerous part of him to have injured.

Flannagan drew a knife from his belt and held it thoughtfully out as though considering it. "I think you need a lesson, Farrell," he said as he approached Raifer. He brought the blade to Raifer's cheek, letting its cold steel side touch the skin. "Do you have any idea what I could do with this, Farrell?" he asked slowly. "Have you any idea how much misery a man can endure without it actually killing him?"

Raifer drew his head back, but with his arms held, there was not very far he could go. The movement seemed to please Flannagan. He seemed to consider it an act of withdrawal.

"Remember, Farrell," he said, and then he smiled, a tight, thin-lipped, threatening smile. He pulled the knife away and resheathed it. Then he motioned to the two men who held Raifer.

They pushed him forward, and he fell into the sand.

"That's better, Farrell," Flannagan said as he considered him. "I like to see a man who knows where he belongs." He smiled again and turned away.

Honor ran to Raifer and dropped to her knees beside him.

"Why did you do that?" she demanded as she offered him her arm to help him to his feet. "You stood no chance against him, manacled like this. He could have killed you."

Raifer smiled crookedly at her. "I just thought he needed another target at that moment, Honor," he told her.

She leaned back on her haunches. "Do you think what he said is true?" she asked him. "Do you think no help will come for us?"

His expression grew sober. "I don't know," he admitted softly.

Then there were hands roughly pushing them both forward into the darkness. Honor thought about what had just happened, about the absent satisfaction that seemed to come over Flannagan's expression as he'd threatened Raifer. *He's right*, she thought with a dully petrified awareness. *There won't be any help for us.*

She plodded forward through the damp sand and up a rock-strewn scarp with the others. It was a terrifying realization. A man without humanity or morals had their lives in his hands.

"My God, it's a crypt. Although modesty prevents a catalogue, I must admit to having slept in odd places before. But never one quite so strange as this."

Prince Edward was trying to remain jovial. He smiled pleasantly at Honor, then nodded at Raifer. "Are you all right, old man?"

Raifer grunted softly as he lowered himself to the heap of straw that was to be his bed. He rubbed his arm thoughtfully. "This is still as sore as hell," he said as he settled himself. "And Flannagan's little helpmates didn't do it much good, I'm afraid." Then he looked up at the prince and smiled. "You know, since the night I first met you, Your Excellency, I've been shot, beaten, threatened, and made to endure sanitary situations that would make any gentleman cringe. I don't suppose anyone's ever told you you weren't exactly a lucky fellow to be around?"

Edward shook his head. "I don't think anyone ever had the emotional wherewithal to say such a thing to me. Unlike you, my dear Raifer, most people seem to be at least a bit impressed by my position."

Honor let her gaze drift between the two men. An easy camaraderie had obviously sprung up between them during their period of confinement on the *Mary Louise*. An odd combination, she thought, a New York City policeman and the heir to the British crown. But then, she told herself, anyone with half a brain would find it more than just a bit odd to find the three of them locked in this dank, musty-smelling hole in the ground.

She made her way to the heavy metal grate that kept them securely from the set of stone steps leading up to the yard above. She put her hands to the bars and shook them only to be rewarded with little more than a dull rattling sound.

"Don't waste your strength, Miss Wainwright," Edward told her gently. "That wrought iron is at least a century and a half old, and they made things to last in those days."

She turned back to face him. "But we can't just sit here. We can't just let them do this to us without at least trying."

She turned and looked at the damp stones that made up the walls of their prison. She could feel the unnerving finger of panic that was creeping into her. It had began when their captors had marched them past the dark outlines of the old church and into the graveyard. She felt as though she were being buried alive being left there. It was all too ominous a feeling for her to dismiss.

As she stared at the stones, she realized she could make out those blocks with roughly carved names, the names of those who had been buried behind the heavy granite.

"I can't sleep here," she murmured shakily.

Raifer stood up and made his way to her. He turned her to face him, lifting her chin with his hand until her eyes met his. Then he smiled gently.

"I'd not thought you the type to fear the odd ghost, Honor," he said softly as he slipped his arms around her.

For a second she hesitated and held herself stiffly away from him. And then Honor felt herself melting toward him, wanting the comfort and warmth of his body close to hers.

"I'm not," she replied shakily. "Only one. Papa's."

She closed her eyes and let her head fall against his chest. But shutting away the light could not shut out her feeling of being in a tomb, and of her own responsibility in the circumstances of her father's death. The awareness of the bodies lying so near to them grew, and with it it brought back the memory of Daniel's still body with painful clarity. If only she'd kept out of it, she thought, if only she'd never accused him, perhaps he'd never have gone to the warehouse that afternoon. If only she could go back and change the events of that day, he might be still alive. Instead, she would forever have the memory of the sight of his body, still and bloodied, lying in the mire of the tunnel. She pressed her eyes more tightly shut and only succeeded in making the image in her mind that much sharper.

Raifer could sense her pain. He held her gently, wishing there were something more he could do to comfort her. "It's at McGowan's and Flannagan's feet, Honor," he whispered softly. "You can't blame yourself for what happened."

She shook her head vehemently. "It's as much

my fault as theirs. He wouldn't have been there but for the things I said to him." She drew back and looked up at him once more as her expression hardened. "It's my fault," she murmured once more.

And mine, he thought as he stared back at her. It was there, in her eyes, even though she left the words unsaid. A sickening realization gripped him, the realization that there would always be that thought standing between them, that his investigation had been the beginning of the chain of events that had led to Daniel's death. He stood and watched her as she turned her back to him and once more wandered slowly to the heavy wrought-iron gate that held them prisoner.

Edward cleared his throat noisily. "There's one note of comfort to all this," he ventured.

Both Raifer and Honor turned to face him.

"Flannagan's got no reason to see any of us dead," he said firmly, "and every reason to keep us alive. That assures me this place is nothing more than a temporary prison." He attempted a pleasant grin which quickly disappeared as neither of his fellows returned it. He stood and made his way to the large heap of hay against the far wall. "I rather relish the thought of a night's rest without the movement of a choppy sea beneath me," he said as he settled himself onto the pile. "And I think there's nothing we can accomplish tonight in any case."

"The prince is right, Honor," Raifer said firmly. He moved to her and put his hand to her shoulder. "Come get some sleep. Tomorrow, in daylight, things will seem a bit easier, perhaps."

She shook her head. "There's no daylight in a tomb," she told him.

But she allowed him to draw her back to the pile of hay. She stood, indecisive, and watched him as he sat and held up his hand to her. Then she shrugged and dropped to her knees beside him. He put his arms around her and they lay side by side in the hay, huddling together for warmth.

"Flannagan won't keep us here long," Edward said as he leaned back and yawned. "I've a feeling he has other plans for us all."

His words had been intended to be comforting, Honor knew, but somehow they, like the surroundings, seemed ominous to her. Whatever Flannagan's plans for them, she felt certain they would bring nothing good.

Edward's prediction was correct. It seemed to Honor that she'd just gotten to sleep when she was wakened by the loud sound of creaking caused by movement of the heavy door at the top of the flight of stairs they'd descended the night before when they'd been brought to their prison. This time the noise was followed by a long shaft of daylight falling down the stairs from the outside yard above. Honor stared at it, almost unbelieving, feeling almost as though she'd forgotten what sunlight looked like.

Flannagan descended the stairs quickly, his footfalls on the old stone steps making a sharp clicking noise as he moved. Behind him, Moynihan and two others followed at a more sedate pace.

"Good morning," Flannagan greeted them with mock cheeriness. "I trust you've all slept well?"

"Like the dead," Raifer replied stonily.

Flannagan laughed. "How appropriate, Farrell. And now it is time for you to join the living."

"Then you're not leaving us here?" Honor asked, almost afraid to believe they were being released from the place.

"But certainly, Miss Wainwright. I've a busy day planned for each of you. It wouldn't do for you to miss even a moment of the activities."

"Activities?" Edward asked as he sat up and reached for his boots.

Flannagan smiled again. "Of course, Your Excellency," he sneered. "You don't think I would let you waste this opportunity I've given you, do you?"

"Opportunity?"

"To address an unfortunate lapse in your education, Eddy." Flannagan drew out the name, expecting, perhaps, the prince would rise to the taunt. He didn't, so Flannagan was forced to continue. "I've appointed myself master," he said evenly, "and you, you see, are student. You are about to learn what it means to be Irish, Catholic, and poor."

Edward finished pulling on his boots and got to his feet. "You're quite mistaken if you think I'm unaware of your grievances. Nor do I think them entirely groundless. I've met with Gladstone on several occasions to address the Irish problem . . ."

"Irish problem, is it, Eddy?" Flannagan interrupted, his tone sharp. He moved forward, his stance threatening. "Shall I show you what I think of your opinion of what you call the Irish problem?" He balled his hands into tight fists.

Edward held his ground, not backing away or giving Flannagan so much as an inch. Honor felt herself mentally applauding his tenacity, even as she realized how futile it was.

"Is that what this is all about?" Edward asked. "To show me how your poor live? Do you think we have no poor in London? There's nothing you can show me that I haven't seen already a hundred times over."

"Oh, you've seen it, Eddy. In the way you see a drama when you go to the theater, as something so remote you can feel yourself secure from contamination. But now you're going to live it. We'll see if that doesn't change your viewpoint just a bit."

Edward shrugged. "Very well," he agreed. "And then what?"

Flannagan smiled his humorless smile. "We shall see, Eddy. I might just send you back to the Queen to tell her what you learned. Or I may perhaps send you back to her in little pieces, as a warning. It all depends on how good a student you are, how well you apply yourself. We begin now. You start by bowing and addressing me as 'sir.'"

For the first time Edward cringed and he colored with anger. Flannagan's threats had made no perceptible effect on him, but the demand that heir to the throne of England act servilely was obviously beyond his ability to ignore.

"You can be damned," he told Flannagan through tightly clamped teeth.

Despite the fact that Edward was taller and broader, Flannagan was the fitter and stronger of the two. There was no doubt in either his mind nor Edward's who the victor would be were it to come to a fight. But Edward simply stood and stared at him, mutely obstinate, refusing to offer up his pride despite the knowledge that Flannagan would extract his price for the act of defiance.

Raifer started to move forward, but Flannagan's escort was at his side, holding a pistol against his ribs, while Moynihan held onto Honor. The two of them were helpless to do anything.

Flannagan smiled at Edward, and as he had the

night before, he drew his knife. But rather than move toward the prince with it, he motioned to Moynihan to bring Honor forward.

"Let's see how much your precious pride means to you, Eddy," Flannagan said slowly. "Is it, perhaps, more important to you than your honor? Would you offer it up for a lady?" He moved the blade close to Honor's face.

Edward was appalled. "Don't hurt her," he shouted at Flannagan.

"On your knees, Eddy," Flannagan ordered him.

"No, don't," Honor protested.

Edward ignored her and did as Flannagan had bid him, falling to his knees.

He eyed Flannagan, silently considering him.

"That's good, Eddy," Flannagan told him calmly. "It's best to think these things out. Now, you will address me as 'sir.' "

"As you like, Sir Flannagan," Edward sneered angrily. But beneath the weak attempt at defiance was the realization that he could not win, the awareness that he was, at least temporarily, defeated. He might defy Flannagan if only he were to suffer for it, but there was no question that he would allow Honor to be hurt for the price of his pride. He knew it, and he knew Flannagan knew it as well.

"Very good, Eddy," Flannagan said as he motioned Moynihan to pull Honor back. "I think it time you and our friend Farrell start to learn a trade." He grinned. "A good, honest, Irish trade." He turned to Raifer. "How do you feel about fish, Farrell?" he asked.

Raifer shrugged. "Quite warmly," he replied. "In fact, it would please me no end to feed you to them." He smiled pleasantly at Flannagan.

Flannagan sobered, his expression turning hard once again, whatever amusement he'd derived from Edward's small defeat immediately vanishing. But he said nothing. Instead, he put a hand to Edward's shoulder and pushed the prince as he stumbled to his feet.

"Hurry up," he said. "It's full dawn and there's work to be done." Then he turned back to Raifer. "And lest you have any brilliant ideas of performing in any manner other than as you are directed, either of you, I will remind you that Miss Wainwright will be held hostage against your actions. She will be made to suffer for the slightest infraction." He strode to where Moynihan held Honor, put his hand to her arm, and twisted it.

Honor paled, but she held back the cry that came to her lips.

"All right, Flannagan," Raifer shouted. "You've made your position clear. Leave her be."

Flannagan released his hold on Honor's arm. "Good," he said, his tone mild now. He motioned to his men, then led the small procession up the damp flight of stone stairs to the graveyard above. The air was thick with the scent of the sea. The sun, although bright, had not had time to burn off a thick mist, and wisps of it lingered, hovering just above the ground, swathing the grave markers. Waiting at the entrance were two more of Flannagan's men, specters in the mist themselves.

"You four, take the men to the boat," Flannagan directed.

He moved to Honor and once again took her arm, his touch this time only slightly more gentle than it had been earlier. Together they stood in the morning damp and watched the group of men as they made off toward the beach. After a while,

Flannagan pulled Honor around and pushed her in the opposite direction.

"Where are you taking me?" she demanded.

"I think you might be in need of a bit of reeducation of your own, Miss Wainwright," he told her. "You are about to learn how to dig potatoes. It should be a pleasant change from the idle life you've led till now."

Honor held her tongue. She could stand digging potatoes, or scrubbing floors, or whatever else he might think it necessary to set her to do. But somehow, deep inside her, she was aware of the nagging suspicion that he intended something worse for her, far worse; this was just a preamble to his real intentions.

Chapter Thirteen

William Ewart Gladstone put the heels of his hands to his temples and rubbed them vigorously, as if the movement might somehow erase the words on the paper on the desk in front of him.

The motion was far from characteristic. The prime minister was known by his staff as being completely controlled, even under the strongest provocation maintaining a perfect aloof British veneer. One of his younger assistants had once, after having overindulged in strong drink, suggested to a companion that the prime minister undoubtedly even made love fully dressed, and managed to do so without so much as wrinkling the crease in his trousers. The remark made the rounds, causing a fair amount of amusement. Unfortunately for its originator, however, it cost the young man his position and his career, precipitating his rather hasty departure to a less than glamorous post in Jaipur, where he labored uselessly, hoping for the reprieve of a posting to a more illustrious office.

Well aware of that young man's fate, the assistant who stood facing Gladstone, one Charles Carter by name, swallowed the comment that came to his lips regarding his superior's previously undisplayed sign of human emotion. Instead, he leaned forward and asked cautiously, "Is something wrong, sir? You aren't ill, are you?"

Gladstone looked up, apparently surprised by the inquiry, then hastily dropped his hands back to a more refined position on the desktop, as if he'd only just realized where they'd wandered to and intended to rebuke them for their folly at his earliest convenience.

"No," he replied quickly. "I'm not ill." He lifted the sheet of neatly printed foolscap. "You've read this, I assume?"

Carter nodded. "Do you think there's any possibility that it's a ruse, sir?" he asked hopefully.

Gladstone shook his head. "Would that it were."

"But the reports from New York, sir . . ."

Gladstone scowled slightly, then once more shook his head, this time vehemently. "Are valueless. Despite their efforts, the authorities there have uncovered nothing. Which only means that this," he pointed to the sheet once again, "is, more than likely, quite genuine."

"Her Highness will not be pleased," Carter ventured with a sympathetic nod of his head.

"No," the prime minister granted, "Her Highness will be most surely displeased." He stood decisively, his action one of will, like that of a brave man facing the last steps to the gallows. "And I have the distinctly unappetizing honor of bearing the tidings." He looked at the younger man thoughtfully. "If you've ever envied the power of this chair, Carter," he said, pointing to the large, heavily carved mahogany armchair he had just vacated, "let this be proof to you that it is not always the most comfortable place to sit."

He turned and stared out the large window behind his desk, at the remains of what was, in milder weather, a scrupulously tended garden. Even now, despite the chill of early November, a few last roses showed brave small splotches of color, red and pink and yellow, amidst the general bareness of the turned-under beds. In the late afternoon drizzle, they seemed wildly out of place, like the sound of laughter at a funeral.

"Shall I have the carriage sent round, sir?" Carter asked softly.

Gladstone turned away from the window and looked at him quizzically. "What was that, Carter?" he asked.

"I wondered if I should have the carriage brought round for you, sir. To take you to Buckingham?"

Gladstone nodded resolutely. "No good putting it off," he murmured. "It certainly won't make it any easier."

As Carter disappeared through the door at the far end of the room to go about arranging for the carriage, the prime minister took a last look at the cold, bare garden. At that moment the empty trees and barren flower beds seemed quite reflective of his own life. Not that he hadn't forseen the eventuality of the letter. From the moment word had reached him describing the circumstances of the prince's disappearance, he knew that eventually the demands would be made. But his expectation in no way made the occasion any the less unpleasant for him. The presence of the actress found drugged in Edward's bed, the dead hall porter, the circumstances all pointed to Irish terrorists, for they had the most to gain by embarrassing the Crown and then hoping to extort concessions from it.

Victoria, of course, had been scandalized at the news of her son's disappearance, even more so when the prime minister had reluctantly revealed the details of the kidnapping to her. Now, with the terrorists' demands to add to her displeasure, he could only look forward to an excruciatingly painful interview. For a moment the thought slipped into his mind that perhaps it would be less cruel to keep the news from her and simply go about the business of doing what he could to get the prince released. But even as he considered the possibility he dismissed it, knowing that it would be not only foolhardy, it would be virtual suicide to try to withhold such information from the Queen.

Resigned at least to the inevitable, he turned, lifted the piece of foolscap from the desk, then crossed the room, following the same path Carter had taken. The young man was waiting just outside his office door, hat, coat, and walking stick at the ready, as well as the sturdy leather case in which the prime minister carried those documents of state that could not be dealt with in the confines of his offices. Gladstone handed him the ransom note, then allowed the younger man to help him into his coat. As he pulled on his gloves and adjusted his hat, he watched Carter open the leather case and place the note carefully inside, then close and lock it.

Carter stood silent, holding out the case. Gladstone eyed it, aware that he seemed to feel something akin to physical revulsion at the thought of taking it. He grasped his gold-tipped walking stick firmly, then took the case with a decisive movement, swallowing his disinclination in the name of duty.

"The carriage will be waiting for you, sir," Carter said as he watched the older man step through the door. Gladstone thought he detected a hint of pity in Carter's tone. What surprised him more than its presence was his own feeling that he rightly deserved it.

The prime minister found his assistant as good as

his word as he stepped out to the white-graveled courtyard. His coach, shiny black lacquer with his coat of arms discreetly emblazoned in gold on the door, was there waiting, the driver sitting with his cloak turned up at the collar to ward off the damp drizzle, the footman standing ready to open the door as Gladstone stepped out into the courtyard.

"The palace, Dick," the prime minister directed, aware of a deep-seated reluctance behind his words. Then he climbed into the dark leather comforts of the carriage and settled himself while the door was gently closed behind him. There was the first sudden jolt as the horses started forward, followed by the comforting clip-clop of their hooves on the cobblestone street.

Unfortunately, the sound ended all too quickly, and he found himself inside the gates of the palace, staring at the familiar face of Dick, the driver, who held the door open for him.

"We're here, sir," the coachman ventured, surprised to see that the prime minister was staring off sightlessly rather than moving briskly, as was his habit.

"Yes, thank you, Dick," Gladstone muttered absently.

He forced himself from the leather-cushioned seat and out of the carriage. He stood before the door only a second, squared his shoulders with sharp determination, and marched forward.

The Queen was busy entertaining her daughter, Princess Beatrice, and her new grandchild, Princess Victoria. The young mother, round and pink-cheeked like her baby, sat and watched as Her Majesty the Queen dandled her child and sang a nonsense song in a rather high-pitched, toneless voice. Plump and neat, dressed in her widow's black, holding the baby and singing, Queen Victoria seemed to the prime minister like any comfortably domestic granny. It was only with great concentration that he told himself she was his sovereign, and likely soon to be a rather unpleasantly cross sovereign at that.

Gladstone knew the Queen relished every opportunity to be with her children and grandchildren, encouraging these visits, but for the life of him he could not quite understand why Victoria had not canceled this particular visit considering the circumstances of Edward's situation. He strode into the Queen's fussily appointed private sitting room, and stood discreetly apart, silently waiting for her to recognize his presence.

Her song finally finished, Victoria reluctantly returned the child to her daughter.

"Beatrice, my dear, I must ask you to excuse me now," the Queen said without so much as turning to Gladstone. "I'm afraid the good prime minister has something very important to tell me, or he would not venture to arrive here unannounced at this hour." She turned, finally, to where Gladstone stood patiently waiting for her. "Is that not so, Mr. Gladstone?"

"I'm afraid it is, Your Majesty," he replied evenly.

Dutifully, Beatrice took the child into her arms and stood. She ventured only the slightest nod toward the prime minister before she left the room. When she had gone, Victoria's round face compressed with the pressure of a scowl. She looked down to her black silk skirt, where Princess Victoria had honored her with the gift of a heavily gummed silver and ivory teething ring. There was a small patch of damp in the royal black silk where the ring had been. The queen lifted the bit of silver, took a white lace-trimmed linen handkerchief from her pocket, and carefully dried the trinket, then dropped it to the table beside her chair before finally looking up to wave the prime minister to the chair opposite hers.

"Well, Mr. Gladstone, shall we dispense with the pleasantries this once?" Victoria asked, peering at him with sharp, round eyes. "What have you come to tell me?"

Gladstone nodded, put his case on his knees, and opened it. "We have received a ransom note, Madame," he said as he withdrew the letter and held it out to her. "The envelope was postmarked Dublin. My people have examined it, but hold little hope of tracing it as the stationery is of a common sort, as is this, as you can see."

Victoria grasped the piece of foolscap gingerly, as though the touch might in some way contaminate her. She stared at it a moment, and her hands began to shake. Reluctantly she returned it to the prime minister.

"I'm afraid I must impose upon you to read it to me, Mr. Gladstone," she said.

He took it from her, daring a small smile of encouragement, then turned his attention to the words on the neatly printed page.

" 'We have the prince,' " he read, " 'and while we do not relish the use of violence, it is a measure we have been forced to take by your indifference to the conditions under which our countrymen must live. Our grievances have been well voiced many times in the past, but your government has until now listened with only a deaf ear and refused to address them. We suggest you see that the official position is changed, if you hold the life of Prince Edward to be of value. Our demands are these: The Church of

Ireland is to be disestablished, with all tithes terminated. Legal and fair limits must be mandated on the rights of landlords over their tenants. If motions to the effect of these demands are not introduced into the Parliament, with the endorsement of both the Crown and the Liberal Party within the fortnight, the prince will die. If, however, you meet our demands, and if the motions are carried, he will be released to you unharmed. Do not believe we will be endlessly patient. We are prepared to send you the prince's right hand to prove our determination. You have fourteen days.'"

Victoria paled. "The blackguards!" she shouted. "The barbarians!"

"Quite, Your Majesty."

"You will send troops to Dublin. They will scour the provinces." Victoria's lips tightened with a bristling anger and fixed determination.

"I do not think that would be wise under the curcumstances, Your Majesty," Gladstone told her calmly.

Victoria glared angrily at him. "Your advice was not sought, Mr. Prime Minister. My son's life is in danger, and I will see every possible measure is taken to have him restored to me."

Gladstone inclined his head respectfully. "Certainly, Madame. It is imperative that the prince be returned unharmed. Which is precisely why it would be imprudent to make a show of force. We would not want to push these people to act precipitously." He stared at her unflinchingly, firm in his stand.

The Queen considered him for a long moment before she turned away, letting her eyes wander until they found the teething ring on the table beside her chair. She lifted it and considered it solemnly before she spoke.

"Of course, Mr. Gladstone, you are absolutely correct. I'm afraid maternal emotion overrode common sense."

"An entirely understandable lapse, Madame, under the circumstances."

"What shall we do?" she asked, her tone turned suddenly submissive.

The prime minister felt a wave of pity for her. He restrained himself from reaching out his hand to pat her plump, shaking one.

"We do as we have been doing, Madame," he replied softly. "We keep this news, like that of the prince's disappearance, strictly among ourselves and those authorities who need to know. The Americans have cooperated in this matter with us, releasing news to their press that the prince has returned to England after his goodwill tour. We shall advise our own press that he has retired to Wales, to do a bit of fishing. We can not chance a collapse of the government due to lack of confidence at this point."

"But Edward," Victoria sighed. "How do we rescue Edward?"

Gladstone settled his shoulders. "I think we should make a show of giving these people what they want. After all, I had intended to introduce a bill disestablishing the C of I a bit later in this parliament. With a bit of work, I should be able to discreetly gather a reasonable show of support. The problem will be forcing a few hands without revealing our reason for haste in the matter."

"Why must these people resort to violence?" Victoria demanded vehemently. "They would have what they want soon enough in any case."

"Perhaps some people find it hard to be patient, Your Majesty."

Victoria's eyes flashed. "I only know I heartily dislike being bullied, Mr. Gladstone."

He allowed himself a small smile. "A most British attitude, Madame."

The fires died from Victoria's eyes, and her tone softened. "I trust you will not be idle, then, in the next few weeks," she said, turning her attention back to the teething ring in her hand.

"Indeed, Madame," he agreed. "Politics oftentimes seems highly inefficient to me, an engine that requires a huge amount of fuel to travel only a few feet. And I must oversee the progress of the team of investigators making discreet inquiry about the prince." He ventured an encouraging smile. "There is little else we can do at present."

Victoria did not seem comforted. "Perhaps you might make some suggestion as to what I should tell Princess Alexandra. She's written, wondering when she might expect to see her fiancé upon his return."

The prime minister considered the dilemma for a moment. "Yes, she would expect to have word from him and will think it odd that he does not visit her once he is supposedly returned from New York. Perhaps you should invite her here for a visit with you, Madame, and tell her what has happened. It might make it easier for you if you had a woman with you in whom you could confide during this time."

Victoria cringed. "How could I tell her about Edward's disappearance?" she asked him sharply. "How could I tell her about that, that actress?"

"You might wish to keep those particular details from her, of course. But I do feel her presence might make it a bit easier for you, Your Grace. And it would certainly forstall any embarrassing suppositions being voiced in the press."

Victoria nodded, obviously resigned. She fingered the ring in her hand, staring at it. The prime minister could see the brightness of impending tears in her round eyes.

"I wish I had Albert with me to lean on now," Victoria whispered.

Gladstone leaned forward to her. "Excuse me, Madame?"

She looked up at him quickly and forced herself into a more composed demeanor.

"I shall do as you suggest, Mr. Gladstone. And let us both pray that our efforts will be enough."

Chapter Fourteen

Honor had never felt so exhausted in her life. Had she had more energy and the inclination to think about it, she would have realized that she'd never been quite as dirty, either. As matters were, though, all she could think about was the empty feeling in her stomach and the myriad aches in her arms, legs, and back.

She had spent the day, like the previous five, digging through the rocky soil of a large field, picking potatoes. She'd not labored alone, but had worked beside a half dozen other women, all of whom made a determined point of ignoring her presence.

All, that is, save one, who had reached into the pocket of her skirt and produced a pistol the first morning when Flannagan had brought Honor to the field's edge. She was dark-eyed and sharp featured, like Flannagan, and although no introductions had been offered, Honor was sure they were brother and sister. They both seemed to have the same remorseless look about them. At first Honor had spent a good deal of her time wondering what had happened to the two of them in the past to sour them so. After the first morning, however, she'd had little thought but for the dull, unending aches the work left in her limbs and her back.

There was one young woman, however, whose

face haunted Honor even when she was brought back to her solitary prison at the end of the day. She was hardly more than a girl, really, dour-faced and painfully thin, and she carried beneath her a shawl a baby so tiny and quiet that Honor had not even realized it was there until the girl had gone to the side of the field to rest and nurse the child. Honor had stared, wondering at a baby that made no sound, no cry. It was only when the skinny girl had turned her eyes up to meet Honor's that she'd realized the baby was simply too small and weak to cry. Half-starved herself, the girl had little milk to give it, and so it clung weakly to life in silence.

"What are ye' starin' at?" the girl had cried out at her.

Honor had turned away, embarrassed, for the first time in her life feeling guilty for all those things she'd always taken for granted—food, and clothing, and a warm, safe place to live. It was suddenly more than obvious to her that the women around her were far less lucky.

When she heard the noise of the door being drawn open above, and saw the flicker of a lantern on the stone stairs, she simply assumed that Moynihan was bringing her dinner as he had the previous nights. She turned around, away from the metal gate, hoping to ignore him. Since they'd returned to the village, the young man had grown more and more surly with her, a fact which completely bewildered her. Close to his own people, he seemed to have come to the conclusion that he had a greater need to hate her.

This evening he was not alone. When he'd dropped the pot on the stone floor and gone back up the steps, she turned to find Flannagan in the cell watching her.

"It seems you've lost your charms, Miss Wainwright," he told her when Moynihan was no longer within earshot, the creaking door at the top of the stairs announcing his departure. "Being back here seems to help him remember who he is and who his enemies are."

"I'm not his enemy. I'm no one's enemy," she protested.

Flannagan only shook his head. "You're one of them, the ones who don't know and don't care. You're as good as the enemy." He considered her thoughtfully for a moment. "Do you know what it is that's eating at young Thomas's gut?" he asked.

Honor shook her head.

"His father had a farm, a tenant farm. And when he failed with his rent because of a bad crop, the landlord had him evicted. Only Tommy's dad, you see, had nothing else. He and his family had been on that land for three generations. There was nothing if they didn't have their land. And so he decided he wouldn't give up so easy, he wouldn't go. He was shot, Miss Wainwright—murdered— trying to protect his family and his home. And his oldest son, Tommy's brother, with him. Since he was twelve that boy has been carrying around that memory, the sight of the two of them dying, watching it in his mind over and over. I'd thought he'd begun to forget, back there in New York. It's good that he's back here. It helps him remember."

Honor drank in his words, the pleased manner in which he uttered them. His complacency suddenly revolted her, and she turned on him.

"No!" she shouted. "You play on his grief and his pain when it only serves to hurt him more, and you do it because it suits your purpose. You don't care about him. You don't care about anyone or anything but your cause."

Flannagan stared at her a long moment before he answered.

"You're right," said finally. "I don't care about his dad or his brother or his pain. Because one man more or less in pain, one man more lying in the ground doesn't matter. All that matters is that we change things."

With that he turned away, leaving her after securely locking the gate behind him.

"Enjoy your dinner, Miss Wainwright," he said. "You'll have company while you eat it this evening. The fishing boats are back."

With that he mounted the stairs. Honor stood, watching the flicker of light from his lantern fade as he mounted the stairs, then finally disappear.

It was only then that she approached the heavy iron pot Moynihan had left on the floor. She opened it gingerly, for the metal was still hot, and peered in hopefully. She tried to quash the feeling of revulsion that came over her as the now familiar aroma of boiled cabbage and potatoes rose to her nostrils. She replaced the top, hardly even noticing the fact that the pot held a good deal more than it had on the previous two nights. She was certainly not so hungry that she couldn't wait until Raifer and the prince was brought back to share her prison and her evening meal.

The thought sent an unexpected burst of pleasure to her. She hadn't realized until that moment how much she'd missed Raifer, how alone she'd felt in the time since they'd taken him and Edward. It's just that those other women treat me like a pariah, she told herself sharply. At least I'm not the enemy to him and Edward. Even if I am little more to him than an unfortunate byproduct of his job, at least he doesn't look at me as though I were the enemy.

Still, despite her rationalization, she could not dismiss the tingle of anticipation she felt at the prospect of his return. She tore off a piece of her now tattered petticoat, rinsed it in a cup of the water from the bucket in the corner of her cell, and proceeded to try to wash her face, feeling suddenly very inept and foolish. The water was cold, and left her face tingling sharply, and the makeshift washcloth, she found, was dark and grimy when she'd done.

She was making a vain attempt to neaten her hair, braiding the long blond tresses and pinning the braid at the nape of her neck, when the noise of the door being drawn open at the head of the stairs told her they'd come. She brushed uselessly at her soiled and rumpled skirt, then stood waiting, watching them descend the flight of stairs.

Her first glimpse of the two men quite startled her. They were both filthy, and rank with the smell of fish. And Raifer sported a thick red scar on his right cheek, just beneath his right eye.

"Is that the way you greet hardworking sailors home from the sea?" Raifer asked as she stood, numbly staring at them after the gate had been opened and they'd entered. She hesitated a moment longer, watching Flannagan as he relocked the gate behind them and disappeared up the stairs. Then she ran to Raifer, letting him enfold her in his arms, burrowing against his chest.

"It's a pleasure to see a pretty face, Miss Wainwright," Edward told her gallantly.

"And if I'd known the stink of fish was so attractive to women," Raifer added with a grin as she pulled away from him, "I'd have taken advantage of the fact a long time ago."

Honor sniffed. "You are a bit gamy," she agreed. "Both of you. But then I doubt I've a right to point fingers. The sanitary facilities in this less-than-fashionable hotel do leave a bit to be desired."

Edward groaned as he lowered himself to the pile of straw. "This is heaven compared to what we've put up with the last five days," he muttered, then sighed as he settled himself into the heap.

Honor put a tentative hand to the thick clot of blood on Raifer's cheek. "How did you get that?" she asked him. "I didn't know that codfish were all that violent."

"If that was all you'd eaten for three days, you might change your opinion," Raifer told her lightly, brushing off her inquiry.

Edward, however, was far less cavalier about the incident. "He got it protecting me," he told Honor. "One of the crew on the fishing boat thought he had a score to settle with me, and decided to do it with a grappling hook. I'd be dead if Raifer hadn't intervened."

Honor paled. "A grappling hook?"

"The prince seems to have a slight tendency to exaggeration, Honor," Raifer told her easily. "He was only a middling-sized sailor, and it was a very small grappling hook."

"You saved my life, Raifer," Edward persisted. "When this is all over, I promise you it will be remembered."

"These people have a bellyful of anger," Raifer said, wanting, obviously, to change the subject.

"After what I've seen in the last few days, it's not so very hard to see why," Honor murmured. She looked sheepishly at Edward. "Excuse me, Your Grace."

Edward smiled. "Please, Miss Wainwright. As we've already shared a bed for one evening," he patted the heap of straw, "and shall again, it appears, I think we can dispense with unnecessary formalities. Besides, I've gotten used to being called Eddy by everyone who finds speech with me bearable during the last few days." He grinned at her. "It would, however, be appreciated if you could manage it in a tone that didn't suggest the desire to kill. I've always felt myself a rather likable fellow. All this has been a rather great blow to my self pride."

"Very well," Honor replied with a smile. "Eddy."

"And I didn't mean to imply you should take the anger personally," Raifer told him. "You're simply a symbol, and suddenly a more than convenient target."

"In any case, there's little we can do about any of it," Edward said slowly. His eyes settled on the iron pot. "I don't suppose there's food in that, is there?" he asked Honor.

"That depends on your definition of the word," Honor told him, thinking of the messy limp heap of cabbage and potatoes.

"Anything even remotely edible," Raifer told her firmly. "With the single exception of boiled fish." He approached the pot and removed the lid. "Vegetables, it would appear," he told the prince.

"Excellent," Edward replied.

"You may not think so once you've tasted it," Honor warned. "If I wasn't absolutely certain there'd be nothing until tomorrow evening except some bread in the morning, I'd advise against eating it."

Edward smiled at her jauntily. "Bread? Did you hear that, Raifer? Can you imagine such luxury? I think Miss Wainwright lacks appreciation for the niceties of her situation."

"Perhaps," Honor said with only a slight grimace. She was surprised at how happy the company of the two men made her, how easy it was for her to accept their banter. She brought bowls and began to spoon up the limp pieces of vegetables. "I wonder what Madame Claudine would say if she could see what it is we're eating?" she mused as she held out a bowl to Raifer.

"Please, Honor, not when we're about to consume this mess," Raifer said as he took the bowl from her, eyed it doubtfully, then handed it along to Edward.

Honor handed him a second bowlful. "Well, I've an idea that might make things a bit nicer for us all," she said slowly as she put a few spoonfuls into her own bowl and considered it dolefully. "I've just been waiting for the two of you to return before trying it."

Raifer's eyes narrowed as he stared at her. "Honor, I think it's time I gave you a lecture on prudence."

She only shook her head. "I'm afraid it's a good deal too late in my life to try to teach me anything like that, Raifer," she said firmly.

"Would you perhaps consider telling us what this idea of yours entails?"

She shook her head once more. "I think talking about it will only make it seem more impossible that it does already," she told him. "It's best, I think, if I don't." *Besides,* she thought, *you'll just try to talk me out of it, and we can't afford to simply sit here and do nothing.*

"I don't think I like this, Honor," Raifer told her as he started to eat.

"It doesn't really matter if you do or not," she replied. "Besides, a man who goes up against a sailor wielding a grappling hook with only his bare hands is hardly in a position to suggest to anyone else that they should be prudent." She smiled at him pleasantly. "Don't you think?"

"I'm afraid she's being perfectly reasonable there, old man," Edward told Raifer with a small laugh.

Raifer scowled, first at the prince, then at Honor. Then he turned his attention to his food.

Honor watched him for a moment, wondering if he was right, if she was being foolish even to consider trying to escape. But then she realized she had little choice. If what she'd overheard Flannagan say to one of his men regarding his intentions for the prince was the truth, then there was little time. Five days, he'd said . . . if there was not news in the papers that Gladstone had managed to force a bill through Parliament disestablishing the Church of Ireland within five days, he would kill Edward and send his body to Victoria. That meant they were, all three of them, under sentence of death. She was under little illusion that he would allow them to live despite his promise to Kevin once he'd taken the prince's life. They would be far too dangerous to him for him to ever allow them to get away from him alive. So it seemed, unless Gladstone could somehow work miracles with the government they would all die within five days. Or unless one of them managed to escape and bring help.

One of them had to make a try, and she had no doubt but that of the three of them, it would be easiest for her. So despite Raifer's admonitions, she knew prudence must be her last concern.

* * *

Honor dropped a half dozen potatoes into her basket, straightened up, then arched her back, stretching, trying to ease the stiff, aching soreness. The cold, damp drizzle only seemed to make the hurt all the more pervasive. She looked around at the field of dark, clodded soil. It seemed to stretch on endlessly. Then she let her eyes wander to the dark-eyed woman, her warder, the one she thought of as Flannagan's sister.

Just as she suspected, the woman's eyes were on her, watching her, and there was the threatening movement of her hand toward the pocket that Honor knew held the pistol. Honor didn't bend back to the long row of potatoes, however, nor did she let her eyes flee those of the woman as she would have wanted them to do. Instead, she stared straight at her.

"I have to go into the woods," she said flatly.

The woman scowled, displeased, but there was little she could do to change the situation. She nodded, then motioned toward a small thicket at the far side of the field.

Honor dropped her hoe to the ground, letting it fall beside the basket, and began trudging through the damp dirt, taking long, purposeful strides over the heaps of clodded earth, taking care not to lose her balance in the uneven footing. She put her hand close to her side, feeling the weight of the rock she'd managed to slip into her pocket earlier that morning as she was digging for the potatoes. Its solidity helped her focus her thoughts, despite the uneven thumping in her chest.

She would have but one chance, she knew. And if it failed, she had little doubt but that this woman jailer would have even less compunction than Flannagan about using the pistol she'd displayed so threateningly. She'd seen the simmering anger in the woman's eyes, felt the silent heat of her hatred. Honor had absolutely no doubt but that she'd use the pistol with no regret whatsoever.

Honor eyed the copse as she neared it, sure that the thick growth of the bushes would mask what she planned to do once inside. If she were careful to make no noise, she need not worry about any of the others noticing. That, at least, was a small comfort. The risky part, she told herself, would be after, when she left the thicket and made her way to the wooded area beyond. The undergrowth there was not very dense, and she would have to skirt through the shadows of the tall trees, hoping they would afford enough shelter for her to move without being seen.

She bit her lip as she considered her escape. The area beneath the trees seemed all too exposed to her.

"Well?"

They'd reached the entrance to the thicket, Honor realized, and she was standing, considering, while her guard watched her. Fool, she said to herself; you're just arousing her suspicions. She darted a quick glance at her warder, then marched off through the narrow path into the thicket.

She found the spot quickly enough, a small hole that had been dug into the earth, the pile of dirt taken from it left to the side to be kicked back into the hole as it was needed. The first time she'd been forced to use it, Honor had found herself a bit revolted by the rudimentary arrangement. After seven nights locked in a hole in the ground, however, she had come to consider the openness of the woods far more congenial.

This time, however, she had no inclination to avail herself of the rustic facilities. She backed into a thick bush that bordered the open space, wedging herself between a tree trunk and the heavy undergrowth. Then she crouched down and waited.

"What be takin' ye' so long?"

Honor didn't answer, didn't even move except to tense herself. She could feel her breath coming in ragged little pants and knew she was afraid.

There was a stir in the bushes along the narrow path, and Honor peered out, waiting for her guard to come closer. Then things seemed to happen very quickly, the woman wandering into the small opening in the center of the thicket, looking around in puzzlement as Honor sprang out, the rock she'd hidden in her pocket now in her hand.

It took only a few seconds, the terrifying movement, the feel of the contact between the stone in her hand and the back of the woman's head. Honor forced away the feeling of revulsion, knowing she had no choice in the matter even as she stood over the woman considering the violence she'd committed.

Then she quickly knelt down, feeling at the woman's neck and finding the pulse, strong and even, and assuring herself there was no bleeding. Honor could only imagine what punishment Flannagan would impose upon his luckless compatriot, sure it would exact greater pain than she had.

She quickly searched the woman's pockets then, finding the pistol and holding it in her hand. She stared at it a moment, unsure. Then the image of her father falling returned to her, the sight of the blood on his chest, the sick, horrible realization that he was dead. With it came a flood of hatred for Kevin McGowan as well as revulsion for Kevin and Flannagan and all the rest of them. She stared at the pistol, realizing that if she took it, if she used it, she would be making the same choices Flannagan and his people had made, choices that negated reason and morality. If she allowed herself to choose violence over reason, she told herself, she would be as bad as the terrorists. She stood and heaved the pistol off into the thicket that surrounded her, hoping it landed deep enough in the underbrush to assure that no one would ever find it.

That done, she turned toward the back of the thicket, toward the side that faced the woods. She would have to force her way through the undergrowth, and she proceeded quickly, ignoring the sharp barbs of the thorns the bushes managed to imbed in her clothing and scrape at her skin. When she broke free of the thicket, she realized her face was marked with several long scratches and that some of them bled. She ignored the discomfort after wiping the drips of red from her cheeks, knowing she had no time to bother with trivialities.

She darted into the shadows of the tall trees that edged the field, eyeing the path at the far side that would take her back to the churchyard and the crypt where Raifer and the prince were still imprisoned, then beyond, toward town. She wished she could go that way, for at least the land was somewhat familiar to her. But that path was barred to her, as she had no way of knowing who in town was part of Flannagan's group. Raifer had told her that he and Edward had been forced through the streets on their way to the wharf, and no one had so much as looked at them, let alone made a move to help. No, if there was to be any help for them anywhere, it would have to be away from the town, inland, and she would have to make her way alone, hoping she could find a town with a constable and find it soon, before Flannagan learned of her escape and resorted to some act of violence against his remaining prisoners.

She started by following the path, only away from the church rather than back toward it. She'd been walking at a steady pace for almost a quarter of an hour when she thought she heard some faint sounds of excitement back from the direction she had come. She assumed her warder had awakened or been found. Now, she thought, now she would have to take care not to be seen. She began to jog along the path, moving as quickly as she could without allowing her own footfalls to drown out any sound from behind her.

It was just as well that she'd taken the precaution. Not more than half an hour after she'd heard the noises that she'd assumed marked the discovery of her escape, she heard the sound of hoofbeats on the trail following her. She ran off into the bushes at the side, ignoring the brambles at the path's edge, forcing her way through them and into the deep brush.

The hoofbeats grew louder, and she fell to the ground, trembling, afraid she'd been seen. It was not until the sound reached a peak and then began to grow weaker once more than she dared raise her head and look out at the path. She made out the shapes of three mounted men on the path in front of her. She was almost positive that one of them was Flannagan.

Honor stayed as she was for a few moments longer, afraid they might return. But as the time passed and the sound of the horses slowly faded away into silence, she forced some courage into herself and slowly stood. The very fact that they had come after her this way, she told herself, meant that it led to some safety. That thought was, at least, a comforting one, and she resolutely brushed away the mud and leaves that clung to her wrinkled, dirty skirt before she set out again, this time with a shade more determination in her step.

She walked now, though, not daring to run, afraid she might miss a sound that would mean she was approaching or being approached by one of her pursuers. The afternoon sunshine had begun to wane when she stepped out of the wooded path and onto a crossroads and well-worn road. There was a marker, arrows fixed to a tall stone pile. One arrow pointed back the way she'd come, and was lettered with the name Kinvarra and the notation 2 miles. The name meant nothing to her, but she assumed it was the town where she'd been held. There were two more arrows, each pointing to her left along the road; Ardrahan, 3 miles, and Loughrea, 7 miles. Honor read them thoughtfully. Three miles to civilization, she told herself, not so terribly far.

She set out with a firm step, telling herself she would be safe in some constable's office before nightfall, telling her story and arranging for help for the prince and Raifer. For the first time since she'd lifted the rock in her hand and let it fall against her guard's neck, she felt as if she might actually escape.

It had already grown dark, and the air, although beginning to clear from the dull dampness of the day, was stingingly cold when Honor realized she had not comprehended how slowly she would travel along the rugged, rutted road, nor how much her own uncertainty would slow her. That, combined with the fact that she'd twice hidden herself off the road as other travelers approached and passed her, combined to slow her progress substantially. She was cold and hungry, and it was fast becoming very dark. Still she had not found a town. Indeed, she'd passed only two farmhouses in the intervening hours, carefully skirting them making sure she was not seen. But now, as the sky around her settled into the dull grayness just before sunset, she realized she would have to make a choice. Either she could try to find some shelter where she could hide for the night and then go on in the morning, or she could take a chance, trust someone, and hope they would help her. Hiding might be safest for her, she knew, but it would also be the most dangerous for Raifer and the prince. The longer Flannagan knew she was gone, the more apt he was to make some move, either changing their hiding place or doing something more desperate. She would have to take the chance, she told herself. She would have to trust someone.

It was with a feeling of relief that she saw the manor house. It seemed to appear out of nowhere, atop a small hillside and surrounded by fields, the windows seeming too brightly inviting in the now almost complete darkness. She moved quickly along the narrow line of trees that lined the drive, not caring any longer if she was seen, not thinking of anything but the warmth and safety the manor seemed to represent. It was only when she was standing before the open door, facing a dour-looking woman in a black dress and a stiff white cap who stared at her with obvious distaste, that she realized it might not be as simple as she'd thought.

"I must speak to your master," she said firmly.

The woman only continued to stare. "Beggars by the kitchen gate," she said through tight lips.

Honor suddenly realized how she must appear, filthy and unkempt, stepping out of the darkness uninvited. No wonder the woman thought her a beggar.

"I am not here to beg," she said firmly, although she realized, in a way, that quite the opposite was true. "I am here on a matter of extreme importance."

Still the housekeeper's face showed distrust, but there was a small crack in her expression, no doubt brought about by Honor's insistence and manner. If she acted in the least cowed, Honor realized, she'd be sent off to the kitchen to beg for a crust. She decided to press her point while she had a small advance to her advantage.

"You will admit me immediately, and then you will summon your master." She might have been the Queen of England herself, she decided, if presumption were a measure of position.

The housekeeper hesitated a moment longer, then stood back, reluctantly admitting Honor into a large, stone-floored hall. "Wait here," the woman told her, punctuating the words with a look that clearly implied there would be penance to pay if Honor disobeyed. Then she crossed the hall to a door at the far end, offered one last glance in Honor's direction to assure herself that the intruder hadn't yet stolen anything or done anything else untoward, and knocked softly at the door and entered.

Honor crossed quickly behind her and listened to the conversation, determined not to lose this chance.

"Squire Blaileigh, there's a person wishing to see

you," the housekeeper announced. "A rather dirty, unkempt person."

"Another beggar," came the sound of a second woman's voice. "I don't know why they all find their way here."

"It's the least we can do, my dear, to offer someone who has nothing a meal and a warm place to sleep. It's our Christian duty."

That was a man's voice, not too low and a bit shaky, the voice of an old man.

"Send him round to the kitchen, Fairchild," he went on, talking now to the housekeeper. "You know the rules."

"She insists upon talking to you, sir," the housekeeper replied.

"A woman, John," the second woman's voice burst in, obviously shocked. "Now there are women out wandering the countryside. And demanding to see you. Of all the cheek."

Honor decided that if she were to await the housekeeper's return she would, indeed, be sent away. So she put her hand to the doorknob, turned it, and quickly entered the room.

"If you please, Squire Blaileigh, I must speak with you. I assure you it is a matter of the greatest urgency."

Three pairs of eyes turned to her with surprise and a bit of shock. Honor found that the voice had, as she'd thought, been a fitting one for an old man. He was a smallish, rather stout, white-haired gentleman with spectacles, and he sat in a large wing chair that seemed to dwarf him. Beside him, firmly settled in a settee, was an equally stout woman, of approximately his age, and wearing a decidedly less congenial expression. She dropped a piece of heavy-looking needlework into her lap and quite simply gaped.

"I'm sorry, sir," the housekeeper muttered as she moved toward Honor. Her intentions were obvious, to remove the foreign creature before she did any damage.

But Honor held up her hand, keeping the black-clad housekeeper at bay. "Please give me just a moment, Squire. If you wish it, when I've had my say, I'll leave. But it is important. I wouldn't barge in this way were it not."

The elderly man blinked twice. "As the, ah, young lady seems determined, Fairchild," he said, waving the housekeeper aside.

Reluctantly the woman backed away from Honor, but she stood ready by the door, obviously sure she would be called on to eject the strange intruder.

Squire Blaileigh peered up at Honor curiously. "Please, won't you sit, Miss . . . ?"

Honor dropped onto a stool by the fireplace, thankful for the warmth.

"My name is Honor Wainwright, sir," she said quickly. "I'm an American. From New York. As you may know, Prince Edward was recently in that city. What you may not know was that he was kidnapped, and is being held for ransom. I and a friend of mine inadvertently stumbled onto the kidnapping, and we were abducted as well."

Squire Blaileigh's face arranged itself in a doubtful scowl. Honor took a deep breath when she saw it, knowing she had little chance left.

"I know all this must sound insane to you, sir," she went on. "And I really don't expect you to believe it. All I'm asking of you is that you send for the authorities. Surely you can extend me the benefit of going that far."

The round little man took a bright white handkerchief from his breast pocket, removed his spectacles, and wiped them vigorously. Honor sat, trying to contain her impatience, watching him slowly replace the spectacles, then return the handkerchief neatly to his pocket. He turned to his wife and offered her a confused glance, one she returned in kind. Finally, he cleared his throat with a loud "Ahem" before turning back to Honor.

"You are perfectly correct in believing that your story, Miss Wainwright, certainly sounds rather bizarre to me. However, your speech confirms your contention that you are an American, and I can accept the fact that if you are mad, you are not, at least, a local madwoman."

Honor smiled at that and felt decidedly grateful for her New York accent. "I assure you, sir, I am not a local madwoman."

"That understood, I am willing to send to Ardrahan for the constable. I hope that will satisfy you?"

Honor heaved a sigh of relief. "It will more than satisfy me, sir. Thank you."

His wife offered Honor an evaluating glance. "Perhaps in the meantime, while we're waiting for the constable to arrive, you might accept our hospitality?" she asked.

Honor saw she was smiling, and realized that, despite the petulance of her voice when she'd spoken about beggars to her husband, she was as determined as he to do her "Christian duty," a fact for which she was profoundly thankful.

"Thank you, ma'am," she replied hastily. "I can't tell you how welcome a bath would be."

"A bath and something to eat, I should think," Mrs. Blaileigh said firmly as she stood, and bustled breathlessly toward the door. "Let's see what arrangements we can make for you."

"In the meantime," the squire said as he, too, rose, "I'll have word sent to the constable."

"I can't tell you, both of you, how grateful I am," Honor told them as she followed Mrs. Blaileigh to the hall.

"Nonsense, my dear," the older woman told her. "It's only our Christian duty."

Honor stifled the smile that almost managed to make its way to her lips and followed after her as she started across the large hall to an enormous flight of stone stairs.

A little more than an hour later, Honor was seated across from Squire Blaileigh in the rather sober dining room of the manor, freshly and comfortably bathed, clothed in a hastily taken in skirt and white linen blouse of Mrs. Blaileigh's, and happily consuming a considerable serving of roast beef. Clean, warm, and with her stomach contentedly full, she felt, for the first time in what seemed years, as though her life might be returning to normalcy. Only a few hours more, she told herself, and all this will have been just an unfortunate memory.

It was not, however, a thought without regrets. Once Raifer and the prince were recovered, she would return home to an empty house to face the reality of life without her father, without Raifer. But even that, she told herself, could seem almost like happiness when she compared it to the previous days.

"My, you were hungry, my dear."

Honor looked up at Mrs. Blaileigh, then down at her now empty plate. "I suppose I was," she replied sheepishly. "It's been weeks since I've eaten any meat." She smiled. "And this was very good. I don't know how I will ever be able to thank you for all you've done."

"Nonsense, my dear," Mrs. Blaileigh replied. Once Honor had proved that she was capable of using the correct fork at table, the woman's fears of her seemed to have vanished. "You have nothing to thank us for."

She was prevented from assuring Honor that she was only doing her Christian duty by the entry of the housekeeper.

"Yes, Fairchild?" the squire asked.

"It's the constable, sir," the black-clad housekeeper replied firmly, her eyes wandering to Honor and wordlessly conveying the admonition that there had never been need to summon a constable to the manor in the past.

"Send him along," Blaileigh bade her.

Fairchild bobbed a quick curtsy and disappeared. Honor dropped her napkin onto the table and pushed her chair back. She stared expectantly as the door opened and a tall young man dressed in a dark uniform entered. She sat frozen as he removed his hat and nodded toward the squire and his wife.

"I'm Constable Regan," he said affably.

"And it was a good thing you suggested I come along, Constable."

A second man entered the room, neatly clad in a dark suit and immaculate white linen shirt. Honor did not even need to look up at him to know who he was. His voice, she found, was unforgettable to her. All she could do was weakly mouth the single word, "No."

"This is the young woman you are searching for?" the constable asked.

"Yes," came the firm reply. "This is the young woman who escaped from the sanitorium."

"No," Honor said once again, this time louder, but with the same sense of disbelief.

"Come, Miss Wainwright," he said as he skirted the table to stand beside her chair. "You've put a great number of people to a great deal of trouble. It's time to return to the hospital."

"No!"

This time Honor screamed as Brian Flannagan put his hand firmly on her arm and pulled her to him.

Chapter Fifteen

Charles Carter pushed the report across the prime minister's desk.

"I thought this was curious enough to bring to you, sir. Of course, it might mean nothing, but at this point, I didn't think we could afford to overlook any possibility."

Gladstone scanned the page quickly, then looked up at the young man. "When did you receive this?" he demanded.

"Just an hour ago. It went through the usual channels, and someone had the good sense to route it to this office. But just the same, it took twenty-four hours to get here."

Gladstone grimaced. "Then the *Mary Louise* and this Captain Keenan will have already sailed," he said, his voice showing decided disappointment.

"I'm afraid so, sir," Carter agreed.

Gladstone turned his attention back to the page. "At least the sergeant had the good sense to be thorough about the particulars," he muttered. "Fifty-three minutes 2 north, 8 minutes 97 west. Let's hope the good captain was accurate. Where is it?"

"Galway Bay, sir. Just west of a small fishing village called Kinvarra."

"I don't suppose he cared to tell us why he waited more than a week to tell us about this unusual debarkation, did he?"

Carter nodded. "It's in the last paragraph of the report, sir. It seems that the officer in charge of the supposed extradition also had in his charge a young woman who was to be taken to a mental hospital near Adrahan for treatment. She insisted she was being kidnapped, and that one of the prisoners was Prince Edward. The captain dismissed her story as lunacy, but after the strange debarkation the officer insisted upon, he began to wonder if perhaps her story might not be true. He really wasn't convinced he wasn't acting like a fool, even though he was reporting the incident. After all, the officer presented him with all the proper papers for the deportation, all neat and legal, sir."

"Too neat," Gladstone muttered. "This isn't some insane terrorist we're dealing with, it's a large and very well-organized group. Extradition papers don't grow on trees."

"No, sir," Carter agreed.

"Well, at least we have a place to start looking, this fishing village, Kinvarra." Still, Gladstone seemed hardly elated. "More than a week. There's probably no trace of them there by now."

"Perhaps there may be, sir. There's been a good deal of violence there over tenant evictions of late. Even some killings, I believe. It sounds like the sort of place that might provide shelter to a terrorist with a plan."

"That's all the worse, Carter. A small town, and much of it with a grudge against the Crown. With a whole town's connivance, we'd be lucky if we could find an elephant in the town square."

The prime minister's brow wrinkled, a situation that seemed all too common of late, Carter thought.

"Shall I have some men sent to this Kinvarra, sir?" he asked.

Gladstone nodded. "With the admonition to be discreet, Carter. We can't afford to take any chances with Edward's life."

"Of course, sir."

Gladstone pushed back his chair, rose, and went to stand by the window. Carter realized that he had spent a good deal of time staring out at the garden during the previous few days.

"How is it going, sir?" he ventured. "With the lords, I mean?"

Gladstone turned to face him. "Slowly, Carter," the prime minister answered. "Nothing, it seems moves slower than Parliament. And with no prod to push them, I don't know if we shall meet the deadline the kidnappers have set for us.

He returned to his desk, and his features settled themselves into their habitual condition of rigid impassivity.

"Shall we get on with it, Carter?" he asked. "And remember to include the cautionary note to the men who are sent to this town, Kinvarra. The prince's life may very well depend upon it."

"What is going on here?" Squire Blaileigh demanded. "You, sir, will take your hand from that woman's arm."

Flannagan shrugged, and made a show of loosening his hold on Honor, but he did not release her. Instead he smiled and turned to the young constable.

"If you would be so kind, Constable?"

"Certainly, sir," Regan replied, then turned to Blaileigh. "This gentleman, sir, is Doctor Powers, from the sanitorium east of Ardrahan. When your man arrived in my office with the news of a strange young woman and a story about kidnappers, the doctor was there, reporting the disappearance of one of his patients, a young American woman, suffering from what the doctor described as delusional paranoia." He paused for a moment, turning to Flannagan for confirmation of this diagnosis, and received a solemn nod for his pains. "As the description seemed to fit, I invited the doctor along, just in case your young woman might be his young woman, sir. As indeed she seems to be."

"No," Honor cried. "It's a lie. His name is Flannagan and he's one of the kidnappers."

Flannagan only smiled easily at Blaileigh. "Unfortunately, Miss Wainwright is completely delusional. But if it would ease your mind, sir, I'd be glad to show you my credentials."

Blaileigh waved his hand. "Of course not, sir. That won't be necessary," he murmured, his gaze drifting sympathetically toward Honor. He seemed perplexed. "Her story, of course, was entirely unbelievable, but her manner was so, well, so convincing . . ." he murmured, almost as though he were making an excuse for his attempt to help her.

"That's often the case with patients of this sort," Flannagan replied, his manner placating, as much as telling the old squire he was not to blame for believing Honor. "Given the opportunity, they can often make one believe the sky is green."

"I am not delusional!" Honor cried angrily. She could not believe what was happening, that these people were talking about her as though she weren't there. "This man is not a doctor, he's a kidnapper, and most probably a murderer."

"Murder?" The squire's expression grew more perplexed. "There was no talk of murder."

"Back in New York," Honor asserted, hoping that

if she gave him a more detailed account, he might once more be convinced. "A hall porter in Prince Edward's hotel was shot. His body was found while I was there. And the murder was most likely committed by the kidnappers." She tried to pull away from Flannagan's grasp. "Please, you must believe me."

She stopped struggling suddenly, breathless, realizing that her agitation only made her seem what Flannagan had presented her to be. Indeed, she could tell from his expression that her outburst had only served to convince Blaileigh of one thing, and that was what Flannagan had told him, that she was totally deranged.

"Such a shame," he said to Flannagan. "Such a lovely young woman. Is there any hope for recovery?"

Flannagan shook his head with a great show of regret. "In these cases, not much, I'm afraid. But we try our best." He began moving toward the door, pulling Honor with him. She had no choice but to go with him. "I regret the inconvenience all this has caused you," Flannagan went on, his manner pleasant, placating, as he approached Blaileigh. "I hold myself entirely responsible."

"Nonsense, sir," Blaileigh replied. His glance wandered to Honor's face, then quickly turned away.

"Please, Squire," she begged him softly as he looked away. "Send word to the authorities in London. Tell them what I've told you."

Flannagan's hold on her arm grew sharp. "Enough of this, Miss Wainwright. You've put these good people to enough bother." He moved her quickly to the door.

The last thing she heard as Flannagan pushed her out into the great hall were Blaileigh's words, assuring the good doctor that he'd been put to no great bother, that he'd only done what any good Christian would do.

"I suppose he's one of your men too?" Honor asked as she sat in the carriage beside Flannagan, waiting for the young constable to join them.

"It pays to have friends in the right places, Miss Wainwright," he replied smugly. "Surely you must know that."

It took only a moment, and then Regan climbed in beside them.

"How could you?" Honor snarled at him as he settled himself across from her. "You're sworn to uphold the law, not foster criminals."

Regan stared at her a moment, then colored and turned away, sitting in silence as the carriage moved steadily through the darkness. It wasn't long before they'd reached the town, and Flannagan had the carriage drawn to a stop.

Regan turned to him. "I thank you for the ride, sir," he said deferentially. "And for clearing up what could have been a very complicated situation."

"And I thank you, Constable, for helping me to find my wayward patient. I shall have the hospital administrator send you a letter of official thanks in the morning. I know such things are sometimes helpful on a young officer's record."

Honor gasped at his words. "Then you aren't one of his men?" she asked Regan.

But it was too late. The damage had already been done. Her accusation had reinforced Regan's acceptance of what Flannagan had told him. He only flushed slightly and turned away from her.

"Thank you again, sir," he said, touching his hand

to his hat as he climbed out of the carriage.

"No, no wait," Honor cried, leaning forward, trying to follow him.

But Flannagan's hand was on her arm, holding her, and the young officer had by this time dismissed her as a madwoman, just as had Blaileigh.

Flannagan pulled her back to the seat, and the carriage started off once again, lurching into motion.

"You told me he was one of your men," Honor said bitterly, mourning her lost chance with Regan.

Flannagan smiled his superior smile. "No, Miss Wainwright. You said that. I just let you believe it."

"Where are we going?" she asked him dully. "Back to Kinvarra?"

"No," he told her. "I'm afraid that particular town might become a bit uncomfortable now, on the off chance that either Blaileigh or our young constable actually took the effort of reporting what happened this evening. I don't like to take chances. And so I've taken the precaution of moving our friends, Mr. Farrell and the prince. And just as well for you, too, I think," he added with a laugh. "It would suit Fiona to get her hands around your neck, I think."

"Fiona? That's her name?" Honor asked. "Did I hurt her badly?"

"Do you care?" Flannagan asked, his tone implying he wouldn't had he been in her place.

"Yes," Honor told him sharply. "If I didn't, that would make me the same as you, wouldn't it?"

"I doubt, my dear Miss Wainwright, that you've the certainty of conviction that is needed to fight for a cause." His glance grew sharp. "And that is the reason why we will win. We do."

She shook her head. "No. It's not conviction. It's

just the willingness to do violence. Any brigand has the same lack of scruples."

His face grew red with anger. So there's something that can reach him, Honor thought. He hates the idea of being thought anything but the righteous rebel leader.

"You haven't answered my question," she said, eager to change the subject, to change the look of outrage she read in his face, sure it would mean violence if she pushed him. "Where are you taking me?"

"Are you so afraid you won't find your accommodations to your liking, Miss Wainwright?"

"On the contrary," she retorted. "I'm sure they could be no worse than the previous ones you provided."

Flannagan smiled at that. "Why, I've arranged the ideal situation for you, actually."

"Where?" she asked again, her interest waning now, but her tone intent.

Flannagan shrugged. "Where would you expect me to bring a madwoman?" he asked her and then punctuated his words with a short, harsh laugh. "In any case, it won't be for long. Two days at the most, and then this whole bloody mess will be over and done with."

Honor's eyes narrowed, and she considered him sharply. "Two days?"

But Flannagan's interest in the path the conversation was taking seemed to have waned. He pursed his lips in thought as he returned Honor's stare. After a moment, his expression sobered and grew decidedly intent.

"You realize you've put me to a good deal of bother. It's lucky for you that neither the squire nor that young idiot of a constable was convinced by your tale. If they had been, I would have been forced to kill them. And that would only make matters all the more dangerous."

Honor paled. "You're serious," she murmured.

"This is a serious game we're playing, Miss Wainwright." He looked at her without blinking. "And landlords and constables are, after all, the enemy. If you want to know, I might even have taken a good deal of satisfaction in dispatching them. But that would only have drawn attention, and that's something I can't afford just yet. So for all our sakes, it's just as well that they believed you to be deranged." He smiled grimly. "Perhaps you should consider the fact that it is quite easy to make people believe you aren't quite balanced, Miss Wainwright."

"Doesn't anything mean anything to you?" Honor demanded. "Don't you feel any compunction whatsoever about taking a human life?"

Once again she could see the anger filling his eyes. "I care, Miss Wainwright. I care about my people. As for the others, this is a war, and they are the enemy. You are the enemy. And in a way, the object is to kill as many of the enemy as you can."

Honor turned away, repulsed by his words and frightened by the certainty she saw in his expression. He knows, he's absolutely certain he's right, she thought. And no one and nothing will sway him. For such a man, no act is too repugnant, as long as he believes it will further his cause. She, Raifer, and the prince were nothing more than objects to him, objects to be manipulated as long as it served him to do so. And to be disposed of once their usefulness was done.

* * *

"For God's sake, Honor, how could you be so stupid as to go off and do this? You could have gotten yourself killed."

Honor hadn't expected this sort of reception. She was shaken and confused after the long ride in the darkness and Flannagan's frightening presence, and she wanted to be petted and comforted. She didn't know what she had expected from him, perhaps to be praised for her attempt. But certainly she had not expected him to blame her.

Tears crept into her eyes. "I was only trying to get help," she protested weakly.

"We told you we'd decided to cooperate," he told her firmly.

Flannagan seemed entirely pleased with the progress of their conversation. "Well," he said, "as you've no doubt a good deal to discuss amongst you, I'll bid you a good evening." He slammed the heavy wooden door behind Honor and locked it.

"I heard him say he was going to kill Edward," Honor went on, ignoring Flannagan's departure. "That if Parliament didn't move to meet his demands, he was going to kill Edward."

She stared at Raifer beseechingly, trying to make him understand, not knowing why, but needing his approval, not his anger.

"That's just talk, Honor," Raifer told her, his tone fairly loud, as he walked past her and looked out the small, barred hole cut in the door. "It's just talk to frighten Gladstone and the queen. No one's going to be hurt."

Honor stared at him, not understanding what he was doing, and sure she hated him for his lack of concern for her.

"Certainly, my dear, you don't think Mr. Flannagan would waste so worthwhile a hostage as I am?" Edward asked her. He was addressing her, Honor realized, but his eyes were on Raifer. "We're all quite safe as long as we cooperate."

Raifer turned away from the door. "It's all right," he said softly. "They've gone." He moved to Honor's side, and this time there was sympathy in his tone, not anger when he spoke to her. "Are you all right, Honor?" he asked. "He didn't hurt you?" He saw the liquid in her eyes and reached out to her, pulling her to him.

She pushed against his chest, backing away from him. "I'm stupid, don't you remember?" she said testily. "I nearly got all of us killed."

"I'm sorry, Honor," he told her evenly. "But I wanted to make Flannagan believe we intend to be perfect prisoners. Your little escapade rather suggested something otherwise. Not to mention being dangerous for you." He put his hand to her chin and pulled her face up to his. "I was worried about you, Honor," he told her softly.

Honor felt a thick thud in her chest. His eyes, his tone, they were telling her more than that he'd felt some vague discomfort for the disappearance of a fellow prisoner. They were telling her that he'd felt real pain, real loss.

"Were you, Raifer?" she asked him. There was a pleasant throb of expectancy within her.

He released his hold on her and stepped back suddenly, as though he realized she were asking him for something he was unwilling to give her.

"Of course I was," he told her abruptly. "We both were."

Honor received his words as if they were lead weights falling into a pond. They were followed by ever-widening ripples of regret, and a feeling of shame that she had allowed herself to think there would be anything else, to wish there might be more.

"Yes, worried and responsible, Honor," Edward spoke up. "If anything had happened to you, I would never have forgiven myself."

Honor didn't turn to him, but continued to stare at Raifer. "You'd neither of you have been to blame. And neither of you have any responsibility for me." Her words were bitter, like her tone.

Raifer's eyes found hers. "Honor," he whispered.

She turned away. "Where are we?" she asked. "It was dark when Flannagan brought me in. There was a gate, but I couldn't see much. Just this building. It looked long and low from the outside, but I can't be sure. And there didn't seem to be much of anything else nearby."

"You're probably right," Raifer told her, his tone dry and businesslike now. "I think we're on an estate of some kind. This place certainly had the feel of stables when they brought us in. And there's a huge old building not far away. I caught sight of it when they were herding us from the wagon and in here. They were quite anxious that Edward and I might be seen, it seemed, not at all like they were back at the fishing village. Which leads me to believe that Flannagan doesn't quite control this area as well as he did Kinvarra."

"And which also suggests that we might be able to find help fairly easily if we can manage to get out of here," Edward said brightly. He looked at Honor sympathetically. "Perhaps more easily than did you, my dear."

Honor shook her head. "If I hadn't made all the wrong choices, said all the wrong things, perhaps we wouldn't be here now. But Flannagan was always one step ahead of me, it seemed." She quickly outlined the events of her day. "He seemed to know just how far I could get, just where I'd go for help. But the worst of it was the way I reacted when he walked into that room. He calmly stood there and called me a madwoman, and all I could do was act in a way that proved to everyone he was right."

"You mustn't blame yourself, Honor," Edward insisted. "Flannagan knows the area, knew where you could go for help, where he could go to keep you from getting it. And the man has far more experience and talent at dissembling. We shall simply have to best him at his own game next time around."

"Next time?" Honor asked. "I thought we were to behave like model prisoners."

"That was for Mr. Flannagan's ears, my dear. A bit of dissembling of our own."

Honor smiled at him. Edward's politeness and perfect manners had begun to endear him to her, as did his seemingly constant British determination to remain cheerful and controlled despite adversity. He'd make one an ideal older brother, stalwartly supportive and dependable. But a man without fire, she decided.

Unlike Raifer, who silently smoldered with his own beliefs, his own thoughts. She turned to him, wondering what it was he was thinking, wondering how after all they'd been through he could still seem such a stranger to her.

"I suggest we all sleep," he said. "Tomorrow we'll have to solve the problem of getting out of here."

Edward nodded, then sniffed slightly. "I think your evaluation of the past of this place is correct, Raifer," he said. "It certainly has the air of a stable. And I'm not quite sure I like Mr. Flannagan's insinuations. First he accommodates us in a crypt, and now in a horse's bed."

"Wouldn't it be pleasant to return the favor?" Honor asked.

Edward's expression sobered. "More than you can imagine, Honor, my dear," he said evenly. There was no question but that he meant it.

"I can't believe how you've bungled this whole operation, Flannagan. First in New York, killing that old man and Wainwright, when we agreed there would be no killing, that unnecessary violence only worked against our cause. And then you get us saddled with two extra hostages, prisoners we don't want and certainly don't need. Now you've let the girl escape, and there are men asking questions in Kinvarra. Government men, most likely."

"If you will recall, I told you that old man Wainwright's death was not to be laid at my door. That was Kevin's doing. And I got the girl back, and no harm done."

Flannagan glared at the well-dressed man seated in front of him. He hated feeling like a recalcitrant schoolboy, hated accounting for himself. Most of all, he hated this man's satisfied smugness, his certainty that he could have done better.

"No harm? What if someone in Kinvarra talks?"

"No one is going to say anything. They're all for us in Kinvarra."

"People make mistakes, Flannagan. Something of which you should be only too aware after the last few weeks. We wouldn't have to worry about any of this if you'd made better arrangements from the start."

"It doesn't matter. We've moved them. Nobody

back in Kinvarra knows anything that can hurt us. And I've sent a message to Gladstone, moving up our deadline. If there's no mention of passage of the bills in Parliament in two days' time, they'll have their prince back, dead. They don't have enough time to do anything that could endanger us."

"You've just made the biggest mistake, Flannagan. You've underestimated your enemy. Do you think Gladstone would send idiots to find Edward for him? Eventually someone will talk about Miss Wainwright's little adventure with the good Squire Blaileigh. It shouldn't take them very long to piece the bits together after that. All of which means we are not as safe as you seem to think we are. I intend to take over, now that I'm here. I'll handle matters directly from here on."

"There's no need for that," Flannagan sputtered angrily. "I know what I'm about."

"I'm sorry to say that you don't, Flannagan. And our cause has no time for you to learn your role just now."

"Our cause?" Flannagan's voice rose. "Where do you find your brotherhood with those of us who are watching our lands taken away, our children starve? What do you know about causes?" He glared at the other man, at his perfectly tailored suit, his pristine white linen. "Rich men have no need for causes."

The other glared back at him, then stood slowly and leaned toward him over the table that separated them. "This whole plan was mine," he said slowly. "Do you remember what you said when I first suggested it? That the crown was inviolate, that you could do anything except move against the royal family. I proved you wrong. I do not intend to let you ruin the opportunity I've made for you. And I do not intend to allow you or anyone else question my dedication or my motives."

Flannagan glowered at him, but said nothing. After all, it was true what he said, about the plan being his. But he'd taken none of the risks, he'd never gotten his hands dirty. All he'd done was talk.

"Bring Edward here, to me. I think it time we induced him to send the proper sort of message to the Queen, one that will convince her to bring some pressure to bear on Parliament."

"I've sent a message to Victoria," Flannagan countered defensively.

"And it obviously was not very effective, was it?"

Flannagan felt the tinge of a flush creep to his cheeks. He hated this man, he decided. And somehow he'd see that there was repayment for the insults that were so freely offered him.

"What of Farrell and the Wainwright woman?" he asked.

The other shook his head. "No, leave them. You can take care of Farrell any way you see fit, and soon. I don't care what you do with him so long as the body isn't found. As for Miss Wainwright, she's not to be harmed. And I don't want her to see me here. I'll arrange for passage back to New York for her. Comfortable, but slow passage. Slow enough so that by the time she arrives there, all this should be over."

He scowled at Flannagan, apparently noting the obstinate, cold stare he was being given and not liking it. He nodded his head toward the door.

"Get Edward," he said sharply. "Now."

Flannagan held the lantern high so it would cast as large a circle of light as possible. Three heads rose, and sleep-blurred eyes opened to look up at him with confusion.

"You, Eddy," Flannagan said sharply, "get up. We've a visitor who wants to talk to you."

Prince Edward rubbed his cheek and eye with the heel of his hand, then groaned slightly as he staggered rudely to his feet. Honor was surprised by his quick acquiescence to Flannagan's orders. Two weeks before, surely, he would have offered some resistance. Now, however, he seemed ready to follow his kidnapper's directions without complaint. How quickly, she thought, we come to accept a situation, no matter how heinous.

"Where are you taking us?" Honor demanded. "Who has come to see us?"

Flannagan crossed the room to her and looked down at her as she sat up in the heap of straw on which she'd been sleeping. An idea was beginning to form in his mind, a way to get back as he'd promised himself he would. The woman, he mused . . . Terrence's precious intended.

"He's here to see Eddy, Miss Wainwright. Not you. But don't worry. We've other amusements for you." He reached down and grasped her arm roughly with his hand.

Raifer lunged towards him, intending apparently to catch him by the knees, to unbalance him and throw him to the ground. But Flannagan heard his movement in the straw and turned just in time. He lifted his foot and brought it down in vicious contact with Raifer's belly. Raifer fell back and rolled himself into a fetal position, grasping his stomach.

"As for you, Farrell," Flannagan told him with apparent satisfaction, "I've plans for you, too. So don't feel as though you're being neglected. It really warms me to know you haven't lost your urge to fight. Somehow, it wouldn't be quite so pleasant if you were cowed and accepting."

Then he motioned to the two men with him, to take the prince's arm and hold him.

"If you would be so kind as to escort Eddy," he instructed then with an unpleasant smile.

They nodded, and pushed the prince out of the room.

Flannagan once again grasped Honor's shoulder and pulled her roughly to her feet. "And you, Miss Wainwright, will come with me."

He pushed her toward the door, then out into the corridor beyond, pulling the door closed behind him, letting it shut with a loud bang behind them, a solid, final sound.

The last glimpse Honor had of Raifer as she turned when Flannagan paused to bolt the door was of him staggering to his feet and running painfully after them. The door, however, was slammed shut before he reached it. Flannagan locked it, drawing the heavy bolt across and dropping it into its slot.

"If you so much as touch her, Flannagan," Raifer shouted, "I'll kill you. With my bare hands, I'll kill you."

"We'll see about that, Farrell," Flannagan replied with a laugh. He stood with his fingers biting into Honor's arm and watched as the prince and his escort disappeared out into the darkness of the night. Once they were gone, Flannagan's grasp on Honor's arm tightened, and his manner grew uncharacteristically agitated. He pushed her along the long, door-lined corridor.

"Terrence's precious, inviolate intended," he snarled angrily.

"It's Kevin, isn't it?" Honor asked him. "He's the one who's come."

She felt herself grow cold with fear. Kevin had

come with the money he'd promised Flannagan, and for some reason the Irishman had determined to reneg on his bargain. Perhaps Kevin hadn't brought as much money as he'd promised, perhaps he'd changed his mind and brought none at all. From the look she saw in Flannagan's eyes, there was no question but that he intended to do her harm.

"You made a bargain with him," she cried weakly as Flannagan pulled open one of the doors and pushed her into a small, empty room. "You gave your word, you promised not to hurt us."

Flannagan sneered at her. "Some bargains are made only to be broken," he hissed as he started toward her.

Chapter Sixteen

It became immediately apparent that Raifer's evaluation that the building had once been a stable was correct. Their small prison had been hastily cleared of stalls, emptied, and altered to accommodate a stout door and bars at the windows. As her eyes adjusted to the light, Honor realized that the room to which Flannagan had brought her had been left untouched. The stall divisions remained, and it was into one of those that Flannagan pushed her, watching her fall back and land against the hard, bare wooden floor with obvious satisfaction.

"I don't think your intended will find you quite as acceptable when I've done with you," he snarled at Honor.

"You, you can't," she stuttered as she tried to edge her way backward, away from him. "Kevin, the money he promised you."

Flannagan's hands fell to his belt buckle. "The hell with McGowan. The hell with his damned money. I've a bill of my own to collect, a personal bill, and you're about to pay it."

Honor scrambled to her feet and backed away from his advance until her feet banged into the wall behind her and she realized there was no place left for her to go.

First she felt his hands on her, pushing her against the hard stone wall, holding her. And then his lips were on her neck and she could feel the hard press of his body close to hers.

"No," she screamed, even though the cry, she knew, was useless. She felt herself flood with panic. There was no one to help her, no one who cared but Raifer, and he was locked into his prison.

She pushed against him, then balled her hands into fists and beat against his chest, only to find that that, too, had no effect on him.

Guided by instinct and her panic, she managed to lift her hands to his face. She dug her nails into his cheeks and drew them downward, feeling a perverse satisfaction at the bright red welts of blood that appeared in their wake.

She'd hurt him, she realized, for he released his hold on her and drew back a bit, putting his fingers to the scratches on his cheek, then staring, rather dazedly it seemed to her, at the drips of red that smudged his fingers. He's used to giving pain, she thought, not feeling it.

Flannagan wiped his bloody fingers on his pants and turned back to stare at her.

"Stupid bitch," he snarled at her through clenched teeth. "You're only making it harder on yourself."

"You'll have to kill me first, Flannagan," she screamed at him.

Her terror, she realized, had begun to fade, pushed aside by the fearful certainty of what he intended for her. As long as she stood, terrified and wondering what he planned to do to her, she had been weakly in his power. Now that she knew, it seemed she had found the strength to defy him.

He started for her, but she managed to dart past him, slipping through his fingers and out of the stall. At first she seemed to be running blind, into shadows and the unknown, for the light that drifted into the room was dim, only the moonlight through the window at the far side, and that was obscured by a drifting layer of night clouds. Then her eyes managed to pick out something in the darkness, the shine of dull metal against the wall, and she ran toward it with all the speed her terror had ignited.

Her hands found the pitchfork, and she pulled it from its hook, scratching her fingers against the rough wooden stall wall as she snatched it. She spun around, that the tines' sharp edges caught Flannagan in the shins as she hefted the fork and brandished it at him.

He backed away a few steps, a look of anger and pain on his face, until he was just beyond her reach.

"Stupid bitch, you can't get away. Put that down," he said very softly, his words very clear, very even, as though he were telling a naughty child how to behave.

Honor lifted the pitchfork slightly, her move clearly threatening. "You stay away from me," she panted. "Come one step closer to me, and I swear, I'll stick it into your heart."

That seemed to amuse him more than anything else. He smiled at her.

"No, you won't," he told her firmly. "You may hate me, but you haven't the stomach it takes for killing. Even if you had the physical strength to do as you suggest, which I seriously doubt." His hand strayed to a leather harness at his shoulder beneath his jacket. When he withdrew it, he was holding a dangerous-looking knife.

"I, on the other hand," he went on, "have absolutely no compunction about carving you up. Now drop that thing, or that is exactly what I will do." He stared calmly at her. Then, pointing the knife at her threateningly, he began to move slowly forward.

Honor knew he was right. The pitchfork offered her little more than a barrier, a way to hold him at bay for a few moments longer. However sharp the tines of the pitchfork might be, they would not simply slice into him, and she lacked both the physical strength and the emotional makeup to take another human's life even were the tines sharp enough to do what she had threatened to do. There was one thing of which she was absolutely certain, however, and that was that she'd be damned before she'd simply stand there and let him do what he wanted without fighting him or trying to escape.

She waited until he was close to her.

"So much for the brave revolutionary, fighting for the freedom of his people," she hissed at him. "You're nothing but a common rapist, masquerading, trying to cover up what you really are."

His reaction was fast, just as it had been in the carriage when she'd made the same suggestion, that he was nothing but a common brigand. His face contorted with anger, and he lunged forward at her, grabbing the pitchfork and attempting to pull it from her grasp. Honor waited for a second, holding tight and struggling, letting his anger take control of him. Then she shifted her weight forward, heaving the pitchfork toward him with all her might, pleased to see the surprise her continued defiance brought him, even more pleased to see the handle of the pitchfork fly forward and strike him on the temple. He stopped, momentarily stunned, dazed by the blow.

Honor began to run, heading for the door that would take her back out to the long, empty corridor, to the room Flannagan had made into a prison, to Raifer. That was her one thought—that if she could only get back to Raifer, somehow she would be safe.

She felt a movement of the air just behind her, and

knew that it was Flannagan's hands reaching out for her. Somehow she managed to evade them, and then there was a clatter in the dimness as just behind her Flannagan tripped over the fallen pitchfork and fell forward.

There was a dull thud, then a sharp, loud moan of pain. She turned and saw Flannagan struggling to his knees. When he'd fallen, he'd obviously landed on the knife he still grasped in his hand. It protruded from his shoulder. Around it there was a sticky, irregular circle of blood.

He stared up at her, and his eyes were filled with undisguised hatred. "I'll kill you, bitch," he hissed at her as he staggered to his feet.

Honor stood, frozen, not quite believing, as she saw him standing unsteadily, staring at her. He raised his hand to the knife hilt and pulled it out, dripping red, and pointed it at her. Then he lunged.

Honor screamed. The echo of her own cry managed to unroot her from the horror of what she'd seen, and she turned and ran, out of the room and into the long central corridor of the empty stable, panting as she fled toward the room where Raifer was imprisoned. She turned back only once, to see Flannagan coming after her, his face contorted with pain and hatred, the red stain on the knife mirroring the thick, dark flow that leaked from his shoulder.

It seemed to take forever, but finally she found the door with the heavy bar across it. Her hands trembled, and she had trouble grasping it. All the while there was the steady advance of Flannagan's footsteps behind her.

Finally, she managed to grasp the bar securely and she lifted it, pulling it up to release the door.

"Damn you."

The words were spoken softly, and close to her, too

close. Without thinking or bothering to look, she turned quickly, swinging the thick wooden bar as she moved.

It came into shattering contact with Flannagan's chest, close to the knife wound. He gasped in pain, then fell, the knife dropping from his hand and clattering to the stone floor at Honor's feet.

She felt the bar being drawn from her hand and looked up, numb, to find Raifer standing beside her.

"Get the knife, Honor," he told her calmly.

She nodded and knelt, her hand reaching out to the bloodstained blade.

But Flannagan, it seemed, had not yet admitted he was bested. He pushed himself away from the wall, toward her, intending to grab her and use her as a shield from Raifer. She felt the touch of his fingers on her hand.

Then things seemed to be happening very slowly. Raifer's fist came in contact with Flannagan's chin, once, then a second time. The Irishman fell back and lay, finally still and blood spattered, on the stone floor. Raifer went to him immediately and put his hands under Flannagan's arms.

"Open the door, Honor," he said evenly as he began to drag Flannagan's still body across the hall and toward the now empty cell. "The door, Honor," he said again, this time sharply, and looked at her when she made no move.

She was staring at Flannagan, her eyes wide.

"Is he dead?" she asked dully.

He shook his head. "No. Only unconscious. And we've got to get him tied up and locked up and ourselves away from here before he comes round. Now will you get the damned door?"

She nodded and moved dazedly to the door, pulling it wide open and holding it for Raifer as he pulled Flannagan through.

"I suppose it would be too much to hope that no one will find him for a while," Raifer said. "There's too much blood out there to be ignored."

Honor looked at the long smear of red against the dull off-white of the floor stones. She turned away quickly, gagging, her stomach heaving. The gore brought back all too vividly the picture of Daniel's body.

Raifer dragged Flannagan over to the pile of straw and then straightened up and stared at Honor. He felt a pang of regret as he recognized the pain in her expression, the lost look of shock. He wished he could go to her, hold her, comfort her hurts. But there was no time for that . . . not if they intended to get away.

"Honor. Come here," he told her firmly. "I need your help."

She responded almost mechanically to him, turning to him and moving into the room. She watched as he stripped off Flannagan's coat and shirt, then tore off a long strip of the linen.

"Here," he said as he handed her the blood-spattered shirt. "Tear off more strips."

She took it from him and watched as he began to tie Flannagan's hands behind his back. The sick feeling still gripped her, but somehow she managed to do as he directed, tearing off long strips of fabric from the shirt and then holding them out to him.

Raifer took the pieces from her and quickly tied Flannagan hand and foot, then made a gag which he tied around the Irishman's head. Honor stared at his work, at Flannagan's still body. The knife wound in his shoulder still bled profusely. She felt sickened to realize that she had been the cause of that dark, thick flow.

"We can't leave him like that," she protested as Raifer stepped back.

He stared at her, not understanding.

"He'll bleed to death," she explained and pointed to the wound.

"It's not that serious, Honor," Raifer protested, and started to take her arm.

But she balked. She wasn't sure why, but she knew she couldn't leave Flannagan like that, not if there was the possibility he might lie there and slowly bleed to death. Perhaps it was the image she'd had of her father's body. She simply knew she couldn't just leave him like that.

"For God's sake, Honor, the man's a kidnapper and a murderer. He killed your father!"

"Kevin killed my father," she told him, and her features hardened. Kevin, she thought, she would gladly watch bleed slowly to death.

Raifer shrugged, then grabbed up the remainder of the torn shirt and knelt beside Flannagan. As he hastily bandaged the wounded shoulder, he realized that she was right, that Flannagan ought to be tried, that he had no right to pass his own death sentence on the man. It irked him to recognize the fact that she had forced it on him, that he'd been too involved in his personal desire for revenge to see what would have been obvious to him under any other circumstances.

When he'd done, he straightened up once more and moved quickly to her side. He put his arm around her shoulder and turned her away, toward the door.

"He'll be all right, Honor," he assured her. "More than well enough to face a jury of his peers. Now we've got to get out of here and find some police, or he'll never face a jury."

This time she let him lead her out of the stables and into the night darkness without protest.

The night air was damp and sharply cold. Honor shivered as she stood beside Raifer at the edge of the circle of light cast by the lantern in the stable. She had no idea where they ought to go, what they ought to do. She turned to him, waiting for him to make the decisions for them.

He hesitated only a moment, taking his bearings. "If I remember correctly," he said as he pointed off toward the right, "the building I saw when they brought us here was in that direction. That must be where they took Edward." He turned to her. "Honor," he said slowly, "I think the best thing is for you to try to get to the nearest town. Bring back some help."

She shook her head vehemently. "I tried that, Raifer. Flannagan made them believe I'm deranged. The town's probably full of it by now—the madwoman who escaped and went to Squire Blaileigh with a tale about a kidnapped Prince Edward. No one will believe me."

He considered her a moment. "Then I want you to stay outside, out of danger. If I manage to get Edward out of there, we'll find you. If not, you get out of here and make your way to safety as best you can." His expression softened as he looked at her. "I wish I could promise you more."

Honor looked up at him, at the blue-gray of his eyes, deciding they were as unfathomable to her as he was. At that moment, she thought she saw tenderness in them, and wistful yearning. She wished she could believe that look meant something, meant that he felt for her what she knew she felt for him. But his eyes had lied to her before, she reminded herself, just as his words had.

She forced her thoughts back to their situation, telling herself she was a fool to think of anything else.

"No," she said slowly and shook her head. "I've as much interest in seeing Edward released as do you. After all, my father died because of this insanity."

He put his hand to hers, cupping it in his own, and stared down at her, wondering why her eyes seemed so mournful, so pained.

"We'll make our decisions when the time comes," he told her gently. "In the meantime, I suggest we get out of here before someone comes looking for Flannagan."

With that, they started off along a well-groomed path, her hand in his, heading in the direction to which he'd pointed moments before. It wasn't long before they saw lights and an indistinct form in the darkness. The shape of the building gradually grew clearer as they neared it, a huge, rambling structure, a small palace, really, with towers and a crenelated battlement at the roofline.

"What is it?" Honor asked, not sure if she was imagining the whole thing. "It looks like something out of a fairy tale."

"No fairy tale, Honor," Raifer replied as he drew her off the path and into the shrubbery when they drew close. "Unless you consider Flannagan an ogre."

"I do," she assured him.

He grinned, then sobered quickly. "It was probably some laird's fortress five hundred years ago, and the country estate of some minor noble for the last century or two," he told her as he considered the mansion.

Honor shook her head slowly. "I don't know what it was in the past, but it certainly looks like it's a prison now. Look."

She pointed to the windows on the upper floors. They were secured with iron bars.

Raifer groaned.

Honor turned to him. "What is it?" she demanded.

"Can you read the sign near the large door?" he asked.

She turned and squinted into the darkness at a large brass plaque at the side of the front entrance.

"Ardrahan Sanatorium," she read aloud. "No wonder Flannagan had no trouble convincing that constable he was a doctor and I his escaped patient. He probably had false papers, like the false extradition papers he showed Captain Keenan."

"And very bad news for us," Raifer said. "We'd never be able to get into a hospital unnoticed, certainly not at night, when the patients are locked in their rooms."

"Then what do we do?" Honor demanded.

"What I wanted you to do in the first place," Raifer told her. "Go to the nearest town and bring back some help."

"I told you, Raifer," Honor replied. "It's impossible. After I told that story about Edward, and Flannagan made me seem to be a lunatic, no one will even listen to any more tales of a kidnapped prince. They'll just lock us up as deranged and cart us back here."

"That just means we'll have to tell them some other story," Raifer said as he put his arm to Honor's waist and began to walk away from the sanatorium entrance.

"What story?" she demanded, hurrying to match her steps to his longer stride.

"When the times comes, we'll know," he told her confidently. "In the meanwhile, I suggest we hurry. I don't imagine they'll let Edward stay here long once they've found Flannagan and realized we're gone."

His words, Honor found, were not the least bit comforting.

"Ardrahan," Raifer read from the signpost when they reached the town. "It doesn't look like much, does it?"

Honor peered into the darkness. There wasn't really very much for her to see, just a few dozen smallish, dark, looming shapes along a not-very-straight street, a dark spire climbing out of the shadows at the end of it, presumably that of the church. There were some lights, mostly carefully husbanded behind closed and curtained windows. Only one building seemed to show any life, the one that sported a crudely lettered sign above its door spelling out the words *The Spotted Calf* and beneath the uneven lettering, a hopeful sketch of a rather lumpy looking animal illogically equipped with both horns and udders.

Despite the uninviting sign, however, Honor looked at the tavern with real envy. She was tired, and incredibly cold. Some alcohol and the warmth of a fire would have a welcome effect on her, she was sure. She turned to Raifer and saw him eyeing the tavern's sign just as she had done.

"What do we do now?" she asked him.

"If I had the wherewithal," he said wistfully, "I'd suggest a brief detour with a strictly medicinal brandy. You look like you could use one, and I sure as hell know I could. But as I was relieved of my coin some two weeks ago, and as I assume credit to an unknown would be unthinkable to the average tavern keeper, I'm afraid it's out of the question." He peered along the narrow street. "So it would seem we get about the business of finding the town police station or gaol or whatever they call it hereabouts." He smiled at her reassuringly, then took her arm and tucked it into the crook of his own. "A pleasant night for a bit of a walk about town, don't you think, Miss Wainwright?" he asked.

His levity was lost on her. "It might be," she responded, "if I had a coat and if the sky showed even the slightest evidence of a few stars or even the moon that seems to have vanished behind all those clouds in the last hour or so. Then again, I seem to be having a hard day today, so perhaps it's unfair of me to pass judgment."

Raifer pressed the hand he held on his arm. "It will all be over soon, Honor," he told her gently. "You'll be able to forget it all ever happened and get on with your life."

Honor looked up at him. He had intended the words to be comforting, she knew, but they only served to remind her that he would soon be only a memory as well. It was an awareness she could accept only with the accompaniment of a numbing feeling of bitterness.

"There it is," he said, and turned to lead her toward what appeared to be a rather bleak storefront.

"What do we tell them, Raifer?" she asked tremulously. "You said you'd know when we got here. Well, we're here."

"So it would seem," he replied dryly. "I suppose it depends on whether your constable, the one who was with Flannagan back at that manor house, is there or not. If he is, I'm afraid it will involve your being incarcerated for a while. If possible, I'd rather avoid that."

"So would I," she agreed vehemently. "I never want to be behind a closed and locked door again in my life."

Raifer grinned. "Well, not one you can't open, anyway," he agreed. "But one meant to keep the world out wouldn't be so unpleasant a thought, now, would it?"

Honor thought of how he'd closed and locked the door to the study of the house where he'd been staying in New York, of what they'd done behind that closed and locked door. More than anything else she wished she could go back to that morning, relive it, make time somehow stand still and never let it end. Had it been in her power, she'd go back to that morning and hold onto it, keep it from turning into an evening that would find her father dead. Her throat filled with a dull, hard lump of hurt at the memory.

"You haven't told me what you plan to tell them inside," she reminded him as she pushed away the thoughts of that morning from her mind.

He considered her pained expression as he led her up to the door. "Just follow my lead," he told her confidently. "If you see the constable who knows you, let me know. Otherwise, do as I do. And try not to talk, if possible. That accent of yours will give us both away."

She swallowed hard and squared her shoulders as he opened the door and they walked in. Whatever the appearance from the outside, inside there was no mistaking the large room for a shop of some kind. There was no question but that was a police station. A low wooden gate separated the front, with its row of empty, hard benches, from the desks beyond. At that moment only one seemed occupied, and that by a barrel-chested, white-haired man in a slightly rumpled dark uniform.

Raifer offered Honor a sidelong glance, and she

responded with a quick shake of her head, assuring him that this was not the constable who had so readily handed her over to Flannagan earlier.

The big man looked up at them at the tinkle of the bell that sounded as Raifer shut the door behind them. It was only when she saw his suspiciously considering look that Honor realized how rumpled and disheveled the two of them must appear.

"How can I be helpin' you?" the officer asked in a tone that implied that he doubted very much if he could help them at all. He pushed aside the evening paper he had been reading. Raifer stepped forward to put his hands on the low wall and leaned toward him.

"Thank the good Lord," he said in the thickest brogue Honor had ever heard. "I was thinkin' I wouldn't be makin' it this far alive."

The constable's brow furrowed. He stood and made his way around his desk to open the narrow gate and let them into the official part of the room.

"What's all this about not bein' alive?" he demanded. "Who are you?"

Raifer pushed Honor forward, then into a chair beside the desk. Then he fell, apparently exhausted, into one himself.

"My name is Raif Farrell," he said. "I'm an orderly out at the Ardrahan Sanatorium. At least I was, until this afternoon. This lady here is Miss Kathleen O'Shaughnessy. She's a nurse out at the sanatorium. And we're both of us lucky to be here alive." He looked up, steely-eyed, into the constable's doubtful stare. "I don't know how it came about happenin', but the inmates from the violent ward have got loose. They're holding the doctors and most of the staff, threatenin' to kill 'em all. It was only pure chance that Miss O'Shaughnessy and I managed to escape."

Honor looked down at her hands and found they were shaking in her lap. This is too preposterous, she thought. They won't believe him. And of all the names to choose, Kathleen O'Shaughnessy! Preposterous.

But apparently the constable seemed quite gullible, or at least a good deal more than Honor felt they had any right to expect. His beefy jaw fell, and his thick cheeks reddened slightly as he listened to Raifer's story.

"How could this happen?" he demanded. "I've had assurances from Doctor Trask himself that the hospital was completely secure."

Raifer leaned forward. "I'll be damned if I know," he said. He turned quickly to Honor. "With your pardon, Miss O'Shaughnessy." Then he turned back to the policeman. "There was a young woman missing early this morning, you see. An American woman."

"Yes, yes I heard about that," the constable interjected, nodding. "Young Constable Regan located her."

"Well, early on, before they thought it necessary to come to you here, most of us orderlies were sent out to look for her. She's not dangerous, you see, but they were afraid she might accidently do herself some harm. So most of us were sent out, like I said, over the local roads, into the woods, to search the area and try to find her. As luck would have it, I fell meself, down a steep scarp. I must have hit my head, because when I woke up it was already gettin' on to dark. So I climbed out and made my way back to the sanatorium only to find that during the day, with most of the orderlies out searchin' for the young woman, somehow one of the more violent patients managed to escape from his cell, then let all the others out. The nurses and the doctors who were left in the hospital tried their best to get them under control, but it was useless. It only aroused their madness, don't you know. Just as I was approachin' the building, I seen Miss O'Shaughnessy makin' a frightful brave effort to escape through a second-story window. She nearly killed herself, but luckily I was there to catch her. She told me what happened, and we decided the only course was to come here for help. And so here we are, shakin' but somehow still in one piece."

"Incredible, incredible," the constable muttered.

Honor could not help but echo the word in her mind. She kept her eyes down, lest the policeman read the truth in them. But her precautions were, apparently, unnecessary.

The constable stirred himself abruptly to a bustling sort of motion and stood. "I'll go round and fetch the rest of the fellows," he said. "I'm afraid we'll be needin' your help, Mr. Farrell, to show us around the hospital."

Raifer nodded. "Of course. Anything I can do to help. Only you must hurry. There's no tellin' what they're doin' by now." He turned and put his hand on Honor's arm. "And Miss O'Shaughnessy . . . there's a safe place for her to stay?"

"Certainly," the constable replied as he moved to a large, sturdy-looking coat tree and removed a heavy coat and hat from it. "And I'll have someone fetch in somethin' for you to eat. You both look like you could use a bite of something."

Raifer smiled. "That would be kind of you, sir," he said. "And perhaps a wee bit of brandy for Miss O'Shaughnessy?" he asked. "I think it might ease her a bit."

"I'll see to it," the constable agreed as he buttoned

his coat. "You both just wait here for us. I won't be more than a few minutes." He moved heavily to the door and out in to the night.

"How could you, Raifer?" Honor fumed. "I can't believe he actually accepted a word of that tripe."

Raifer grinned. "It's been my experience, Honor, that if you play on people's fears, they will accept as gospel the most preposterous tales. And what could strike fear into the heart of a constable of a town that is home to a mental asylum?" he asked.

Honor laughed. "The possibility that the inmates have taken control of the madhouse?" she offered.

"Precisely," he said with a nod.

"And have I thanked you for the brave and gallant way you saved me by catching me as I fell from that window?" she asked him, her tone a bit arch.

Raifer shrugged. "Nothing. Actually, it was quite brave of you to take the leap. Admittedly you were fleeing a fate worse than death at the hands of a half dozen crazed fiends, but still."

Honor's face fell. His description was a shade too close to reality for her to find anything amusing in the thought. She leaned forward to the police constable's desk and scanned the evening paper he had been reading when they came in.

"I think the inmates may really have taken over the asylum, Raifer," she said softly. She pointed to an article near the top of the front page.

Raifer leaned forward and read the paragraph:

> *Prince Edward retired to Scotland for a short fishing holiday following his return from a successful visit to the United States and Canada today. Fotheringay Castle will be host to the future king for the next several days as he rests and relaxes from the rigors of his long trip . . .*

Raifer's eyes drifted away from the paper and to Honor's bewildered expression.

"Why would they print such fabrications?" she demanded. "He's not in Scotland. He's here."

"I assume the Queen and Gladstone are attempting to keep the kidnapping a secret, Honor," he replied. "News of it could only undermine the stability of the current government. I think that's something they especially don't need just now."

"But it will just make it harder," Honor said. "Don't you see? Even if we get the police out there, no one will accept that Edward is who he is."

Raifer made a calming motion with his hands. "Let's just get past one thing at a time, Honor. Once the police are out there, and Flannagan and his friends are in hand, I think we can depend on Edward to impress the right people with whatever regal manner seems necessary to him. I've no doubt but that he can do whatever is necessary."

Honor shook her head. "He hardly looks regal in those old fisherman's clothes he's wearing. And God only knows what they're doing to him," she countered.

"We haven't much choice just now, Honor," Raifer replied.

Honor stood and walked to the window, then stared out into the night. He was right, she knew. But still she wished there could be a bit more certainty about things. Too much had happened in the previous weeks for her to feel easy at the prospect of yet another disappointment, another loss to Flannagan and his people. And her experience with Squire Blaileigh made her realize just how possible that might be.

The darkness outside had become total, she realized, for she could see absolutely nothing, not another building, not the barest of outlines of the rolling hills beyond the town. This wasn't what she'd intended when she'd longed for an adventure that afternoon back in her father's library. She'd thought it would be filled with starlit nights and moments of excitement to thrill her. Reality was like the night outside the window, simply dull blackness, fear punctuated by panic, discomfort, and hunger.

She closed her eyes, wishing fervently that she could open them and find herself safe in her father's house. When she did, she found nothing had changed, that she was still facing the window, looking out into an ink-black night.

"The Sargeant sent me round with some food for you folks."

The words were punctuated by a draft of cold air from the outside. Honor could see in the window the reflection of a young officer entering the office bearing a large tray which he set down in front of Raifer on the desk.

"That's most kind of you, sir," Raifer replied, the careful singsong brogue once more flowing from his lips like some kind of absurd caricature. He turned to face Honor's back. "Won't you be comin' and have somethin', Miss O'Shaughnessy?" he asked.

For a second Honor was frozen. The face she saw reflected back at her in the mirror of the window was familiar, too familiar.

It's over, she thought. Just like that, so foolishly, over.

"Miss O'Shaughnessy?"

She managed to collect herself. "Aye," she replied, her voice weak, the accent uncertain. "You go right ahead. I'll be right there."

The young constable was staring at her back.

Honor could almost feel his eyes boring into her. And for some reason she could not quite explain, she knew, despite the fact that he had not even seen her face, he knew.

There was a moment of silence with both men turned to her. She stood, stiff and unmoving, still staring out the window, her back to them. And then the young constable touched his hand to his hat, nodded toward Raifer, and turned to the door.

"Well, the sergeant will be wonderin' what it is I'm at," he said before he put his hand to the doorknob. "We won't be much longer. Enjoy your supper."

"Thank you," Raifer called out after him as he opened the door and left.

When he was gone, and the door firmly closed behind him, Honor spun round. "Raifer, we have to get out of here," she cried softly.

He looked up at her, startled, the spoonful of stew halfway to his mouth. "Why?" he demanded sharply.

"That was the one. And he recognized me," she replied.

"But he never saw your face, Honor," he said softly. "You simply keep out of his sight until we've gone. I'll wait for the rest of them outside."

She shook her head. "He recognized me, Raifer. I'm sure of it."

He stared at her a long moment. "You're positive?" he asked her.

She nodded. "Yes, Positive."

He stood, obviously having decided to trust her intuition, made his way to the front of the office, and darted a quick look out the window. Then he turned back and strode to the desk.

"You're right," he said softly. "He's out there. Talking to the other one, the one who was here with us." He quickly gathered up a half loaf of bread and two pieces of cheese that were on the tray and handed them to Honor. "Here," he said as he gave them to her. Then he went to the window she'd been standing beside, unlatched it, and pulled it open. "Out, Honor. Quickly."

She nodded and went to the window, sitting on the sill ledge and then swinging her legs over it. Raifer put his hands to her waist and lowered her gently to the ground. Then he leaped out quickly and took her hand.

"It seems we're going to have to do this by ourselves after all, Honor," he said.

She nodded, unable to find any words. There was nothing but as thick numbness in her at the prospect.

Chapter Seventeen

Charles Carter cleared his throat discreetly. The noise, as he suspected, was just loud enough to rouse the prime minister from the heap of papers that littered his desk.

"Yes?" Gladstone asked warily.

Carter regarded his superior with a growing feeling of remorse. Gladstone had come to have, over the previous few days, the look of a felled deer gazing up at the hunter and waiting for the coup de grace. Carter found himself sincerely wishing that he were not once again the bearer of bad tidings.

"The report, sir. From the men we sent out to Kinvarra."

Gladstone's eyes studied his for some sign, anything that might be construed as positive, only to find nothing. His assistant's expression was as barren of hope as he himself felt. Resigned, he held out his hand.

"I suppose we have nothing to celebrate, Carter?" he asked, but it was obvious from his tone that he realized there wasn't. The inquiry, they both knew, was nothing more than a wan attempt at conversation.

"I'm afraid not, sir," Carter responded as he handed the short report across the prime minister's cluttered desk. The clutter, he realized, disturbed him. The heaps of papers were unprecedented, at least in his memory. It was the prime minister's habit to attend to matters serially and with dispatch. He had never before seen more than one folder on the desk at a time, never before been aware of any physical evidence of confusion in the office at all.

He knew it wouldn't take the prime minister long to read the report. A half dozen lines only, outlining the inquiries made by the agents and the little result they had produced. The closing line was, of course, hopeful, mentioning the steps the men planned to take next, but the sum total of the report was that no trace of Edward had been found in Kinvarra and, despite suspicion that the villagers knew more than they seemed willing to divulge, none would be forthcoming in the near future. All of which, Carter knew, was a very dangerous prospect. Since the second note from the kidnappers had arrived, that announcing their deadline was being pushed up, Gladstone had been placing a good deal of his hope in the possibility that the agents might discover something that would lead them to the kidnappers' hiding place. Now that seemed unlikely.

"Is there any possibility, sir, that we might get the press to cooperate, not print the results of tomorrow's vote?" he asked. His question was halfhearted. He knew the answer as well as the prime minister.

Gladstone shook his head. "Not without giving them some sort of an acceptable reason. The arrogance of the third estate is unswayable. Besides, even if they were to do as you suggest, news would still be broadcast. Simply too many people would be privy to the information. So you see, we're in that proverbial position, damned if we do and damned if we don't." He threw himself against the back of his chair and sat looking up at the ceiling. "It would have been perfect if the Foreign Office had found some trace of Edward, but I suppose that was too much to hope for. But as for keeping the vote quiet, that's impossible. I'm sure our

Irish friends will know shortly after we do that the motion will be defeated. God help us, for all we know, there might even be an MP involved in this mess." He shook his head. "No," he went on thoughtfully, "tomorrow's headlines will give the usual account of the session, and the kidnappers will know the exact count and that the motion was duly introduced, voted upon, and defeated by a narrow margin." He slammed his fist against the desk. "Damn them. If they'd given me more time, I could have done it."

"I don't suppose, sir," Carter offered, "that the Queen could perhaps issue an edict?"

Gladstone looked up at him with the same expression he'd use to stare up at the devil himself. "Are you mad, Carter?" he asked. "Do you want to start a civil war? Or haven't you ever heard of Magna Carta?"

Carter backed away, cowed by the prime minister's withering glance. "That was stupid of me, sir," he muttered.

"Yes, Carter, it was. Better Edward's death than trying to change the rule of law. After all, this is England."

He spoke the last words with the sort of defensive pride that he knew his countrymen had used to proclaim their superiority to the world for the previous five centuries, the kind of pride that meant England was willing to send any number of her sons to their deaths rather than submit to an outsider's will. But this time, he knew, it was not just any son who would die, it was the future king. And if nothing intervened in the next few hours, he was sure the kidnappers would do as they promised, begin to carve up Edward and send the parts home one by one.

Honor stumbled.
The darkness was almost absolute now, unrelieved

by visible stars or moon, and only exacerbated by a steadily thickening mist. Raifer's hands were quick to find her waist and keep her from falling, but it hardly seemed worthwhile to her. She felt she was too cold, too tired to go much further in any case.

"We'll find some shelter and get a few hours' sleep," Raifer said abruptly, breaking the long silence that had settled between them as they walked.

"But Edward . . ." she began to protest.

Raifer shook his head. "They won't be taking him anyplace. Not in this soup. If we can find someplace to rest, I think all three of us ought to be safe for the night at least."

Honor didn't make any effort to protest further. She thought longingly of the small farmhouse they'd seen as they'd trudged from the sanatorium to Ardrahan. They should be approaching it soon on this oddly determined return journey. She wondered if he remembered seeing it.

"There was a farmhouse," she ventured.

Raifer nodded. "So I recall," he told her. "It can't be much further. And just as well." He looked at her critically. "You look just about played out, Honor," he told her gently.

Honor squared her shoulders. "I'm fine," she assured him perhaps a shade too sharply, but she knew he was right. She wasn't fine. She was cold and hungry and near to exhaustion. The thought of food and a warm bed was almost too much for her to contemplate.

They trudged on in silence for a while. Honor felt the cold beginning to creep into her, and she no longer had the strength to throw it off. She began to shiver.

"Is this any better, Honor?" Raifer asked her softly as he put his arm around her.

She was startled by the sudden warmth that started to fill her at the contact. "Yes," she admitted. She found herself smiling foolishly up at him. His eyes, she found, were not on her, but were fastened to the road ahead of them. His gesture, she realized, had simply been one of kindness, nothing more than an offer to share his body heat. She found herself wondering how the contact could strongly affect her and yet leave him so apparently indifferent. She set about trying to convince herself that the growing feeling of warmth within her was not strictly hers alone, but that he felt it within him, too. She did not quite succeed.

"Honor," he said suddenly, and then paused.

She felt her heart thumping in her chest. She wasn't quite sure why, but she had the distinct feeling that he was about to ask her something, something important, and she felt her breath catch in her throat with an oddly expectant elation. It's not just me, she thought. He feels it, too.

"Yes, Raifer?"

"There's something I've been thinking about, something I have to ask you."

There it was again, that strangely pleasant thudding in her chest. "Yes, Raifer?" She stared up at him, waiting.

"Back at the asylum. You said something about Flannagan having forged papers, forged extradition papers."

It seems he did have something to ask her after all, she thought, but not quite what she'd expected. The thudding ended abruptly. Almost without realizing what she was doing, she drew away from him.

"Yes," she told him. "He had extradition papers. Captain Keenan mentioned them. That was why he was so ready to agree with Flannagan's story about taking me to be treated here, that I was deranged. Because he'd seen the papers."

"You're sure?" he pressed. "He had extradition papers?"

She found his manner irked her far more than she

would have thought possible.

"Yes," she snapped. "That's what he said, I'm sure of it." She turned away, vexed with herself and with her reaction to him, but more vexed with him for being so oblivious to her, for being so concerned with what seemed to her trivialities. "Why?"

He shook his head. "I don't know. It sounds wrong to me. Extradition papers would be very hard to falsify." He concentrated on the road once more. "I'll have to think about it."

Honor darted an angry glance at him. You do that, she thought. Think about where those papers might have come from. Think about your precious job. That's all that matters to you in any case.

She trudged on, carefully keeping her distance from him, just enough to remind herself that she mustn't let herself think of anything but the immediate situation, of where they were and what it was they intended to do. For that was all that mattered to him, and she would be a fool if she let anything else matter to her. She felt the cold beginning to creep into her once more, but she refused to allow herself to shiver, to give him any indication that she was anything less than completely self-sufficient.

The fog began to thicken considerably. It quite bewildered Honor, for she'd never seen fog like this before in her life. Certainly there were days in New York when the mist rolled in off the ocean, but this mist was far more invasive, almost as though it was a wooly curtain that had settled around them and obscured everything around them beyond a few feet's distance. Honor doubted they would be able to find the farmhouse at all, and was sure they'd spend the night wandering around in the darkness and the fog.

But then it suddenly appeared, a hazy, dark shadow that floated near the road. Honor started forward, pleased and anxious, but Raifer grabbed her arm and held her back as he considered it warily.

"It has to be well past midnight," he said as the two of them stood, not a hundred feet from the rickety-looking front door.

It was obvious, even from the little they could discern in the darkness, that this was not a very prosperous farm. The front gate and fence were in disrepair, and Honor could see dark stains, darker shadows, really, along the side walls where the paint had long ago peeled and not been patched.

From somewhere in the rear of the house a dog sent up a ragged, unpleasant howl. It was an eerie, unsettling sound in the thick, misty darkness.

"I don't think these people would welcome strange visitors, Honor," Raifer told her. "Certainly not ones that appear out of the mist in the middle of the night." He pulled her gently away from the house and toward an equally disreputable-looking barn. "I suggest we make ourselves as comfortable as we can out here, and make sure we're gone before there's any chance of our being seen in the morning."

The prospect was not quite as inviting as Honor had expected, but she was far too tired to argue with him. The dog's howling went on sporadically, making her feel more and more uneasy. It was with relief she realized the animal was obviously tied or penned in the rear of the house, for it made no move to investigate the cause of whatever noise they had made that roused it in the first place.

They entered the barn warily, trying to keep as quiet as they could. It was dark and filled with the not quite pleasant odor of fresh manure, but it was warm, and Honor told herself she could content herself with that.

"Stay here," Raifer whispered to her, then wandered off into the darkness.

His sudden disappearance startled her, but she made no move to follow him. Her legs were trembling with weariness and she found herself with absolutely no will or desire to investigate on her own. Instead she stood, breathing shallowly, trying to accustom herself to the odor of the manure and the animals.

It wasn't long before there was a touch on her shoulder and she jumped, for the darkness was deep enough so that she had not seen Raifer return to her.

"It's all right," he whispered gently, realizing he had frightened her. "It's only me."

"Who else would it be?" she replied a touch peevishly, refusing to admit her fear to him, knowing it was childish of her to be frightened of the dark.

"I found an empty stall," he said to her as he found her hand with his. "And it's not even very dirty."

"That's incredibly reassuring," she told him wryly. "Not that a bit more dirt would matter."

She followed him forward, depending on his hand to guide her, for she found her night vision completely inadequate.

"Here, Honor," he said after they'd brushed past a half dozen slumbering sheep and a single cow. "I think we ought to be safe enough here."

She let his hands guide her to the heap of straw, then she dropped down and lay back, feeling the release of the muscles in her limbs as they slowly eased.

"Hungry?"

Raifer's voice seemed to be coming out of a mist, not right beside her where he'd settled himself in the straw.

"Please, don't let me think about food. Of course I'm hungry."

"Then don't think about it," he laughed softly as he pressed a chunk of something cold and moist into her hand. "Just eat."

She sniffed the piece suspiciously. "Cheese," she said finally, and gnawed hungrily at the chunk. "I'd forgotten. You were brilliant to take it before we left the police station."

"I'd have been brilliant if I'd managed to take away the stew," he told her. "Here, wash it down with this."

His hand found hers again, and this time deposited a jagged piece of bread.

"Do you remember what real food tastes like, Raifer?" she asked him ruminatively through the bites of bread and cheese. "Maman Claudine's cassoulet?"

"Don't torture yourself, Honor," Raifer replied with a small laugh. "This is all we're likely to get tonight." He chewed his own bread thoughtfully. "Besides, whatever happens, you should be back in New York soon enough. You'll forget all about this once you've had a bath and a decent meal."

"I've had a bath and a decent meal," she told him. "At Squire Blaileigh's, remember? And it hasn't made me forget a thing," she finished bitterly.

"I'm sorry, Honor," he whispered. "Believe me, I am."

She turned to him, wishing she could see more than the pale outline of his eyes in the darkness, wondering what his expression showed, if there was relief in it at the prospect of being rid of her, or even the smallest tinge of regret. Suddenly she found she had lost her appetite, and her hands dropped to her lap with the remainder of the bread and cheese.

They sat in silence for a few moments, a silence that seemed to grow thicker and more pressing as it dragged on. Finally Raifer swallowed the last of his share of the food. He turned to face her and found her watching him.

"I think, Honor, that when I leave here tomorrow morning, you should stay. It was stupid of me to take you away from Ardrahan. At least you'd be safe there."

"Safe?" she snorted. "They think I'm insane. They would have just sent me back to Flannagan, back to the asylum."

"Ardrahan isn't the world. Tomorrow you can start making your way eastward. You'll come to a town eventually. You could send back help."

"No," she told him decisively. "You yourself said they won't keep Edward at the sanatorium very much longer once they find Flannagan and learn we're gone. They might not be able to move him tonight in this fog, but they will as soon as they can in the morning."

"Honor, you'll just get in the way of whatever I can do to help Edward."

She felt a sudden rush of anger at the offhanded way he told her to please just go. As though she were nothing to him but an unpleasant responsibility of which he'd be only too happy to divest himself as soon as possible.

"You can't be quit of me just like that," she snapped back. "I won't just go off and disappear from your life that easily. I'm as much a part of this as you are. And if you intend to go back for Edward, so do I. After it's over, you can return to your precious job and forget I exist. But I won't simply walk away from all this simply because you want to be rid of me." She quieted suddenly, surprised at her outburst. She'd not meant to say any of it, but somehow it had been said nonetheless.

Raifer put his hand to her shoulder. "Is that what you think, Honor?" he asked. "That I want to be rid of you?"

"What else is there for me to think?" she sniffed.

She could feel a catch in her throat and tried to force it away even as she told herself that she didn't care, not about him, not about anything but getting Edward away from Flannagan and his people. She tried to push his hand away from her shoulder and started to turn away from him.

He caught her, his hands on her shoulders. "Honor," he said softly, his voice suddenly very gentle. Then he lowered his lips to hers and kissed her softly.

She hadn't prepared herself for that, she realized. Indifference, even outright disdain, that she could deal with, but not this gentleness, not this pretense that he actually cared.

"Don't," she cried softly.

But she had lost her will to pull away from him. Somehow all she wanted at that moment, no matter how wrong, was the feel of his arms around her, the press of his body close to hers. It doesn't matter, she told herself, that it's not real. Nothing matters, not tomorrow, not the truth, nothing. She only knew that at that moment she was lost, and needed him to find herself.

Somehow she found herself lying back in the straw, although she didn't remember moving, and somehow he was kissing her, kissing her lips and her eyelids and her neck. All she could feel were the arrows of sweet fire that shot through her at his touch.

Slowly, trembling, her hands made their way along his chest to his shoulders, then, more determined as she pressed her lips to his, to his back where they clung to him. Whatever happened on the morrow, she realized, whether they managed to get Edward away from Flannagan or not, it would all be over one way or another. This, then, was to be her last night with him, and she would have nothing left when it was done. At the least, she told herself, she could bring away a memory, a sweet memory that held something more than an image of the darkness and sharp odors of the ramshackle barn.

She pulled him to her, aware that his fingers were unfastening the buttons of her blouse, knowing only that she wished he would hurry and have done with the distraction. She slid her hands back to his chest, furiously intent now, as she unfastened his shirt buttons. That done, she put her hands against his skin, then her lips, kissing his neck, his chest, tasting his skin and the wiry hair.

I'll remember this always, she told herself, the taste of his skin, the feel of it. She knew it was true, that whatever happened those things would be imprinted on her mind for as long as she lived, that his mark was on her, like a brand, something that would never wash away.

He was pushing away the linen of her blouse, and she pulled back from him to help him, letting him bare her shoulders and her breasts, anxious for the feel of his lips against them, for the sweetly exciting provocation of his tongue against her nipples. She wondered fleetingly how many other women he'd stirred to passion this way, how he'd learned all the right places to touch, all the right movements to make with such deft sureness. For there was no doubt in her mind that he knew just what he was doing to her, or that he could not help but feel the growing fire that was seeping through her body.

Make him remember, too, a voice inside her said. Leave him at least to someday have some regrets at what he left behind him.

She drew him down to her, her hands caressing, urging, inviting his touch. She bent her knee, sliding her leg along his thigh, then guided his hand to the softness of her flesh. He seemed more than willing to oblige her, and she felt the warmth of his hand against her inner thigh, the fire slowly drifting through her. What started as a gentle stroking caress of her thigh grew steadily stronger, more insistent. She brought her lips to his neck, breathing her own fire, feeling it reflected in him, in the heat of his skin and the steady, determined throb of his pulse beneath her lips.

Finally he brought his hands to her hair, twining his fingers in the thick tangle, and pulling her face away from him. She could feel his breath as he stared down at her in silence for a moment, could hear his ragged panting. There seemed to be a question in his expression, or perhaps surprise. She stared up at him, wondering what it was she saw in his eyes, wondering if it was passion or lust or just a trick of the darkness.

When he lowered his lips once more to hers, however, she forgot her questions and told herself she didn't care.

All there was for her at that moment was the heat of his hand against her flesh, the taste of his tongue and his lips, and the sweet, honeyed lava that seemed to fill her veins. She spread herself beneath him and waited, breathless and expectant, for the hot, sweet probe.

But he pulled back from her as he had moments before and stared down at her, the same question in his expression, as though he were unsure.

She decided to answer his questions before he could ask them. "I'm not asking for pledges, Raifer," she whispered, feeling the words come hard and sharp in her throat. "I don't want them."

"Honor, I . . ."

She shook her head vehemently. "No. Not now . . . it's not important."

Then she put her hands to the back of his head, pulling him down to her lips, telling herself that this was what she wanted, only this hour, and then nothing more.

He slid inside her, driving thought from her mind, leaving it filled instead with the rising tide of flowing fire, the narcotic netherworld where nothing else but the feel of him mattered. She raised her legs and wrapped them around his waist, and let her body move with the rhythms of the eternal dance.

Raifer had never felt before as he did at that moment, he never lost himself so entirely to the power of a woman's arms, had never felt himself so completely a part of another person's body. He'd thought he knew her, understood her, but now he realized that she was, would always be, a mystery to him. The idea was as bewildering as it was intriguing, the realization that she would forever be as unfathomable to him as the passion that now gripped him, that she roused in him some well of feeling he had never even known was there.

He made love to her with an intentness that startled and shook him, that separated him completely from the reality of where they were and what was happening to their lives. All that mattered for those endless, precious moments when time seemed to stop was the feel of her in his arms, the feeling of being a part of her, of knowing she was joined to him. And when he finally felt her body arch to his, when he heard the long, deep moan and knew that her moment had come, he allowed himself the sweet pleasure of release, felt himself consumed by it as he had never felt before.

From somewhere outside himself, he heard himself whisper, "I love you, Honor."

The words were a surprise to him. He'd thought to say them before they'd started, but she'd stopped him and he'd decided it was just as well, that it couldn't mean anything to her. After all, she'd made it perfectly clear what she thought of him, that she neither wanted nor expected anything from him. But somehow the words would be said despite the reticence, and once he'd uttered them, he realized how true they were and how much she meant to him. *No matter,* he told himself, *what she thinks of me now, that she thinks me low enough to desert her, to use her. When all this is over somehow I'll convince her that she's wrong.*

If Raifer's words startled him, they completely shattered Honor. What his body had done to hers was minor compared to the reaction she had to those three simple words. Once she'd heard them, she allowed herself to dare to hope that it might actually be true, that it wasn't simply just another lie like all the others he'd told her.

He stared down at her, his eyes on hers, his hands gently smoothing away the damp curls that clung to her cheeks. She was beautiful, far more beautiful to him at that moment than she'd ever seemed to him before. He felt a sudden stab of pain as he looked down at her, for all he could see was doubt in her eyes.

"I love you," he said again, this time more vehemently.

"I told you, Raifer," she told him. "I don't want any of that, don't need it."

He silenced her with a finger to her lips. "I heard," he said with a smile. "No pledges, no promises. Not now." He sighed. "It's just as well, Honor, because I'm in no position to make any promises." Then he lowered his lips to her eyes, wanting to close them, to shut away the doubt he saw in them. When she opened them again, he saw it had faded, at least a bit, and that seemed to be enough for him, at least for that moment.

He lowered himself to the straw beside her and put his arm around her shoulders, drawing her near to him. "Are you warm enough?" he asked her as he languidly stroked her arms and her back, finding himself inordinately pleased with the contact, with the way her skin felt to his touch.

Honor nodded. "Hmm," she replied sleepily as she nuzzled close to him.

Perhaps it's true, she thought. Perhaps she should let herself believe him. She knew she wanted that, knew there was nothing in the world she wanted more.

After a few moments she raised her face to his and found him staring dully up at the barn's rafters, his gaze preoccupied and far away. Don't ask, a voice inside her warned, but she knew she would not heed it.

"What is it, Raifer?" she asked him softly. "What are

you thinking about?"

He turned and looked at her, and it seemed to her that his look was a bit startled, almost as though he had forgotten she was there, that he was not expecting to find her beside him.

"I was just thinking," he said with a grin, "however unexpected the prospect."

She refused to be put off. "About what?" she pushed.

He shrugged. "About those extradition papers you mentioned, Honor," he said slowly. "Someone would have had to have gotten them for Flannagan, someone in the New York government, someone important. That means Flannagan had accomplices, others besides McGowan. It may just be the tie that puts Fitzpatrick in the middle of this mess."

Honor turned away. I should have known, she thought. That's all that matters to him, his job. And what happened, that was just words, words that meant nothing to him.

Raifer pushed himself up onto his elbows and leaned over her.

"Honor," he said. "Is there something wrong?"

"No," she replied as she shook her head. "Nothing's wrong."

He put his hand to her shoulder, but she refused to turn back to him and face him. He waited a moment, then he released his hold of her.

"We should get some sleep," he said.

"Yes," she agreed dully. "We should sleep."

She settled herself on her side, her back to him, her hands under her cheek. Raifer stared at her a moment, then rummaged around in the pile of their cast-off clothing. He took her skirt and spread it over her, gently drawing it up to her neck.

"Good night, Honor," he said softly.

She gave him no answer. Her own words were repeating themselves silently in her mind, nothing's wrong, over and over, nothing's wrong. She forced her eyes tightly shut. Nothing's wrong, she told herself firmly, but she could not stop the tears that slowly trickled down her cheek, nor the sure knowledge that absolutely everything was completely and absolutely wrong.

There was the sound of the barn door shutting.

Honor's eyes popped open, and she found herself completely awake. For a moment she thought it might be the farmer, and that they would be found, trespassers in the barn. Then she realized it was still dark, before dawn. When she turned to where Raifer had lain at her side, she realized she was now alone.

It was him at the barn door, she realized abruptly. He'd gone and left her there, abandoned her while he went back to the sanatorium for Edward.

She scrambled hastily into her clothing, surprised to find that her night vision had finally cleared and that she could discern objects in the near complete darkness. Dressed, she slipped out of the barn and ran to the road, then started off at a trot in the direction of the sanatorium.

The mist from the night before had nearly disappeared. What little of it remained skimmed the ground to about knee height. As the first pale dawn light began to relieve the darkness, Honor realized she was running through what appeared to be an eddying pool of gray smoke. Had the circumstances been different, she would have found the effect fascinating.

As it was, however, she was intent upon finding Raifer before he reached the sanatorium. However she felt about his act of desertion, she knew she did not want to face Flannagan's domain alone. She needed Raifer, more than she could easily accept at that moment, far more than she wished she did. That need would not end when Edward was found, when they all returned to their own lives.

Her thoughts drew up sharply. She had gone on through the past weeks believing herself ultimately inviolate, satisfied that Kevin's bribe would protect her, if not from discomfort and embarrassment, then certainly from the threat of any real violence. But as the image of Flannagan returned to her, the knife in his hand ready, his eyes filled with hatred, she realized her assumption had been groundless. Surely that was what Flannagan had intended for Edward if his demands were not met. She no longer had any reason to assume the terrorist would stop at her death and Raifer's.

The thought was chilling. However much she might have dreaded the thought of going on without him, the possibility of Raifer's death filled her with a sickening dread that she knew would never fade. Nothing could be worse than that, she realized, not the thought of his abandonment, not even her own death. With an awful lurch, she realized that no matter what had happened between them, she loved him, that she would always love him. She'd been a fool to think that their lovemaking the night before would somehow change any of that, would purge her of the need she felt for him.

She pushed the thought out of her mind, forcing herself to concentrate on running, on not letting herself tire. The effort served to settle her, and she plodded doggedly on. By the time it was near full dawn, she could just make out the gate of the sanatorium in the mist-shrouded distance. The pedestrian passage, just to the left of the larger, barred carriage entry, was ajar just as she and Raifer had found it the night before. And slipping through onto the sanatorium grounds, Honor could make out Raifer's familiar form. He was moving with stealth, but fairly quickly, she noted. She forced her now tired legs to move faster, determined to reach him before he disappeared into the huge labyrinth of the sanatorium itself.

She wasn't quite fast enough. She was breathless and panting, and completely damp with perspiration, when she reached the thick hedge of bushes that fronted the sanatorium. She stood for a moment trying to catch her breath, becoming painfully aware of the cold she'd been able to ignore as she ran, and watched Raifer march openly up to the main entry and pull open the huge carved door.

She shivered in the cold and wondered how he could be such a fool as to boldly enter that way. She knew, if she were to ask him, he'd tell her as he had several times before, that when he encountered someone, he'd know what story to tell. And a tiny voice inside her added that chances are they'd believe him, too. After all, she had firsthand experience of just how convincing he could be when he wanted to be. She allowed herself a smile despite her fear.

If I stay here, she thought with a surprising calm as she hugged herself trying to keep warm, I'll freeze to death. Refusing to allow herself the opportunity to consider the foolhardiness of her actions, she stepped through the line of thick bushes and started after him.

Oddly enough, there seemed to be no one about. The hallway on either side of her was quiet, the front desk empty. Around her was nothing but quiet—nothing, that was, except for the muffled sound of a single set of footfalls.

The noise was coming from her right, and Honor decided she had no choice but to follow it. If it was Raifer, all would be well, she told herself. If it wasn't, well, she really could think of nothing else to do.

The place surprised her. She passed long rows of closed doors, all silent at this early hour. She realized she had absolutely no idea of what she might find inside the sanatorium, but somewhere there had been the picture of barred and locked doors, the expectation that those imprisoned beyond the doors would be crying out in anguish. It was only after a few moments that she noted the doors she passed were carefully lettered with the names of doctors. This would be the way visitors entered, she realized. Here, at least, all would be clean and calm. If there were poor, deranged patients locked away behind bolted doors, they would be carefully hidden, far away from anyplace where friends and relatives come to inquire about their loved ones might see such unpleasantness.

She wondered if she ought to enter one of those closed offices and consider for a moment just what it was she could do now that she was inside. The place seemed even more enormous than it had from the outside, and she was beginning to think that running after Raifer willy-nilly as she had, with no idea what it was he was about or where he was headed, was an extremely foolish thing to do.

It was an assessment that was immediately and unpleasantly confirmed.

"Who are you, and where are you going?"

Honor whirled around. A door just behind her and to her left had opened. Now a large, solid, matronly-looking woman dressed in black with a white apron and prim little cap sitting squarely on her gray-streaked hair was standing and staring at her with the sort of suspicious look that chilled Honor with fear. She stood for a moment, foolishly gaping and speechless, staring at the nurse. And then instinct took over where she ought never to have let it invade. She turned and ran.

It was the last thing she ought to have done. She was tired and hungry and had absolutely no idea of where she was going. The woman, besides being none of those things, had had a great number of years' experience dealing with disoriented, fleeing patients. She stood for a moment, watching Honor reach the end of the corridor and turn to the left. Then she took after her with a speed that was completely out of proportion to her age and bulk.

Honor heard the soft pad of the woman's sensible shoes following her and knew she hadn't much time. She headed for a large door at the end of the corridor that she prayed led to the outside, hoping desperately she could reach it before the nurse caught her.

With the sound of the woman's footsteps filling her ears, and expecting to feel her grasp at any moment, Honor reached the door with her last burst of energy. She put her hand to the knob and flung her body against the wooden panel to push it open. She'd been right, she discovered. In front of her was a small vestibule and a large windowed door that opened onto the sanatorium grounds.

She darted to this second door and put her hand to the knob, sure she could make it outside and to safety before the nurse could reach her. Her heart was thumping wildly as she turned the heavy brass knob only to find it did not budge. She looked down at the lock, then began banging against it irrationally with her hands as she turned and saw the door from the corridor opening behind her. The door refused to give.

"Now, you weren't thinking of going anywhere, were you?"

The hand that gripped Honor's arm was strong and ungiving. It pulled sharply, jerking her away from the door to the outside.

"Now let me see," the nurse went on calmly, as though this were an occurrence that happened daily. "You don't seem familiar to me. You must be one of that new doctor's patients. Is that right? Doctor Flannagan?"

She had reopened the door to the corridor and was pushing Honor along in front of her, through it, back into the heart of the building.

Honor's heart fell at the mention of Flannagan's name. Her resistance drained from her, and she allowed herself to be pushed along into the corridor with no further show of protest. But then a small shred of hope began to form within her. The nurse had called Flannagan "Doctor." Perhaps she didn't know. Perhaps there still might be some small chance of convincing her of the truth.

"You don't understand," she said, turning to the woman, trying to sound rational when the whole matter seemed totally insane, even in her own mind. "Flannagan isn't a doctor. He's a kidnapper. He's holding Prince Edward. He kidnapped me."

The woman smiled pleasantly. "Of course, my dear," she said evenly.

"It's true," Honor protested, hating the sound of hysteria that seemed to be creeping into her voice.

"Now come along," the nurse went on, nudging her forward. "We'll get you settled in your room and have a nice chat, and you can tell me all about it."

The nurse's tone was friendly, but there was a look of iron determination in her eyes, and her grasp of Honor's arm tightened.

Honor's hopes disintegrated. Why, she wondered, had she been such a fool as to barge into this place alone? Why did she always act before she thought out the consequences? Now they would lock her up and put her in Flannagan's hands. *Flannagan*. She shivered at the thought of the man. After what had happened the night before, she had little doubt as to what he would arrange for her once he got his hands on her. And no one knew she was there, not Raifer, not the prince, no one. Even if Raifer somehow managed to escape with Edward, neither of them would know she was still there, under Flannagan's control.

She was trapped, and she had no one to blame but herself.

Chapter Eighteen

"Well, thank the good Lord you've found her. I'd be out of a job for sure if I lost her, and me only just started here."

Honor heaved a sigh of relief at the familiar, if slightly exaggerated, brogue. The nurse, however, did not share her relief at the sight of Raifer.

"What is this patient doing roaming around the halls unattended?" she snapped. "And at this hour of the morning." Her eyes narrowed contemplatively as she considered Raifer. She gave no indication that she intended to turn over her newly acquired charge to the tall man in attendant's garb who had managed to appear in the quiet, empty corridor without her noticing.

Honor, too, eyed him. He looked a bit unkempt, but not so bad that it would lead to any messy questions. That was, if he could somehow convince the nurse that he belonged there in the first place.

"I was supposed to bring her round to Doctor Flannagan's office," he offered with a slightly foolish grin that somehow managed to make him appear just a bit simpleminded. "But I seem to have gotten myself a bit lost. I am new, you see." He repeated the grin, and the look, boyish and slightly dense.

"So you mentioned," the nurse said dryly, obviously not in the least charmed by his meager attempt. "Why would the doctor want to see a patient at this hour of the morning?" she demanded suspiciously.

Raifer simply shrugged. "Ain't my place to question, now, is it?" he asked.

The woman's expression hardened. "I don't like it," she said, and her lips tightened. "Not any of it. I haven't since the whole thing started. But Doctor Trask would have this Flannagan person here. And now all sorts of irregular things are happening. Well, if you intend to bring this one to Flannagan, you'll have to see the Director," she pronounced firmly.

Raifer only looked a bit befuddled.

"Doctor Trask," the nurse snapped at him. "Along the corridor to the left. And keep yourself and your Doctor Flannagan's patients out of this wing. I'll not have my patients disturbed, do you understand?"

Raifer nodded meekly, putting his hand to Honor's wrist as the nurse released her hold.

"I'll be careful, ma'am," he said, and started down the corridor quickly, dragging Honor along his wake.

"What the hell are you doing here, Honor?" he hissed at her under his breath.

"Why did you leave me?" she countered with equal vehemence.

"Damn it, to keep you safe," he retorted.

She had no time to tell him that she didn't believe him. He had stopped in front of a door near the entry hall. A large brass plaque announced that it was the portal to the offices of Doctor Hubert Trask, Director.

Raifer darted a quick glance back along the corridor and saw the nurse was still there, watching. He smiled at her, then knocked at the door and stood patiently waiting until a voice from within called out, "Enter."

"What are we doing?" Honor demanded in a panicked whisper.

"Just what's expected of us," Raifer whispered back as he opened the door and pushed her into the office in front of him.

It was a large room, filled just a bit too full with leather-covered furniture and lined with bookcases crammed with thick volumes with gold embossed titles and an excess of Latin names. In the center of the room was a large, square mahogany desk behind which sat a man in shirtsleeves studiously applying himself to the perusal of a pile of papers that littered the surface while he consumed a large cup of coffee and a goodly quantity of bread liberally spread with butter and a dark red jam. Honor's stomach churned enviously as she considered the good doctor's breakfast.

He looked up and adjusted the spectacles that had slipped down his nose. Sharp, dark eyes considered them as he pushed himself back from the desk.

"What is this?" he demanded.

Raifer cleared his throat and gave him the same weak smile he'd given the nurse, the one that seemed to say he was simply a poor working bloke doing as he was told and only managing to make a mess of it despite his efforts.

"I was supposed to bring the young woman to Doctor Flannagan, sir," he replied.

Trask stood up. "Doctor Flannagan, is it?" he asked. "I thought you people were to stay out of the sanitorium proper. What do you think you're doing here?"

"I was told to bring her to Flannagan, that's all, sir," Raifer replied weakly.

"This whole thing has gotten out of hand," Trask went on, obviously perturbed. "Flannagan was to tell you people to keep to the west wing and nowhere else. I have a hospital to run here, and despite the importance of your Mr. Flannagan's charge, I won't have routine disturbed."

"No, sir," Raifer agreed readily.

Trask considered Honor a moment. "This is the American woman?" he asked.

Raifer nodded. "Aye, sir."

"Well, I suppose Flannagan wants her to see the other one, the American. Room 303, west wing. Do you have that?"

Raifer nodded again. "Aye, sir, 303, west wing." He tugged at Honor's arm and backed into the door, pulling her with him. Then he stopped and motioned with his free hand. "That way, sir?"

Trask banged his fist against the desk top. "Damn it, man, I'll show you. And once I've done that, I want you to tell your Mr. Flannagan I'll have no more invasions into this part of the hospital." He stood, his expression showing obvious anger. "Is that clear?" he demanded as he moved toward Raifer.

Raifer smiled pleasantly, and nodded. "Yes, sir," he agreed as he backed away from the door to let Trask pass.

Then he pushed Honor behind him and very quickly brought the side of his outstretched hand down on the back of Trask's neck. The doctor seemed to freeze for a moment, and then he simply collapsed.

Honor watched him fall to the floor at their feet with a kind of numbed fascination. She looked up at Raifer.

"Why did you do that?" she asked him, dazed.

Raifer knelt at Trask's side. "He's obviously helping Flannagan," he replied. "That ought to be reason enough. But it seems only practical to remove one of the opposition at the moment. And I have a feeling his sudden disappearance might create a little havoc around here sooner or later." He was busily removing the carefully tied cravat from around Trask's neck and using it to secure the man's hands behind his back. "A little confusion can only help the situation, I think," he added when he'd done. He straightened up and looked around the office. "There," he said, pointing to a door at the far side of the room. "See what's behind that."

Honor nodded and ran to the door, opening it to

reveal a half empty closet.

"Excellent," Raifer said with a smile as he stood and grasped Trask under the arms. "A nice cozy spot for the good doctor, I think."

Raifer dragged Trask across the room and pushed him haphazardly into the closet, then arranged him with his knees bent and his head against the closet wall. Then he closed the door, turned the key in the lock, and pocketed the key.

"Now what are you doing?" Honor demanded as she watched him move to Trask's desk and rifle through the drawers.

"Just seeing if there's something that might come in handy," he replied. He straightened and held up a large key ring. "And I think I've found it."

He grinned at her as he crossed to her and put his hand to her waist. He looked down at her thoughtfully. "Honor, I want you to get out of here now, find someplace secluded and hide."

Honor shook her head. "No," she told him vehemently. "Kevin's here. You heard him say so, the American, he said. It has to be Kevin. And I intend to see him again. To tell him how much I hate him. To show him how much misery he's caused."

"Honor, we've no reason to believe the man he was referring to was Kevin. It could be anyone."

She shook her head. "It's Kevin. I know it is. And if you try to stop me or send me away, I'll just follow after you. This isn't over yet for me, not until Edward's freed and I've seen Kevin."

Raifer considered her fixed expression and decided there was no hope of dissuading her. He shrugged with resignation.

"Very well," he agreed. "But try to follow directions. And stay out of my way."

She glared up at him. "Yes, sir, Mr. Farrell. You have but to command," she said, her tone just a bit snippy.

Raifer grinned. "Shall we, then, Miss Wainwright? I believe it was room 303, west wing."

Raifer pushed her against the wall beside the door marked 303.

"Stay put," he whispered. Then he pulled a blade from the inside breast pocket of the stolen white orderly's coat.

Honor looked down at it with dull surprise. "Where did you get that?" she asked him.

"The same place I got this," he replied, touching the lapel of the jacket.

It was a medical instrument, she realized, a scalpel. The sight of it made her shiver with distaste.

"I don't suppose you were expecting me to smile and suggest they let Edward go with nothing more than my charm to persuade them?" Raifer hissed at her. "Now be quiet."

He moved quickly to the door, put his hand to the knob, and turned it, bursting into the room quickly, hoping to surprise whoever might be inside.

He did. Kevin McGowan lifted his head and stared bleary-eyed at him from where he lay on the hospital bed that had been pushed against the far wall of the room.

"What?"

Kevin moved to get to his feet, but his reactions were far too slow. Raifer crossed the room to him and hit him once, pushing him back to the bed, and holding the knife he'd taken from his pocket to the older man's neck.

"Don't make me use this," he warned, his voice a tense whisper.

Kevin nodded silently and fell back, limp, making no further protest.

Honor crept into the room and watched the procedure with a dull sense of shock. Kevin seemed old and tired and very worn to her, his face gray and his body somehow shrunken. She realized she'd begun to think of him as some horrible monster over the previous few weeks since her father's death, something larger than life. Now, as she gazed at him, she realized that he was nothing more than a beaten old man. She closed the door quietly behind her and then moved to Raifer's side.

"Honor?"

Kevin seemed confused, disoriented, as though the sight of her completely bewildered him. The sound of his voice was a dry, rasping croak.

Honor stared at the knife in Raifer's hand, so close to Kevin's neck. She concentrated on it, mesmerized by the dull gleam from it. For a second she imagined it slipping into the wrinkled gray flesh. Then she drew back from the thought with horror. A wave of pity swept over her.

"Honor?" Kevin croaked once more, then cleared his throat. "You're all right, Honor?"

The words seemed so puny, so foolish to her, they drove away the spurt of pity. She smiled a darkly angry smile at him.

"Of course I'm all right, Kevin," she told him sharply. "I saw you kill my father. Then you turn me over to a ruthless murderer. How could I be anything but perfectly fine?"

"Get back, Honor," Raifer hissed at her.

When she didn't move, he repeated his order, his tone harsher this time, "Get back."

She took a few steps backward, watching still as Raifer returned his full attention to Kevin.

"Where do they have Edward?" he demanded and he pressed the scalpel closer to Kevin's flesh.

"In the next room," the old man replied, and nodded

toward the door at the side of the room. He seemed resigned to the situation, apparently willing to cooperate.

"Who's with him?" Raifer demanded. "How many guards?"

"Two. Flannagan and one of his men," Kevin replied. He turned his eyes back toward Honor. "I thought you'd gotten away. I thought you'd at least be safe."

He looked pitiful, Honor thought, old and pitiful.

"I never wanted any of this," Kevin went on. "It was all supposed to be so easy. Gladstone was supposed to give in without any fuss."

"Is that what all this is?" Raifer asked. "A fuss?"

Kevin started to reach up to him. Then, as Raifer pressed the knife closer to his neck, he lowered his hand once more. "They intend to kill Edward," he whispered. His own words seemed to shake him. "It wasn't to have happened like this."

"I knew it," Honor murmured. "Flannagan is insane. He'll stop at nothing. I heard him say that if Gladstone didn't give him what he wanted, he'd carve up Edward and send Victoria the pieces as a warning."

Raifer put his hand to Kevin's shoulder and pulled him up out of the bed. "Why don't we see if we can't convince Mr. Flannagan that killing Edward isn't quite the thing to do?" he hissed as he pushed Kevin towards the door, then glanced quickly at Honor. "Stay here," he ordered.

Honor watched as Raifer urged Kevin toward the door to the adjoining room. It amazed her just how little she felt at that moment, just how empty she was inside. It was as though the previous weeks, her father's death, Raifer's dismissal of her, all of it had combined to strip away her ability to feel, leaving her emotionless and separate. She hated the feeling. Even hurt, she thought, would be better than feeling nothing.

Just before Raifer reached the door she heard her own voice, and she was amazed at how calm it sounded.

"Unless you intend to use Kevin as a shield, he'll do you no good with Flannagan," she said. "I doubt his own mother would be a hostage he'd consider worth saving if it came to a choice involving his precious cause."

Raifer stopped with his hand on the knob. "I think you're right," he agreed thoughtfully. "It seems you were right to make me bring you along after all, Honor."

A week before Honor would have been pleased by even so simple a word of praise as the one he'd given her. At the moment, however, it seemed she felt as indifferent to his words as to everything else.

"See what you can find to tie him up with," Raifer told her as he escorted Kevin back to the single metal chair beside the bed.

Honor looked around, then pulled the sheet off the bed and tore off a long strip. Kevin sat quietly, as though he had no more will to fight, to even make an attempt at resistance. He looked up at Honor as Raifer pulled his hands behind his back and tied them.

"You can still get away, Honor," he said softly. "I won't tell Flannagan you've been here. He plans to take Edward away in an ambulance coach anyway, as soon as it's full morning. To Galway. To wait for the results of the vote in Parliament."

"Vote?" Raifer asked. "What vote?"

"On the disestablishment of the Church of Ireland," Kevin told him. "If it passes, Edward is to be released. If not . . ." He shrugged.

"So that's what this is all about," Honor said softly. "Trying to force the British hand."

Kevin nodded. "It's a fair cause, Honor. A righteous

cause."

She stared at him coldly. "As righteous as my father's death?" she asked and her voice rose.

Raifer put a hand to her arm. "Quietly, Honor," he murmured. "They're not deaf in there, after all." He nodded toward the closed door to the next room.

"You must believe me, Honor," Kevin began, but she turned away and his words faded. He realized they were useless in any case.

Raifer fixed a gag around his mouth. "Just in case you decide to try for one last blow for the cause," Raifer muttered as he tied it.

Kevin only shook his head slowly. Whatever fight he might have had in him was gone. It had been that way since the previous day, since the moment he'd realized that Flannagan fully intended to carry out his threat to kill Edward. It seemed all he could do was to stare at Honor's rigid back.

She didn't turn until she heard Raifer walk slowly toward the window.

"What do we do now?" she asked.

Raifer stood and stared out in silence for a moment. Then he turned back to face her.

"I think we go for a little ride," he said with an easy grin.

She threw him a puzzled look. "This is not the time for a joke, Raifer," she hissed.

He motioned her to his side and she went to him, her step wary.

"Look, Honor," he said, and he pointed down to the dark coach that stood waiting near the small side door at ground level just below them. "Edward is to be taken away in an ambulance coach. You don't think it might be that one, do you?"

A slow smile spread across her lips. "I think it just might," she agreed.

Raifer put his hand to Kevin's arm. "A little fresh

morning air?" he said as he fished about in his orderly's jacket. "I think we might spread a bit more confusion," he added as he pulled out the ring of keys he'd taken from Trask's desk and handed them to Honor.

"What do I do with these?" she asked.

"I think we may find something useful," he told her cryptically.

She took the keys, not sure what he intended, but knowing better than to ask. Then Raifer pulled the door to the corridor open and stared out, assuring himself that it was still empty. They started out and to the stairs.

They silently descended one flight. The sign on the door leading to the corridor of the ward bore the words *Nonviolent Ward*. Raifer smiled when he saw it.

"I think those keys might come in handy here, Honor," he told her. "A few open doors might lead to a bit of confusion, don't you think?" he asked with a smile.

She nodded as she removed the key marked *second floor pass* from the ring. Then, leaving Raifer waiting in the stairwell with Kevin, she moved along the corridor, opening those doors that were locked with the passkey.

The patients were mostly asleep. Only one old woman was sitting up, awake, in her bed.

"What are you doin'?" she demanded as Honor opened her door and began to leave.

"I thought you might like a little walk," Honor replied brightly and pushed the door wide open as an invitation to her to come out.

The old woman scowled. "Has Robespierre been overthrown, then?" she asked. "Is the revolt over?"

Honor nodded vaguely. "Yes," she replied.

The woman scrambled out of bed, pulling on a thick, flowered robe with long-fingered, shaking hands.

"Thank goodness," the woman told her and offered her a toothy grin. "I'm to be one of the Queen's ladies, you know. Now the revolt's over, I will be." She wagged her head enthusiastically. "There'll be fancy-dress balls and handsome young men to dance with me." She smiled as she touched the unruly tufts of her thin gray hair, a sadly coquettish gesture.

"Of course," Honor agreed. She darted a quick look out into the hall. Raifer would be wondering where she was, and she didn't want to waste any more time in the room with this old woman who'd lost herself somewhere in the French Revolution. She started to back away.

The woman reached out a bony hand to her. "Where is she?" she demanded.

"Who?" Honor asked.

"Marie," the old woman replied. "The Queen. She's a prisoner, too. They have her here somewhere."

Honor nodded. "Yes, yes, of course. I don't know which room she's in, but it must be one of these. Would you like to be the one to release her?"

The skin of the old woman's face crinkled as she smiled and she blushed as though she were a young girl. "It would be such a great honor," she said devoutly, as though whispering a prayer.

"Here," Honor said, pressing the key into her hand. "You can free all the prisoners, if you like. They're in the rooms along this corridor."

"Thank you, child," the old woman answered as she pressed the key to her flower-wrapped bosom. "I won't forget this day, not ever."

The woman bobbed her head and started out to the hall. Honor followed, wondering if she'd manage to be able to work the locks with her unsure-looking hands. Honor stood aside and watched the woman apply herself to the lock of the next door along the corridor. Miraculously, she seemed to be far more nimble than she appeared. She swung the door open wide. Honor, satisfied that she would manage, turned to go.

"You've done the Queen a great service," the old woman called after her. "She won't forget you."

Honor turned and saw the old woman staring after her, smiling. She returned the smile, then started off to the stairwell where Raifer waited with Kevin.

"Done?" he asked, surprised at the speed with which she'd returned.

She smiled. "Marie Antoinette's lady-in-waiting is finishing up for me," she said with a touch of glee. "And it seems the Queen is in my debt. I'm told she won't forget."

Raifer darted her an uneasy glance as he took Kevin's shoulder and urged him toward the next flight of stairs.

"Let's hope a living Queen will soon share her sentiments," he said as he motioned her to follow.

Honor stood huddled with Kevin beside the door to the outside as Raifer crept beneath the window and stood for a moment, locating the driver and guard who waited beside the ambulance.

The large, dark carriage cast a sharp shadow in the early morning sunshine. The two men stood close together and passed a dull-colored metal flask from hand to hand, apparently in an effort to keep themselves warm. They were both, Raifer had no trouble realizing, Flannagan's men. He and Edward had had an unfortunate acquaintanceship with them during their stint on board the fishing boat.

"It's time," one of them was saying as he took a last swallow from the flask. "You'd best go up and fetch them."

The second man eyed the bottle, watching the first replace the stopper and then deposit the flask in his jacket pocket. Then he nodded. "I'll go," he said once he was convinced the whiskey would not be offered again, and he started for the door.

Raifer quickly flattened himself beside the door and motioned to Honor to back away. When the man entered, he was ready, and as soon as the door swung shut behind the terrorist, he brought the side of his hand down hard on the back of the man's neck.

Honor thought it odd, how the terrorist simply fell, his expression unchanged, almost, only his eyes suddenly closing. There was a small thud as he fell, and Raifer darted a glance at the man outside waiting by the carriage, to see if he'd heard. Flannagan's man, however, seemed preoccupied with the contents of the flask which had once again appeared, and oblivious to the noise within.

Raifer motioned to Honor to be silent, then he quickly pulled the fallen man into the stairwell. He pulled the man's jacket off him and quickly shrugged into it. It was a bit tight across the shoulders, but he assumed no one would have the opportunity to make a thorough examination of his sartorial condition. He took the man's pistol, then appropriated his cap, pulling it firmly onto his head. Then he went back to join Honor.

"When I motion to you," he whispered, "you come out and bring McGowan."

She nodded, then watched him pull the cap low across his forehead, hoping to obscure his face a bit. He strode outside.

"Are they comin'?"

Raifer had expected the inquiry. He nodded, then moved quickly to the rear of the ambulance. As he hoped, the second terrorist seemed more interested in the prospect of seeing Edward than he was in what he assumed was his fellow's sudden urge to investigate the rear door of the coach. He moved to the side of the entrance door and peered in, waiting for a glance of Flannagan and the prince.

The man's eyes seemed to take a few seconds to focus on the forms just inside the entry, that of Honor and Kevin, staring back at him in fear-tinged surprise. When he did, he started forward, his hand to the door.

"What the . . . ?"

He never finished the question. Raifer sprang out at him and felled him from the rear, using the butt of the pistol he'd taken from the first man. Like his fellow, he dropped to the ground without making a further sound.

Raifer grabbed him under the arms and pulled him back out into the garden hedge that edged the wall of the sanitorium. Then he motioned to Honor. She darted out, and he motioned to her to get into the driver's seat. He removed the terrorist's jacket and cap and handed them up to her as she settled herself on the plank bench.

"Do you think you can handle this thing?" he asked, motioning toward the reins.

She nodded, not quite decisively, but with some show of determination.

Raifer smiled his encouragement, then darted a look toward the entryway where Kevin still stood, trussed and apparently bewildered. "Good," he told her. "If it's possible, I'll try to get up here and take over, but if we have to leave in a hurry, you may have to drive. I'll get Kevin and the other one, get them hidden with the one in the bushes."

"No," she interrupted. "He comes with us. He has to answer for my father's death."

"It won't be that easy, Honor," he told her evenly.

She shook her head. "He killed Papa. That was easy enough."

There was no time to argue with her, of that Raifer was absolutely certain. "All right, he comes with us.

When Flannagan comes down with the prince, I'll somehow get Edward into the coach. When you hear me shout, you get us out of here. Fast, unless you want us all dead. Clear?"

She nodded.

"And put those on," he said, pointing to the cap and jacket. "Cover up your hair before someone sees you."

She reached for the cap and piled her hair onto the top of her head, tucking it under the rough wool. She was pulling on the thick, rough jacket as Raifer turned away. He climbed down and made his way back to where Kevin still stood.

"You get in the rear," he told the older man, motioning toward the coach. He pulled the door open and once again motioned for Kevin to get inside.

Kevin only shook his head, for the first time since they'd descended the stairs beginning to show some sign of defiance. Raifer realized he could go nowhere at that moment, so he let him stand as he was while he returned to the stairwell and retrieved the unconscious body of the first terrorist. He pulled him back out through the entry and deposited him with his fellow with no more care than he'd show a sack of potatoes or one of the crates he'd handled back in Honor's father's warehouse in New York. The similarity occurred to him with a kind of detached amusement. All that seemed years before to him and somehow too hard to precisely recall. He returned to the entryway for Kevin.

This time he made no requests, but simply pulled out the pistol and pointed it. The older man's eyes went wide when he saw it and dully he moved as Raifer directed him, out the door and to the back of the waiting ambulance. Raifer held the door open and then was forced to help him climb inside. He fastened the door, then went around to the front of the carriage and climbed up once more beside Honor.

He sat silent for a moment, and stared at her. She seemed to be shivering despite the warmth of the stolen jacket, and it took him a few seconds to realize that it wasn't the cold that caused the trembling, but fear. He put his hand to hers, stilling the movement of her fingers with his own.

"Do you think you can do this, Honor?" he asked her softly. "Do you think you can drive this team?" If she was too frightened to do it, he knew, it would be a good deal more difficult.

She didn't turn to face him, but sat, as she had been, staring at the rumps of the two horses hitched to the ambulance coach. Then she nodded, her eyes still fixed to the front.

"Yes," she said in a hoarse sort of a whisper. "I can do it."

His hand pressed hers quickly, and she finally looked down to where his large hand covered hers and held it. If only it would always be so between them, she thought. If only I could think I would always be able to reach out and find his hand close to mine. The thought, she found, only made her feel miserable, and she forced her thoughts to the words she realized he was speaking.

"It won't be for long," he promised. "We'll get Edward away, and then we'll all be able to leave this behind."

She found she couldn't answer him, but only nodded once more. There was a dull thickness in her throat as she heard the words repeated only slightly differently from the way he'd said them. Yes, the echo in her mind taunted her, we'll be able to leave this behind, and he'll leave you behind as well. She knew the lump in her throat was not caused by her fear alone, but something else as well.

Raifer darted a quick glance up to the window on the third floor where he knew Flannagan waited with

Edward for word that the ambulance had arrived and awaited them.

"Perhaps I'd better go up there and give him the word," he murmured thoughtfully.

Honor put her hand to his sleeve and grasped it. "No," she cried softly. "He'll realize it's not one of his men, he'll kill you!"

"There ought to be a good bit of confusion up there by now," he began to protest, but then he quieted. He pulled the cap lower, over his eyes, and waved quickly up at the shadow of a man who had appeared at the window. Then he turned away and stared, as Honor had, at the horses' rumps.

"It seems they know we're here without any effort on my part after all," he told her evenly. He released the hand that had been holding hers. "When I call out to you, Honor," he reminded her as he began to climb down from the diver's seat, "slap the reins, hard, and get us out of here as fast as you can."

"As fast as I can," she repeated numbly. She watched him walk to the rear of the carriage. "You forgot to add, and pray," she muttered softly when he'd disappeared from her view.

Chapter Nineteen

Constable Regan had just removed his jacket and hung it on the rack by the door when the two strangers appeared, opening the door and entering just behind him. At first he seemed a bit stunned at the sight of them, for by their appearance they were certainly not the usual inhabitants of Ardrahan, or even anyplace close by. Their clothes spoke of Belfast, or perhaps even London, more than of the Irish countryside.

"We'll be speakin' to yer chief," the first said.

His words were right, the sound of them familiar enough, and that put Regan at his ease a bit, although his curiosity was certainly still raised.

"He'll be along in a bit," Regan replied, still eyeing the two. "His wife is ailin' of late. Her hip. She's a touch of arthritis, and the first cold mornings of the winter, don't you know. But Chief Grogran settles her in in the mornin', and then he comes along."

He stopped then, realizing he had talked too much, rambling on, that the explanations were unnecessary and unwanted. He wasn't sure why, but the two men made him nervous. He always seemed to talk too much when he was nervous.

"We'll wait," the second man told him, walking by him and settling himself familiarly at Grogan's desk.

The two words were pronounced with a clipped, short accent, but they were far too few for Regan to catch their impact, especially as he had become a bit flustered at the proprietary manner the men seemed to assume.

"You can't be sittin' there," he started, and motioned to the hard wooden benches that edged the wall.

"We'll sit where it pleases us, Constable," the man told him firmly as he leaned forward and extracted a leather case from his breast pocket.

The sentence was long enough to tell Regan what the first two words had not, that this one was an Englishman, and one accustomed to being in charge at that. His nervousness turned to near panic.

"I'm Commander Stainforth, Foreign Office," the seated man informed him with a look that said clearly that so lowly a person as Regan was entitled to nothing more. "This is my assistant, Lieutenant Coriarty. We have a few questions to ask your chief."

Regan felt his stomach heave queasily, and he stood, foolishly staring, as the second man, the one identified as Coriarty, settled himself in the only remaining almost comfortable chair in the room, his chair.

"If you could trouble yourself to make us a cup of tea?" Stainforth suggested pointedly, waking the young constable from his stupor. His expression suggested he would be doing Regan an honor were he to drink it.

"Yes, sir," Regan agreed, moving quickly to the coal stove and shoving a large scoop of coal from the scuttle into its belly, nearly managing to completely stifle the embers that remained there from the previous evening before he thought to stir them and the flame caught. He fussed a good deal over the tea, taking a far longer time to make it than would have otherwise been necessary, but was glad of the diversion. He'd just set down the mugs in front of Stainforth and Coriarty and set about filling the milk jug when Grogan arrived, and he offered up the responsibility for hospitality as well as the local police honor to his superior.

Grogan mumbled a good deal as he inspected the identification Stainforth offered him. He finally handed it back, holding it out to the Englishman deferentially.

"You'll excuse me, sir, but we've never had anyone from the Foreign Office here in Ardrahan."

"I daresay you'll have a good number more if there's any truth to my suspicions," Stainforth told him sharply.

"Suspicions?" Grogan was starting to feel as nervous as his underling had earlier.

Coriarty pulled from his breast pocket a sheet of paper which he proceeded to unfold with exaggerated slowness.

"This report, submitted by you, to the regional office in Galway," he said.

Grogan's eyes scanned the sheet, recognizing it immediately.

"Yes, sir," he agreed deferentially. "The weekly report. I sent it along yesterday, as I do every week on Thursday."

It wasn't much, he realized, and he mentally reviewed the lot, three drunks, one brawl, and that business Regan had tended to, about that young woman who'd escaped from the sanatorium, the same one who'd shown up the previous night. The last reminded him that he and Regan would doubtless have their work cut out for them that day, that was assuming he received notice from the sanatorium that the two patients were on the loose. If the fog had been less thick the night before, he'd have gone out to find the pair despite the lack of notification and saved themselves, unquestionably, a bit of time. But there was little thought that he and Regan could have found the two of them in the fog and there was really no need for him to put himself to the bother of a search, at least not until there was an official request from the hospital.

At that moment, however, he could only hope he and Regan would have the leisure to search for a few harmless crazy folk that day. The look in the Englishman's eyes seemed to tell him he might have other duties to perform. He considered the report, and wondered what in it could possibly be of any interest to the men from the Foreign Office.

Coriarty was quick to inform him. "There's an item

here about a young woman," he said, staring at Grogan with a look that implied the man should have recognized the importance of the particular situation all along.

The constable nodded. "Yes, sir. From the sanatorium just to the north of town, she was. Pretty wee bit of a thing. But mad as a hatter."

Coriarty made a show of completely ignoring him.

"This woman had a tale of having seen Prince Edward?" Stainforth cut in sharply.

Grogan nodded, eager to be of whatever use he could. "Yes, sir. But that was just tales, sir. The prince is in Scotland. It was in the papers only yesterday, it was."

"And where did she say she'd seen the prince?" Stainforth demanded.

Grogan turned to Regan for an answer. The younger man considered for a moment before he replied.

"I believe there was some mention of the old churchyard, in Kinvarra," he said.

Stainforth turned to stare at Coriarty, and then the two men began to rise.

Regan went on, not aware of their movement. "But then, last evenin', it was some story about the patients rioting at the sanatorium. She just seemed to want to get the police out on one wild-goose chase or another. Her and the man with her." He looked up at Stainforth. This time he could not miss the look that passed between the two Foreign Office men.

"Come along," Stainforth ordered as he moved toward the door. "The both of you. We just might have need of your services, for whatever they're worth."

Grogan darted Regan a look of perplexed vexation, but he started after the two Englishmen. All he offered by way of objection was a rather weak, "If you think it's really necessary, sir."

Flannagan got out of the chair and stretched. As he moved, the sharp stab of pain from his wounded shoulder sent a tremor through his torso. He hated the hurt, but more than that, he hated the awareness that he was not entirely in control, not of the situation, not even of his own body.

He turned abruptly to where Edward sat, neatly trussed and tied into a hospital straitjacket, in the corner. The prince almost looked like a madman, he thought. Between the restraining jacket, the disheveled and uncombed hair, and the untrimmed brush of his beard, he had a wild and entirely uncertain air. The fact pleased Flannagan. He began to consider the possibility of arranging for a final portrait of the prince, one that could be sent to Victoria as a reminder of her son's final hours.

The noise from the hall outside the room distracted him. "See what that brouhaha is about, Moynihan," he said crisply to the younger man who sat with a dejected sort of indifference facing the prince.

Moynihan nodded, rose, and went to the door, opening it slowly and peering out for a moment before he stepped back and reclosed it behind him.

"There's something wrong," he said slowly. "There's people out there, patients. Just roaming around unattended."

Flannagan turned to him sharply, the movement causing him to wince with the pain from his shoulder. "Where is that damned carriage?" he muttered angrily. He moved toward the window, but stopped as he passed Edward. "And what, may I ask, are you smiling about, Eddy? You're going to die today, or have I forgotten to tell you?"

Edward shook his head slowly. "No," he replied evenly. "You've made quite a point of mentioning it. But it seems something might go wrong for you after all. It seems already to be starting, doesn't it?" He offered Flannagan the widest of grins.

"Damn you," Flannagan snarled. He knelt and pulled out his knife. "Push me one step more, Eddy, and we won't wait for word of the vote in Parliament. I'll kill you here and now."

Edward's eyes were fixed on the knife. He'd seen it so often in Flannagan's hands, heard the threat so many times, he'd begun to think of how it would feel were Flannagan to press the blade between his ribs. He wondered if the fear could be worse than the reality.

Flannagan stood, obviously placated with Edward's thoughtful withdrawal. He continued on to the window and glanced down. The carriage was below, and he could just see one of the drivers, huddled into his jacket as he sat at the driver's seat. The man looked up briefly at him, then lowered his gaze back to the waiting animals.

"They're here," he said to Moynihan as he waved quickly to the man below. "The fools, they were to have come up and told me when they arrived. Let's be quick about this. Whatever's happening here, I don't like it."

"Not afraid, are you, Flannagan?" Edward suggested, his voice edged with a tinge of scorn as he once again found his courage. Funny, he thought, as matters seemed to grow worse and worse, he had begun to grow calmer and more certain of himself. Despite his awareness of the man's violent nature, despite the certainty that he would in most likelihood die soon, he had begun to lose his fear of Flannagan.

"Shut your mouth," Flannagan shouted at him. He turned and approached Edward, his fist raised.

But Moynihan caught it with his own. "That's not necessary," the younger man told him sharply.

Flannagan turned to face him, surprised at the determination he heard in Moynihan's tone. He stared at him as if he'd never seen the younger man before.

"Are you turnin' on me too, Thomas?" Flannagan asked him. "Is that it, now? You've forgotten all about your father? Your brother?"

Moynihan shook his head. "No," he replied evenly. "What must be done, must be done. I'm with you, and you know it. But there's no need for the rest of it," he said. "I'm sick of the violence. Theirs and ours."

" 'Tis a thin meal that sates you, Thomas," Flannagan told him thoughtfully.

Moynihan shrugged as though the words meant nothing to him. Then he crossed to Edward and pulled the prince to his feet.

"Let's be gettin' down, then. You said yourself you didn't like what was goin' on here."

He pushed Edward toward the door without glancing back to see the look of sharp consideration Flannagan leveled at him.

"It's seems you've forgotten the costs, Thomas, the reasons," Flannagan said to his back.

Moynihan turned and faced him, then he shook his head slowly. "No, I've forgotten nothing," he said. "Except, perhaps, my humanity."

"We've no use for their values, Thomas," Flannagan preached to him. "They're empty baggage to us, needless burdens we can't afford to carry."

"Are they?" the younger man asked. "Perhaps. I can't say they're doin' me much good just now. But somehow I simply can't be so easily shut of them as you seem to be."

There was bitterness in his tone, and a sharply critical look in his eyes as he stared at Flannagan. Then he shrugged once more and turned away, apparently done with the conversation.

"We'd best be goin'."

By the time they'd descended the stairs to the second floor, they'd encountered half a dozen patients, all unaccompanied and obviously enjoying their unexpected stint of freedom. Noise drifted from the second-floor corridor, attesting to the fact that there were quite a few more in a similar position, and that whatever nurses and orderlies were on duty at that hour were completely overwhelmed with the situation. There were several shrieks, not all of them of glee.

"It's like Bedlam," Moynihan muttered, his manner

agitated from the sounds and the unexpected appearance of so many of the patients. "We'd better get out of here fast." He hurried Edward along on the stairs.

"What would you expect it to be like, Thomas?" Flannagan asked him. "It isn't like Bedlam; it is Bedlam." His tone grew bitter. "It's all Bedlam. We can't escape it."

Moynihan turned to him and gave him a perplexed look, but said nothing. Before starting down again, however, he was struck with the fact that they were leaving one of their number behind.

"Hadn't someone better go back for McGowan?" he asked.

Flannagan seemed to consider the question for a moment, as though he might be just as willing to leave McGowan where he was and forget him. But he nodded.

"You take our precious Eddy on out safely to the coach," he said. "I'll go back for McGowan."

Then he turned and began to climb as Moynihan, his hand firmly holding the prince's shoulder, proceeded on down the stairs and to the side door.

"Hurry yourself, man," Moynihan muttered as they neared the entry. The shouts seemed to have been growing louder from the floor above, and he realized that they disturbed him a great deal more than he would care to admit. He took his pistol from his pocket, suddenly wary, and held it ready in his free hand. Then he quickly pushed the door to the outside open and proceeded to the back of the carriage.

He was surprised to find the door closed, having expected it to be open and awaiting the prince, but he pulled it open, too, and pushed Edward forward to it. It wasn't until the prince had half climbed in that he looked inside and saw the unexpected vision of Kevin McGowan, trussed and gagged, sitting on the wooden bench inside.

"What's going on here?" Moynihan demanded as he dropped his hand from Edward's arm and looked around.

There was a small movement, and without really thinking, he fired at it, his action one of reflex, not thought. If he'd had the chance to consider, he'd have noticed Raifer's pistol aimed for his heart.

All of which was very lucky for Raifer. Had Moynihan taken the time to aim, Raifer surely would have been shot dead, for there was no possibility that the young terrorist could have missed the mark at such close range. When he'd seen the pistol in Moynihan's hand turn to him, Raifer had immediately aimed the weapon he'd taken from the driver he'd left unconscious in the bushes. But this pistol wasn't like the police arms he'd been accustomed to using in the past. It was cheap and not very well tended. It misfired, and the awareness of that fact was immediately followed by the sensation of pain in his upper arm.

The pistol dropped from Raifer's hand. He was pushed backward by the force of the blow.

Moynihan considered him dully for only a second, but during that second he seemed to have drawn the conclusion that Raifer and Honor had reached the authorities, somehow convinced them that the prince was indeed in Ardrahan after all and in need of rescue, and the whole of the local police force was about to descend upon him, Flannagan and the others. It was an eventuality he'd come to expect over the previous few days, most especially after he'd found Flannagan the night before, wounded and tied up in the cell where the Americans had been imprisoned. The thought of losing when they were so close, the realization that it had been for nothing, was more than Moynihan could stand. He pointed the pistol at Edward.

"For my father," he said as he put his finger to the trigger. "For my brother."

He pressed.

Kevin saw him turn and raise the pistol. He knew immediately what Moynihan was about to do, and he knew just as certainly that he could not allow it to happen, that if Edward were killed there would never be any peace for the Irish. The whole attempt had been insane, he realized, and it had all gone too far, much further than any of them had anticipated at the start.

He leaped forward, letting his bulk fall against Edward, knocking the prince forward to the ground at the foot of the carriage. As he fell after Edward, Kevin felt a sharp, burning pain in his stomach, and knew Moynihan's bullet had found a mark, if not the one he'd expected. He fell forward, aware of the pain, and realizing that he didn't care. He'd come to consider himself dead since the moment he'd caused Daniel Wainwright's death. All Moynihan's bullet had done was finalize that death. Nothing, he realized, mattered but that Edward not be killed.

Honor heard the first shot and felt a sudden staggering surge of panic. She dropped the reins and began to scramble down from the driver's seat, unaware that she was praying aloud, "Please, Lord, don't let it be Raifer." As her foot touched the ground, she heard the report of the second shot. She turned and saw him lying on the ground. The feeling of loss hit her like a blow. But then she saw him move, his hand reaching out and grasping the fallen pistol. It was then she looked up and saw Moynihan, aiming his own weapon for a second shot at the prince. She stood, immobile with fear, and for a third time the sound of a shot tore through the air.

For a second everything seemed frozen, unmoving. Then the pistol fell from Moynihan's hand and the big young man slumped and fell.

It was then that Honor realized Raifer was getting painfully to his feet, saw the pistol in his hand, and saw he'd managed to fire before Moynihan had the chance. She ran forward to him only to find her glance filled with the spectacle of the three fallen men, Edward, Moynihan, and Kevin. Together, she and Raifer moved forward, reaching out to Edward who, impeded by his bound arms, was trying unsuccessfully to get to his feet.

Then Raifer knelt by Kevin and drew away the gag from his mouth.

"Why did you do it?" he asked. He smiled gently. It was only too obvious to him that Kevin was dying.

The older man looked up and found Honor's wide, terrified glance. "It was wrong," he told her. "It was all wrong from the start. I didn't realize it until I saw him raise the pistol. But I knew this was the only way I could make amends for what I've done."

Honor's eyes moved down his body to the blood-smeared front of his shirt and jacket. She fell to her knees beside him. For all the times in the previous weeks she'd thought she wanted to see him dead, to see him killed as her father had been killed, she realized at that moment that death, most especially Kevin's death, could do nothing to remedy what had happened.

"Oh, Kevin," she murmured as she reached out her hand to his cheek. It was only when she saw the drop fall to his shirt that she realized she was crying.

"Sweet Honor," he whispered. "I do love you like my own." Then he struggled to move, to lift himself.

"No, don't," she cried.

He shook his head. "I'm dead, Honor. But you, you and Farrell must get away. Take the prince and go." He looked around wildly, searching for Raifer's face. "Take her and go," he panted when his eyes had found Raifer's. "Now. Flannagan is still here." His eyes grew wild. It was obvious he was in great pain. "And *him*."

Those words said, he fell back and grew suddenly very still. Honor stared at him, not quite understanding.

"He's dead," Raifer told her softly as he put a hand to her shoulder and drew her up. "Get into the carriage with Edward."

She stood shakily, but once she was back on her feet, she realized that they were still far from safe.

"No," she told him, staring at the bloodied arm. "You're hurt. You can't drive."

He considered her for a few seconds. "Are you sure you

can handle the team?" he asked her.

She nodded. "I'm sure."

Raifer turned to Edward. "Inside," he said. "We'll see about removing that thing there," he added, referring to the straitjacket. "No time now."

Honor watched as the two of them climbed into the carriage, then turned and began to move to the front. She paused as she passed Moynihan's body, then knelt and gingerly retrieved his fallen pistol, not quite aware of what it was she was doing, but subconsciously realizing there might be need of it. Then she ran to the front of the carriage, climbed hastily up into the driver's seat, took up the reins, and slapped them sharply on the horses' rumps.

Flannagan ran out of the building in time to see the carriage disappear into the greenery of the lane leading to the sanatorium grounds gate. He looked down dully at the still bodies of Kevin and Thomas Moynihan. Kevin's he ignored, but he fell to his knees beside Moynihan.

"Oh, Thomas, lad," he moaned softly. "Why did you have to go and get yourself killed?" He could feel an unaccustomed thickening in his throat, and for a second he wondered how long it had been since he'd cried. "I'll get them for you, Tommy. I'll kill them all for you," he murmured softly as he gazed into the sightless eyes. Finally he reached out and closed Moynihan's eyes, unable to stare at them any longer. Then he leaned forward and kissed the still cheek, realizing that it was already beginning to grow cold.

"What the hell do you think you're doing, Flannagan?"

He looked up and felt the urge to weep fading as it was replaced by the familiar feeling of a more potent emotion, the sharp, vengeful surge of hatred.

"He's dead. They're both dead," he said to the man who had followed him from the inside.

"They can't get far," the other man told him. "Horses.

We can still catch them and salvage this fiasco." He stared at Flannagan sharply. "Move, man. There's no more time to lose."

He walked past the two still bodies as if they weren't there, without even wasting a glance on them.

Honor drove the horses furiously. When she reached the sanatorium gate, she pulled them to an abrupt halt. Raifer jumped down from the carriage and swung the gate open so the carriage could pass through. Honor watched him with a kind of detached curiosity, noting the dark red stain of his blood on his sleeve, the way his arm hung useless and limp at his side. She could do this, she told herself fiercely. She could do whatever she had to do. The three of them had suffered too much only to lose to Flannagan in the end. She would not allow herself fear, nor the thought of defeat.

"Which way?" she shouted to Raifer.

He hesitated for a moment, then pointed in the direction away from Ardrahan. Honor nodded, understanding. She could only imagine the sort of reception they might expect to receive in the town, the same sort they'd found the evening before, and their protestations as to Edward's identity would only be looked upon as further ravings of escaped maniacs. She had to admit that the whole situation must seem preposterous. And anyone seeing Edward at that moment would have no difficulty branding him a madman were he to claim to be a prince. He hardly looked princely.

Had she known that the entirety of the Ardrahan constabulary, under the leadership of two agents Gladstone had sent and who were more than willing to accept the possibility of the prince's presence, was leaving the town for the sanatorium at that very moment, Honor would happily have chosen that direction, would gladly have given herself over to their authority. As it was, however, both she and Raifer were ignorant of the fact that anyone in Ireland might seriously consider their story true, and so chose to turn the carriage in the direction of Galway.

She waited until Raifer was back inside the coach and then slapped the reins once more, urging the horses onto the road, turning them far too quickly and nearly tipping the coach in her inexperience and haste. But they were lucky, the carriage settled itself, the horses set to their work, and Honor intently concentrated on the driving.

They'd ridden for nearly half an hour, and Honor was just considering the possibility of stopping the carriage and seeing how Raifer and the prince were doing. After the panic of the first few minutes, she'd begun to feel at her ease. She found it was far easier than she'd anticipated handling the team, and she was beginning to think Flannagan had made no effort at pursuit. After all, it was now full morning, a brightly sunny morning, and the carriage was traveling through a country of rolling green hillsides. Nothing could happen to them in such a place, out in the open, she told herself.

It was then she heard the sound of the shot. There was no mistaking it, not after the events she'd witnessed on the sanatorium grounds. She darted a glance backward and saw them, two horsemen, galloping after the coach. She could tell they were growing closer even as she watched them. The one to the front, the closest, was Flannagan. She couldn't see the face of the second man.

She turned back to the horses, gripped the reins more firmly in her hands, and slapped them against the horses' flanks, urging them forward. Whatever feeling of calm and certainty she'd been feeling disappeared. She should have realized that Flannagan wouldn't simply let them walk away with the prince. And this time, she knew if he caught them, he wouldn't stop until they were all dead.

If Honor was surprised at her first glimpse of Flannagan following them, Raifer was not. He'd expected pursuit, had imagined the sound of horses' hooves beating on the road behind them, since they'd left the sanatorium. He'd been working furiously at the knots of the straps that held the straitjacket in which Edward was confined. It was a near impossible task for him, for the knots had been tied securely and his right hand was virtually useless, the loss of blood from the wound in his arm making his fingers unresponsive. It was an agony to him to lift the arm. The wound was still bleeding profusely, and he knew he would have to do something about it fairly quickly, or he would be of no use whatsoever. Despite his efforts, Edward was still entrapped in the jacket when they heard the first shot.

"Honor," Raifer muttered, and he felt a thick throb of panic, of fear that she might be hurt.

Then he felt the carriage pick up speed. He and the prince were jostled against the side of the carriage. He made his way to the rear door and pulled it open so that he could see out. His left hand gingerly grabbed for the pistol he'd used when he'd shot Moynihan. He wondered if he would be able to aim left-handed. And then he began to wonder if the pistol would even fire, or if it would jam again or misfire, as it had done before.

"Only one way to find out," he muttered, half aloud, as he steadied himself, leaning against the side of the carriage as it bumped along the uneven road. He took as careful aim as he could and pulled the trigger.

Nothing happened. As it had before, the firing mechanism of the pistol jammed, and this time the condition seemed to be permanent.

"Damn," Raifer muttered angrily.

He darted a glance out the door and realized that Flannagan was closing the gap between them. He could see the man's upraised hand and the metallic glint of the pistol. And then he could hear the report of two more shots, and felt the stinging bite of a bullet as it nicked his cheek.

He jumped back, slamming the carriage door shut. There was the sound of another bullet, and the dull crack it made as it came into contact with the wood of the carriage door.

"What do we do?"

Edward was staring at him, Raifer realized, obviously expecting him to make the decision, to somehow provide some idea for escape. Raifer looked around them.

The carriage had been fitted out as a conveyance for the sick. A cot was bolted to one side, and a wooden bench to the other. There was nothing else.

"That," he said, pointing to the bench. "Help me pull it from the wall."

Edward stared at him as if he were a bit mad after all, but he did as Raifer asked, standing with his back to the front of the coach and using his feet to push the bench free. Between the two of them they managed to tear it loose of its bolts.

"Now what?" Edward asked as Raifer used his good arm to drag the bench to the rear of the carriage.

"Now we see if Mr. Flannagan has ever had the opportunity to refine his skills at steeplechase," Raifer told him.

He pushed the door wide open and threw the bench out.

At first he was surprised at how close Flannagan had come, then he realized that was to their advantage. The long bench rolled from the carriage onto the dirt road, bouncing once, and then coming into sharp contact with Flannagan's horse's front legs.

Both animal and rider were unprepared for the blow. The horse fell to its knees and Flannagan slid forward, landing on his face and then rolling over. His horse returned quickly to his feet, limped for a few steps as though testing himself for injury, and then trotted toward the hillside that edged the road, obviously intent now on rest and a few mouthfuls of the rye grass growing there. Flannagan, however, lay where he had landed, on his back in the middle of the road, his eyes staring dully upward.

From where they watched, both Raifer and Edward

could see what happened next, as the second rider, as little prepared for the obstacles that now littered his path as Flannagan had been, attempted a jump to save himself from the same fate. His animal cleared the thrown bench. It didn't clear Flannagan's body.

The last thing Flannagan saw were the hooves, the certainty of his own death. There was only time for a short scream, and then that, too, was cut short by the impact.

The second rider's horse went down on his front knees, his weight completing what the contact of his hooves had begun. His rider, however, clung tight and held his seat. The horse got back to its feet, and the rider urged him on after the fleeing coach. After giving Flannagan's bloody body only a brief glance, he seemed to forget him altogether.

It was about that moment that Honor turned and saw the crumpled heap of Flannagan's body on the road, and the second rider still coming after them.

"Oh, God," she murmured as she realized what had happened to Flannagan, somehow sure that his death would have to be paid for if the second man managed to reach them. She turned back quickly to the horses. The woolen cap flew free as she turned, letting her long, burnished gold curls escape to the grasping fingers of the wind.

"One down," Raifer muttered as he darted a glance out the door. A shot rang through the coach, this time fired by their one remaining pursuer. Raifer slammed the door shut.

"And one to go," Edward added doggedly. "Shall we try the cot?"

Raifer shook his head. "No good," he replied as he saw the second terrorist nudge his horse toward the edge of the road. "He's keeping to the side. He won't fall for the same ploy."

As he dared another look back, Raifer realized the rider had slowed his horse and seemed to be drawing the animal to a stop as he sat simply staring after the carriage while the animal came to a chest-heaving halt at the side of the road.

"What is he doing?" Edward asked, as he too came to realize the man was no longer pursuing.

"I don't know," Raifer admitted slowly. "He's got the advantage now. He could close in for the kill."

They continued to watch as the terrorist raised himself in the saddle, staring at the mane of Honor's hair which floated golden in the morning sunshine.

Chapter Twenty

Honor realized that flight was no longer necessary as she darted quick glances back, noticing the last of the terrorists sitting, staring at the quickly growing distance that separated him from the carriage. She allowed the horses to slow a bit, eventually bringing them to a halt several minutes later when they were well out of view of the horseman and the place where Flannagan had fallen. The road had come to a division, parting left and right, and edging a narrow stream.

Honor jumped down and raced to the back of the carriage just as Edward and Raifer were climbing out.

"We're safe," she shouted to them, her tone filled with glee and relief.

"So it would seem," Raifer muttered in response, his words not at all as assured as hers had been.

She stopped suddenly and stood staring at him. "Raifer," she whispered, reaching out to the cut on his face.

He winced and drew back, then brought his good hand to the cut and gingerly wiped away the dark line of dripped blood that lined his cheek.

"It's just a scratch," he told her as he considered the red stain it left on his fingers. "If you could manage, freeing Edward might be useful." He nodded toward the still securely fastened restraining jacket.

Honor emitted a small, nervous laugh as she moved toward the prince. "We must look a regal threesome, the lot of us," she said as she worked at the knotted straps at Edward's back. She darted a look at Raifer and saw him staring back, obviously keeping watch for the last of the terrorists. The road behind them seemed quiet and still.

"He was probably one of Flannagan's underlings," Edward suggested, "who decided the cost wasn't worth the game."

Raifer kept his eyes to the place where the road curved behind them. "Perhaps," he muttered. "In any case, I don't think we should stay here too long."

"We are safe, aren't we?" Honor asked him softly when it occurred to her, as it obviously had to Raifer, that the terrorist might not have given up after all.

He turned to face her and offered her a distant smile. "Certainly," he told her when he saw the shadow of fear returning to her expression. Then he grinned. "It would seem your adventure is finally at an end, Honor."

She swallowed, suddenly aware of the thick feeling in her throat. "Yes," she managed. "At an end."

She turned back to loosening the knots at Edward's back, trying to concentrate on what her fingers were doing, trying not to think the words, that it was more than the adventure that was over, but whatever she and Raifer had shared was now ended, too.

The knots were finally all untied, and Edward's arms fell limp at his sides. She helped him remove the heavy canvas jacket.

"We've still to find some authorities who will believe us," he began. "Not that I'd much blame them if they were to take the same attitude as your friends in Ardrahan." He smiled pleasantly at Honor. "Remind me in the future never, under any circumstances, to remove my clothing. It seems that clothes do make the man, after all."

He laughed, and Honor managed a weak accompaniment. Then Edward fell silent, offering her a weak smile by way of apology for his poor joke, and concentrated on rubbing his sore arms and wrists to return the circulation to them. He seemed to realize that something was happening between Raifer and Honor, and he could see the hurt in her eyes, but he was not quite sure what it was, nor what he could do to help.

Raifer moved to the stream and began to daub some of the cold water to the cut on his cheek. When Honor saw him, she followed.

"Let me do that," she said. She pulled his hand away from the cut. "It looks like it hurts," she said.

Then she lifted the hem of her skirt and pulled off a piece of her petticoat, wondering vaguely as she did so what Squire Blaileigh's wife would think if she were to see to what use her charity was being put. Then she noticed the way that Raifer stared at the bit of exposed calf, and the way he suddenly tore his glance from it to stare determinedly at the flow of the water in the stream.

She wet the cloth and wiped Raifer's cheek clean. "I think this is nothing compared to your arm," she told him, letting her glance fall to the blood-soaked sleeve of his jacket.

"You're probably right," he agreed as he pulled off the jacket, then sat, staring at the limp, gory mess of his arm. There was a dark, angry scar just above the wound, attesting to the just-healed hole where the first wound had been. "This is getting to be a bad habit, I think," he muttered dryly.

Edward paled a bit as he stared at the wound, grimly fascinated, and then turned away. Honor began to wash the wound, aware of the way Raifer flinched at the contact. Her stomach heaved at the sight of the blood and the pale, broken flesh.

"We should take you to a doctor, Raifer," she told him.

He only shook his head. "I think what we do is make our way to London. I don't think Edward will be safe until he's out of Ireland."

"Why?" she demanded sharply. "Flannagan's dead. He couldn't have lived after the way that horse trod him. You said yourself it was over."

Raifer offered her a grim stare. "Flannagan wasn't alone in this. The sanatorium, the apparent ease with which it was all done . . . the more I think about it, the surer I am about Fitzpatrick in New York. But we've no idea who was involved here. We can't afford to trust anyone."

She sat back on her heels for a moment, staring at him. That's all that he thinks about, she thought, and not for the first time, all that matters to him, that he figure it all out, find the culprits. There's nothing else for him but his damned job. Grimly, she set about the task of bandaging the hole in his arm.

"And just how do you propose we get there?" she asked. "Or am I supposed to drive this thing all the way to the coast?" She nodded towards the carriage with its dark identification on the side, the word *ambulance* printed in flat, clear letters.

"No," he told her. "It's too noticeable. We'll have to leave it somewhere, and soon."

"Then what?" she demanded, a note of exasperation creeping into her voice. She pulled the long piece of petticoat she was using as a bandage too tight, tight enough to make him wince in pain, but she didn't seem to notice.

"Britian has a fine rail system, Honor," he told her. "We take a train to Dublin, a ferry to Liverpool, then the train again to London."

"But unfortunately, old man, all that isn't free," Edward broke in. His expression seemed a bit apologetic "And we've no money."

"But if Honor would be willing to part with this," Raifer replied as he reached out and caught her hand with his good one, "we should be able to manage," he said evenly

Honor looked down at the hand he was holding. It wa bare, save for the ring Terrence McGowan had placed o her finger all those long weeks before. Funny, she thought, she'd not even noticed it was there, not for th whole of that time. She'd not thought of the ring, nor o Terrence, not since the evening he'd given it to her There'd been so many other things to think about. An now, with her thoughts forced to him, she realized she fel nothing, no anger, no affection, nothing at all. There wa just the uncomfortable feeling that she would someday be forced to tell him of the circumstances surrounding his father's death.

"Certainly," she said, putting the ring from her finger and holding it out to Raifer.

Edward stepped forward. "We can't do that," he said. His manner seemed to convey shock. "We can't take a lady's jewels. It wouldn't be gentlemanly."

Raifer looked up at him and grinned. "You're not doing it, Edward. I am. And I have no doubt that Honor is completely resigned to the fact that I'm not a gentleman."

She finished bandaging the arm and tied the ends tight.

"Ouch," Raifer complained as she pulled the ends to form the knot.

She smiled at him grimly. "You're quite right, Mr. Farrell," she said primly. "I've never been of the opinion that you were a gentleman. I see no reason to start now."

Raifer grinned, tossed the ring in the air, and caught it. "Then it's settled," he said. "Let's move on. It's still a long ride to Galway."

It was late afternoon by the time they reached Galway, too late to try to sell the ring at any of the half dozen curio, antique, or jewelry shops they passed.

"Now what?" Honor demanded as she stared at the closed and shuttered storefronts.

"We find the station," Raifer told her.

"But we've no money to pay for tickets," she countered.

"I'll think of something when I get there," was his not unexpected reply.

When they reached the station, Raifer directed Edward to drive on past. It wasn't until they'd reached a quiet, nearly empty residential street that he told the prince to pull the coach to a halt.

"The ambulance will call less attention here," he explained as Edward tied up the reins and then helped

Honor to the ground.

Honor was decidedly grateful for the emptiness of the street as she stretched her legs. They'd doubtless seemed an odd threesome, she thought, riding through the town, all perched on the driver's seat of the ambulance. She'd noticed more than one curious glance.

More than just uncomfortable at feeling herself an object of curiosity, she was tired and cramped and sore from the long ride. The walk back to the train station seemed almost pleasant by comparison, a welcome change. And she was hungry, she realized, ravenously hungry.

"Can we get something to eat, do you think?" she asked Raifer. "That is, once you've worked your magic and gotten us onto the train?" She looked up at him walking between her and Edward. She was shocked to see how pale he looked in the waning light. His face seemed drained, and his step was not his usual strong stride.

"Raifer," she asked him softly. "Are you all right?"

He looked down at her and smiled, a warm, gentle smile that lit up his eyes. "I think we could all use a good dinner and a warm bed," he replied.

The smile left his lips as he said the last word, but something about the way he peered at her, the way his eyes seemed to look into her, made Honor's heart jump. She turned away quickly, not wanting him to see her tremble, to notice the surge of hope that filled her. That's all he's interested in you for, she told herself sharply, one last time in bed, a final hour's amusement. Then he'll go back to his real love, his job. And he'll go wreathed in the glory of his success. He couldn't ask for anything more.

When they reached the station, Honor and Edward stood to one side as Raifer approached the ticket clerk.

"Three to London," he said easily.

The clerk looked up at him, his sharp eyes taking in the rumpled clothing, the dark, rust-colored stain on the torn sleeve of the rough jacket.

"You got money?" he asked Raifer unceremoniously, with no hint of appology for the affront in his tone.

Raifer stared at him, his eyes hard. The ticket clerk found himself turning away, more than a bit disturbed by the intensity of the look. This was not a man who would accept insult, he realized. And by the looks of him, he was not afraid of a bit of trouble.

"I have something better than money," Raifer told him as he held out the sapphire ring Honor had given him.

The clerk's eyes found the stone and seemed unable to tear themselves away. It was obvious that the ring was worth a small fortune, more money than he'd ever see in one place in his lifetime. And it was equally obvious to him that Raifer could not have come by such a piece of jewelry honestly.

For a second the man's greed battled with his conscience. It didn't take very long. Greed won out easily.

"This ain't no jewelry store," he told Raifer softly, conspiratorially, as though he did not want to be overheard. "But then, I suppose you couldn't sell it at no jewelry store."

Raifer smiled. "Oh, but I could. That is, if I were willing to wait until morning. But I see there's a train tonight," he said, looking up at the departure schedule behind the clerk's seat, "and we want to be on it." He leaned forward and lowered his voice to a near whisper. "You see," he said, nodding toward Honor and Edward, "the ring belongs to that young lady. She and my friend are running away to be married. They can't afford to wait until the morning, until her father and brother come after them. You know how it is." He stayed as he was a moment longer, leaning across the counter, his smile challenging the clerk to believe him. Then he smiled as he drew back, a knowing, humorless smile. He raised his wounded arm and let it drop to the counter as the clerk continued to stare, aware that the man's eyes were as intrigued by the bloodstain as they had been by the sight of the sapphire. "Don't worry," he added. "No one is going to report this ring stolen."

The clerk looked up at him then, at the intent look in Raifer's eyes and the knowing smile. He needed nothing more to convince him that Raifer was a thief, and a murderer, too, most likely. He decided to accept the story. If it were ever to come to it, he told himself, he could tell the authorities that he'd been forced to the exchange. And if he was lucky, he stood to make a small fortune on the exchange.

He took out his ticket book and wrote out the three sets of tickets, then pushed them across to Raifer's waiting hand.

"Third class to Dublin, packet to Liverpool, third class to London," he said as he delivered the tickets.

Raifer didn't bother to even look down at the handful of paper. "And I'll be needing ten pounds," he told the clerk. "You wouldn't want me to go hungry, now, would you?" He allowed his good hand to drift menacingly to the inside of his coat, aware that the clerk inferred he was reaching for a weapon.

"Ten pounds," the man repeated nervously as his hands moved toward the cash drawer. "Certainly. The ring's worth that."

"And more," Raifer assured him. "At least a hundred times more."

The clerk took a ten-pound note from the drawer and pushed it across the counter to him, keeping his eyes on the way Raifer's hand returned to the inside of his coat after he'd picked up the bill.

"Track two," he said hoarsely. "You can board in ten minutes."

Raifer backed away from the counter, then grasped Honor's arm and led her and Edward off into the interior of the station, toward the tea table at the far wall.

"How did you do it?" Honor demanded. "What did you tell him?"

Raifer allowed himself the luxury of laughter. "I told him the ring was yours, and you and Edward were running away to marry. And I let him believe that I'd done some violence and stolen the thing and needed to leave. What he believes is up to him, but I think he leaned toward the implication, rather than the story."

They'd reached the tea table by the time he'd finished his explanation, and the three of them surveyed the savaged trays of sandwiches and breads that remained at that late hour of the day. At the sight of food, Honor's stomach began to growl rather loudly. Edward grinned at that, causing her to blush and back away while Raifer had the vendor put a half dozen rather limp-looking sandwiches and an equal number of nondescript muffins into a bag. When he'd paid with the note the ticket clerk had given him and collected the change, they started toward the track to board the train.

"Wait," Raifer said, pointing to an issue of the evening paper that had been left on one of the waiting area benches. "This must have been what they were trying to do."

Edward and Honor stood and scanned the headline, *"Parliament Narrowly Defeats Vote to Disestablish C of I."* Then Edward shook his head.

"Gladstone was only two votes short," he said as he finished the article. "If they'd given him more time, he probably could have done it."

"I think this has as much to do with power as it does with the vote," Raifer mused. "Whoever engineered this thing, he intends to prove himself as strong and as powerful as the crown. This was just his way of proving it."

His words seemed to startle Edward, for he stared at Raifer without answering.

"I think we'd better go," Honor told them.

Edward dropped the paper and they moved on. The conductor was ringing the bell to announce that their train was being boarded. They followed the stream of passengers to the edge of the track, where a porter pointed them to the four rear cars, then left them to find their own way, obviously deciding they were without funds to provide him with a tip and therefore not worth the exertion of any further effort. They moved along amidst the flow of the rest of the third-class passengers, their bag of food looking at home with the cardboard valises and packages tied up with bits of rope and string others carried.

When they'd disappeared, a man who had been sitting quietly absorbed with his evening paper rose and moved to the ticket window where Raifer had purchased their tickets.

"There was a man here a few minutes ago," he told the clerk with a sharp, low tone. "He bought three tickets and paid in a rather unusual manner."

The clerk felt a flush of fear creep into his cheeks. The woman's father, he thought in a panic. Or brother, he amended as he judged the man's age.

"He said it belonged to the woman, that it wasn't stolen," the clerk pleaded, his voice rising into an unpleasant whine as he considered the possibility that he might be entrapped, involved with some crime.

The man smiled at him. "Indeed," he said as he removed his wallet from his breast pocket. Slowly, he counted out twenty ten-pound notes and placed them on the counter in front of the clerk. "And I'm sure we both wish to see it returned to her."

The clerk, his eyes on the pile of crisp notes, managed to nod. "Indeed, sir."

"They were going to London?"

"Yes," the clerk nodded once more.

"Then I suppose I shall have to do the same," the man said, pushing the notes forward. "I shall bring the ring to her," he added, his eyes sharp, intimidating.

The clerk pulled out his ticket book. "Yes, sir," he said as he somehow managed to produce the proper combination despite the shaking in his hands, and then pushed them across the counter.

"Aren't you forgetting something?"

The clerk looked terrified for a moment, staring down at the tickets he'd authorized, wondering what it was he'd done wrong.

"The lady's property," the man reminded him.

"Yes, sir," he replied, his voice shaky, as he reached into his pocket and withdrew the ring. He placed it on top of the tickets.

The man smiled. "Very good," he said as he pocketed the ring and the tickets.

When he'd turned away, the clerk leaned back into his chair and felt his heart racing. Then he reached out to the neat stack of bills on the counter in front of him, counted out the price of the tickets, and quickly pocketed the rest.

Once they'd boarded the train, Honor, Raifer, and the prince made their way into one of the third-class cars, crowded and jostled by the press of anxious travelers, and found themselves lucky to find three empty seats together. Honor and Raifer fell into the two seats together on one bench, and Edward sat facing them. The fourth seat, the one beside Edward, was quickly occupied by a large, unkempt man in a plaid suit and bowler hat who smelled strongly of beer. He stared at the three of them as the train left the station. Then, losing his curiosity, he pulled his hat down low over his face and proceeded to fall into a deep and very noisy sleep.

As soon as the scenery outside her window had turned from cityscape to the darkness of countryside night, Honor turned her attention to the activities in the car around them. Dinner pails had been brought out and opened, and the air had quickly become redolent with the smells of sausage and beer.

Edward leaned across the narrow passage between the benches, toward Raifer. "I don't suppose I could persuade you to produce that magnificent feast you purchased for us, could I, old man?" he asked.

Honor nodded enthusiastically. "I'm hungry enough to eat a horse," she announced.

"You may be doing just that," Raifer replied as he produced the sandwiches. "These are supposed to be beef, but I have my doubts."

Despite the warning, the three of them fell to quickly consuming the entire contents of the bag. While they ate, the conductor passed through the car, collecting and punching tickets with an air of supreme indifference.

Raifer noticed that among the third-class passengers, his torn and bloodied sleeve seemed no longer an object of curiosity. Poverty, he realized, provided one with a certain measure of invisibility.

When Honor had finished the last of her share of the food, she put her hand to her mouth. "I have never been so tired in my life," she said as she yawned and then leaned against Raifer's shoulder. The image of the snoring man across from her seemed an inspiration. She was asleep almost immediately.

Edward gazed at her as Raifer put his arm around her and held her.

"I hope I'll be able to make all this up to the both of you once we've reached London. I know all you've both been through on my account."

Raifer looked down at Honor thoughtfully before he replied. "I think we'll concentrate on getting back to London before we talk about debts," he said softly. Then he lifted his head and his eyes roamed the length of the railroad car. "We're not there yet."

Despite his vigilance, Raifer finally gave in to sleep, and so did not see the darkly dressed, red-haired man who strolled through the length of the car later that night. The car was quiet by that time, the travelers all sated from their train meal and, having made themselves as comfortable as possible, succumbed to sleep. Not that the man seemed out of the ordinary. Red-haired, blue-eyed, he seemed just another struggling Irish businessman off on some hopeful venture. But the careful observer would have noticed that he seemed a bit too interested in the faces of the sleeping travelers as he meandered down the length of the long, central aisle of the car. He would have seen that the man's face contorted with emotion as he paused momentarily beside the seats where Honor, Edward, Raifer, and their noisily snoring companion dozed, that it took him a moment to settle himself before he continued on his solitary constitutional. As it was, the occupants of the car all slept, save for the conductor, and he had little interest to spare for the people in his charge other than to assure himself that they did not perpetrate any grave or undue damage upon the rolling stock of the railroad that had been placed in his charge.

"It seems your concerns were all for nothing," Edward said between bites to Honor and Raifer.

They were sitting at a small wharfside tavern, devouring a huge breakfast of coffee, eggs, ham, and fresh rolls.

"Hmm," Honor agreed, her mouth full of roll and butter. "It seems Raifer can't get past being a policeman, not even for a few hours," she added once she'd swallowed. She forked a large piece of ham and held it up. "This almost makes up for sleeping sitting up all night, don't you think?"

Edward grinned. "Best meal I've ever eaten," he agreed.

Funny, Honor thought as she watched the prince eat, I don't think either of us has ever really appreciated a meal before. It shocked her to think that it required a month such as the one they'd just endured to make them aware of how much they'd taken for granted all their lives, of just how much they had, and of how much so many others lacked. She darted a quick glance at Raifer. He was eating with a determined seriousness, but none of the delight she and Edward had with the first real meal they'd had in weeks. He still thinks we're not safe, she mused.

Edward apparently read Raifer's expression quite differently. "Is the arm bothering you?" he asked.

"We should have gone to a doctor," Honor added.

When they'd reached Dublin and left the train, she'd begged Raifer to see a doctor, but he'd rejected the idea immediately. "It'd take too much time," he'd told her. "And there'd be too many questions." She had had to satisfy herself with cleaning and rebandaging the wound.

"I'll see a doctor in London," Raifer told her now, obviously a bit vexed with the continued discussion of his arm.

"Well, a few hours on the packet, and then a half day on

the train. We'll be there by nightfall," Edward mused aloud. "It all seems safe enough now. Why not relax a bit?"

Raifer pushed his empty plate away from him and picked up his coffee cup. "I will," he replied. "Just as soon as I'm sure everyone involved in this matter is where they belong, in jail."

"You'll never be able to be certain, Raifer," Honor told him slowly, watching the way his eyes considered her, the way he seemed to be rejecting her words even as she spoke them.

He darted a quick glance toward the pier where the packet was tied. "It seems they're allowing passengers to board," he said as he took a last long swallow of his coffee. "I think we should go."

Honor hurriedly addressed herself to the remainder of her breakfast, realizing that there was nothing she could do or say to him that would in any way effect his determination. Perhaps it's just as well, she mused as she ate the last of her eggs, that it's over. There was no way she could ever be just an appendage to a man's life, an afterthought that came only when he'd nothing more important to occupy his thoughts. Still, there was a thick numbness inside her at the thought, the recognition that despite everything, still she loved him.

She pushed away the thought along with her nearly emptied plate, telling herself that she could make her own life for herself, that she had no need of a man's affections to make her existence worthwhile. For a second her thoughts drifted to Terrence McGowan, and the ease with which she'd given up the ring he'd given her. No, she thought, there was no possibility her life could ever be tied to Terry's despite the grief they now shared.

"Honor? Are you coming?"

She looked up, startled to realize that she'd been so deep in thought that she'd hardly noticed them rise from the table, nor Raifer leave a scattering of coins by his plate to pay for the meal. She stood hastily.

"I'm ready," she told the two men, and they started out

across the wharf to the waiting packet.

Fog set in as soon as they were offshore, and no amount of morning sun seemed capable of dispelling it. The air was filled with an eerie light that filtered through the mist-laden sky. Edward assured Honor it was hardly unusual, considering the time of the year. Still, she decided it could only bode ill.

The light was soon completely obliterated by a dull drizzle, and that was no more comforting. Honor peered out the lounge window at the grayness, a color that seemed pervasive, gray air, gray water, everywhere she looked it seemed gray.

The interior of the packet quickly became uncomfortable, the air rank with the odors of damp wool, perspiration, and beer. Crowded and smoke-filled, the large interior cabin began to lurch more and more as the boat drew away from land and out into the open waters of the Irish Sea. It was with great relief that Honor agreed to a walk on deck when Edward suggested it. It seemed that like her, the prince could not quite command his stomach to peaceful stillness with the deck lurching beneath them and the air so close and so unpleasantly scented.

Honor stepped through the door, out onto the deck after Edward, with Raifer just behind her, and buttoned up the thick wool jacket, still the same too-large jacket Raifer had taken from Flannagan's man back at the the Ardrahan sanatorium, against the cold of the stiff breeze on the water and the damp of the drizzle.

"We needn't go out," Edward said when he realized just how raw the afternoon had turned.

But Honor shook her head. The cold, she found, didn't bother her. On the contrary, she was quite pleased to inhale the clean, salty smell of the sea air.

The three of them moved along the side to the rear of the boat and stood staring at the churning, foam-tipped waves in their wake. Honor grasped the rail with one hand as she smoothed back the loose curls the wind had blown to her face.

"This is so much more pleasant," she said. "I wonder why no one else is out here." She nodded back toward the empty deck.

Raifer shrugged. "I suppose that they just prefer to be warm and dry," he ventured wryly.

Honor looked up at him and saw that he was staring at her, his expression oddly intent. "Well," she replied with a nervous laugh, "I choose clean air to warm and dry anytime."

She quickly turned away, to stare once more at the dull gray water. She found herself wishing that it was all over, that they were finally in London and had finished saying their good-byes. She wondered how she would manage to survive his leaving, wondered how she'd managed to think of it with any semblance of calmness over the previous few days. At that moment, the thought made her tremble and feel weak and alone.

Raifer, misunderstanding the cause of her tremor he saw in her hands, moved closer to her and put his arm around her.

"And I thought you preferred the cold, Honor," he said softly, his lips against her ear.

Edward turned to them and smiled. "It's not a long trip," he assured them. "A few hours more, and if the fog lifts a bit, we should be able to catch a glimpse of the coast a good while before we reach Liverpool."

"I'm afraid that's an experience not all of us will be fortunate enough to enjoy."

The three of them turned around at the sound of the unexpected voice. Honor gasped. Standing on the deck facing them was Terrence McGowan. He made no effort to hide the pistol he was holding in his hand.

Chapter Twenty-one

Gladstone sat silent for a moment and stared at the report he'd taken from his brief. He'd already read the five pages of neatly written script several times and hardly needed the review. What he was really doing was trying to decide one the best means of dealing with these new developments without unduly upsetting Victoria yet again.

"Well, Mr. Gladstone. You promised me you'd have news for me this morning. I sincerely hope it is good news."

Gladstone cleared his throat. "At least it is not bad news, Madame," he replied.

He realized his tone was a bit waspish, and he regretted the fact. He'd come to resent the Queen's implications that he was not doing everything that could be done, that he'd not pressured the members of Parliament as hard as he might have and pushed the vote through.

"Am I to understand that Edward was not found at his, this sanatorium your agents discovered?"

"I'm afraid not, Your Majesty," the prime minister replied. "When our agents arrived, they found the hospital in an uproar, hundreds of patients running about at liberty, and the staff making a vain attempt to contain them. The director was finally located, bound and locked in the closet of his own office."

The image brought a look of distaste to Victoria's

expression, a far cry from the hint of amusement Gladstone himself felt upon consideration of the situation. ("Good for them," his assistant, Carter, had exclaimed. "Getting a bit of their own back." Although he'd remained silent, the prime minister had echoed the sentiment.)

"They searched the grounds? Everywhere? Surely there must have been some trace?"

"Your Majesty, a thorough search was made. Two men, presumed part of the group who kidnapped the prince, were found tied and gagged near a rear entrance to the hospital. They've been taken into custody but so far have refused to tell us anything useful. The bodies of two more were also found not far from the same entrance. But there was no trace of either the prince nor the man and young woman who had gone to the Ardrahan police the previous evening trying to persuade them to go out to the sanatorium, the same young woman, I might add, who had appeared at the door of a local squire with the story of Edward being kidnapped."

"So we have no more information than we did two days ago?" Victoria asked sharply.

Gladstone dismissed the touch of anger in her tone, knowing it was the result of fear.

"There is a bit more, Madame. A man, the same who claimed to be a doctor at the hospital and thus persuaded the local constable that the woman's story was simply the ravings of a lunatic, was found dead on the road to Galway, apparently trampled by his own mount. The hospital director, one Dr. Trask, identified the man as the leader of the group who had forced their way onto the sanatorium grounds and demanded his cooperation, threatening to kill him, the staff, and the patients if he did not comply. If that is true, then perhaps Edward managed to escape, and the leader of the conspiracy is dead."

Victoria was unconvinced. She shook her head ponderously. "If that were true, Mr. Gladstone, he'd have gone to the authorities. We'd surely have heard something by now."

She stood and crossed the room to a large table laden with silver-framed photographs. She lifted one, a childhood portrait of Edward that she'd taken to staring at a great deal in the previous days, and peered at it as though she were searching for something in the small sepia-toned face. "That is, he'd have gone to them if he were able," she said softly.

The prime minister stood and crossed the room to her. For a moment he stood, his hand outstretched, feeling the human desire to comfort another one sees in pain. But his reticence and his sure knowledge that she would resent the gesture overcame his pity. He let the hand fall to his side before he spoke.

"We can still hope, Madame. If Edward is not sure just whom he can trust, a not unreasonable supposition, considering the circumstances, he might try to make his way back to London."

Victoria's short, rounded, black-clad body seemed to tremble for a moment, then she collected herself sharply and turned to face him. Her features were composed, although Gladstone thought he heard a slight tremor in her voice when she spoke.

"Let us all hope so, Mr. Gladstone. Let us sincerely pray that is true. I, of course, have personal reasons to wish for the restoration of my son. But do not believe the position of the crown will ever be quite secure again if these monsters succeed in their assault upon it. That is a legacy I'm sure neither of us would wish to leave to the Empire."

Gladstone nodded, struck with just how accurately she'd weighed the situation. He watched her as she turned and made her way out of the room, feeling all the time the full weight of her words on his shoulders. She had been, he knew, absolutely right, not only in assessing the loss in stature to the British crown, but also his reluctance to leave such a disaster behind him as legacy of his years in office. And the worst of it, he realized, was the simple fact that there was nothing else he could do. Except, as Victoria had suggested, pray.

"Terry!"

At first, Honor was simply bewildered, surprised at seeing him there, wondering how he'd appeared out of nowhere. But then her eyes fell to the weapon in his hand and she felt a dread, icy panic start to run through her.

"How did you get here?" she asked. "What are you doing here?"

Before she had even finished the words, she realized that she didn't want to know, that the answers would bring her no comfort.

Terrence smiled at her, but there was no warmth, no pleasure conveyed by the expression. "I came to return something to you, Honor," he told her as he put his hand to his pocket and withdrew a small box.

He threw it toward them. Edward caught it, opened it, and handed it to her. Honor hesitated a moment. Somehow she knew even before she took it, she knew the box would contain the sapphire ring. She began to move forward, toward Terrence, but Raifer put his hand to her arm and pulled her back.

"Don't, Honor," he told her flatly.

"What is it?" she murmured, staring first at Raifer then back at Terrence. "What's happening?"

"He knows," Terrence said with a thin smile. "Don't you, Farrell? You finally have it all figured out."

Raifer shrugged. "I'm ashamed to admit that until this moment I'd really thought it was Kevin. But now I realize it was you behind the whole thing. You just used your father." He turned steely eyes to Terrence. "You used them all—Flannagan, Fitzpatrick, even your own father."

Terrence scowled. "You really thought it was m

father?" he asked. There was disgust in his tone at the thought. "My father was a fool. He was fit only for that puny little shipping business of his. He had no idea what a man can do if he's only willing to dare."

"He's dead," Honor murmured, shocked at the indifference she heard in Terrence's voice. "Do you understand? This thing you've done, it's killed your father."

He sneered. "He's been dead for years, dead and buried, along with his money, under that heap of his grand new house, his mansion. He was a fool."

Honor drew back, not quite believing what she heard, dumbfounded by his casual cruelty. "He was your father," she protested weakly.

"Spare me, Honor. I've no patience for maudlin sentimentality. This little game with Gladstone and Edward was intended to make me the most powerful man in Ireland." His eyes grew sharp and evaluating as he turned his glance to the prince. "It still will. Once Edward's body is found, Gladstone will realize he has to deal with me."

Edward shook his head. "None of this is necessary. Gladstone has every intention of addressing the Irish complaints. I've spoken to him. He'd already drafted measures to disestablish the Church of Ireland and restrict the power of the lords."

"Lip service," Terrence interrupted. "All you British offer is talk. I intend to get more than that. And when I do, perhaps there will be kings in Ireland once again, Irish kings." His eyes traveled back to find Honor's. "And you could have been at my side. I loved you, Honor. And you betrayed me." His eyes became wild and bright as he stared at her. Honor could almost feel the hatred and the anger welling up inside him, like a great blast of heat from an open, stoked furnace.

"Don't try to deny what you've done," Terrence went on, his voice rising. "I saw you asleep in his arms on the train. You looked comfortable there, as if you were used to being there. How many times have you slept that way,

Honor? And what did you do with him before you slept?" he asked her sharply. "What freedoms did you allow him that you denied me?"

She felt only shock at that moment, as though there was a growing distance between them that she could only think came from the disbelief she felt that he would say such things to her.

"You've no right to question me, Terry. I never made any promises to you."

His face grew red. "We had an understanding. And you chose to throw away the life I would have given you for a nobody, a policeman. *Whore*. It sickens me to think that I loved you."

Honor felt a surge of her own anger. "You loved me?" she retorted. "Is that why you let Flannagan take me? Did you give him leave to try to rape me?" She was shaking now, trembling with rage. "And even with all that, he was better than you are, Terry. He was, if nothing else, honest about what he was. He didn't lie, didn't use and pretend innocence."

"Be quiet," he shouted at her. The pistol was trembling in his hands. He seemed to be fighting with himself, forcing himself to become calm. When he spoke again, his voice was just under control. "I was almost ready to forgive you, Honor, to take you back. When I saw your hair, when I realized it was you driving that carriage, I was stricken that I might have shot you, hurt you. And then I find you gave away the ring I gave you; I find you lying in another man's arms." His words grew slowly harsher, more menacing. "Since you enjoy the feel of his arms around you, perhaps it will comfort you to know that I intend to let you die in them."

Raifer put his hand to Honor's arm and drew her back beside him, then stepped in front of her. "Nothing happened between us, McGowan. I tried, but she wouldn't have it. What you saw on the train was exhaustion, nothing more. If you have a score to settle, it's with me, not Honor."

At first, Honor could see only that he was trying to protect her. Then she realized he was trying to distract Terrence, misdirect his attention as he moved slowly forward. She somehow realized he was going to do something, something stupid, rush Terrence and the gun, hoping to save her and Edward. She didn't know how she knew, but as she realized the distance between the two of them was growing as Raifer edged closer to Terrence, she could see it in her mind's eye, Raifer suddenly leaping forward and the pistol being fired.

Just as surely as she knew what it was he intended, she knew she couldn't stand there and watch him die. She'd seen far too much death in the previous weeks — her father's, Kevin's, Moynihan's, the glimpse she'd had of Flannagan's as the horses' hooves had struck him, stifling his single, last cry. It seemed her vision had been blurred by a veil of blood. At that moment, she knew only that she couldn't bear to see Raifer's as well.

She darted around him, surprising both men and herself, as she threw herself forward, toward Terrence. For a moment, she expected to feel the searing bite of a bullet, expected to hear the thundering report of the shot. But there was nothing, only Terrence's arm reaching out and grabbing her, turning her around and holding her roughly to him, his hand hard at her waist. If he had prepared himself to see her die, as indeed it had seemed to her, apparently he was not quite ready to watch her bleed to death at his feet.

He pressed the barrel of the pistol to her head. "Get back," he screamed.

Raifer and Edward had no choice but to obey him. Honor realized that she had, yet again, made the wrong choice, had given Terrence a second weapon to hold over Raifer and the prince, to force their obedience. Still, she realized she did not regret what she'd done. She knew that if it had been Raifer Terrence had seen running toward him, there would have been no hesitation, no indecision. Terrence would have fired.

He pulled her back until they were against the rail. Honor felt it pressing cold and hard against her thigh.

"What do you intend to do, Terry?" she asked softly. She realized her voice was trembling, but there was nothing she could do to steady it. Her question seemed to amuse him.

"I'm going to let you watch your lover die, Honor," he told her. Then he motioned with the pistol. "You, Farrell. Climb over."

Raifer moved close to the rail, his eyes on Terrence as he swung one leg over and straddled it.

"Please, Terry, don't," Honor whispered, begging, aware she'd done little more than buy Raifer a few moments of life.

"You plead for his life, Honor? Is that what you're doing?"

"Yes," she cried weakly. "Let him go. Let them both go."

"And what would you do to convince me to let him live?" Terrence hissed at her.

Honor heard the madness in his voice, then realized that he'd somehow slipped over the edge of the line between sanity and derangement.

"Anything, Terry," she told him. "I'll do anything."

His hand dropped away from her waist and clamped itself to her shoulder, pushing her down. "Then kneel before me, Honor," he told her, "and plead with me."

She sank slowly to her knees, the cold, hard feel of the pistol barrel still at her temple.

"Now beg," he told her.

She looked up at him, at the madness in his eyes. "I beg you, Terry," she pleaded softly. She could feel the tears filling her eyes, yet she kept them on him. "Let them go."

"The ring," he directed. "Put on the ring."

She realized that she still held it, wrapped in her tightly clasped fingers. She opened them and found it lying in her palm. Her hands were shaking, but she managed to force it onto her finger.

"Now, beg my forgiveness."

"I beg you," she murmured shakily.

He interrupted her. "No, first confess your sins, Honor. How can I forgive you, if you don't confess how you've sinned against me?"

"I've sinned against you, Terry," she said, reciting the words numbly. "But I was wrong. And I beg your forgiveness."

He shook his head. "You must have forgotten, Honor. Perhaps you need a reminder." He darted an angry glance at Raifer, and realized he was moving, forward, closer to them. "Get back," he shouted, and pressed the pistol to Honor's temple. Raifer did as he directed, staring with impotent rage at Terrence as he turned his attention back to Honor. "You lay with that man," he hissed at her. "You behaved no better than a whore."

"Honor, don't!"

Raifer leaned forward to them once again, but Terrence cocked the pistol and pushed it against her temple, forcing her head back.

"Say it, Honor," Terrence shouted at her.

Honor took a deep breath, trying to still her trembling. As she knelt on the cold, damp plank deck, she felt a weight in the pocket of the jacket, pressing against her thigh. And with a dull sense of shock she remembered that it was a pistol, Moynihan's pistol, that she'd taken from the ground beside his body. She'd forgotten until that moment that she had it, and realized what a fool she'd been not to give it to Raifer at the very start. Now the weight of it seemed to bear down on her leg, and she felt it like a fire against her skin, condemning her for her stupidity.

She looked down, at Terrence's feet. "I lay with him, Terry," she repeated his words dully. "I behaved like a whore. I beg you to forgive me." Her eyes strayed, from Terrence's boots to her own trembling hands.

"Now kiss my foot, Honor," Terrence hissed at her.

She darted a look up, saw the malice in his eyes. But he nudged the pistol he held against her temple once more, and she knew she had no choice but to do as he bade her. She leaned forward and put her lips to the grimy tip of his boot.

When she looked up, she saw Terrence was smiling, but not at her, at Raifer. The pistol was raised, too, and pointed at him where he sat, straddling the rail. Terror filled her, but somehow she managed to control it, to put her hand to her pocket, and force her fingers to find the pistol. Somehow they distinguished the wooden butt and wrapped themselves around it, her thumb finding the hammer and pulling it back, her index finger locating the trigger.

"Did you hear her, Farrell? She admits you lied."

There was an edge of hysteria in Terrence's voice now, but Honor could see his hand was steady as he pointed the pistol at Raifer.

"For that alone you deserve to die," Terrence shouted, and his fingers began to squeeze.

There was the sound of a shot, the concussion from it seemed to tear the air around her. Then her nostrils filled with the scents of powder and burnt wool, the dank, wet air holding it close to her, not letting her escape it. Honor thought she would smother from the smell of it.

And then the pistol dropped from Terrence's hand and fell downward, into the roiling water at the packet's wake. He looked down, a look of shock and disbelief filling his face, as he stared at the red circle on his chest. Then he turned his eyes to her as he fell backward, over the rail and into the dark, grey waves.

She stayed as she was, kneeling on the cold planks of the deck, shaking. It was only when Raifer was beside her, when she felt his arms enfold her, that she was able to look down at the hole in the pocket of the woolen jacket. She pulled her hand from the pocket, bringing with it the pistol. It felt hot to her, seemed to burn her fingers, and she dropped it. Edward moved quickly forward and kicked it over the side. Honor leaned forward and watched it fall until it, too, like Terrence, was swallowed by the waves and the dull gray fog.

"What was that noise? What's goin' on here?"

The three of them turned to find a burly member of the packet's crew running along the side deck toward them.

Raifer looked up at him. "Noise? I didn't hear any noise. The young lady just fell, that's all."

The sailor wrinkled his brow as he came to a halt beside the three of them, but it was obvious he was as pleased as not that there seemed to be nothing seriously wrong. "Well, what do ye expect, takin' her out here, with the decks all slippery from the wet? What do ye want to be doin' out here at all in this weather?" He knelt down beside Honor. "Are ye all right, miss?" he asked as he offered her his hand.

Honor nodded her head slowly. "Yes, thank you. I'm not hurt. It was foolish of me to fall."

Her words, she realized, seemed absent, as though they'd been spoken by someone else. It struck her sharply that she was different, someone she'd not been before. She remembered taking the pistol from the woman Fiona when she'd managed to escape into the woods, and throwing it away, telling herself that using it would make her as bad as the terrorists. At that moment she realized she'd used a pistol, taken a man's life with it. Flannagan and his men had had a cause that they'd used to excuse their killing. Terrence had been willing to kill for his own power. At that moment Honor realized that there was, after all, something important enough to her to kill for, something important enough to be willing to die for. She looked up at Raifer and knew she'd killed for love. Was her cause, she wondered, any more righteous than any other?

She took the sailor's hand and got slowly to her feet.

"Ye ought to be gettin' inside where it's warm and dry,"

he told her with an almost shy smile.

She nodded soberly at his words. "Yes," she murmured, "yes, we will."

He stared at her a moment longer. "Ye're sure ye ain't hurt, miss?" he asked.

She nodded. "I'm fine, thank you," she replied mechanically. How could she tell him that in firing at Terrence, she'd killed whatever remained of her innocence? How could she ever make anyone understand what was only vaguely clear in her own mind?

She looked down at her shaking hands, and realized that the ring, Terrence's ring, was on her finger. She pulled it off. Then, staring out at the dull wall of grey fog behind the packet, she threw it as hard as she could, watching it fall to be swallowed by the waves, knowing it would soon find the bottom, along with Terrence and the pistol that had killed him.

"I think we should go inside now, Honor," Raifer told her gently. He put his hand to her arm.

She nodded and turned, more than willing to let him take her away from there. They moved toward the door to the packet's lounge, leaving behind them the sailor staring bewilderedly into the gray waters and wondering just what it was he'd seen her cast off to a dull, wet grave.

Chapter Twenty-two

They used the last of the money Raifer had gotten from the ticket seller to hire a hansom from Victoria Station to Buckingham Palace. The cab driver had been at first reluctant to take them, eyeing them rudely and demanding to see the money for the fare before he allowed them to climb into the carriage. When he let them off in front of the palace gates, he watched them with amusement as they turned to the walk to the guardhouse.

He pocketed the coins that Raifer had given him. "Maniacs," he muttered to himself as he considered their shabby, rumpled appearance, "expectin' to walk up to the palace and be greeted like they was lady and gentlemen."

His words hung in the damp evening air for a moment before he turned the horse and drove away.

He would have been far more greatly intrigued had he lingered a moment longer. If he had, he would have seen an officer of the guard stand, bewildered for a moment, staring at one of his unkempt passengers before ordering that the gate be drawn open and the trio allowed to enter.

Honor had to admit that she felt a bit bewildered at the way Edward was recognized, as though the guard had been ordered to be on watch for him, regardless of the guise.

She found herself walking along in a dazed, bemused

fog. Had Raifer not been holding firmly onto her arm, she doubted she could possibly have kept up. She was, she realized, feeling just a bit peculiar, flushed and warm, and a bit dizzy. It hardly seemed to matter. After the events of the previous days, a touch of dizziness could hardly give her much cause for alarm.

She had no idea how they managed to arrive at the large, improbably cluttered room. With all that space, she mused, the room ought to seem airy, not weighted and crushingly full. She realized her thoughts were wandering and managed to force her attention to Edward as he approached a short, roundish woman dressed in rather old fashioned silk, all black, a dark little gnome who held out her arms to him in bewildered greeting. But as much as she tried to concentrate on the words that were spoken all around her, none of it made any sense.

The thought of the room's clutter forced its way back into her mind, as though the bibelots and lace-covered pillows and welter of silver framed pictures were pressing themselves down upon her, suffocating her.

"No," she protested weakly, and waved an arm at a chintz-covered sofa that seemed to be pulsing, coming ever closer, threatening the space where she stood.

A dozen eyes turned to stare at her, strange eyes, most especially one pair, darkly intent and distrustful. She closed her eyes, trying to avoid the stare, and when she reopened them, the room was spinning around her, faster and faster, until it seemed she was falling into blackness.

When she awoke, the same eyes were peering down at her. Honor drew back, not understanding, and feeling too weak and disoriented to fight the power with which they seemed to peer into her.

"Don't be afraid. You're safe now."

A face formed around the eyes, a high forehead, a long, aquiline nose, a pleasant if not terribly strong chin. The lips were smiling, but there was still that look of distrust about the eyes, a look Honor could not understand.

"Who are you?" she demanded as she pushed herself into a sitting position, her back against a heap of linen covered down pillows. "What happened?"

"You fainted. But don't worry. You had a touch of fever, and the doctor said you were suffering from exhaustion. He assured us you would be just fine, with a bit of rest."

Honor put her hand to her temple. "Fainted? I don't remember," she murmured. "Where's Raifer? And Edward?"

The lips lost whatever bit of smile they'd worn. "Mr. Farrell went off with Mr. Gladstone and some gentlemen from Scotland Yard as soon as the doctor had seen you and pronounced you in no danger. I don't think they've returned yet to the palace this morning."

Honor turned away. Of course, she mused . . . Scotland Yard. His precious job. It wouldn't be over for him until the ends were nearly tied up and explained.

"And Edward?" she asked, turning back to the young woman.

The lips were drawn suddenly tight and the questioning, distrustful stare seemed to grow sharper. "He's with the Queen. They were both here earlier this morning, but there are matters to be tended to, matters of state."

"Of course," Honor murmured.

"I stayed because I wanted to talk to you."

This last was said with a bit of hesitancy, as though the woman distrusted even the thought of exchanging a few words with her, as though they might somehow prove to be disastrous.

"Who are you?" Honor asked her softly once again.

"I've not introduced myself, have I? How rude of me."

She seemed ruffled now, but she continued to stare at Honor. "I'm Alexandra, the prince's fiancée."

Honor managed a smile. "Of course. Edward spoke a great deal about you," she ventured, wondering, still, why Alexandra seemed so distrustful of her.

The smile wasn't returned. "I wanted to speak with you because of something I overheard."

Alexandra finally drew her eyes away from Honor's and stared down at her hands. Her fingers were clasping and unclasping themselves, and Honor could not help but see the woman's distress.

"How can I help you?" Honor asked her gently.

"Mr. Gladstone told Her Majesty that a woman was found in Edward's room after he was kidnapped. The situation appeared rather," she swallowed, obviously forcing herself to find the strength to go on, "rather compromising. She was, I believe, an actress." Alexandra looked up again, and this time there was pleading in her eyes.

"Yes," Honor replied softly. "Mr. Farrell believes she might have been part of the conspiracy. That's all I know."

Alexandra's expression grew once again sharp. "I am not a fool, Miss Wainwright. I know I'm not a great beauty. And I am also well aware that Edward has what is genteelly referred to as a roving eye."

"I'm afraid I can offer you no advice on that matter," Honor told her firmly. She was bewildered by the questions, but she was also firmly convinced it was not an argument in which she wished to become embroiled. She had her own miseries to deal with, she told herself. Alexandra would have to tend to hers by herself.

But she was mistaken if she assumed it was information about Edward's relationship with the actress Diana Wells that interested his fiancée.

"You're a very beautiful woman, Miss Wainwright," Alexandra went on with obvious distaste, but decided determination. "You have spent a great deal of time in forced proximity to the prince in the last few weeks. And you speak of him quite familiarly. As he speaks of you. With warmth and affection."

Honor bristled. "If you are asking me what I think you're asking," Honor told her sharply, "I can assure you, despite the situation, the prince behaved in a completely gentlemanly fashion. If I speak of him in what seems to you a familiar fashion, it is because we became friends. And his friendship is the only vestige of the experience I hold with any affection."

Honor was surprised by her own bitterness, realizing as she did that the only other cause for her to think any good had come out of the previous weeks, the possibility that there might be something between her and Raifer, was just delusion.

Alexandra seemed shocked by the vehemence in Honor's words. She colored with embarrassment. "I'm truly sorry. I really meant no offense," she murmured. "I simply had to know."

Honor stared at her a moment, then she, too, felt a touch of shame at her reaction. She had no reason to condemn this woman for wanting to know her future husband was faithful to her. She knew, she told herself, as well as anyone, how painful was the knowledge of loving someone who felt nothing in return.

"I'm sorry, too," Honor told her. She smiled weakly. "Perhaps the fever? Or is that not ample excuse?"

Alexandra turned to her and smiled, the first sincere smile Honor had had from her.

"More than ample," she replied. She stood and stared down at Honor. "I'll have some tea fetched for you. Then, perhaps you should rest a bit more. The Queen hopes you'll be well enough to dine with the family this evening."

Honor watched her leave on her mission to locate someone who might be empowered to fetch the offered tea, then fell back into the heap of pillows. She was not at all sure she wanted to be well enough to dine with the family that evening. She was not at all sure she wanted to do anything but sleep ever again.

When she awoke, Honor found, much to her surprise, that she was hungry, hungry enough to face even the formidable presence of Queen Victoria, if food was in the offing. She felt much stronger, well enough to refuse the help of a solicitous maid and make her way herself to the bath.

As she bathed, she wavered between hoping that Raifer would still be off with the gentlemen from Scotland Yard that Alexandra had mentioned, and yearning to see him again. A part of her knew it would be wiser to try to forget him, to go back to New York as quickly as possible, back to her students at the Settlement House, back to a life with some measure of sanity about it. But no matter how much she might throw herself into the classes she taught at the Settlement House, no matter how much she might try to force herself to find some meaning in her life, she knew her whole existence was in a shambles. She would never be able to forget the vision of her father's death, or those of Kevin and Terrence, either. Too much had happened to her to make the possibility of returning alone to New York anything but one more horror she knew she was unprepared to face. With Raifer's help she could possibly cope; without it she knew she was lost.

She climbed reluctantly from the bath and, wrapped in a thick terry robe, followed the maid back into the bedroom. She was startled to find a gown of heavy, pale green silk trimmed with dark green velvet laid out on the bed for her, along with all the necessary underthings, all silk, all beautifully soft and lavishly trimmed with lace.

"Where did all this come from?" she asked.

"Her Majesty ordered a wardrobe for you, miss," the

maid informed her. "The dressmakers have been working all day to finish this gown by evening."

Honor stared at the display of silk and velvet. It was a very handsome gown, the silk a soft iridescent shade that shimmered in the lamplight. She thought ruefully of the way the Queen must have perceived her the evening before, a tattered street urchin with worn, filthy clothing, her too-large wool jacket bearing a large burn over the pocket where the bullet had passed through it. No wonder Victoria had ordered some proper clothing be prepared for her. After all, it wouldn't do for the British royal family to be served their dinner along with such a harridan.

She suddenly laughed aloud, realizing that she'd appeared the evening before in the Queen's presence, and she could remember nothing of the experience save for the impression of the clutter of the room. Half of New York society plotted for the honor of being presented at the Court of St. James, and when the occasion arose in her life, she'd appeared looking like a hag and carried away no memory of the event at all.

The maid helped her into the gown, and Honor found it fit surprisingly well, despite the absence of any fittings. A queen, she mused as she sat at the dressing table and allowed the maid to dress her hair, could order miracles, it seemed.

"There, miss," the maid told her as she stood back and surveyed her handiwork.

Honor nodded a polite thank you and quickly examined the arrangement. Her hair had been piled in thick, loose curls on her head, and soft, wavy wisps framed her face. The arrangement was quite becoming, she realized, and the awareness only made her regret more painfully that Raifer would have no interest in admiring

Her thoughts were disturbed by a loud knocking at the door. The maid quickly answered it and turned to

435

inform her, with a slightly flustered expression, "The Prince of Wales, miss. And Mr. Farrell." She then stirred herself to manage a small curtsy as Edward and Raifer entered, followed by a servant bearing a tray with a wine bucket and three glasses. Then, darting one more openly envious glance at Honor, she bobbed once more and left the room, followed by the slightly more decorous departure of the servant who had set the tray down on a table at the far end of the room.

"Honor," Edward exclaimed as he clasped her hand. "You look lovely. Are you quite recovered?"

She nodded. "Yes, thank you, Edward," she said as she watched Raifer, apparently completely at his ease, stride to the table with the wine, withdraw the bottle from the ice bucket, and proceed to expunge the cork with a loud pop.

"She did scrub up rather well, didn't she, Edward?" he said with a grin. "I told you she could be fairly nice to look at if she's taken in hand," he went on casually as he filled the three glasses. "I understand your questioning the possibility, as you've seen her looking quite scruffy lately. But the raw material is there, needing only a firm hand with a scrub brush and a bit of silk to give her the appearance, at least, of a respectable lady." He lifted one of the glasses and sampled the wine. "Although appearances, I'm told, are sometimes deceiving." He smiled at them, then settled himself into a chair, obviously waiting for them to follow suit.

Honor stared at him mutely, aware that her heart was pounding so hard it almost hurt. He looked terribly handsome in elegant black evening attire. It hurt her suddenly more than she could have thought possible to see how indifferent he seemed, how easily he could mock her.

"Don't listen to a word he's saying, Honor," Edward told her pleasantly. "He simply doesn't want to admit that he's been worried about you." He smiled. "Cham pagne, my dear?"

He led her across the room, lifted the two remaining glasses, and handed one to her. Honor accepted the glass and sipped the wine.

"Oh, I've no doubt but that Mr. Farrell had other matters on his mind, and no time to waste thoughts on me," she replied. "Isn't that true, Mr. Farrell? All those messy details to be handled. It must have been wonderful for you to have all of Scotland Yard at your beck and call." She smiled archly, then brought the glass back to her lips.

Raifer raised his brow. For a moment Honor thought there was hurt in his eyes, and perhaps a touch of regret. But then he shrugged, and his expression became impassive once more.

"Actually it was rather frightening. All that power at my fingertips. I could almost understand what might have gone through your friend Terrence's mind. Almost, but not quite."

Honor drew back, hurt by his seeming callousness. She turned, crossed to the settee facing his chair, and settled herself into it before finding enough composure for speech.

"Then everything is settled?" she asked him.

"So it would seem," he replied. "Fitzpatrick is no longer Chief of Police. He resigned and is being investigated for his involvement in the illegal exportation of arms. It seems there's not enough evidence to tie him to the kidnapping, but this will be enough to remove him from a position to do any more damage. And knowing him, he'll not take the blame alone, but bring along those who were part of it with him."

"And you'll have your job back when you return?" she asked. He should be delighted, she thought, ecstatic. There's nothing else he wants.

His response, however, surprised her. "I'm not sure I'll take it," he said as he stood and crossed the room to stand in front of her. "I've somehow gotten the faint impression that my future wife is not very happy about my career choice." He sat down beside her and leaned toward her. "Although I'm hoping she might change her mind if I promise to draw a firm line separating work from pleasure. But if not, I'm a flexible man. And the woman in question means more to me than the New York City Police Department. I could always go back to reading the law. Or maybe even mining. I did a good bit of working in an iron mine before I met her."

Honor realized her hands, all of her, was shaking. The champagne splashed over the rim of her glass and onto the pale silk of her skirt. "Your, your future wife?" she sputtered.

He took the glass from her hand and put it firmly on the table beside the settee where it could do no further damage.

"Although as far as reading the law is concerned," he went on as though she'd said nothing, "I can't help but feel I'm a bit old to be a student. And since my father retired and left the management of the family mines to my brother, he's become rather set in his habits and might not like me pushing my nose into a very comfortably profitable business. I could spend my days gambling at my club, I suppose, and maybe indulge in a bit of drinking, and live off my share of the income. It's more than enough to maintain my house in the city. There certainly wouldn't be any problem with providing for a wife and a few children as well. But I do feel a man's sons should be able to think of their father as something more than a wastrel, don't you, Edward?"

The prince smiled, nodded, and emptied his glass. "Personally, I have little to say against a wastrel's life," he said as he refilled his glass. "But I do understand the sentiment."

"Your father's mines?" Honor repeated numbly. "Your house?"

Raifer looked up at Edward and grinned. "I think Honor's not quite recovered from that touch of fever, Edward. She doesn't seem to be able to conduct a rational conversation. Perhaps I should put her back to bed?"

The prince nodded sagely. "Perhaps that would be best," he said as he moved toward the door. "I'll be glad to make your excuses, old man." He paused, his hand on the knob. "Do you think she'll be well enough for the wedding tomorrow?" he asked. "Mother's already sent for the Archbishop of Canterbury to perform the ceremony. She'll be most disappointed if it must be put off."

"Oh, I'm sure she'll be recovered by then," Raifer told him. "Neither of us would want to disappoint the Queen." He turned then to Honor and put his arm around her waist and drew her close to him. "You will, won't you, Honor?" he asked her softly, his lips close to her ear.

"Recovered?" she repeated, her mind still in a daze.

Raifer put his hand to his pocket and withdrew a ring, a gold ring with a very large, very sparkling diamond which he proceeded to slid onto her finger. She looked down at it, not quite sure she believed what it was she was seeing there.

Raifer put his hand to her chin and pulled her face up to meet his. "You will be well enough to participate in a wedding ceremony tomorrow, won't you, Honor?" he asked her softly before he kissed her, gently, on the lips.

She stared up at him for a moment when his lips left hers, losing herself in what she saw in his eyes.

"Won't you, Honor?" he asked her once again.

She nodded. "Yes," she exclaimed softly. "Oh, yes."

She put her arms around his neck and pressed her lips to his.

For just a moment, Edward stood at the door, peering at them and smiling. Then he slipped out of the room and into the hall, closing the door firmly behind him.

Edward took a step or two along the corridor, then stopped for a second as he heard the click of the key turning in the lock behind him. He grinned, aware that he felt decidedly happy that matters had settled themselves so satisfactorily, and began to compose the excuse he would make to the Queen before he continued along the carpeted hall.

On the other side of the door, Raifer turned, lifted the key that was now in his hand, and smiled as he slipped it into his pocket. Then he moved quickly to the settee where Honor still sat.

"Edward is about to tell the Queen that you had a touch of a relapse and were taken to your bed," he told her evenly. "You wouldn't want to be the cause of his telling a lie, would you, Honor?" He stopped in front of her and held out his hands to her.

She looked up at him and smiled. "Certainly not," she agreed as she stood, all the confusion gone now, his intention clear to her. She was, she realized, more than willing, even anxious, to be accommodating.

He put his arms around her and pulled her close. His lips, when they found hers, were hungry and certain. There was the sweet, liquid heat beginning to fill her as his tongue found hers, the warmth of his breath mingling with her own, heady with the hint of champagne.

She twined her arms around his neck as he lifted her in his arms and carried her across the room to the large bed.

"Do you think you could manage to become a policeman's wife, Honor?" he asked as he set her down on the satin coverlet. "I do rather enjoy being a detective. After all, if it hadn't been for that, I'd never have found you."

She smiled up at him. "I suppose I could manage," she whispered as he lowered himself to her.

He kissed her, first on the lips, then on her neck, letting his lips find the gently racing pulse there before he spoke.

"You're sure?" he demanded as he pulled himself away and smiled down at her.

Honor gazed up at his face, reading the certainty in his expression. He knew perfectly well that at that moment she would deny him nothing. And she knew he knew it.

"Yes," she told him, and she returned his smile.

When he touched her again, she closed her eyes and for a moment just let herself float on the pleasant heat that filled her as she felt his hands and his lips against her skin. She'd never thought to feel this way again, never thought to find herself in his arms like this again. And now she suddenly found herself anticipating a lifetime beside him, a lifetime of loving him. It seemed almost more happiness than she could bear.

She felt his lips, warm against her neck, slowly trailing a path of liquid fire down to her cleavage. She reached up to him, wrapping her fingers in his dark curls, pulling him close, encouraging the gentle exploration his lips and tongue had begun.

He pulled away from her suddenly and her eyes popped open. She stared numbly up at him, questioning.

He smiled down at her. "It wouldn't do to ruin that lovely gown, Honor," he told her with only a hint of amusement. "I'm told the Queen went to a good deal of trouble to see you were properly bedecked this evening."

"I suppose it wouldn't," she agreed, and she guided his hands to the buttons, secure that he would have no trouble with them.

He didn't. In a moment the bodice hung loose, and he swept the gown aside, casting it on a nearby chair with far less interest in its preservation than his words had indicated. She sat in her shift and stared at him.

"If we're to begin our honeymoon," she said as she lifted her hands to the buttons of his shirt and slowly began to free them, "I think it only right we begin properly."

He straddled her where she sat on the bed, one knee close to each of her thighs, feeling the sweet rising tide within him as her fingers slowly bared his chest. It was a strange pleasure to him, he found, to watch her face as she concentrated on the task at hand, the oddly innocent intensity of her expression. When she'd finished with the shirt, she looked up at him, smiling, and the look of innocence was replaced with one of amused impishness. She proceeded to his trousers, freeing the buttons slowly, letting her fingers linger against him. He threw his head back and let the fire fill him, aware that she knew just what it was she was doing to him.

When she'd completed her task, she slid her hands beneath his loosened clothing letting them slide along the even muscles of his hips to his back. Then she leaned forward and pressed her lips to the hard wall of his belly. She inhaled the scent of him, drinking it in, tasting him with her lips and her tongue, suddenly wanting to touch, to taste all of him.

She felt his fingers twining themselves in her hair, then sliding to her cheeks. She looked up at him to find his gray-blue eyes staring down at hers. There was fire in them, she realized, and undisguised passion.

He smiled suddenly. "I thought we were beginning this honeymoon properly," he said.

Then he shrugged quickly out of his clothing, taking even less care than he had with hers and simply dropping it to the floor beside the bed. He returned to her quickly, straddling her, pushing her gently down to the bed and following her.

"Do you think the Queen would approve?" she asked him with a grin as he wound the fingers of one hand in her thick curls and cupped her breast with the other. "The honeymoon begun before the wedding?"

He smiled down at her wryly. "Most probably not," he admitted. "But if I don't tell her and neither do you, she won't ever know. Besides, I intend to make an honest woman of you tomorrow afternoon, Honor. Let's not quibble about a few hours." He sobered and gazed at her thoughtfully. "Have I told you how much I love you, Honor?" he asked her, his voice suddenly very husky.

She shook her head, then spread herself beneath him. "Show me," she told him softly.

He smiled again as he slid into her. She moaned softly at that first sweet thrust. Then he held himself still as he brought her chin upward, until her eyes found his.

"I love you," he whispered to her. "I'll never stop loving you."

"You're my life," she replied. "You're every breath I take, every beat of my heart."

She reached her hands up to his neck, pressed herself to him, and let her lips find his. He began to move slowly inside her, and she felt a tide of passion within herself, a tide that surged through her with a heady, unexpected speed. It swept through her with devastating certainty, filling her, overwhelming her.

The agonies of terror and uncertainty she'd borne through the previous weeks might never have existed. All that mattered now was the way she felt when she was in his arms, that and the unutterably sweet knowledge that she had a lifetime to explore the endless world the circle of his arms made for her.

Raifer felt her tremble beneath him. He lowered his lips to hers, allowing himself to share her sweet ecstasy. As it filled him, consumed him, he knew suddenly that nothing in his life before had ever felt quite so right, so perfect.

He stilled, not wanting to leave her yet, not willing to let it end.

"I love loving you," he told her softly.

"I love when you love me," she replied in a ragged whisper.

He kissed her again, certain that he would never cease

to feel the way he did at that moment, not in ten years, not in a hundred. His eyes found hers, and he realized then that it had somehow been fated, ordained from that very first moment he'd stared into those magnificent eyes. They were looking up at him now, deep and round and glazed with passion. They set adrift a current within him. He felt it rising in himself and welcomed it.

Honor reached her fingers up to his cheeks, caressing them softly, her eyes surprised and questioning as she became aware that he had already begun to stir the tide within her once more.

He looked down at her and grinned. "A proper honeymoon, my love," he whispered.

In answer, Honor smiled.

ROMANTIC GEMS
BY F. ROSANNE BITTNER

HEART'S SURRENDER (2945, $4.50)
Beautiful Andrea Sanders was frightened to be living so close to the Cherokee—and terrified by turbulent passions the handsome Indian warrior, Adam, aroused within her!

PRAIRIE EMBRACE (2035, $3.95)
Katie Russell kept reminding herself that her savage Indian captor was beneath her contempt—but deep inside she longed to yield to his passionate caress!

ARIZONA ECSTASY (2810, $4.50)
Lovely Lisa Powers hated the Indian who captured her, but as time passed in the arid Southwest, she began to turn to him first for survival, then for love!

Available wherever paperbacks are sold, or order direct from the Publisher. Send cover price plus 50¢ per copy for mailing and handling to Zebra Books, Dept. 2975, 475 Park Avenue South, New York, N.Y. 10016. Residents of New York, New Jersey and Pennsylvania must include sales tax. DO NOT SEND CASH.

HISTORICAL ROMANCES BY EMMA MERRITT

RESTLESS FLAMES (2203, $3.95)
Having lost her husband six months before, determined Brenna Allen couldn't afford to lose her freight company, too. Outfitted as wagon captain with revolver, knife and whip, the single-minded beauty relentlessly drove her caravan, desperate to reach Santa Fe. Then she crossed paths with insolent Logan Mac-Dougald. The taciturn Texas Ranger was as primitive as the surrounding Comanche Territory, and he didn't hesitate to let the tantalizing trail boss know what he wanted from her. Yet despite her outrage with his brazen ways, jet-haired Brenna couldn't suppress the scorching passions surging through her ... and suddenly she never wanted this trip to end!

COMANCHE BRIDE (2549, $3.95)
When stunning Dr. Zoe Randolph headed to Mexico to halt a cholera epidemic, she didn't think twice about traversing Comanche territory ... until a band of bloodthirsty savages attacked her caravan. The gorgeous physician was furious that her mission had been interrupted, but nothing compared to the rage she felt on meeting the barbaric warrior who made her his slave. Determined to return to civilization, the ivory-skinned blonde decided to make a woman's ultimate sacrifice to gain her freedom—and never admit that deep down inside she burned to be loved by the handsome brute!

SWEET, WILD LOVE (2834, $4.50)
It was hard enough for Eleanor Hunt to get men to take her seriously in sophisticated Chicago—it was going to be impossible in Blissful, Kansas! These cowboys couldn't believe she was a real attorney, here to try a cattle rustling case. They just looked her up and down and grinned. Especially that Bradley Smith. The man worked for her father and he still had the audacity to stare at her with those lust-filled green eyes. Every time she turned around, he was trying to trap her in his strong embrace.

Available wherever paperbacks are sold, or order direct from the Publisher. Send cover price plus 50¢ per copy for mailing and handling to Zebra Books, Dept. 2975, 475 Park Avenue South, New York, N.Y. 10016. Residents of New York, New Jersey and Pennsylvania must include sales tax. DO NOT SEND CASH.

HISTORICAL ROMANCES BY VICTORIA THOMPSON

BOLD TEXAS EMBRACE (2835, $4.50)

Art teacher Catherine Eaton could hardly believe how stubborn Sam Connors was! Even though the rancher's young stepbrother was an exceptionally talented painter, Sam forbade Catherine to instruct him, fearing that art would make a sissy out of him. Spunky and determined, the blond schoolmarm confronted the muleheaded cowboy . . . only to find that he was as handsome as he was hard-headed and as desirable as he was dictatorial. Before long she had nearly forgotten what she'd come for, as Sam's brash, breathless embrace drove from her mind all thought of anything save wanting him . . .

TEXAS BLONDE (2183, $3.95)

When dashing Josh Logan resuced her from death by exposure, petite Felicity Morrow realized she'd never survive rugged frontier life without a man by her side. And when she gazed at the Texas rancher's lean hard frame and strong rippling muscles, the determined beauty decided he was the one for her. To reach her goal, feisty Felicity pretended to be meek and mild: the only kind of gal Josh proclaimed he'd wed. But after she'd won his hand, the blue-eyed temptress swore she'd quit playing his game—and still win his heart!

ANGEL HEART (2426, $3.95)

Ever since Angelica's father died, Harlan Snyder had been angling to get his hands on her ranch, the Diamond R. And now, just when she had an important government contract to fulfill, she couldn't find a single cowhand to hire on—all because of Snyder's threats. It was only a matter of time before she lost the ranch. . . . That is, until the legendary gunfighter Kid Collins turned up on her doorstep, badly wounded. Angelica assessed his firmly muscled physique and stared into his startling blue eyes. Beneath all that blood and dirt he was the handsomest man she had ever seen, and the one person who could help her beat Snyder at his own game—if the price were not too high. . . .

Available wherever paperbacks are sold, or order direct from the Publisher. Send cover price plus 50¢ per copy for mailing and handling to Zebra Books, Dept. 2975, 475 Park Avenue South, New York, N.Y. 10016. Residents of New York, New Jersey and Pennsylvania must include sales tax. DO NOT SEND CASH.

ZEBRA ROMANCES FOR ALL SEASONS
From Bobbi Smith

ARIZONA TEMPTRESS (1785, $3.95)

Rick Peralta found the freedom he craved only in his disguise as El Cazador. Then he saw the exquisitely alluring Jennie among his compadres and the hotblooded male swore she'd belong just to him.

CAPTIVE PRIDE (2160, $3.95)

Committed to the Colonial cause, the gorgeous and independent Cecelia Demorest swore she'd divert Captain Noah Kincade's weapons to help out the American rebels. But the moment that the womanizing British privateer first touched her, her scheming thoughts gave way to burning need.

DESERT HEART (2010, $3.95)

Rancher Rand McAllister was furious when he became the guardian of a scrawny girl from Arizona's mining country. But when he finds that the pig-tailed brat is really a voluptuous beauty, his resentment turns to intense interest; Laura Lee knew it would be the biggest mistake in her life to succumb to the cowboy—but she can't fight against giving him her wild DESERT HEART.

Available wherever paperbacks are sold, or order direct from the Publisher. Send cover price plus 50¢ per copy for mailing and handling to Zebra Books, Dept. 2975, 475 Park Avenue South, New York, N.Y. 10016. Residents of New York, New Jersey and Pennsylvania must include sales tax. DO NOT SEND CASH.

She shook her head. "It must be Mr. Farrell," she said. "Detective Farrell," she amended, recalling that he had given Raifer that title. She stared at him, her eyes wide and pleading. "Please," she whispered.

He stood looking at her for a long moment as he hesitated. "I don't know if I should be doing this," he said, then added, "Wait here."

He disappeared then, leaving Honor to wonder if he'd left her there to mull over the impropriety of her request, or perhaps even her actions of the previous afternoon. Perhaps he thought it only fitting that she spend a bit of time amidst the chaos of the station house, a fitting place for her to consider the extent of her sins.

But he was back in a few minutes, a small piece of paper in his hand. He held it out to her. "Detective Farrell has been suspended because of what happened yesterday," he said slowly before he released the paper to her.

His eyes were edged with accusation that Honor felt as a chilling bite of guilt. That was her fault, at least in good part, she realized, even without his terse reminder.

"Both Detective Farrell and Captain Ryan," he finished.

"Perhaps what I have to tell Detective Farrell might help to rectify that situation," she offered, hoping that might mollify him.

Apparently her words had the effect she wanted, because he handed her the slip of paper and then even offered her a small smile as she took it.

"Thank you," Honor said.

"Whatever you're going to do, Miss Wainwright, I suggest you do it fast," he told her in a hoarse whisper. "Word here is that the Chief is out to get Ryan's blood, and he won't mind spilling a bit of

"Have you any idea where I can find him?" she asked. "It's very important," she added, hoping he would feel that enough of an inducement.

She had no desire to relate to him her experiences of the previous two hours, the fruitless and embarrassing trip to the seedy rooming house and the words she'd exchanged with the greasy-looking landlord, with his shiny dark little eyes and dirty vest and shirt sleeves, his smilingly suggestive questions and final, useless admission that Raifer had offered up his rooms and left no forwarding address the evening before.

"I believe he's taken some rooms near Lafayette Street," the young policeman told her.

"I've already been there," Honor replied, feeling the blush of red that crept to her cheeks as she remembered. She looked down at her gloved hands, concentrating on a small thread that had come free from the leather at the tip of her right thumb. "He's gone and left no forwarding address." She dared look back up at him. "It really is important."

"Perhaps another officer," he suggested, obviously deciding that it would be wisest to be as accommodating as possible. After all, he'd seen the chief of police apologize to her and her father, something that he'd never heard Fitzpatrick had ever done before.

Honor hesitated. Perhaps she could tell another officer. After all, she had little desire to see Raifer, to feel the shame and hurt surging through her, to know how he had used her and see it in his eyes. But somehow she knew he would deal with her, would accept her word that Daniel had had no part in the matter if she traded her information about the terrorists' identities. She had no such faith that another policeman would be so accommodating.

the front step.

"I'm looking for Mr. Farrell," she replied, her tone slightly hesitant. "Mr. Raif Farrell."

He did not, as she expected, reply that no Mr. Raif Farrell lived there and close the door on her. Instead, he stood back, allowing her room to enter a marble-floored and mahogany-walled entry.

"Whom shall I say is calling, miss?" he asked as soon as she had stepped inside.

"Honor," she said. "Honor Wainwright."

"If you'll wait here, Miss Wainwright," he said. "I'll see if Detective Farrell will see you."

With a small bow, he turned and crossed to a heavy mahogany door. Honor watched as he knocked gently, then entered, closing the door behind him. He'd returned before she had time to consider what she would do if Raifer did not want to see her. She was forced to consider that possibility quite quickly as he told her, with his unchanging tone, just that.

"I'm afraid Detective Farrell is not receiving visitors just now, miss."

Honor shook her head as though she'd not heard him correctly. "Tell him it's a police matter," she insisted. "And very important."

He shrugged, and then turned to do her bidding, his manner suggesting that he was complying more to induce her to leave without further fuss than for any other reason. But when he'd disappeared behind the mahogany door, Honor followed him, opening it in time to hear Raifer's voice, dark and bitter, "Tell her to find a policeman if that's what she wants."

"I thought that's what you were, a policeman," she said, and watched as he turned to find her standing in the doorway.

Detective Farrell's along the way." His eyes grew hard as he stared at her. "And that would be a waste, because they're both very good men."

With that he nodded stiffly, then turned on his heel and walked away from her. Honor followed him with her eyes. Ryan, Chief Fitzpatrick, they were all simply names to her, names that only confused the matter. She turned to the front door and walked slowly to it, then out into the sharp sunshine and the noise and grime of the city street. She raised the piece of paper she still clutched in her hand and read the address that was printed in neat block letters on it. Squaring her shoulders, she gathered her determination back once more, then raised her hand to a passing hansom.

Honor thought the young police officer must have made a mistake when she arrived at the address he had given her. It was a large house, brick fronted, admittedly not on the avenue, but just off it. She double checked the address, then decided there was nothing for her to do but go to the door and inquire.

She got out of the cab, paid off the hansom driver, and walked up the front steps, finding herself feeling a bit foolish but no less determined. When she reached the door, she raised her hand to the knocker and sounded it firmly.

The door was opened, if not immediately, quite promptly, by a youngish old servant in proper butler's livery, a man very nearly the image of Fraser who stood official guard at her own house, if not quite so stern eyed.

"How may I help you, miss?" he asked with a slightly bored drawl when he found her standing on